# THE VIKING HOSTAGE

# THE VIKING
# HOSTAGE

*Tracey Warr*

IMPRESS
BOOKS

First published in 2014
by Impress Books

Innovation Centre, Rennes Drive, University of Exeter Campus
Exeter EX4 4RN

© Tracey Warr 2014

Typeset in Garamond by Swales & Willis Ltd, Exeter, Devon

Printed and bound in England by imprintdigital.net

British Library Cataloguing in Publication Data
A catalogue record for this book is available from the British Library

ISBN 13: 978–1–907605–59–8 (pbk)
ISBN 13: 978–1–907605–60–4 (ebk)

# CONTENTS

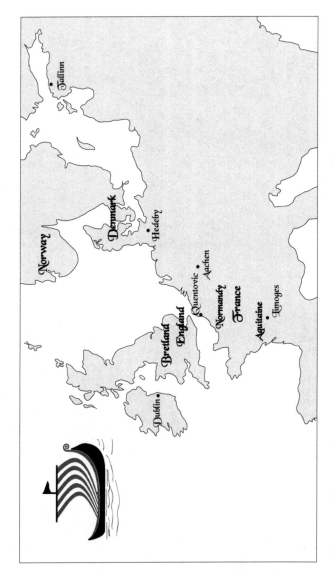

10th century Northern Europe

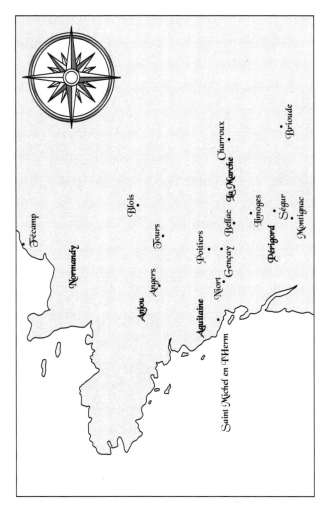

Central France at the time of Sigrid and Aina

# Main Characters

(Genealogies are on pages 377–386)

**Sigrid Thorolfsdottir**, Norwegian slave
**Thorgils Thorolfsson**, Sigrid's brother
**Olafr**, Sigrid's foster-brother

**Ademar of Ségur**, Viscount of Ségur, cousin of Gerard of Limoges, custodian of Limoges
**Melisende**, Viscountess of Ségur, wife of Ademar and their child
   **Aina**

**Gerard of Limoges**, dispossessed Viscount
**Rothilde of Brosse**, wife of Gerard and their children:
   **Guy**
   **Hildegaire**
   **Aimery**
   **Adalmode**
   **Hilduin** and six others

The sons of the Count of La Marche:
**Helie**
**Audebert**
**Boson**
and two others

**Guillaume IV 'Strong Arm,'** Duke of Aquitaine and Count of Poitou

**Emma of Blois**, sister of the Count of Blois, Duchess of Aquitaine, wife of Guillaume IV and their son **Guillaume**

**Aldearde d'Aulnay**, Viscountess of Thouars, mistress to Guillaume IV Duke of Aquitaine

**Geoffrey 'Greymantle,'** Count of Anjou and his son **Fulk 'The Black,'** heir to the county of Anjou

**Blanche of Anjou**, sister of Count Geoffrey of Anjou, Countess of Gévaudan

**Bishop Guy of Le Puy**, brother of Count Geoffrey of Anjou

**Lothaire**, King of the Franks, descended from Charlemagne his son **Louis**, heir to the kingdom of the Franks and other members of the last Carolingian royal family

**Hugh 'Capet,'** Duke of France and his son **Robert**

**Richard I 'The Fearless,'** Duke of Normandy

**Gunnora**, Duchess of Normandy and their son **Richard**, heir to the duchy of Normandy

**Maredudd ap Owain**, King of Gwynedd and Deheubarth and his daughter **Angharad**

And various clergy, vikings, servants, serfs and slaves.

# Part One

# FREEDOM

## 972–988

*'Know that things did not happen as I have written them
but that everything could have happened thus.'*

# 1

# Tallinn

## Summer 972

A list of items for sale was called out in the marketplace. I was described as one female Northchild, but my name is Sigrid Thorolfsdottir. I am for sale along with my brothers, Thorgils and Olafr, who stand either side, holding my hands.

'Ease up Sigrid,' Thorgils whispers to me, 'you're crunching the bones of my hand. It will be alright.'

I try to relax my grip on his knuckles and look out at the few buyers staring up at the platform where we stand barefoot. Most of the crowd have gone since we are the last and least interesting item. Around the edges of the market square tall, thin houses are painted in gay colours. Awnings above the stalls flap in the slight breeze, their colours leached out by sun. Apples, nuts and cheeses are carefully arranged in small mounds and circles. Chickens are panicking in wooden cages. If I squint my eyes I can just see the sun sparkling on the sea in the distance, beyond the square and the buildings, and the buyers.

'Three fine children of the Northmen, already growing muscled and hard-working,' Klerkon, the slaver, shouts to the sparse audience, pushing up the grimy sleeve of Thorgils' shift and pinching the flesh of his bicep, leaving white fingerprints against the brown skin. I glance up at the angry muscle shifting in my brother's cheek. Olafr and I are nine and we still have the scrawniness of childhood, but Thorgils is strong for his twelve years, with arms and thighs filled out from rowing and working on boats. Me and Thorgils are red-haired, and Thorgils' face is reddened and splattered with freckles from the sun at sea. Olafr has blond, curling hair like a sunny nimbus but it is not shining today. The crowd is silent and Klerkon encourages them: 'Have you ever seen more perfect physical specimens! Blond and ruddy. They will soon be tall as date palms.' He raises his hand above his head to demonstrate how tall we will be. 'They will do all your hard, nasty work for you. Come *on*! Give me an offer here!'

A woman in a fine scarlet cloak with black hair caught into a flimsy, transparent veil is staring at me with a look of pity. All three of us belie the slaver's description. We are grimy, starving, exhausted, humiliated. My red braid clings flatly to my neck in a greasy hank, my face is streaked with dirt, my blue eyes swim with tears that I frequently sniff back from falling. I stink of the pigpen where we were kept for a week on Smaeland Island after the pirates captured our ship and killed our father. Thorgils told me that Father is with Freya and the other gods now. Olafr is our foster-brother and his father was also murdered and his mother sold as a slave. Klerkon threw a few buckets of cold water over us this morning to smarten us up but our misery is ingrained by now. A slave is reduced from a person to a thing, Thorgils said bitterly as we watched the sale of the adults before us.

'I'll give you a cloak,' a man shouts from the crowd and I turn to see what he looks like.

'Two!' shouts back Klerkon.

'I've only got the one,' the man says, unpinning it from his shoulders and sweeping it around, 'but it's a fine one.'

'A cloak!' mutters Thorgils, 'for us!'

'Done,' says the slaver, 'for the two boys.' He swiftly cuts down twice on the rope that ties me at the neck to my brothers and hands the two ends to the now cloakless man.

It happens so fast and we do not know all the words of this language. 'My sister!' Thorgils shouts but he and Olafr are already being pulled roughly from the platform, Thorgils' ankles tangling as he struggles to stay upright against the rope. No one understands or cares what he is saying. Coming slowly to the realisation that I am losing them, I begin to wail, my voice small and cracked by thirst and fear. 'Be brave Sigrid!' Thorgils shouts. He bends one knee and digs his toes into the dust to stand and speak to me, resisting the drag of the rope at his neck that is already circled with red and purple bruises and sores. 'We will come for you! This I promise.'

'We will Sigrid!' shouts Olafr. 'We will find you.'

I press my lips together desperately, grip my hands around each other, willing the tears to stay in my eyes as Thorgils and Olafr are pulled farther and farther off into the crowd. Thorgils has promised, I tell myself emphatically, but a chill grips my body and my teeth start to chatter.

'I will take the girl!' calls the woman in the scarlet cloak and the portly man next to her puts a hand on her arm, speaks to her, but she shakes her head and calls out 'two *solidi*,' walking up to the edge of the dais, showing the coins on the flat of her hand. The slaver slaps his sword hilt to confirm that a bargain is struck. I weave my head from side to side trying to see around the backs and hats of people, past the rear-ends of horses and the piles of produce but I can no longer see the red head and fair head of my brothers. They are gone. I am panting like a hot dog but my heart wears the thick ice of the fjord in deepest winter.

Money chinks into Klerkon's hand. I look at my new owner, trying to control my lower lip, scrubbing at the drip of my nose. The woman smiles and reaches to take my hand but seeing how filthy it is she thinks better of it. 'Ademar,' she says softly.

The finely dressed man accompanying her takes hold of my rope and beckons me to come with him. He leads me down from the platform, through the milling people browsing and bartering at the stalls, to a water spigot. He unclips a ceramic cup hanging at his waist, fills it and offers it to me, saying in Norse, 'Drink!' I take a few sips, looking into the crowd for a glimpse of Thorgils. The man, my owner, acts out throwing his head back and drinking to indicate that I should drink more. I guess that he only has a few words of my language. The man's hair and beard are dark grey, streaked here and there with the deep red vestiges of the hair colour of his youth. His dark blue tunic stretches over a rotund belly. I study him and he raises his eyebrows and smiles at me but I do not smile back. There is humour and perhaps kindness in his grey eyes, or maybe he is laughing at me.

'Will you tell us your name, child?' says the man called Ademar. I listen and understand but I do not speak. I feel dazed, as if I have forgotten something but I cannot remember what it is.

Ademar turns to his wife who is pretty and much younger than he is: 'She has suffered. That is why she is silent, Melisende. She lost her brothers. You saw that, and who knows what went before.'

The woman sighs and peers down sympathetically at me. 'Or perhaps she does not understand. Our language is Occitan,' she says to me, slowly and a little loud. I stare stonily at her and watch how she looks me over and grimaces. 'Her hair crawls with lice.'

I try to maintain my stony face as Ademar draws a sharp knife from the scabbard at his belt, grasps my thick red braid close to my neck, saws at it, and drops it in the dust at my feet where I look at it, bereft, doubly humiliated, a shorn slave.

'It will grow back clean and not itching,' Melisende reassures me, untying a comb from her girdle and running it over my cropped head to remove the rest of the vermin. Her touch is gentle. Minutes ago the braid was part of me; now it is abandoned, like a snake's old skin. Everything is gone.

Ademar concludes some business with a group of Moor traders, weighing out silver and then folding up his scales which fit neatly into an oval clasped box made from the two cups of the contraption.

'Are you taking the *majus* home with you to Francia?' one of the men asks Ademar, gesturing towards me.

'*Majus*?' says Ademar.

'Fire-worshipper.'

'Oh. Yes we are.'

'Haven't you had enough of those visiting you already with swords and axes?' grins the Moor.

'Yes,' sighs Ademar, 'we have, but the Northmen raids are not so frequent now in Francia.'

'I hear the slave trade is falling off in the West,' the man remarks.

Ademar nods politely but seems keen not to be drawn into a conversation.

'There is still good trade in the East though, especially for young bed-slaves, but on the other hand enough breeding goes on amongst slaves that it renders the buying of new ones unnecessary really, or at least the price is very low. I'll give you one *solidi* for it,' says the man, gesturing at me again.

'She's not for sale,' Ademar tells him, and I realise that I have been holding my breath since the man's question and let it out with relief. Ademar steps up onto his horse and leans down to grip my arm. I put one foot on his and swing up behind him as I used to with my father.

At the tavern where they are staying, Melisende orders a warm bath, food and water for me. She is smiling broadly, pleased at the outcome of my scrubbing and combing. Despite myself I like her face, but I determine to continue not speaking to them. Somehow my muteness keeps Thorgils and Olafr with me, denies that I am made a slave, a nothing, owned by these people. I run my hands over my shorn head which feels strangely light and naked without my hair. Even Ademar who had seemed doubtful about my purchase at the market is grinning. They watch me as I wolf down the bread and meat set in front of me.

'She's extremely hungry,' says Melisende, smiling.

Ademar bends to tie one end of a long rope to my ankle and attaches the other end to his belt. I lift the rope, examining the knot, admiring how well-made it is. In response to his wife's doubtful expression, he tells her, 'If a runaway slave is captured they are killed immediately. You don't want that to happen to her and naturally she would run if she could. She wants to be with her brothers, your Northchild.'

I keep my face expressionless, as if I do not understand him. What I feel is not his business.

'Melisende, Melisende!' he says indulgently, shaking his head. 'What do you think we are going to do with her?'

'I couldn't leave her there, Ademar. Look at her. That shapely red head, those huge eyes, blue as a summer sky in the little triangle of her face, and the way her nose tilts up at the end? She looks like a scalped fairy. How could I abandon her to just anyone who might take her?'

'You speak of her as if she were a doll.'

7

'No. You saw how she was wrenched from her kin. She is near enough the same age as our own daughter. I could *not* leave her there.'

There is vexation with him in her tone now and I look between them. I listen hard, catching some words, guessing some others perhaps wrongly.

'No,' Ademar says finally, 'you could not. Nevertheless, what shall we do with her? There is no place for a slave in our household, nor should there be. Some bishops have rightly railed against this traffic, even when the unfortunates are pagans, as she no doubt is.'

'Well she is not a slave through any fault of her own, at her age. We will see what we shall do with our Northchild, when we return to Ségur, when we grow to know her.'

Melisende's maid, who bathed me, takes advantage of the lull in their conversation to step forward holding out her hand to her master. 'I found this unchristian thing on her, my Lord.'

I watch the flash of the silver as she passes my serpent brooch to Ademar and curse her in my head with the worst curse I know.

'Bit my hand she did when I took it.' She turns her hand to show them the marks of my teeth on the soft part between her thumb and index finger, and Ademar lifts his eyes from the serpent in his palm, to glance briefly at me before returning his gaze to my gleaming brooch.

I tried to hold tightly to the filthy shift where the silver serpent was hidden, but the maid wrestled it from me, bent my fingers back painfully from the brooch, prising it out of my grip. The slavers stripped us of everything of value: my rings, knife, thimble and shoulder brooches, but my father pinned his great serpent brooch inside my belt when he saw the billowing orange sail of the pirate ship coming fast upon us. I transferred the brooch to the hem of my shift, keeping it safe until now and this stupid maid.

Ademar weighs the heft of the silver in his palm, runs a finger along its finely wrought serpentine curves, and peers at the runes that Thorgils scratched on its underside for me when we were in the pirates' pigpen.

'What do the marks say?' asks Melisende.

Ademar shrugs and looks the question to me. Leap from the fetters! Escape from the foes! I recite the runic charm in my head but keep my face blank. Ademar nods at my silence and hands the serpent back to me. I cannot keep the surprise from my face now, so I look down swiftly instead, pinning the brooch onto the new belt they have given me, nodding my thanks curtly. From the corner of my eye, I see Ademar raise his eyebrows at me again. 'That is a brooch of great value and workmanship,' he tells Melisende. 'How quickly and utterly our fortunes may shift,' he says thoughtfully, and I see the reflection of my shorn head in the dark pupil of his eye. 'It seems your Northchild comes of good stock. Either that, or she is a wondrous good thief.'

# 2

## Montignac

### September 972

'Must you pace up and down like a hungry hound?'

Hearing the irritation in his brother's voice, Audebert stopped, his face close to the wall. The heavy chain at his ankle was pulled taut to its full extent. Above his head a sheer rock wall fifty foot high reached up into cold air and a circle of distant blue sky. He placed his palms and forehead on the cold, damp stone letting the misery it had witnessed over the years seep into his skin and mingle with his own.

'Sorry,' said his brother, Helie, relenting. 'I know. We are like caged beasts. We should be out there, riding down a stag.' He gestured upwards in the direction of the sky.

Audebert suppressed the grief that rose in his throat at his brother's words. He turned and paced back the ten strides which was all the hole allowed, the hole they had been imprisoned in for many months. Helie's beard reached to his belt. Audebert's thick black hair stood up from his forehead, aside from one dangling lock. His hair rolled over the top of his head in dense, turbulent waves, and snaked in matted twists and hanks down his back. At least it warmed his neck in the frigid nights.

'How much longer can they keep us here?' Audebert said for the hundredth time. Helie looked at him exasperated but did not reply. There was no good reason to ever let them out. Since Helie's reckless raid had inadvertently led to the blinding of a priest, their captor, Gerard of Limoges, was within his rights to keep them prisoner. No doubt their father had tried to treat for their release but he must be angry with Helie for his actions. And he has other sons, Audebert told himself bleakly.

'I've barely begun,' he said. 'I can't end my life here, like this, in this hole.' Audebert was sixteen when they were captured and by his reckoning his seventeenth birthday was last week.

Helie said nothing. A search of the dungeon for any means of escape took them less than an hour on their first day. It had no weaknesses. It was a deep pit with a small opening high above their heads, covered with a metal grate. At least they could see the distant circle of day fading to night and stars, and occasionally they heard geese honking and glimpsed a flurry of white flying overhead. The hole was a natural rock formation adjacent to the castle, its surfaces giving no purchase. At the beginning of their imprisonment Audebert had tried over and over to find hand-holds in the rough grey stone to climb up, but he never got higher than a few feet and his hands were cut and bloody, his knees and shoulders bruised from his repeated falls. The jailor reporting on these attempts, had come and fitted them with ankle shackles. 'Now look what you've done,' said Helie, picking at the scabs forming on the sores around the iron cuff on his leg.

The jailor lowered down a jug of water, bread and other scant provisions now and then. Audebert had been in peak physical condition when they were captured but now his clothes hung on his large bones and the muscles of his sword-arm were gone. He tried to persuade his brother to pace and wrestle every day but Helie was morose and lethargic. Audebert conceded that it was difficult to want to exercise when you were starving and your stomach muscles clenched on air. 'You haven't eaten each other yet then!' the jailor called down to them cheerfully. His visits were erratic: some days he came, others he did not.

The jug of water was not enough for washing, so they had to exist in their own filth. Audebert found a flint on the ground with a fine edge and scraped his body in the fashion of the Romans, although he lacked their sweet perfumed oils. He set up a latrine near a small crack in one stone corner. When it rained their waste sluiced away into the moat and the rain washed them too. If Aude-bert had a vessel down here he could have collected rainwater but his attempts to fashion something from loose stones had so far failed and the jailor insisted on pulling the jug up each time he gave them water. The jailor repulsed Audebert's efforts to talk to him, to ask for a vessel to wash with. 'I'm not here to chat with murderers,' he said. When it did not rain for days, they must ferment in the soil of their own bodies and breathe the stench of their excrement and urine. So Audebert was grateful that it had rained the night before when the jailer yelled, 'Oi! You've got a visitor!'

Audebert pushed himself to his feet and thought that the sun had come down to visit him as the bright face of a young girl with a shining tumble of abundant golden hair, peered down from high above him.

'Hello,' she called tentatively.

'Hello,' Audebert called up, his voice ricocheting on the stone. 'Who are you, Lady?' Even at this distance he could see her face was pensive and sensitive, her large green eyes framed by dark brown lashes and brows.

'Adalmode. My father is Lord Gerard.'

He guessed that she was around twelve – on the brink of womanhood. She was beautiful as the day, as the sky, as freedom. She looked down with a frankly curious expression.

'Hello Lady Adalmode. I am Audebert, son of the Count of La Marche. What brings you to my hearth?' he laughed, gesturing around himself.

Adalmode peered down into the deep hole at the two young men. One sat huddled on the floor leaning against the wall and the other who had called out to her was standing in the middle of the circular floor his face turned up, catching the sparse light. She grimaced at the boy's description of the awful place he was in. In the gloom at the bottom of the dungeon pit, Audebert's smile lit his face, crinkling startling blue eyes that sloped downwards at their corners, lifting his mouth into a perfect curve and a glimpse of even white teeth, dimpling one cheek.

'Is that your brother?'

'Yes Lady.'

'Is he ill?'

Helie glanced briefly up at her and resumed his hunched position.

12

'No Lady Adalmode, he is merely miserable. His ailment is in his shackles.'

The brothers bore a strong resemblance to one another, but whilst the vivid blue of Audebert's eyes against his black hair and his strong masculine features contradicted by boyishness gave him beauty, the similar features were merely compiled on Helie's face.

'Goodbye,' she said and suddenly her fair head was gone, the circle of sky was empty.

'Goodbye Lady Adalmode,' Audebert shouted, raising a hand towards the empty sky, hoping that she was still within earshot. 'Come again!'

The only reply was a shower of bread and bruised apples from the jailer. Audebert rescued the food, dusted off as much of the dirt as he could with the dirty sleeve of his tunic and placed it on a large flat stone that he had designated as 'the table.'

'To table,' he announced cheerfully. 'At least today we have something nice to talk about, rather than rats and regrets.'

'Nice!' said Helie, reaching for a lump of bread. 'She came to gloat.'

'I don't think so. I hope she will come again. Did you see how pretty she was?'

'Hope will kill you Audebert,' said Helie.

The next morning Audebert did hope. It rained in the night and he was grateful again for that. He took his flint scraper and with difficulty cut off hanks of his hair. Helie sniggered at him from his corner. He had taken up that corner early in their captivity and rarely moved from it. It was the only spot that received a splinter of sun when there was any. 'Audebert, I'm sorry to tell you that even with your barbering and your rain-wash, you are not looking your best in the unlikely event that your sweetheart calls again.'

Audebert carried on hacking off small chunks of black hair and studied the corpse-pallor of his brother's face. No doubt he looked the same, like a thing found under a turned stone, his nut-brown tan leached from his skin by captivity.

'If she does visit again,' said Helie, 'she'll like as not let down a long skein of spittle on your hopeful face. She is the spawn of our enemy you fool.'

Audebert kept silent and waited, but Adalmode did not return.

In the cold night Audebert felt the agony of his imprisonment more sharply because he had glimpsed life beyond this stone place. He wept quietly in the dark, allowing the tears to trickle coldly down his cheeks, hearing his brother's gentle snores, the occasional distant sounds of the night-time castle above, the lap of the moat waters against the stone, the hoot of an owl. He remembered his life before: the pampered life of the lord's son, and thought of his mother at home in Bellac, worrying over her two lost boys. He pictured his bed piled with thick brown bear skins, his wooden chest filled with clean, fine clothes, his horses and dogs, the bread baking in the kitchen and the cook scolding him for 'testing' her works in progress. How could he go on bearing this? He wished that Adalmode had not shown her face and reminded him of the wife and children he might never have now. He looked with self-disgust at the 'chess pieces' he had made from bits of stone and mud. His brother only condescended to play infrequently. You fool, he told himself, to be so full of hope. The season was growing colder and soon the rain would be replaced with wind, hail and snow. How would they survive that down here?

They would moulder, take ill and die, or grow thinner and thinner and starve. Or one day Gerard of Limoges would come and convict them. They would be pulled, blinking and filthy from the hole, pelted with rotten food by howling, laughing people, made to walk barefoot as criminals, blinded probably – their eyes for the eyes that Helie had taken from the priest, and then hanged on the gallows, their legs dancing and jerking briefly.

Audebert licked at the salt tears on his mouth, cuffed them away from his cheeks, clenched his fists and fought hard to see some glimmer of hope. Helie was wrong. Hope would keep him alive. The memory of Adalmode's face and her voice – the few words she had spoken – would keep him alive.

He took up his flint and scratched another line on the wall in the place that was his 'calendar.' His name was scratched there too. He thought before this that his name would ring in the halls of lords as they toasted his victories and war-feats – Audebert of La Marche! – he imagined men shouting, the goblets clashing and the drinking horns raised in his direction, the beer dribbling in the glossy beards of his soldiers. He thought that his name would ring through history, down the generations of his sons and daughters. Now perhaps, it would be just this hole and starvation, pain, shame, death. He peered at the wall in the moonlight, at the count of, so far, one hundred and ninety-seven days. One hundred and ninety-seven nights when the damp seeped into his bones and his fingers were swollen red and ugly with the cold – fingers, he thought, looking at them, that should be tracing the soft curve of a young woman's breast, a young woman lying next to him on a fine white sheet. Audebert wrapped his painful hands around his knees and assumed his brother's habitual position. 'Stop whimpering,' he told himself aloud.

In the chamber Adalmode shared with her sisters, the door was slightly ajar as she stood guard peering into the passageway, whilst her oldest brother Guy stood at a lectern placed close to the window. He put the goose quill back into the ink horn and rubbed at the brown ink stain on the callus on his right middle finger – his writing bump. The lump was permanent and had been there since he was ten and started writing his Annals. The ink stain was fairly permanent too – and only really came off in the summer when he swam every day in the river. Guy learnt to read and write in the cathedral school in Limoges and saw in the library the records and genealogy of his family who had been dispossessed of their right to rule the city. He determined to do his best to keep those records up to date in his own small way until the family honours were restored. Only Adalmode knew about his scribing. His father would be angered by it. Writing was for clerks, not for the sons of noblemen, he would shout. If his brother Hilde-gaire came to know of Guy's Annals he would tell their father, so

15

Adalmode was on the watch for anyone coming and then she would hiss to Guy to conceal his writing.

The bumpy sheets of parchment were folded in half around each other in gathers, forming a small book. The pages of this gather were nearly filled and Guy reminded himself to buy more used parchment at the next fair in Limoges so that he could wash the old writing from it with milk and oat bran as the monks had shown him, and make himself a new book, a second book of Annals. He wondered how many books he would fill in his lifetime and if he would ever write there: 'In this year Guy became Viscount of Limoges.' He retrieved the quill and added 'Book I' to the title on the front page. He lent down close to the manuscript, moving a clear glass filled with water over the parchment to help him read through his earlier entries.

*The Annals of Guy of Limoges Book I*

**+ 966** In this year of the reign of King Lothaire of the Franks who is descended of Charlemagne, Gerard of Limoges, his wife Rothilde of Brosse and their family continued in exile at the castle of Montignac, dispossessed of their rights to the viscounty of Limoges, through the continuing anger of the Duke of Aquitaine caused by the disloyalty of Gerard's grandfather in the time of Ebles Mancer. The great city of Limoges continued in the custodianship of Gerard's cousin, Ademar of Ségur, who prospers with trading in the lands of the northern seas. Just after mid-winter the nursemaid at Montignac, Editha, died at a great age, that she did not know herself but it looked like over a hundred. A hot summer.

**+ 967** In this year King Lothaire and Queen Emma rejoiced at the birth of their son, Louis. A monk named Bede has explained some mysteries of the world in his books *The Reckoning of Time* and *On the Nature of Things*. It is written by the Anglo-Saxons that the earth resembles a pine nut and the sun glides about it, although some country folk say instead that the sun dives into the ocean each night and rises up again from the waters in the morning. The firmament is adorned with many stars and is perpetually turning around us. In June a large circle surrounded the sun with the colours of the rainbow and four brighter circles embraced it.

+ 968 In this year, after the negotiations of his uncle Ebles, Bishop of Limoges, Duke Guillaume IV of Aquitaine, known as 'Strong Arm,' took Emma, the sister of the Count of Blois, as his wife. Around mid-summer the hound, Egil, had eight pups at Montignac, one white, which went to Gerard's daughter, Adalmode of Limoges.

+ 969 In this year, Emma of Blois bore an heir for the Duchy of Aquitaine. The fortress at Brantôme was struck by lightning and badly burnt. The head groom at Montignac died. The bread failed in the villages of the Limousin. It was reported that vermin like moles with two teeth fell from the air and ate everything up and were driven out by a priest through fasting and prayer.

+ 970 In this year the day before the *nonas* of April, at the end of the night, while the brothers were singing the divine office of the night, innumerable stars were seen to fall as a rain from the sky over the whole world.

+ 971 In this year the Vienne rose up over its banks, covered the water meadows and lapped at houses, bridges and churches and then retreated leaving a great slick of mud in its wake. It seems that as the veins lie in a man's body so lie the veins of water that run through the earth, the great rivers such as the Vienne in Limoges.

Guy smiled at the comical mix of youthful earnestness and everyday concerns in the entries for the early years, and frowned at the errors that he had scraped at with a knife, leaving ugly patches on the parchment. He moved the glass of water to one side and picked up his quill again to write this year's entry, bending with his face an inch from the surface. He had been composing this year's entry in his head since his conversation with his father at breakfast and he scribed it carefully now, only needing to scrape at two errors.

17

**+ 972** In this year Helie and Audebert, the sons of Count Boso of La Marche, blinded Benedict, a priest under the protection of the Bishop of Limoges and the Duke of Aquitaine. The sun was covered by the passing of the moon and day turned to night. The Duke of Aquitaine held Assembly in Limoges. Gerard of Limoges pledged allegiance and asked for the return of his rights and was again refused. Gerard, on the advice of his eldest son, Guy, continued to hold Helie and Audebert of La Marche, in his dungeon, in hopes of winning favour in time. Rothilde, wife to Gerard of Limoges, gave birth to an eleventh child, a daughter named Calva. An heir named Robert was born to Hugh Capet, Duke of France and his Duchess Adelais who is sister to the Duke of Aquitaine.

Guy read the entry back over and closed the book, retied the black ribbon around it in a cross shape and put it back in its hiding place in the locked casket under Adalmode's bed.

With one hand Adalmode held her thick fair hair bunched behind her head, away from her face, stood at a distance of three paces from the long trestle in the Great Hall and expertly spat an olive pit into a metal bowl. She loosed her hair, smiling smugly at the loud ping the stone made as it hit the dead centre of the bowl and swirled around its own momentum before coming to a stop. She giggled as Guy stepped up beside her, ostentatiously chewing on his olive.

'Stop laughing,' he said, his voice muffled around the olive in his mouth, 'you'll make me swallow it.' His pit, spat in response to Adalmode's, inevitably missed the bowl and the trestle and struck a disgruntled old lurcher sleeping in front of the fire.

'What did I get?' Guy called out triumphantly.

'You hit the dog, you idiot.'

'Best of three?' asked Guy, as the dog staggered to its feet, stared balefully at them, and moved towards the doorway where a patch of sunlight gleamed on the worn stone floor.

'Poor dog,' Adalmode called after it. 'You are wise to move out of the way!'

'Adalmode! Are you doing anything useful?' She turned to the sharp note of anxiety in her mother's voice and removed the mirth from her face. 'And Guy, shouldn't you be out practicing in the bailey with your brothers at this hour?'

'I am on my way there, Mother,' declared Guy with gusto, and Adalmode automatically stepped to his side so that he could lay his hand on her arm in what appeared to be a gesture of affectionate companionship but was in fact a gesture of necessity to conceal his extreme short-sightedness. Guy was tall and thin, gangly, with light brown, tousled hair. The lines of his features were distinctive, too sharply angled for beauty, but it was an intelligent, humourous face.

'I'm going with Guy, Mother, as Sergeant Rufus has asked me to take them wine to relieve their sweaty exertions,' Adalmode lied smoothly, picking up an empty jug from the table with her free hand.

'Very well,' said Rothilde. Adalmode watched with concern as the tense lines around her mother's mouth smoothed briefly into a vague smile, before she sat and placed both elbows on the table, dropping her forehead into her upturned palms.

Adalmode picked her way carefully to the door, guiding Guy's feet away from the mounds of dog faeces and discarded, congealing food, which littered the thin rushes on the floor, giving off a sweet, sickly odour. Between them they had made shift for years to conceal the extreme weakness of Guy's vision from the rest of the family, and above all from their father. Adalmode was six when she realised her favourite brother needed her help. He was hopeless at all physical activities: swordplay, quintain, games of chase. He played *boule* erratically, winning through sheer fluke or losing and never hitting the ball. In chess he had to peer closely at the board and make excuses for it: 'I thought I saw a spider on the board; I thought I saw an ant.' It was a family joke. 'You are checkmated and no insects about it!' his brother Hildegaire would shout. His younger brothers teased him relentlessly over his lack of physical ability which they were acquiring so well, just as they teased Adalmode simply because she was a girl. Guy and Adalmode were allies against The Brothers. His tongue and seniority, as the oldest son, protected her; her eyes served him.

'This hall is in a terrible mess and poor Mother is exhausted and dejected again,' she told Guy in a low voice.

'Can you help her?' he murmured back. 'I can manage.' They were at the doorway and Guy reached his fingers to the cold stone reassurance of the doorjamb.

'Are you sure?' Adalmode asked doubtfully. The ring of sword-play in the bailey struck her ears and she looked to where their brothers Hildegaire and Aimery were practicing.

'Yes, go and help Mother.'

She watched anxiously as Guy felt his way down the steps, his hand tracing the rough stones of the wall as his guide. She knew he was surefooted in a place such as this, that was familiar, and yet she liked to stick to him as much as possible. 'Hildegaire is on the left and Aimery the right,' she called softly to him, as he reached the cobbles. 'Sergeant Rufus has set up the quintain and practice rings to the left of the well. Aimery is winning.' Guy smiled back in her direction but his gaze did not quite connect with her eyes. She knew her face was just a blur to him and he was locating her from the vivid red of her dress, which she wore deliberately that he might pick her out in a crowd or at a distance.

'I'll come back and help you when I've seen to Mother,' she said and Guy turned his face towards the sound of his broth-ers' fighting. Adalmode returned to the chaos of the hall, call-ing crossly to a gossiping huddle of maids as she passed: 'The state of this hall is a disgrace. I feel sure that I have spiders liv-ing in my hair. Get it cleaned immediately! Swipe the cobwebs from the corners and strew fresh rushes. I want to see the stone flags gleaming and to smell rosemary within the hour!' The girls jumped to their feet, making apologies and yeses, bumping into each other as they hunted for brooms that lent and lay neglected in the corners.

Adalmode walked back to where her mother was still hunched over the trestle. She wrapped her arms around her mother's shoulders, laid her cheek against Rothilde's and felt cold tears there. 'All will soon be . . .' Adalmode began but she was inter-rupted by the sudden loud scream of a baby and felt her mother flinch. 'Don't worry, I'll go and fetch her,' Adalmode said. She ran to the cradle, lifting her baby sister, Calva, rocking and cooing and then called for the wetnurse. 'Gerda, Gerda, where are you? Calva needs you.' Gerda came running and took the grisling baby from Adalmode, placing her to her breast so that everyone in the hall relaxed again as the insistent wail was abruptly switched off. Adalmode sat down next to her mother and took her hand.

'Thank you my love,' Rothilde said, 'you are such a good girl.' She smoothed a stray curling lock of Adalmode's honey-gold hair behind her ear. 'Your father's plea for reinstatement has been refused again,' she sighed, explaining her particular dejection this morning. Adalmode had already heard the news from Guy who had attended their father in his audience with the Duke. They had all hoped so earnestly that this year, finally, Gerard would be returned to his rights.

'What happened?' she asked. Many years before, Adalmode's grandfather had chosen the wrong side to support in the battle between Ebles Mancer, Count of Poitou and his rivals, the Counts of Toulouse and Auvergne, in their struggle over the throne of Aquitaine. As a consequence her grandfather had lost his family rights to the rich holdings of the Viscounty of Limoges. All her life, Adalmode's father had been trying to convince Guillaume, the present Count of Poitou and Duke of Aquitaine, of his loyalty. Every year he sued for the restitution of Limoges, but always returned from the assemblies empty-handed. Meanwhile his family grew and the meagre resources at Montignac where they were exiled, grew no larger. Her father's chances of restitution from the Duke were not helped by his reckless kidnap of her mother for wife, and the Duke was still bearing a grudge for this too.

It was a romantic story that her parents liked to tell to their gathered children and retainers, but it had worsened the family's situation. In the days when Adalmode's grandfather was still in favour with the Poitou overlords, still the Viscount of Limoges, Gerard was betrothed to Rothilde, heiress to the rich castle of Brosse, but when Adalmode's grandfather fell out of favour, the Duke reneged on the betrothal oath and married Rothilde to Archimbaud of Camborn instead. Adalmode's father lost the Viscounty and the wealthy bride that should have been his. When

Rothilde was widowed, instead of watching her married to yet another man, Gerard rashly abducted and married her himself. This act further entrenched the Duke's disgust and impoverished Rothilde. Now there were eleven children and the soup grew thinner and thinner and the Duke's face did not grow any friendlier to Gerard.

The blessing of her parents' fertility should have been the envy of their neighbours but instead it stressed the family's severely constrained resources. Every year, more servants and soldiers left them for better conditions elsewhere, and every year Adalmode and her mother must do more of the work themselves. Rothilde whispered to Adalmode that she prayed to God, Calva would be her last child.

Adalmode's older brothers should have left home long ago to be apprenticed to neighbouring lords but nobody wanted to take the sons of a disgraced family. Guy tried to find positive solutions to their dilemma, but Hildegaire grew angrier, along with their father, bitterly watching as Duke Guillaume allowed their cousin, Ademar of Ségur, to administer their birthright in Limoges and grow rich on it.

Of course, Adalmode, thought glumly, just as no one will take the sons, who would want the undowried daughters of Gerard and Rothilde? Adalmode's betrothal should be in negotiation by now. Would she have to be married off to the cloddish son of the castellan who looked at her golden hair with lust and would touch her rudely as she passed if it were not for the threats and fists of her brothers, or would she have to go into a nunnery? She wanted to stay with Guy always, but she knew that a marriage to someone significantly lower in status was her likely fate, and soon. Her brother, Hilduin, went to the monks last year, as soon as her father could scrape together the necessary endowment for him, and Geoffrey and little Hugh, the youngest boys at eleven and three, would join him in the monastery before long.

Last year Adalmode and Guy accompanied their father to the Assembly at Poitiers. When her father petitioned for the return of Limoges the Duke said, 'Show me some true allegiance, and I'll reward that, but for now all I see before me is the son of a traitor, a kidnapper defying me.' Gerard prostrated himself in supplication in vain. Once out of the Duke's sight and ear-shot, Adalmode watched her father shout, kick and smash their paltry possessions in his anger at the Duke's refusal. 'I would sooner eat grass in the mountains than spend one more day at this court!' he yelled.

'This is not the way, Father,' Guy told him. Her brother was near-blind but far from stupid. He listened intently to the currents and eddies of debate and nuance around him.

'What is the way then?' shouted their father. 'You know this way do you boy?'

'I can make a suggestion,' said Guy.

His father kicked the chest once more doing more damage to himself than the solid wood, swept a few more of their mother's precious goblets to the ground, and slumped into a chair. Guy waited. Eventually his father looked up. 'You're still here. Speak it then – your suggestion.'

'The Duke's priest was assaulted just recently and blinded by Helie of La Marche.'

'Yes, I know that,' said Gerard. 'The entire country knows that Helie of La Marche attacked the unarmed priest Benedict. Of what interest is it to me if La Marche cannot control his sons?'

'If you captured Helie, brought him to justice,' said Guy, 'Duke Guillaume would reward you.'

A long silence followed whilst Gerard considered this. Adalmode saw that her father was looking intently at Guy. 'That's brilliant, boy,' said Gerard finally, 'That could work.'

Gerard and Guy sent spies to search out Helie. They found him with his brother Audebert in the forest of Gençay, not daring to go home after Helie's sacrilegious act, the smoke of their fire giving away their position, a small group of men huddled around it. Gerard and Guy quietly surrounded the camp and captured the two La Marche sons without bloodshed. Guy told Adalmode that he sat his horse and hoped he would not be required to engage in any serious combat, and on this occasion he had been lucky. The stealth and surprise paid off. Helie and Audebert languished now in the dungeon.

Helie of La Marche's crime had outraged the counties, the story told in horror from hall to hall. Gerard held the La Marche boys at the pleasure of the Duke, and at some considerable risk of reprisal and rescue from their pugnacious father, the Count of La Marche.

'What did the Duke say about the captives?' Adalmode asked her mother.

'He was pleased,' Rothilde said, 'but that's all. He promised nothing and simply told your father to continue their captivity.'

Adalmode sighed. The cost of mounting the foray had been a tremendous gamble urged by Guy and the risk of keeping them captive was more than the impoverished family could really bear. The Duke's wily prevarications, playing one vassal off against another and giving nothing, were notorious. 'If Duke Guillaume will not reward us with the return of our birthright to Limoges, then Father must treat with the Count of La Marche for their ransom,' said Adalmode. She feared for the young man she recently saw in the pit – so cheerful despite his dire situation. Her father could not afford to keep them for long and perhaps if the gambit failed he would hang them in disappointed anger, but then that would exacerbate the feuding that already existed between her family and that of the Count of La Marche, leaving her family worse off, torn between two infuriated lords.

The troop of Adalmode's younger brothers and sisters burst loudly into the room. Adalmode rose rapidly to manage them and keep them from upsetting her mother. The children settled to play in the fresh rushes on the floor, drawing circles, faces and wavy lines with their fingers in the sweetly pungent dust. Adalmode realised she should check on the dubious military exploits of Guy outside in the bailey. At the door she turned back to ask her mother, 'Why is the La Marche younger brother in the dungeon too?'

'Because they are both violent ruffians who laid murderous hands on a sainted man of God,' Rothilde replied.

'He told me his name is Audebert.'

'Yes . . .' Rothilde began. 'You talked to them? What are you doing talking to them? I forbid you to go near there again.'

Adalmode looked innocently at her mother, her green eyes wide, and resolved that she would take a basket of the last pears from the orchard for the young man with the funny black hair, the red smiling mouth and the brilliant blue eyes, and perhaps she would put her second-best ivory comb in the basket too.

In the bailey Guy was wearing chain mail over the training gambeson that bulked him up, and a beautifully crafted sword, an heirloom from his grandfather from the days when the family ruled Limoges, with its green jewelled hilt knocking against his thigh. Guy liked how his high black boots with their metal inlaid soles, rang out his steps on the cobbles. A breeze ruffled his brown hair. He felt the slight warmth of the early morning sun on his face. He looked out onto the bailey with large dark brown eyes and saw next to nothing: a wash of grey and black, splashes of green here and there, a small and low dark movement that must be the cat, a melee of pink and brown movement in the centre of the courtyard near the vague shape of the well, that must be his brothers Hildegaire and Aimery at practice. Guy heard the ring of their weapons, their heavy breathing and occasional shouts of triumph or grunts of defeat. He heard the water dripping from the leaky bucket hung over the well resounding in the pool far below. He heard a bird squawk overhead. He heard a woman's voice singing off to his left – one of the servants washing or cooking.

Guy could glean a great deal with his ears, with the touch of his fingertips, even feeling shifts in the textures beneath his feet. He could sense the proximity of obstacles and people. He knew every inch of Montignac fortress having learnt the steps, the twists and turns, the routes, but outside of his familiar environments, he needed to rely on his sister to avoid exposure. Visiting Poitiers, it had taken him days to learn the alien spaces and too long to find his way from one place to another. 'What is wrong with you boy?' demanded his father. 'You have been lax of late.' Guy's sensitive hearing picked up the muffled snort of derision that Hildegaire thought he was sharing only with himself. Any loss of standing on Guy's part, Hildegaire saw as his own gain.

Now Hildegaire called from the courtyard: 'Join us Guy! Give that fancy sword an outing for once, instead of playing with girls.'

'Yes join us,' echoed Aimery in a voice more friendly than Hildegaire's sarcasm.

'Not now, I have to practice with Rufus,' Guy replied but he crossed the bailey and stood close to the panting fighters. He could smell their sweat. He saw that Hildegaire's shape was low and huddled, so he must be bent over, with his hands on his knees, catching his breath. 'Aimery bested you again,' Guy guessed.

'Yes!' exclaimed Aimery, pleased with himself and Guy saw that Aimery held out his arm towards Hildegaire. 'A good fight though, Hild.'

Hildegaire did not take the proffered hand but instead straightened up and stalked off, kicking a pebble in his path that ricocheted against the stone of the well. Guy listened to the trajectory of the pebble and the way its sound continued to vibrate for seconds afterwards. He walked to his saddled horse to train with Rufus, the castle's sergeant-at-arms. Rufus had done his best over the years to improve on Guy's profound incapability.

'*Scandere equos*,' shouted Rufus. Guy used his hand to steady the horse, find the stirrup and step up into it. 'Remember, sire, stick solidly to the saddle, you are forming a veritable iron-clad whole with your horse.' In the saddle Guy was confident, in silent communication with his mount, using his knees and relying on the horse's skills and practice, if not his own.

He swung his lance in the direction of the practice ring. He knew its rough location, could see the outline of the contraption, and was satisfied to feel his lance connect with the dangling ring, not well, not in the centre, but somewhere in the vicinity rather than with the air for once. That was good enough.

'Well done, my lord, a hit,' called the sergeant. The oldest son in a family, the heir, needed to be strong and capable, not only to withstand the enemies without but to withstand the enemies within: six brothers and the future husbands of four sisters. Any of them might gladly step on him to get their hands on the throne of Limoges, if their father ever succeeded in regaining it, and if any of them knew the truth about his eyesight, they would do just that. Guy could not see much beyond the end of his nose. To read he had to hold a book or parchment right up to his eyes. His humiliations on the practice ground were notorious. Hildegaire told him yesterday that he would gladly see Guy in a monastery, 'where weaklings belong.'

26

Guy was shocked at the blasphemy. 'A monk is not a weakling,' he said, 'he is stronger and braver than you or I, abjuring this world to purify his soul for the next, for the kingdom of Heaven.'

'Why not go into a monastery if you feel that way?' retorted Hildegaire.

Guy admired the discipline and devotion of the monks but he did not want to be one of them. He was the eldest son, the heir. To inherit his father's viscounty was his right, and he knew that he could do a good job of it, if the family were ever reinstated.

Adalmode ran down the steps to the bailey to see Guy turning his horse from the quintain and looked with pity at her brother's knobbled knees below his heavy chainmail and his scrawny forearms struggling to wield the weight of the lance.

'No, no, master Guy,' shouted Rufus, 'lift it higher,' and Guy made an effort to comply.

Adalmode sighed. She knew the drill, had been watching Guy's training for years, and with her lithe, strong body she could perform it much better than her brother. His hair was flattened in places at the back of his head, and sticking up in tufts on the top. He obviously woke late and had not had time to run a damp comb through it.

'That'll do for today, Lord Guy,' Rufus said, looking decidedly unimpressed.

Guy smiled broadly in the direction of Adalmode and she ran to help him pull off the oily chainmail. He winched up a bucket of water from the well, lent over to grope for the rope and pulled the bucket towards himself, sluicing the sweat from his face and chest. 'That's over with for another day then,' he said cheerfully, taking her hand and strolling with her towards the castle's postern gate that let out in the direction of the wooded banks of the river.

The sun was sparkling on the water's surface but the season was turning to autumn and the water was chilly now. Today, instead of wading in as they sometimes did, they strolled along the bank in the dappled shade. Three ducks floated by effortlessly in the current and turned their heads curiously towards them. A large fish leapt and plopped back down so fast Adalmode wondered if she had actually seen it. The creak of frogs and insects buzzed in the air. Guy bent down at the water's edge to dip his hands in and run them over his grimy face and tousled hair, glancing up and now looking sleek as an otter. 'Lovely,' he said.

'Me you mean?' asked Adalmode and he flicked a spray of water at her, leaving damp circles on her skirt.

'What was it like in Limoges, when you saw the Duke?'

'Oh you know. Terrible as always. Father asked for the return of his rights – not with much grace I must say – the Duke was rudely forthright and rapid in refusing him.'

'Despite the prisoners?'

Guy nodded.

'Did you see Ademar of Ségur there, our cousin, who rules in Limoges in our father's stead?'

'No, he was away on one of his trading trips in the north but his little daughter was there, a red-head, accompanied by Ademar's steward. The Duke made a big fuss of how pretty she was.'

'Aina isn't it?'

Guy nodded again.

'Ademar has no sons. That's something.'

Guy shrugged. Sons could come after all.

'I'm worried about your military prowess,' said Adalmode, laying heavy sarcasm on her final word, hauling herself up onto a large flat rock, determined to talk through her brother's problems.

Guy grimaced.

'If Father isn't convinced you can command the men,' Adalmode told him, 'you'll find yourself in a monastery and Hildegaire will be the new Viscount in waiting.'

'Do we have to talk about this again,' groaned Guy. 'It's such a lovely day. Look at that eagle soaring there.'

'It's a cormorant, Guy,' she said exasperated. 'Do you want to be a monk then?'

'Of course not,' Guy said, finally serious.

'Well then?'

'What can I do though?'

Adalmode looked at his thin body stretched out next to her. He was all knobs of bone: elbows, knees, wrists. Her own limbs were muscular, rounded and tanned a golden olive colour, whereas Guy's skin was pinkish brown in places, burnt and peeling in others and shockingly white in the rest. Physically he took after their mother and not their rugged warrior father. Their mother sometimes referred affectionately to Guy as a long streak of nothing. 'You need to bulk up,' Adalmode said without conviction, 'but you already eat like a goat. More meat perhaps?'

'I doubt if eating more or exercising more is going to transform me,' said Guy. 'I'm just hopeless at the quintain.' They laughed, remembering his latest humiliation with the shield and dummy suspended from a swinging pole. Guy managed to charge and hit the shield but then failed to avoid the rotating arms with their heavy sandbag that so frequently winded him and knocked him from the saddle.

'You're hopeless at all of it,' Adalmode interjected affectionately.

'Yes, but I can't see the quintain at all, not until my horse is more or less right underneath it, so I completely fumble that, and of course, then there's the archery . . .'

Adalmode smothered a yelp of laughter remembering how her brother had been forced by Hildegaire to the game of penny prick last week, shooting an arrow at a hanging penny coin, but accidentally shooting his arrow into the rump of a passing horse.

'It's not funny,' he remonstrated, 'I spent all night in the stable with that poor horse and his groom, dressing the wound and trying to say sorry.'

'You are safe, for now,' said Adalmode, 'because of the capture of Helie of La Marche and your advice to Father. He appreciates your political astuteness and we must hope that taking these prisoners will pay off in time.' She closed her eyes and lent back basking on her elbows, thinking about the blue gaze of the black haired young man in the dungeon, a contradictory gaze full of laughter and desperation.

Guy looked around. Everything was a green, blue-grey blur. He knew that the green was the bushes, trees and grass and the blue-grey was the water, the rocks and sky, and he could discern the brilliant blonde head of his sister in the vague wash of his vision, but there was no detail. He could not see the contours of her face unless he brought his own up very close to hers, and he had learnt not to do that in public.

# 3

# Hedeby

## September 972

To be clean and fed by Lord Ademar and Lady Melisende should feel marvellous after the horrors I have been through, but I am numb at the loss of my brothers. The day after the slave market I wake in the saddle, held to Melisende's breast, covered by her warm cloak. I tried not to sleep, to look and look at everything we passed, hoping I would remember the way back when I escape to search for Thorgils, but I was so bone-tired that eventually my eyelids drooped and I dreamt I was home in Viken playing and my father was calling us in to come and eat. Waking, I feel devastatingly miserable as the knowledge of my losses floods back upon me. Seeing that I am awake, Melisende kisses the top of my head and strokes my cheek. She smells of lemons.

At the port Ademar concludes his business with the Estonian merchants, aided by his servant, Phillippe, a big man with a bushy brown beard. Phillippe smiles often in my direction and eventually he comes and gives me a sweetmeat. I pop it whole into my mouth where it swells my cheek. 'She's a little beauty, my Lady.'

'Yes,' says Melisende.

'The face of a cherub and the mien of a matron,' says Phillippe, and I pretend not to understand him, whilst Melisende laughs, amused at his assessment.

Ademar and Phillippe are overseeing the unloading of barrels of salt and wine from Ademar's ship. In exchange he is loading goods from the Estonians to take back to his homeland. Sometimes the barter is unbalanced on one side or the other and

Phillippe weighs out silver in the scales to conclude the deal. Melisende leads me to a stack of chests and opens one, showing the marvellous coloured jewels inside – white, blue and gold with pictures of men, women and horses. 'Enamels,' she tells me, 'from Limoges.' She lifts the lid of another chest from Ademar's stock and I see translucent green drinking vessels packed in straw. Melisende draws one out to show me how it glints in the sun. I admire its funnel shape and the air bubbles captured inside the glass as she twirls it carefully around. She leads me to the goods that Ademar has purchased to take back to Francia. Several chests stand open, filled with furs and skins – lush brown and white bear skins, red-brown hides of elk and reindeer. I put out a finger to stroke the white fur that reminds me of home, and all the while I am looking around for any sign of Olafr or Thorgils. 'Here, look,' says Melisende showing me a chest with hundreds of walrus tusks, and another gleaming warmly with blocks of amber, like a vast vat of honey. The final chest is full of tiny soft feathers, pale grey and white, for stuffing into pillows. A few escape and flit away on the breeze. The unloading and loading and the checking and negotiations take several hours. I know that soon I too will be loaded onto a ship.

When we go on board I step carefully around the cargo that has been stowed in the sunken centre, around the mast. Old skins are tied on top to protect Ademar's goods from sea spray and rain. A goat is led up the plank to provide us with milk for the journey. The large square sail is striped yellow and black and whips back and forth in the wind that sings zinging in its rigging.

After we leave the port and make for the open sea, Melisende suffers with sea sickness and Ademar holds her head, keeping her hair and veil from her face as she vomits from the side of the ship. Recovering from the latest bout of nausea, Melisende is propped against the side of the ship and looks to where I stand in the bow of the boat, staring back to the coastline, trying to memorise the outline of the port, imprinting it onto the map in my mind, the map back to Thorgils and Olafr. I curl my palm and fingers around the sharp edges of the serpent brooch in my pocket, pressing its unyielding points into my soft flesh. I know that a slave crouches at the very bottom of the social order but I will never forget that I am the daughter and sister of noble men. I will harbour my worth secretly between me and my silver serpent. Thorgils will find me.

Now that we are on the boat, Ademar has removed the rope from my ankle. A heavy grey cloud hangs over the roofscape of Tallinn. I think that if the cloud comes down a few inches lower to be pierced by the needle of the tallest church spire, then it will rain.

'Look how well she rides the sea, Ademar, on her Northchild legs,' says Melisende.

I do not acknowledge her comment, but I feel the up and down swell of the sea in the balance of my feet and hips and that, at least, makes me feel at home and in control of something for myself.

At night I sleep with Melisende and Ademar, wrapped in a reindeer skin cocoon. Waking in the mornings in 'snuggle warmth' as my father used to call it – the night's accumulation of body heat – it is hard to emerge out of that chrysalis into the cold air. The September days are warm but the nights at sea are chill. In the morning I grip the gunwale watching the rosy sun coming up like a great fiery ball, reminding me of reflected firelight slinking across Thorgils' red hair. Without my braid I cannot even pull my hair over my shoulder to look at its colour and remind myself of my brother, and without my braid, my head and neck are cold in the wind.

We sail within view of the coast on our left and some nights the sailors use the oars to bring the ship closer in and anchor off a beach, so that they can go ashore in a small boat, pitch tents and build a fire. There are five crew members: the helmsman, the lookout, two to manage the sail and one bailer. Phillippe and I help the bailer. We form a chain with me in the middle and two buckets passing up and down the chain, one empty and one full. Phillippe dips a bucket in the water swilling in the hold, passes it to me and I pass it to the bailer who throws it over the side. Phillippe and the other man sing songs to help them keep a rhythm and I join in which makes them laugh kindly at me. I am used to sailors singing at sea and I sing my own words to their melodies. My lyrics are words of sorrow at the loss of my freedom and my brothers.

Ademar and Melisende regard me singing. 'She has a voice, then,' says Ademar.

'A sweet, sad voice,' says Melisende.

After three days at sea the ship is rowed up the estuary of a broad river: 'The Schlei,' Phillippe tells me. Then we reach a shallow lake and approach a town built on the shore. I stare in amazement at the largest settlement I have ever seen. 'Hedeby,' Phillippe says, noticing the change in my expression.

The town is surrounded by an enormous semi-circular earthwork at its back that runs down on both sides to the sea. On the side nearest to us it continues into the sea as a wooden structure. There are wooden watch-towers at intervals along the earthwork and beyond that, there is a vast ditch.

'They're protecting it from your relatives,' Phillippe laughs.

As we round the palisade arm and pull towards the wooden pier I see a stream running through the centre of the half-circular town, crowded with small boats. The stream's banks are covered with wooden planking and on either side are many, many houses laid out in straight lines with narrow streets running between them. Many of the houses are large with curls of grey smoke escaping from holes in their reed-thatched roofs. Some houses are built from timber planks and others have timber frames and wattle panel walls daubed with clay or dung. Near the water's edge I can see the fire and smoke of blacksmiths at work and hear the chang! chang! of their hammers. The crew sling and knot the ship's ropes to the bollards and hand us onto the pier.

Melisende has succeeded in persuading Ademar not to rope me again. 'Do not humiliate her so,' she begged him on the ship. I kept my eyes down, pretending not to understand or care what they said. I have hidden my serpent again in the hem of my chemise where its ostentation will not attract the attentions of a thief. I run my fingers around its curves through the flimsy material. Upside down, its shape is the same as the first letter of my name. Leap from the fetters! If I lay my hand flat against it, it is as big as my hand and I can feel one edge against my wrist and touch its top edge with the tips of my longest fingers.

'Is your silver serpent safely hidden away?' Ademar asks, noticing its absence from my belt.

I nod once.

'Good girl. That is sensible when we are travelling and amongst strangers. Was it your father's?' he asks me gently, but I give him no response.

At the port the business of unloading Ademar's goods for sale begins again, supervised by Phillippe, whilst Ademar and Melisende take me with them to find lodging for the night and to buy horses. The house they choose to stay in has a timber-lined well and a bread oven out the back. On either side are craftsmen's houses – one working with textiles, and the other with metal. I can hear snatches of my own language being spoken around me. I wonder if I might escape like a rat down one of the narrow alleys between the houses but everything is so hemmed in, I fear I would soon be cornered and decide to wait for a better opportunity. When Ademar has settled Melisende to her satisfaction, and seen to the stabling of their new horses, he goes out again to assist Phillippe. The women of the house roll out dough for bread and prepare food in a cauldron suspended above the hearth on chains from the roof beam. The houses are crammed so close together that I can hear two women next door arguing about whose turn it is to carry in wood.

When Ademar and Phillippe return, Ademar has gifts: an amber necklace for Melisende which she exclaims over with pleasure, trying it on, and a glass bead necklace for me. I stare down for a long time at the complex patterns of orange, yellow, black, red and grey running through the string of beads that Ademar loops over my head. I look up at him at last and smile my thanks, and he briefly cups my chin in an affectionate gesture, choosing to ape my mute communication himself.

'Did you get something for Aina?' asks Melisende and he nods patting the scrip pouch at his waist.

Our host hands round wooden bowls filled with mutton stew and cabbage, peas and onions. The firelight plays on the circle of faces around the hearth.

'A welcome change from salted fish,' declares Phillippe.

Melisende passes me a horn filled with mead. 'Take a little of this Northchild,' she says. After the stew, come bowls of sweet berries which I eat so quickly that all the people in the house laugh at me.

The other travellers staying here are all men. As the beer passes round, the conversation grows louder and several men are staring at Melisende. Phillippe leans forward suddenly and tells them in Norse, 'Be cautious with beer and another man's wife.' The conversation quietens down again after that and Melisende and Ademar lead me with them to a separate room that the hostess has prepared. Melisende takes a round polished metal mirror from her baggage and holds it up to smile at the amber beads against her black hair and then she turns it around so that I can see myself. My shorn red hair caps my head like a helmet, emphasising my wide face and high cheekbones. My blue eyes swim in the blurry mirror, chiming with the central blue bead on my necklace.

The next morning breakfast is chunks of warm bread with goose eggs cooked in soapstone bowls placed in the embers of the hearth. Ademar's chests and barrels of goods are carefully packed onto carts drawn by oxen and Phillippe sets off with a train of loosely roped pack-horses, carts and wagons, and an armed escort along the road to the west, turning in the saddle to wave goodbye to me. 'Where is Phillippe going?' I ask in a flat voice. Ademar turns to me. They are the first words I have spoken since Tallinn and I pronounce the strange Occitan carefully. I conceal my smugness at his surprise.

He answers quickly as if he is afraid I might lose the power of speech again. 'Phillippe will go with the carts ten miles to the River Treene, then onto the River Eider and then out onto the North Sea. He will ship the merchandise to Quentovic where he will take on wheat, wool, tin and silver from England in trade for more of my salt, wine and drinking glasses and then sail towards Noirmoutier, down the Loire and meet us again eventually at our home in Ségur, God willing.' He stops, waiting to see if I will say anything more in response but I just nod my head and look at him, expressionless.

'We are journeying on the Haervej road towards Aachen,' says Melisende. 'Our journey is a pilgrimage as well as for trade. Ademar and I need a son and we are going to pray at the shrine of Charlemagne and lay hands on all the marvellous holy relics there to entreat for the saints' help.'

I guess that Melisende is speaking of her gods and I touch the Thor's hammer on the thong around my neck. Klerkon dropped it over my head before the slave market began and placed similar pendants on Olafr and Thorgils to show we were heathens and could legitimately be sold as slaves to Christians. Melisende glances at Ademar. 'We must see to the Northchild's religious instruction when we reach home.'

In my mind, I promise the Aesir that I will never be untrue to them and adopt the Christians' god, if they will only help me get free and rejoin my brothers.

# 4

# Montignac

## August 973

Audebert woke and looked at the empty corner of the dungeon where his brother had been. He slapped his thighs and jiggled his knees to try to get the blood warmed up, before rising painfully to his feet to begin his morning walk, as he called it, to amuse himself. A few months ago a new jailor arrived and this one talked to them. A change came over Helie who sensed something that might be used to his advantage.

'Yer father's died,' the jailor told them abruptly one day.

'That makes me the Count of La Marche,' Helie called up, 'and rich.'

Little by little each day Audebert saw that Helie was priming the jailor to help him escape, and one morning Audebert woke to find his brother gone. Just like that. No message, no words of farewell. It was possible that Helie had been taken out and hung, but it seemed more likely that the courting of the jailor had borne fruit and Helie had not seen fit to include his younger brother in either his escape or his plans.

Audebert knew the surface of the rock in the pit as if it were his own skin, every crack where a morsel of glistening brilliant moss clung, every fissure where insects scurried, every smooth projecting round stone that he could wrap his hand around, every jagged edge. Some days he studied the pit and its minimal lifeforms: the ants, lichen and mosquitos. He traced with his finger a thin, pale pink vein that ran through the damp, dark rock, close to the ground, rising upwards shaped like an eyebrow. Some days he sat and stared at the circle of sky and the infrequent events there: the brightening of dawn, the flight of birds and clouds, the darkling of twilight, and once in a while he saw the moon there – beautiful, beyond reach. Some days he kept his eyes shut and watched the play of light blobs and sparks floating behind his eyelids, or he remembered, or he imagined. Whatever he did, in the end it led to grief, the knowledge that the world was going on without him. The worst thing was not touching anything warm and living – no person, no hound, no horse, not being in the proximity of anything else breathing. He longed to hold someone in his arms – his mother, his little brother Gausbert, but mostly Adalmode, and feel the heat of their warm skin against his cheek. He longed for a bath to ease his knotted muscles and his joints stiff with inactivity and cold. He longed for a bed since he never truly slept here, only slipped into unconsciousness, waking slumped painfully against rock and fetters.

Audebert's existence in the hole had been eased by Adalmode's occasional visits and gifts: blankets, food, balm for the sores on his fettered ankle, and he treasured the broken ivory comb she gave him, even though it was impossible to make much use of it on his matted hair and beard. It helped a little with the lice. He told himself stories about the frieze of people and animals carved along its top and then he told those stories to Adalmode and made her laugh. She confirmed his guess, that Helie had escaped, and was on his way to Rome to seek absolution. The marks scratched on the stone behind Audebert's head were numerous now, so many that he tried not to let his glance graze against that wall too often. It had become like a suppurating wound, something he must avert his eyes from, and yet he must keep count. He set up a rhythm to get him through the days and nights, speaking softly to himself for company and to confirm his existence.

As the morning wore on the heat in the pit became stifling, still and stolid like an almost visible thing, the sun boiling up the sky's bowl above his head and the stones soaking up and holding the brilliant rays, no breeze to give him relief. It was impossible to do anything except doze and feel leaden, lethargic. He tried to decide whether this was any better or worse than the bitter winter he had just shivered through, with hail clattering down against the stone and lingering in cracks and corners like frogspawn. It was hard to remember that cold now, in this heat. Audebert sat with his bare legs extended before him, thinking how thin and filthy they were, watching a slender line of sweat trickle down his arm towards his bony wrist, catching in his peripheral vision another bead of sweat dropping from his nose onto his chest. It would be best to sit here naked but then Adalmode might come and so he retained his ragged shirt and loincloth, not wanting to offend her with the sight of his exposed, emaciated body. He maintained his exercise regime in the early mornings when the temperature was cooler and it was possible to move without immediately becoming a waterfall of sweat, and worse, developing a terrible thirst that could not be slaked. It grieved him to see how little power he had left in his limbs. Perhaps he would die soon. Sometimes Adalmode came every day for a week and talked with him, sometimes she was gone for many more weeks and he wondered if she would ever come again.

'Audebert!'

Her voice. He blinked up into the blinding sunlight. 'Lady Adalmode, it is a great pleasure to see you, although I cannot actually see you at the moment,' he said shielding his eyes from the glare, and slowly rising to his feet, to be a few inches nearer to her. 'I have missed you these last twenty days.' Audebert did his best to inject optimism and insouciance into his voice but he knew that she could hear the desperation in its timbre just as he could.

'I'm sorry Audebert, to have left you alone so long. I was visiting a neighbouring family with my mother.'

'Of course,' smiled Audebert. 'You have a life to lead.' Again his cheerfulness rang false in his own ears.

'It must be very hard now you are alone,' said Adalmode, and he saw she was looking him over with concern.

'Well, my brother was not the best of companions, but yes, he was a companion. Slightly more responsive than this rock I suppose.'

She laughed a little with him but then her expression suddenly sobered. 'I want to ask you something Audebert.'

'Yes?'

'Did you actually blind and murder that priest as everyone says?'

There was a silence between them. Audebert sighed. 'No, Lady. I was not there when my brother attacked the priest. As you know, some have taken advantage of the poor state of repair in the countryside and at the monasteries left in the wake of the invasions of the Northmen, and they have looted and rendered the ruination even worse.' He paused. It was not a good thing to admit of his brother, but it was true, and he needed Adalmode to know the truth. 'Helie thought to take treasure from the undefended monastery of Charroux, to gain independence that my father did not allow him, and he was angered by your father and brother's defeat of him in a skirmish at Brosse. He wanted revenge. The priest Benedict came upon him and Helie blinded him, mistaking him for an armed man.' Audebert spoke reluctantly of the crime that his brother had enacted. 'When Helie realised with horror the sin he had committed he did not know what to do. He sent a messenger to me saying he had made an error and to come and help him. I didn't know until I got there what the error was.' Audebert paused again. 'But I swear to you Adalmode, that Helie did not murder the priest. He lives still but in darkness in a monastery. The account that he was murdered is an exaggeration.' The sun shifted so he could look up and see the concentration on Adalmode's face as she listened to his story. 'I had only been there for a short time, talking with Helie, telling him that he must go home to our father and confess his actions and seek penance, when your father and brother suddenly arrived and took us by surprise.' He paused again. 'This is the truth, Lady Adalmode.'

'I know it,' she said with conviction. 'I pray for you to Saint Léonard of Noblat. I would not give you hope when I do not know of any, but perhaps this escape of your brother's will in time lead to some change in your own circumstances.'

'I try not to hope. My brother warned me against doing so, and yet I must, especially when I see your kind and lovely face, Adalmode.'

He could not be sure at this distance but he thought her cheeks reddened a little at his words. From down here in the hole he had watched her blooming from a girl to a young woman, a very lovely young woman. He caught a flicker of movement from the corner of his eye. A small lizard was darting its way up from the pit towards Adalmode and Audebert willed it to reach that destination, that opening to freedom. Take her a gentle touch on her boot from me, he thought, if you reach that high.

'Tell me something of the world, Lady Adalmode.'

'What do you want to know about?'

'What is happening at the courts of the great families?'

Adalmode considered for a moment. She knew some things that a peddlar had told her and Guy recently, but perhaps Audebert knew much more of the world than she, and she did not want to appear foolish. 'Well, they say Hugh, the young Duke of France, is the power behind the throne of the weak King Lothaire,' she ventured.

Audebert laughed shortly and Adalmode feared she had got things wrong. 'Nothing much has changed then. His father before him was king in all but name. Charlemagne was a great king with a great empire and a long reign but it all began to be torn apart by his descendents the minute Charlemagne died, and now we just have the runts of his litter as our kings. They rule only the northeast corner of the Frankish lands now,' he said dismissively.

Adalmode took a breath of relief. She had it right after all.

'I'm sorry Audebert, my source is merely the peddlar who brings silks and needles for my mother to buy. I fear this is not a very good quality of news for you!'

Audebert shook his head. 'Better than the spiders and rats who are all I have to hear from otherwise. Is Lothaire as weak a king as everyone thought he would be when the nobles sat him on his throne as a boy?'

'He doesn't seem to command a great deal of admiration. There are fears that his little son, Louis, may be witless too. My brother says the great nobles to the north – the Duke of France, the Counts of Normandy, Anjou, Blois and the others, that they vie for control of the king and the prince. The Duke of France's sister, Emma, was married to the Viking Count Richard of Normandy but she has died and now they say he has taken his concubine, Gunnora as wife and legitimised their bastard children.'

41

Audebert nodded at the last piece of information which judging by the expression on his face was something he had not known.

'Yes it's a sad state of things when Charlemagne's descendents have to give Frankish lands to Viking marauders because the northern lords are not strong enough to repel them.'

'As you say,' Adalmode went on, 'we hear very little about the king here. The power in these lands is the Duke of Aquitaine, called Iron Arm.'

Audebert frowned but said, 'Yes. My ancestors were appointed Counts by King Rudolph many years ago in an attempt to curb the power of that family.' He was silent for a moment. 'Do you go to the Duke's Assembly in Poitiers?'

'I went once and my brother Guy goes most years.'

'What news there then?'

'The Duke's sister, Adelais, is married to Hugh, the Duke of France, and Adelais has just borne a son.' Adalmode tried to remember what else she had overheard at table or anything else the peddlar had told her mother. 'Duke Guillaume of Aquitaine and his wife Emma have a baby son, but the Duke has a mistress, Lady Aldearde of Aulnay and Duchess Emma does not like it.'

Adalmode stopped, embarrassed again. Audebert was laughing. Of course he did not want to hear this tittle-tattle. He needed to know who was at war with who.

'There is no news regarding La Marche that I know of. I suppose your brothers, Gausbert and Boson are holding it, whilst Helie is on pilgrimage to Rome.'

Audebert nodded. On her last visit Adalmode told him that before he died his father had done penance and offered a donation to a monastery in recompense for his son's crime but it had come to nothing in relation to his own freedom.

'My brother says the marriage of Emma of Blois to Guillaume of Aquitaine was engineered by her brother, the Count of Blois, to give some balance against the power of the Duke of France and that Geoffrey Count of Anjou is the other great power in the land. He has an heir named Fulk and the peddlar told us the Count's sister, Blanche, who is married to the Count of Gévaudan, is a very great beauty.'

'Indeed she is,' Audebert said. 'I saw her once when I went with my father to Angers, the year before I was captured, and it was a sorry thing to see such a lovely young woman yoked with the old Count of Gévaudan, who is many years her senior.'

Adalmode felt embarrassed again at her ignorance. She was dealing second-hand gossip about people that he had actually met.

'Geoffrey of Anjou won a victory against Duke William this year at Les Roches,' Adalmode faltered, trying hard to remember the details. 'And the Duke conceded to Anjou lands south of the river Vienne and even rights in the Convent of the Holy Cross.'

'In Poitiers! St Radegund's Convent?'

'Yes.'

'Well that can't please Guillaume to have this Count from Anjou holding rights in the very heart of the Duke's own territory.'

Adalmode shook her head in agreement, pleased that she had managed to distract him for a while with her news, pleased that he was still interested in the world, despite his long confinement. 'I brought you these things.' She signalled to the jailor who was standing at a discreet distance out of Audebert's line of sight and out of earshot, and a basket was lowered on a rope, a rope that was too flimsy to bear the weight of a man, even a starved one such as Audebert. He drew out the bundle inside and the basket was raised up again.

'Thank you Lady.'

'Won't you see what it is?'

Audebert wiped his dusty hands one at a time on his shirt and unfolded the cloth revealing a small illuminated book, some good bread and cheese, a small bladder of wine. He smiled up his thanks to Adalmode. The book would keep him busy for hours. It was the third she had brought to him. He did his best to keep them clean and dry and returned each to her on the next visit, so that nobody would notice her illicit borrowings from the Montignac book chest.

'Bless you Adalmode for your great kindness to me.'

'It's my birthday,' she said. 'I wanted to celebrate with you.' He saw her hesitate before saying, 'I am thirteen now. Of an age to be betrothed.' She waited for his response.

'My sincere good wishes on your birth day, Lady!' Audebert would have liked to say more, but what could he say to her when he was down here, filthy and shamed. A priest occasionally came to look down into the hole and pronounce anathema against him: 'Your arms are accursed, your horses are accursed. You will be refused Christian burial.' Although he did not commit the crime, he must pay for the actions of his kin. He looked up at Adalmode perplexed. Her mention of betrothal was intentionally suggestive perhaps, but why, apart from Christian kindness, would she be interested in a half-dead criminal. He was familiar enough with her by now to know that she would not taunt him. He frowned an enquiry to her, 'Adalmode . . .' She was gazing anxiously at him with those beautiful green eyes, the colour of young grass after rain. If he were not in this dungeon, if he were restored, clean, well-fed, the brother of the Count of La Marche, perhaps he could ask for her hand in marriage, but now, in this hole, in this sorry condition? He heard a mutter from the jailor and knew that his time with Adalmode was up again.

'I have to go,' she said and raised her hand to him, her gaze lingering on his upturned face and the doubtful expression there.

# 5

## Ségur

### February 974

Aina and I are seated on the long wooden chest at the foot of her bed, and I am sewing together two pieces of cloth to make a skirt. Aina looks up as her mother, Lady Melisende, comes into the room.

'Here is my new gown Aina, that your father bought for my birthday. What do you think?' She twirls around, holding the train of the gown in one hand. It is a dark velvety brown with intricate golden embroidery at the hem, cuffs and neckline.

'Lovely!' exclaims Aina, 'but whatever you do, Mother, don't ask *her* opinion,' she giggles, pointing at me.

I look up from my work, perplexed.

'And why is that Aina?' asks Melisende, with a look of mock disapproval on her face.

'*She* will tell you the absolute truth, with no frills. She cannot tell a lie, even a kind one.'

I frown at this description of myself. Melisende draws a stool close to me, and sits down companionably close, glancing at the stitching in my hands. 'Your sewing is very fine, my Northchild,' she says and I am aware of Aina in my peripheral vision, scowling at her mother's use of my petname.

'Thank you, my Lady.'

'And is this so, Sigrid? You cannot tell a lie.'

'I can't see any good reason to do so,' I answer staunchly, 'but I can keep a still tongue if that is a better route.'

Melisende smiles and cups her hand affectionately around

mine. 'Indeed!' she says warmly, looking with an amused expression to her daughter. 'Truth-saying is virtuous, Aina, and we should all admire Sigrid's example.'

Aina tosses her thick red hair over her shoulder and laughs. 'Mother, every silly maid in the place would be crying their hearts out and every man-servant would be too depressed to get out of bed and go to work, if Sigrid's truths were spoken everywhere.'

Melisende shakes her head at her daughter and pats my knee before standing up. 'You stick to your truths, Northchild. There is no malice in you, I know.'

'I *do* like your new dress, Lady Melisende,' I call out rapidly as she reaches the door, and turns back to me. I frown crossly at Aina. 'The colour is so rich and becoming and the golden stitching is beautiful. I would like to copy it for the dress I am making for Aina.'

'See!' says Aina. 'The truth, the absolute truth, Mama!'

They both laugh and Melisende wiggles her fingers to us as she goes out.

'Forgive me, Sigrid, for teasing you,' Aina says, sorry for only a fleeting moment. 'Tell me the story of your arrival here again, won't you?'

I look at her indulgently and draw a deep breath, poking my needle carefully into the fabric on my lap. I will need my hands to tell my story. I am famed in the household for storytelling. 'I wintered in Aachen with your parents and I learnt my serving duties. When the spring came we began the long journey back here. After many, many days and weeks of travelling we saw a fortress on the horizon, etched grey against the pale morning sky, besieged by the black gnarled twists of vines and framed on either side by limestone cliffs tinted rose and lavender. In the nearby fields there were dark red cattle and I watched oxen plant their feet slowly, their eyes protected from the sun and flies by hemp rags. "Ségur!" Lord Ademar called to me. "Home!" But it was not my home then. Not yet. We rode past tall poplars alongside a fishy stream and the river held the trees up and then down in reflection. We rode through a village straggling and winding around the steep sides of the fortifications and the villagers came out to watch us and call greetings to Ademar and Melisende. Inside the walls of the castle the steward, Renaud, came to greet his master and mistress, and just behind him a young girl about the same age as me came tripping and skipping down pale stone steps.'

Aina laughs at this description of herself.

'"Aina!" Lady Melisende called out gladly. The girl had thick red hair that hung and swung straight down her back like a gorgeous silk curtain, and I thought with regret of my own lost braid lying in the dust on the road somewhere near Quentovic.' Though Aina is ten and a girl still, she should be wearing a veil over her hair but she rarely does what she should. I continue my description of my first meeting with her. 'The girl had large grey eyes and a fine gown that was tucked short into her belt, showing her legs like a boy. In her hand she held a small, calf-bound white book. I had only ever seen Christian priests with books at home, trying to convert us. You stared at me Aina.' I mimic her glare and she giggles. '"You brought a boy!" you said resentfully to your father.'

'I truly thought,' says Aina, 'that Mama and Papa had gone on a journey and brought back a boy because they needed one and I was merely a girl. I was most put out at first until I heard my mistake.'

'Your father chucked you under the chin. "The Northchild is not a boy, silly," he said. "We had to cut her hair short to get rid of the lice. She's a girl like you. A girl you can play with." "Not like me," you asserted, screwing up your nose at me.'

Aina leans forward and kisses my cheek to make up for her initial resentment of me.

'Steward Renaud crouched to slice through the rope at my ankle. "You run," he said, "and", he mimed a hanging, his tongue lolling, and I heard the tinkle of your laughter. I lent around Renaud to glower at you.' I reenact the glower that I greeted Aina with at our first meeting and she stretches her small pink mouth wide in glee, her shoulders shaking.

'"Girl!"' I mimic Renaud's voice and tone of command. 'He shook his head at me and his expression was fierce. I looked miserably to where Lady Melisende had already forgotten me and was entering the hall with you, her chattering daughter excited at her side.'

Aina sighs. 'Poor Sigrid, the poor friendless slave at first.'

'Not friendless now,' I say smiling warmly to her. We fall silent and I turn back to my sewing whilst Aina picks up a scroll telling the story of an explorer in a distant land. Aina's words, 'poor slave,' echo in my head along with the conjured images of my arrival here last year. I felt what seemed to me like the sudden withdrawal of Melisende and Ademar's affection as they were wrapped up in their reunion with their daughter Aina, and the daily business of Ségur. I became just another part of a large household of servants, the lowest part. I felt the weight of my slavery fresh on me then.

The steward Renaud had a pendulous and quaggy belly that swayed when he walked and he never liked me. He beckoned to me in the courtyard on that first day. I followed him to the hot kitchen where a delicious smelling meal was in preparation. Ten sets of eyes turned towards me. Renaud pointed to a table where I sat alone and ate the bread and cheese put before me. I looked surreptiously at the strangers, under my eyelashes, for my experience of slaves was that I might be put to sacrifice, or at least when I was a few years older I expected to be sent unwilling to the beds of men who might treat me badly.

'This girl here,' Renaud told the assembled servants, 'is a pagan slave.' They murmured and frowned and crossed themselves. 'We've never had a slave or a pagan here before,' he went on, 'and the work of a slave is to lug firewood, feed pigs, cut peat, clean shoes, sift cinders, all the dirty work.'

The cook tutted at him. 'Renaud! The girl may be a pagan, but she's a child nonetheless and I'll have no cruelty to no one in my kitchen.'

'You'll do as you please, Becky, I've no doubt as you always do, but I'm telling you this girl is related to them who have devastated our monasteries and coastal towns, and carried our own folk away into slavery and our daughters into prostitution. We all know monks who'll tell us they are glad of a gale that keeps the Vikings off the sea.'

'From the Fury of the Norsemen O Lord deliver us!' recited one of the men sitting near the fire.

'I know all about your subversive tricks, you slaves,' Renaud said addressing me again, 'sabotaging tools, thieving, burning the harvest, mutilating yourself, trying to kill yourself or your unborn babies.'

I stared at him with my mouth open.

'Don't try any of it here,' he said fiercely waving his fist close to my nose, and I shook my head, my eyes wide.

The next morning there was a general agreement in the household that I needed to bathe. The cook accompanied Aina and me through the postern gate and down to the bank of a broad green river that ran around three sides of the castle.

'What's it called?' I asked.

'I'll tell you if you tell me your name,' Aina said.

I hesitated. My initial muteness and the continued withholding of my name were small acts of power in my powerlessness, but there was something about the girl I liked and I wanted her to like me. 'Sigrid Thorolfsdottir,' I said.

'Sigrid,' she said with satisfaction, and did not attempt to pronounce the second more difficult part of my name. 'Well, Sigrid, the river is called the Auvézère and flows down towards Périgueux through this plateau which is named the Bocage. Can you swim?'

I nodded, suppressing my contempt at this ridiculous question.

'Don't try to escape,' Aina said. 'I'll catch you and you'll get a whipping so bad you won't sit down for a fortnight.'

'Alright,' I told her.

The place we had come to was a placid sheet of water created by a small waterfall the breadth of the river, just before the bridge. Water roared down in glassy sheer sheets over black boulders. Behind the waterfall, the green placid pool was easy to enter from flat rocks extending towards the river. White fluffy flowers gathered in clumps on the water's surface and in rocky crevices on the bank. A frog leapt in ahead of me. A few leaves twisted and turned on the surface. Aina and I stripped to our shifts and waded in.

I swam out to the deep centre of the river, revelling in the sun on my face and the silky liquid sliding over my grimed skin, soaking at my tangled muscles and heart. I breathed in smelling the scent of soil suspended in the water. The sunlight striped the pale skin of my arm under the light green water. Thorgils will find me I told myself. He will come and take me back to my freedom.

The castle stood above us on a rise in the bend of the Auvézère, banners flying on the towers and at intervals along the steep path leading up to it. A double-arched stone bridge crossed the water a little way upstream and the small village clustered at the foot of the hill near the bridge with irregular height houses and gaily coloured roofs. Two small boats bobbed, tied to the opposite bank, one painted curious patterns in black and white and the other painted brown. Next time if I took a knife from the kitchen to slice their moorings, if I could be sure the oars were in the boat, I could escape.

Green leaves hung in thick swathes from trees leaning from the bank. Reflected light danced. The church bells chimed the hour – seven strokes and then a joyful pealing calling us to breakfast. The water was surprisingly warm for one who had grown up swimming in icy fjords. I swam round and round in large circles. Aina hauled herself out onto one of the flat stones and sat drying, watching me suspiciously, ready to leap in and give chase if I showed signs of escape. Wait. Watch and wait. Be patient. My father's voice was in my head, from the times he taught me to hunt. Better to run when I am sure than to risk a beating or worse, a maiming that might ruin my chances of freedom forever. I swam back, shook myself like a dog on the bank and put on my clothes. They were a good fit but old and threadbare in places – Aina's cast-offs.

A few days after my arrival Ademar took me to see the castle chaplain, Father Dominic, and explained that I would be instructed as a Christian and then I could be freed and would no longer be a slave.

'No,' I said firmly.

'Sigrid . . .' Ademar began and the chaplain tutted and reached for a wide leather strap hanging on the wall. Ademar stayed the chaplain's arm and looked enquiring at me. 'It's for the best Sigrid. You are in a Christian land now.'

I eyed the strap but clutched my Thor hammer. I had to remember my brothers, my father, and my homeland at all costs. I must keep something of myself that could not be bought or commanded and I had resolved with myself that I would not lie or compromise concerning my gods.

'No,' I said loudly, looking with steel into Ademar's eyes, 'I am a Northchild.'

'Hmmpf, let me see to this my Lord,' said the priest, 'We are told in the Psalms: Thou shalt bruise the heathen with a rod of iron and break them in pieces like a potter's vessel.'

'No,' said Ademar, holding up a hand to Father Dominic. 'I'll not have her compelled or ill-treated. Very well Sigrid, then you will continue as a slave if that is your wish. We will ask you again when you have been here a while longer.'

The other servants were all free, so I was the lowliest person, which meant that I had the worst, most unpleasant jobs that nobody else wanted to do. If the privy needed cleaning that was my job, or if the field needed dunging then I must go and do the work.

On the rare occasions when I saw Ademar he winked at me and asked me how I did. 'Well,' I said, 'thank you sir.' He remembered me shackled and dishevelled at the slave market and I felt shame for that.

'*Bonne!*' he said.

When I went to the spigot, Aina sometimes came to stare at me. She sat on the steps, watching me go back and forth between the well and the kitchen. 'What does it feel like to be a slave?' Aina asked eventually.

'I wouldn't know,' I said smugly watching Aina's eyebrows crease together in confusion.

The humiliation of my enslavement was hard to bear. In my dreams the silver coils of my brooch transformed into a splendid ship with a serpent masthead and I rode across the sea to Thorgils and Olafr shouting: 'Leap from the fetters! Escape from the foes!,' but then my dream turned to nightmare, for I found them harshly used as slaves, working in a mine or sometimes a treadmill. Their backs were streaked purple from the lash and the rest of their flesh had a hideous pallor. The pupils of their eyes were eaten away by smoke so that they could hardly see and groped at me, asking, 'Is that you Sigrid?' I woke from such dreams sweating, my eyelashes clumped wet with grief.

'Tell me about your homeland,' Aina tried when she saw me the next day.

I considered shaking my head in refusal but I wanted to speak of it. 'I am from Viken in Norway. My countrymen have travelled all around the world and seen many strange things.'

'What things?' said Aina in an avid voice.

'On Iceland there are twenty volcanos. They erupt with lava and ash and black sand.' I searched my memory for what I had heard as a small child and my recollections had no connections, one to another. 'We had a neighbour who was called Halfdan the Generous with Money but Stingy with Food.'

Aina laughed, bending over and pressing her hand to her side. 'You're making my face ache Sigrid, stop!' she cried.

'Well it's not all funny,' I said. 'In Norway winters are sometimes so cruel we had to carry the livestock out to the fields in the spring because they were so enfeebled by lack of feed, and if the harvest failed we had to make bread from the bark of trees.'

'That sounds foul,' she said, pulling a face. 'What about your gods? You have lots of them?'

'Odinn has a horse called Sleipner with eight legs – very fast. The Gods live in Asgard and they travel across Bifrost the Rainbow Bridge to our world, to Midgard. The underworld is called Niflheim.'

'A rainbow bridge!' exclaimed Aina and I could see the imagining of it dancing in her eyes. 'You have goddesses too don't you?'

'Frigg is the wife of Odinn and the mother of Baldr.' Aina was staring at me agog. 'Freyja has a chariot drawn by two cats and she is the goddess of love.'

'Cats?' queried Aina.

I nodded yes, my blue eyes wide to express my awe and reverence of my Aesir. 'Gerdr is the wife of Freyr and she was once a giantess. Sif has golden hair and is the wife of Thor. Skadi used to be married to Njordr the god of the sea but she separated from him and she lives in the mountains and hunts on skis with a bow.'

Aina's eyebrows were raised high as she took in this information. Her small mouth was open in a perfect O and she shook her head slowly from side to side. 'We have Mary,' she said, 'she is the mother of Jesus, the son of God, but she was a Virgin and wasn't married to God. She was married to Joseph a carpenter.'

'Are you sure?' I asked, bemused.

'Yes,' said Aina and shrugged her shoulders. 'Tell me more about Skadi who hunts on skis.'

In return for my tales of gods, Aina told me how one of the Ségur gardeners talked to the plants. 'And listens to them talking to him too!' she exclaimed, and she told me that Renaud is known as the Ségur Chronicle because he hears and retails all the gossip. 'And,' she said, 'I overheard my mother's maid telling the kitchen maid that she would *do* Phillippe if she got the chance.' We exchanged baffled looks. Phillippe had just returned from his trading trip.

'I hope she doesn't mean that she would hurt him,' I said. 'I like him.'

'Me too,' said Aina.

When I was set to clean the Lord and Lady's chamber one day, I was astonished by the array of toys Aina possessed: miniature spoons, jugs and goblets for her dolls, glove puppets, a rocking bird that stuck its tongue out from its beak, brightly coloured spinning tops and a hobby-horse with little bells on its harness. Aina showed them to me and let me hold the bird and make its tongue stick out at her.

On another day Renaud took me and the priest with him out to the sheep who were suffering from murrain disease. Father Dominic opened his Bible and solemnly began to recite from its pages to the stricken flock. I remembered my father telling me that Christians were fools, and I kept the laughter from my face. Sometimes I was sent with the dogs to guard the flock from wolves, to lead sheep and goats back to the sheds and milk them, to do the arm-aching work of making butter and cheese.

'It's a life of sweat and dirt, maid, but it will soon be over,' the cook told me, which gave me no comfort. I had to find my brothers and avenge my father before my days were over, and I was just wasting my time here. When I thought of making an escape my heart sank for it had been a journey of many months to come here, through lands that I knew nothing of. There was no sight of the sea. If there had been sea I think I would have just made away in a boat as soon as possible and trusted myself to Odinn. Here I could only think to escape on the river, but I needed to wait and find out more about where it would take me.

My work was to tend sheep and pigs, help with the harvest, cook, brew beer, wait at table, nurse those in the household who were sick, spin, weave, dye, sew, work in the garden and vineyard and look after the animals in the courtyard. Most of the time I was covered in soot and smuts from cleaning fires or some of my other work and it was near impossible to keep my face, hands and apron clean. I went short on the milk and scraps given to me, leaving them instead for the house spirits hoping they would help me with my chores. I was sorry but also smug when another maid had a misfortune – bruising her hip on the corner of the table in her hurry, scalding her fingers on a hot dish, or dropping and breaking a precious glass – for it was obvious, since they were Christians, that they were not leaving the necessary gifts for the helpful house spirits, whereas I often saw the spirits disappearing around distant corners, little old men with wrinkled faces and pointy hoods, carrying brooms and doing some of my work for me.

Preparing food in the kitchen that would be carried into the hall, I poured the broth carefully from the pan into three bowls for Ademar, Melisende and Aina, breathing in deeply, savouring the scent of the rich brown soup flecked with orange and white chunks of vegetable. My stomach rumbled, anticipating my own meagre portion of the leftovers later. I slept in the kitchen at nights with the household dogs. I dreamt of my father standing on the far side of the fjord calling to me in the cold, clear air, of the sledge that he made for us one year that we could hitch to a pony and drive through the snow, of Thorgils and I running through dark, slender trees, encumbered by our thick fur cloaks. I dreamt of racing downhill on skis with Olafr to try to get back in time for something urgent – what was it? I woke trying to clutch at the mystery of what we were racing towards, unable to grasp it.

It was my job to keep an eye on the fire, to riddle it and stoke it up in the mornings before anyone else was up and about. Sometimes I woke late with the cook's boot poking in my ribs. She was cross that there would be a delay in baking the morning bread. At night, when I finally lay down after my hard labours of the day, I tried to stay awake to spend a little time in the longed for privacy of my own head, and I would trace my serpent's curves through its flimsy cotton pocket. I liked to think this caress woke the serpent and it spoke to me telling stories of my homeland and my kin. As the months at Ségur wore on, my recall of my father's face and voice became vague and he seemed to slip away from me, more and more just a dim reflection in a murky pond, but Thorgils was always vivid, his aquamarine eyes – now green, now blue, depending on whether or not we were on the water – his freckles clustered densely together all over his face.

Ségur was a mostly harmonious place presided over by Ademar and Melisende. There were subtle gradations of everybody there which I learnt in time. The dairy maid was considered superior to the girl who tended the pigs and she in her turn was considered to have more standing than the maid who looked after the poultry, taking them out for daily walks behind her like a gaggle of school children. The steward Renaud was the most important of Ademar's servants, and after him came Phillippe, who assisted with the trading, and then the miller, the smith, the foresters, and the herdmen. There were so many servants each with their own duties and rights that it took me a long time to get to know them all and to understand the strange customs. There was a ploughman, a bee-keeper, an oxherd, a cowherd, shepherds, a cheesemaker, a barnman, a woodward, a hayward and sowers.

Aina told me: 'Each sower gets to keep one basket of wheat for themselves, for their own strips of field. The cowherd can pasture his cow with ours. If a tree blows down in the forest it belongs to the woodman and the corn that falls by the barndoor belongs to the barnman.'

I frowned at her, thinking there seemed room for cheating in these rules, but Ademar was respected by his household and Renaud kept a tight rein. Some servants were free and some were unfree serfs, but as a slave I was the most lowly. Ademar, Melisende, Aina, and many of the servants treated me with kindness but some of the lesser servants took advantage of for once having someone lower than them, and they looked on me with contempt and suspicion, muttering that a pagan would soon go straight to hell.

There was a large chestnut tree on the riverbank, some distance from the castle gate and not visible from the walls. I decided that this would be my sacred tree and as often as I could I left small offerings there to the Aesir and the Vanir, begging that they would keep Thorgils and Olafr safe and help me to find them very soon. I could not push the toleration of Ademar too far and if anyone found out I was sacrificing to my gods I would be badly beaten, so I left things that if noticed I could say I had just dropped them: a shiny pin, a strand of scarlet thread, a lump of bread. I would be punished for carelessness too, but it would be mild compared to the fury that would be unleashed against me if I were caught in my solitary rites. I prayed to the Aesir in my head and assured them of my secret loyalty and hoped they would be loyal to me and give me my freedom, and I looked for the omens of birds and tried to hear the raven's sayings.

Father Dominic sometimes railed in the chapel against pagan gods who were demons according to him, and he always looked at me then and the whole household, excepting Ademar and Melisende, would turn around and stare at me. Aina would also turn and stare at me but with frank interest on her face. Margareta, the poultry girl, who envied me Phillippe's kindnesses, said I needed to be exorcised and I gave her the hebegeebies because I looked like a carrot. I tried to keep my head down and keep my own counsel but I was stubborn in my beliefs as in everything else.

'Saint Paul said let women keep silence in the churches,' bellowed Father Dominic in his sermon that I was made to sit through, 'Adam was not deceived, but the woman was deceived, and was in sin. We see prostitutes all around us wearing fine clothes.' To my mind, Father Dominic and his god spoke ill of women and I would have none of them.

Every now and then Ademar or Melisende would try gentle persuasion. 'There are many of your countrymen, Sigrid,' Ademar told me, 'who accept that Christ is a God, one among many, alongside your Aesir – could you start with that perhaps? And let Father Dominic tell you about Christ in that way and then make up your own mind – I know you will make up your own mind.'

56

I shook my head. I had taken my ground and I was going to stand it. Nothing would change my mind – not beatings, not harangues, not alienation and ostracising. Eventually they gave up. I wore them down or they forgot about my secret resistance as I went through the motions, attending their church services.

Phillippe recognised that I clung to my own traditions and each time he returned from a trip North he brought me something: two oval brooches, a decorated book in Norse, a rune-carved mirror.

'What do the marks say?' Aina asked, excited, but I pretended that I could not read them, for they simply said Toka made this for Inga, and that was a little disappointing. If I were at home Thorgils would have made me such a gift and the runes would say Thorgils Thorolfsson carved this for his sister Sigrid Thorolfsdottir. Instead I had to worry about what had happened to Inga that she had lost her mirror. Was she made a slave like me?

'Why do you resist converting Sigrid?' Aina asked. 'Would it not go better for you to do so, with Father Dominic, but also with the other servants who do not accept you because you are stubbornly pagan.'

'I cannot say I believe in your god and not in mine when that is not the truth. I cannot lie.'

'Don't you like it here?'

'Yes, your parents and many people are kind to me but I don't belong here. I am ripped from my life. I belong on a boat, in a fjord, on a mountain, in sun or snow and ice.'

At night, lonely for Thorgils and Olafr, I sometimes sat by the well and sang songs in Norse. The sound of my singing carried in the night air to Aina where she lay on a pallet in her parents' room, until one night she asked, 'Mother, may I sleep in the other chamber to myself and may I have Sigrid for my own maid?'

Everybody in Ségur was stacked up in their proper order, but I saw noblemen come to visit the household who were not noble and spoke unkindly or lasciviously to the maids, and I saw the lowest, like me, who could be as noble as a king and as kind as an angel. Sometimes Melisende sent Aina and I on an errand to the village to the chandlers or the fishmongers and I witnessed the orders of the people there. In the house of a weaver there were five women spinning for him and children worked sorting and carding the wool. The women had to work hard, scouring flax and combing hemp. The butcher was a widow woman and though she had two boys who were apprentices, she also had her two young daughters under her tutelage. One of the boys told me that apprentices had to swear not to marry, frequent taverns, tell their mistress or master's secrets or to rob the master. I nodded. This seemed reasonable. I considered that everyone in a way was indentured to someone else – even the lords owed a duty to their overlords, and if they were good men as Ademar was, then they owed a duty of protection to their servants, tenants and serfs too. Some mornings I woke longing with a desperate intensity to be able to do, just for one day, only what I wished and not what I was told. I saved those feelings up, promising myself that one day they would have their chance, they would be able to soar out.

Walking to the village one morning Aina and I stopped to exchange gossip with the laundresses at the river as they washed and wrung out clothes, their arms and hands red and chaffed. Aina called a hello to two men thatching on the roof of a house. In the fields men, women and children were weeding. The peasants here lived frugal lives, with a few pigs, cows and sheep, slender meals and rough clothes. When times were good they lived a simple life but if the harvest was poor they would be wretched and hungry and Ademar did what he could to bring the families relief. We stopped off that morning in the inn, because Melisende had sent a tonic to the innkeeper's wife who was recovering from a difficult birth. The innkeeper sat us down in his warm kitchen with two small beakers of hot mead to warm us and chunks of fresh bread. We could hear snatches of men's conversations from the main room of the inn.

'These rich lords,' an angry voice exclaimed, grown loud with drinking, 'they are either raiding us: killing, stealing, slaving, or they offer us their "protection".' His last word was said with a sneer. 'And the price of our "gratitude" for their so-called protection is our submission to their unjust commands and their greedy tolls and tithes.'

'Hush, man!' I heard the innkeeper cry, no doubt conscious of Lady Aina listening in his kitchen. 'You speak unwisely and here in these lands, unreasonably, for our lord, Lord Ademar is a fair man and we are all truly glad of his protection of us.'

The drunken man began to argue with this, but we could not hear properly, as the innkeeper nudged the kitchen door shut with his shoulder as he passed with two beakers of ale in his hands.

'My father is not greedy and unjust!' Aina said indignantly to me.

'No, but many lords are, and this man speaks of those others. He is right that the inequalities are not right.'

'How can you speak so, Sigrid? The orders of the people are the will of God.'

'Your God,' I say and she rolls her eyes at me and tears off another chunk of the warm bread with her teeth, in an unlady-like manner that Lady Melisende would not allow at the hall table.

Ademar and Melisende had Aina and me educated together by Father Dominic since there was no boy in the family to teach instead. Father Dominic protested to Ademar that women should not read and write. 'Their minds should be constricted,' he said, 'because they can't be trusted.' Ademar diplomatically but firmly rebutted his arguments.

In our classes Aina ran rings around him. She was good at counting and I was good at stories. If Father Dominic set us something to write for our task that day, Aina would pout and say to her mother, 'I want Sigrid to do it for me.'

Melisende would widen her eyes and shake her head. 'What a daughter, eh, Sigrid?' she'd say.

The thought of spending time in the company of Father Dominic held no charm for either of us, but for me, there was an added grief. Since he was forbidden by Ademar to beat me for my failure to accept Christianity, he took full advantage of the opportunities presented to him in my schooling instead and most days he made me put out my hands and hit them with a leather strap for any reason he could concoct. Aina took me into the kitchen afterwards and applied butter to my swollen fingers.

After one particularly vicious beating, she marched me to her father where he sat with his clerk, surrounded by accounts, in the

Great Hall, and held my palms out under his nose. '*Enough* of that mean priest, Father! I'll not tolerate this more. We need to go to the nunnery once a week for our lessons now. Father Dominic is barely literate or numerate himself anyways!'

Ademar looked at my hands and then at his daughter's impassioned face in astonishment, and after that we did indeed go to the nunnery for our lessons.

I look up at Aina now and smile, catching her eye. She pushes herself up from her seat and steps close, bending to kiss the top of my head. 'We are so different, you and I, and I love you for it,' she says. The long hanks of Aina's loose hair mingle with my red braids, as she bends over me and it is difficult to tell where the hair of each of us begins and the other ends in the tawny mass of our two heads together. Aina's hair is the dark red of an autumn leaf or the depths of a rich red wine held up in a glass towards the light, whilst mine is brighter, tending more towards the colour of amber. Aina's hair is straight but mine has grown back curling. My skin has a thickness and a ruddy tint about it, stretched smoothly across my prominent high cheekbones. If you knew to think about it, mine is clearly a Scandinavian face. My eyelashes and eyebrows are light brown. Phillippe told me that when the sun touches my head there is a red aura coming from my hair and skin. Aina's pale skin, on the other hand, does not take the sun as well as mine. She sometimes suffers with sunburn if she uncovers any part of herself for too long outside.

'Yes,' I say, agreeing placidly that we are different, reaching up to smooth her hair from her face with both my hands.

Aina sits back down on the chest and sighs. There are three hours yet until supper. 'Tell me about it again, Sigrid,' she says. 'I know it was so hard on you, but tell me again. I love to hear of the sea and the ship and the strangers.'

'Perhaps another time my Lady,' I demur. Aina swings one foot back and forth, but contains her frustration. I watch her do it and relent. 'Alright,' I say, and my mistress sits up straight instantly, her face brightening, 'I will tell you again. I am Sigrid Thorolfsdottir,' I say, and then wait for the rustling of Aina's skirts to stop as she wriggles expectantly on her stool and clasps her hands together beneath her chin.

'This is the story of my childhood, before I was enslaved. Long ago and far away in the snowy lands of Norway where the wolf howls at the *nidjaros* – the northern lights in the sky . . .'

'It wasn't all *that* long ago.'

'Do you want to hear the story or not?'

She presses her lips together, pulling a comical face and twirls her wrist and hand around in the air to indicate that I should continue.

'In Norway in the kingdom of Viken, King Tryggve was the grandson of Harald Finehair who had ruled all Norway and conquered all the world.'

'*All* the world, Sigrid?' Aina's voice is laden with scepticism.

'Are you taking this seriously?' I ask crossly.

'Absolutely!'

I pause for a while to make her worry.

She opens her big grey eyes at me. 'Sigrid, please!'

'I was a baby just born and my mother dead in birthing me, and my father a great lord in Viken, when murderers came from Denmark, greedy for land.'

Aina sighs happily. She has heard the story many times before and the sound of the names of people and places strange to her fills her with delight. She repeats them after me, which I find a little annoying but I indulge her.

'My father took the lady he served who was heavy with child, me and my brother, Thorgils, and we fled by boat in the night to hide from the murderers. My father was renowned for his piloting skills and his knowledge of the sea routes. We sailed north and then west with no sight of land for three days and my father steered us by the sun and the stars, the moon and the flight of birds, until we came to the islands of Orkney and we concealed ourselves there.'

'You can't remember any of that?' Aina interjects, excited at the vision of the sea voyage that she is conjuring in her mind's eye.

'No, my Lady, I was a newborn. Thorgils was three years old and little as he was himself, he had to carry me, while my father helped the Lady Astrid whose birthing time was near. As I grew older and began to understand, my father or brother would tell

61

the story of our escape when we gathered around the hearth at night-times, so that I came to know it and tell it to you now.' I draw breath to continue, mimicking the hand gestures and mannerisms of the skalds from my childhood as I tell my story. 'My father took us to the homestead of his kinsman on the Brough of Birsay.'

'Brough of Birsay,' Aina echoes the name. 'What was that place like?'

'It was a tidal island. Twice daily when the tides rose the homesteads were surrounded by roiling waters and cut off from the main island, so that we must live our lives to that rhythm of the sea. When Lady Astrid's time came, the women slung curtains to give her privacy and the men were banished to the neighbouring farmstead. She gave birth to a son and named him Olafr. We stayed there all summer and Thorgils said it was a good time. He watched the warriors set out to go viking and played with the sons of the fishermen and farmers, and me and Olafr, the two babies, we grew strong. My father waited as long as he could to give Lady Astrid time to recover, but he knew we could not stay because the murderers were searching for us everywhere, wanting to kill us.

Before the viking warriors returned home, as the nights began to wax cold and long, we set sail back the way we had come and travelled by night and hid in farmsteads that were friendly to my father, but when the spring tides came, the spies were out looking for us once more. Sailors came in with the tide and the tidings that we were hunted.'

Aina shakes her head from side to side, her eyes wide, impressed as always, at the drama of my young life. 'Nothing so dramatic ever happens here,' she says. 'Why did they hunt so hard for you?'

'Because we were important,' I say mysteriously. 'We travelled by night, in the clothes of plain people and slept in ruined barns and under hedges to avoid speaking with anyone who might betray us. We were exhausted and hungry and in Skaun a man named Biorn turned us away, guessing we were fugitives. We travelled on weary, and came to his neighbour Thorstein's homestead, and he made us welcome, but then a travelling workman came and said the search party were hard by. Biorn had told them of strangers travelling with small children. "Quickly," Thorstein said to us, rousing us from our sleep, "bestir yourselves. You must go now". He sent us with a guide into the forest and we heard the thuds and cracking branches of many horsemen close behind. The guide led us to the edge of a lake and gestured for us to wade into the cold water. My brother held me on his shoulders and my father held Olafr aloft who laughed all the time at this adventure, though the rest of us were solemn and begged him to hush. In the middle of the lake was a small overgrown islet and we hid in the high rushes there, shivering in the water, with my father's hand gentling on Olafr's chattering mouth, as the soldiers searched for us. We heard their calls in the clarity of the morning air, and the snorts and tramp of their horses. We saw their breath white in the cold. I peeked through the reeds and looked mute and anxious into the eyes of my brother Thorgils. The men searching had Thorstein with them and he led them in the wrong direction, away from our hiding place.'

I pause and Aina reaches for the wine jug, pouring a cup for each of us. 'Were you very afraid Sigrid?'

'Oh yes,' I say, 'my heart was thumping hard. My knees were knocking together in the water. I feared that I might, by accident, betray us all, with a sneeze, or the loud sound of my teeth chattering together, or a cry if a frog should jump on my foot, and then we would be killed.

Then father kept us safe at the homestead of Hakon the Old. Olafr and I ran in and out of the longhouses playing and Thorgils learnt the skills of the warrior and pilot from my father. Astrid hid her jewels and fine silks and lived a quiet life. My father showed Thorgils the craft of making a good ship and Olafr and I watched as the boat took shape under their hands. When Olafr and I were eight the enemy soldiers found us.'

Aina gasped even though she had heard the story before.

'My father looked to where his sword stood in the corner. One of the warriors made to grasp Olafr by the arm, but Hakon's thrall, Bristle, jumped between them and slapped down the warrior's hand. Bristle was unarmed but he was a mountain of a man and could do them damage. My father's men were making ready to fight, the warriors backed down and left. Bristle got his freedom for that brave act, but decided to stay with his master in any case. We knew we could not remain there so my father determined to take us to Holmgard to the east.'

'If you were freed, Sigrid, would you stay with us?'

'I am a pagan Northgirl and I need to find my brothers.'

Aina stares steadily at me, disappointment evident in the pout of her mouth. To distract her I say: 'What about the map?' She nods and jumps up to find the large rolled map on the shelf, bringing it back and pinning it down on the table with pebbles, tracing with her finger our voyage. I help her locate the starting point: Viken in Norway, and nod as Aina's finger moves first around the coast of Norway westwards to Orkney, and then back again to Oprostad, then eastwards into southern Sweden and Hakon's homestead near Uppsala, then out into the open sea towards Holmgard.

'Can you remember that voyage?' Aina asks.

'Yes,' I say, miserable, wishing I could not remember it. 'I was near nine years old by then and I can remember every gust of wind and every sparkle of sunlight on the sea as we set sail from the harbour. I remember the sailors calling, the gulls, the sail whipping against the ropes and filling with the sluggish breeze as the sea opened up before us. I remember the hope in the eyes of Lady Astrid as she looked across the expanses of blue sky and sea.' I pause and wipe at the tears on my cheeks.

'Perhaps you should not continue, Sigrid. It's upsetting you.'

I sniff and shake my head. 'It's alright. I've started now so I must tell the tale, and its telling is for the honour of my father and Astrid.' I look back down at the coloured map, my eyes lingering on the green of Viken and conjuring a vision of mountains laced with fjords and longhouses with smoke curling up out of their roofs. 'Perhaps I will go back one day,' I say.

'I should like to come with you,' Aina says eagerly. 'Why don't we go on an adventure together?'

I smile at her but this hardly seems likely, that we would be allowed to go where we wished, or that her parents would not soon send men to chase and bring us back if we ran away. I carry on with my story. 'We set sail and were at sea four days and entered the Baltic Sea, which we called the Eystrasalt, but then we saw the dreaded orange sail of a pirate ship. My father did what he could but there were few fighting men on board and very soon the Eistland pirate ship hauled alongside, the men boarded and killed near everyone. My father was disarmed and forced to his knees before the leader who was named Klerkon. The pirate lifted his sword to strike my father dead. "Give me my sword to hold," cried my father, but the pirate just killed him.' Aina knows from previous tellings of the story on cold winter nights that a Norse warrior must die with his sword in his hand if he is to go to Valhalla and feast with the gods.

Tears are falling down my cheeks and I do not tell Aina of my numb terror at seeing my father killed and thrown into the sea. 'Astrid covered my eyes but her hand was shaking and I saw it all nevertheless. I wished to see it, to burn the image of those men on my eyes so that I could seek revenge upon them. My brothers, Thorgils and Olafr, were doing the same, staring at their faces. My father's lifeless body disappeared into the grey depths, into Niflheim.'

I take a gulp of wine and wipe away my tears with the flat of my palm. The story is on its way now and must flow on. 'The pirates turned to us, especially looking at Astrid who was a beautiful woman.'

'Wouldn't they have been careful with her if she was worth a good ransom?' asks Aina, desperately hopeful as she always is at this part of the story.

'Perhaps,' I say, 'but we knew there was a price on our heads and if she revealed her identity her son would be murdered, so she did what she had to, to protect Olafr. The leader took her away and we did not see her again. I heard she was sold as a bed-slave.'

We are both silent for a moment.

'They didn't show much interest in us: three bedraggled and distraught children. They tied us together with thick, harsh ropes around our ankles and necks, and lashed us to the side of the ship. When the sea was high the waves washed cold and salty over us. At night when the temperature dropped, we clung together for warmth and comfort and had no coverings. They gave us water and stale bread sometimes. The voyage was two days more and in the shivering nights Thorgils murmured stories to distract and reassure me and Olafr until his voice failed from grief and cold. On the third day we arrived at their pirates' nest on Smaeland island and they put us, still roped, in the pig-pen.'

Aina screws up her nose at the imagined smell of it.

'We were there for a few days, sitting and sleeping as best we could. Thorgils shoved the pigs away from us with his foot and shouted when they got too near and the pirates came and laughed at us. At night it was freezing and we huddled together while Thorgils told us that my father was with Freya and we would avenge him and find Olafr's mother. I sang songs that my father had taught me and when Olafr wept and sniffed we pretended we couldn't hear him.

One morning Klerkon came and took us out of the pen. He stripped our tunics from us and threw buckets of cold water over us, as we stood there in our shifts. Then he hung a Thor's hammer on a thong about each of our necks, and put clean, rough tunics on us. We had no shoes and the burn marks from the ropes were red and raw on our necks and wrists. "Hmm," he said, hands on his hips.' I place my hands on my own hips, mimicking the pirate. '"They will do," he said. He tied us again but with a finer rope and pulled us onboard the ship and we sailed for some hours until we came to a large port called Tallinn.'

'And that is where you met my mother and father,' says Aina.

'Yes,' I say and am silent for a while. I look up to see the expectation on my lady's face. For Aina this is the 'good' part of the story, where I am rescued by her parents, but for me this is the worst part and it hurts me to allow the word-pictures to cross my lips and hang there becoming visible in the still air of the chamber. I do not tell of my terror, even greater than when my father died, at being ripped from Thorgils and Olafr.

'And so I was sold to Lord Ademar and Lady Melisende and came here to Ségur with my head cropped, tied with a rope, a louse-bitten slave.' I end my story abruptly, unable to inject heroism into this part, and not wishing to linger on it.

'Sigrid, you can't see anymore to sew in this light,' Aina says, moving the candle as close to me as she dares. 'Looking at the great flame of your hair now, it's hard to remember you as that miserable, shorn-headed child last year. Will you show me the serpent?'

I push back the folds of my dress to show my brooch pinned on my belt. 'It was my father's.'

She touches the curves of the brooch, and then my cheek. 'It's beautiful, Sigrid. Very fine work.'

The dinner bell begins to peal in the Great Hall below, and we stand up, smoothing our skirts.

# 6

# Poitiers

## Easter 974

'Father, I would like to make a new attempt to regain our family honour at this Assembly,' Guy said the week before the family were due to undertake their annual journey to Poitiers. 'A fresh voice and face may sway Duke Guillaume?'

Gerard was silent for a long time. 'Alright son. I have made no headway with the Duke for years. Now it is your turn to try.'

They travelled to the city by river – down the Vienne and then onto the Clain until they reached the outskirts where they disembarked to prepare for their entry into the city, through the gateway in the great Roman walls, past the pale pink brick of the Baptistry of St John where the early Christian Poitevins had been immersed in the baptismal pool, past Saint Radegund's Holy Cross Abbey, past the church of Sancta Maria Maior and onto the Palace of Poitiers with its elegant slender white towers and long slivers of windows.

Riding into the courtyard of the Palace the family were dressed, according to Guy's strategy, in their best finery and Adalmode was loaded with all that remained of Rothilde's jewellery. She wore a dress of fine gold silk, a head veil of gossamer thin gold net held in place with a thick gold circlet, three necklaces of gold, gold bracelets and golden earrings. Thick honey tendrils of her hair showed beneath the veil. There were gold and jewels on each of her fingers and thumbs, gold buckles on her shoes and at her girdle. 'I can hardly move, Guy!' she protested.

'Bear up, Addy,' he said, 'you look splendid, shining like a golden icon.' Guy led the best horse from Montignac, covered with a fine saddle cloth as a gift for the Duke.

'If this doesn't work,' Gerard grumbled, 'you've finally broken us lad.'

Their arrival made the impact that Guy had intended. The Duke received the horse graciously and Gerard looked distressed as it was led off to the already very well stocked stables. The Duke's little son was greatly impressed with Adalmode. 'Golden lady, golden lady!' he shouted with glee, jumping up and down, clapping his hands, stretching out his grubby fingers to touch her, until his nursemaid restrained him.

The following morning the family prepared to make their case. In the Great Hall, the Duke sat on the raised dais surrounded by nobles. Duke Guillaume's nickname was Iron Arm, gained from his youthful prowess on the battlefield, but there was no evidence of that now in the raddled and overweight face of the middle-aged man looking down on Adalmode. Geoffrey, the tall, upright, Count of Anjou stood close to the Duke's throne, splendidly dressed in brown brocade and grey fur, his long grey hair falling below his shoulders. Some two hundred people were crammed into Duke Guillaume's hall to hear the justice cases before him at this Easter Assembly. In the crowd of people Adalmode caught sight of their kinsman, Ademar of Ségur who was administering Limoges at the Duke's behest, in place of her father. He was here with his young daugher Aina, whose beautiful dark red hair, hung uncovered down her back. Despite herself, Adalmode exchanged a smile with Aina and a nod with Ademar. She noticed that another red-haired girl, with a long graceful neck, accompanied them. A maid perhaps.

'Gerard, formerly of Limoges!' the steward called out and Adalmode made her way to the front of the crowd of people with her brother and father.

Amongst the richly dressed people seated with the Duke there were three very striking women. The Duke's young wife, Emma of Blois, seated to his left, was not a beauty. Her nose was too long, her forehead too high, her expression too stern, but she had tremendous imperious presence. Next to her, was the sister of the Count of Anjou, Lady Blanche, Countess of Gévaudan, whose beauty was legendary, and Adalmode thought, in this case not exaggerated. Blanche's hair was as golden as Adalmode's own. Her face was a perfect oval with large brown eyes, a shapely nose and a small mouth with full lips that reminded Adalmode of a ripe raspberry. But Adalmode's eyes were drawn to another lady who sat at the far end of the dais. She knew from gossip that this was Aldearde d'Aulnay, the Viscountess of Thouars, the Duke's favoured concubine since they were both very young. There were rumours that Guillaume and Aldearde had wanted to marry but the Duke's uncle, Bishop Ebles, brokered powerful political marriages for both of his brother's children, Adelais to Duke Hugh Capet and Guillaume to Emma of Blois. Emma had been a small child at the time of the betrothal and so Guillaume, having to wait a long time to marry, took 'comfort' with Aldearde in the meantime. However he had continued to take the same comfort after his marriage too, and after Aldearde's own marriage. Aldearde was a decade older than the Duchess and Countess Blanche, but her face and presence still had power to hold the eye. Her brown hair was thick and lustrous, her face shapely and her brown eyes alight with humour. It was rumoured that the Duke paid Aldearde's father and husband handsomely to connive at the affair. Adalmode watched the Duke and Aldearde exchange a fond glance and she saw how Duchess Emma also registered this glance, but Adalmode had no more time for conjecture on the scandals of the Aquitaine court for her brother was beginning his plea.

'Lord Guillaume, my father, myself and all our family suffer great pain that there was anger between our ancestors. Now I ask you, let there be friendship between us. Hear our plea. As descendents of Charlemagne and his county officers we of noble blood should support each other. My family is reduced and not able to sustain a noble life without the honour of Limoges that is rightfully ours.' Guy's voice rang out confidently in the hall. The murmur of activity and private conversations behind them stilled as her brother captured the attention of everyone there. Guy paused and looked to the Duke, who gestured with a slight movement of his wrist and hand that Guy should continue. Throughout Guy's speech the Duke's eyes had roved over Adalmode and she looked down at her feet in embarrassment.

'My ancestors,' Guy resumed, 'received the viscounty of Limoges from King Eudes many generations ago and held it in good faith and peace with your ancestors, until the offence of my grandfather. We are related by blood and marriage to the lords of Aurillac, Brosse and Thouars. We ask that you take account of our descent from the noble officers of Charlemagne, pardon the offence and restore us to our rights, that we might serve you well.'

Duke Guillaume held up his palm for Guy to halt and called out: 'Is there a man of great years who knows the full history of this story?'

A grey-haired and wrinkled man from the ranks of knights assembled in the hall stepped forward. 'I know it!' he declared.

'Knows Duke Guillaume's desired version no doubt,' muttered Gerard.

'We will hear this story through again then,' said the Duke, 'and resume the question in two days.'

Gerard groaned quietly. 'So now he will listen to a litany of the wrongs of my father and his betrayals. This gains us nothing Guy,' he said in a low tone.

'Be patient, Father, there is much negotiation to come yet over the next few days.'

On the following days the Duke was supposedly hearing other plaints, but he seemed, instead to spend only a few hours in the hall and most of his time hunting, drinking with his doctor Madelme, singing with Viscountess Aldearde. On the third day of the Assembly Adalmode and her family were summoned again to the hall.

'Your grandfather committed a gross breach of loyalty to mine,' stated the Duke.

Guy put a restraining arm on his father's and stepped forward. 'Yet my father and I offer you nothing but unwavering loyalty. We captured and held Helie of La Marche prisoner who so wickedly offended against your kinsman and God.'

The Duke inclined his head, with a smug expression on his face. 'Indeed. I hear that he has unfortunately escaped now.' There was an awkward pause. 'Yes your loyalty is proved but your cousin Ademar of Ségur, and his father before him, have administered

71

Limoges well on my behalf these many years. Can you continue to give me this same yield? And how would he be recompensed if I were to restore the honour of Limoges to you?'

Lord Ademar stepped forward, and the two red-haired girls stood hand in hand behind him. 'May I be heard, Lord Guillaume? Sire as you know my father and I have given you stalwart service as vicars of Limoges.'

'Yes,' said the Duke, 'and I would not wish to see my revenues there decreased, or my defences weakened, or to offer damage to a family that has always chosen mine.'

'Dammit,' Gerard muttered, his face growing red with anger.

'No, father,' Guy cautioned. 'I spoke with Ademar last night and he speaks now on our behalf.'

Gerard and Adalmode looked at him in astonishment. 'Why would he?' asked Adalmode.

'You will see.'

'Lord Guillaume I am alas suffering from an illness that weakens me and the doctors say there is no cure for it,' pronounced Ademar.

'I'm sorry to hear that Ademar,' said the Duke, lazily. 'Madelme here is a miracle worker. Get him to look you over.' He gestured to the Italian who was asleep crumpled in a corner with his mouth open after a hard night drinking with his patron.

'I will,' said Ademar, in a neutral voice, glancing unimpressed at Madelme. 'However, Lord Guillaume, in the meantime, I must make arrangements for the future.'

'I see,' said the Duke, sitting up straight.

'As you know Lord I have no son. My daughter Aina is my heiress.' Ademar drew the girl with darker red hair forward, and put an arm around her shoulders, showing her to the Duke.

'Hmm,' said Duke Guillaume, who obviously was surprised to hear this but did not say so. 'No nephews or brothers, Ademar?'

'No sire, but I would have Guy here as son-in-law if you permit it, and then the honour of Limoges might pass back into his family and yet my daughter will retain the prosperity and position that I and my father have worked for.'

Adalmode turned her head to glance at Aina and saw how the girl was looking at Guy with a shocked expression on her face.

Everyone it seemed, including Aina, had been taken by surprise at this revelation.

Duke Guillaume cleared his throat. 'Well, well, I will think on it.' He looked towards Gerard with dislike.

'My lord,' said Guy, deciding that he had to carry their case home now or never, 'if we cannot reach concord, with this suggestion of Lord Ademar's, then I must regrettably ask that we agree to settle this dispute by judicial duel.'

Adalmode gasped and placed her hand urgently on Guy's arm. 'No, Guy!'

Guy glanced briefly at her, and she was surprised to read amusement in his eyes.

'You distress your golden sister,' said Duke Guillaume, looking at her again with frank sexual interest. 'I will think on it and command you to hear our decision in some days,' he said, waving to dismiss them.

Back in their chamber Guy flung himself down on the bed laughing, 'Excellent gasping there, Addy!' whilst their father took to pacing up and down the small room with a great frown on his face and then without speaking a word to them, left, evidently in search of Rothilde.

'What on earth are you thinking Guy? You can't fight a judicial duel. You know you won't win that. I will have to fight it disguised as you.'

Guy laughed loudly. 'You aren't wearing the right kind of shoes for fighting, darling! Don't worry if the Duke insists on the duel then we have a serf who will do the fighting on our behalf, but very often a contender will back down from a duel and then we would win by default. What do you think about Aina? She's pretty isn't she?'

The question was genuine. Guy could not really see Aina, only that she had red hair. 'Yes, she is,' Adalmode said, distracted, considering the ramifications of their recent audience with the Duke.

Adalmode skipped past a smiling guard in the passage, one hand balancing her weight and the other clutching the bladder of good wine her mother had sent her to fetch for the exulted visitors to their chambers, the Duchess of Aquitaine and Lady Blanche of Gévaudan. Adalmode gazed in awe at the ladies' fine clothes and jewellery when they arrived: Emma's red wool cloak was lined with soft white fleece and her green silk tunic had intricate gold thread running around the hem, cuffs and neck.

Lady Blanche had stroked Adalmode's cheek, 'What a beautiful child,' she said to Rothilde.

Aldamode was entranced by Duchess Emma's curly brown hair, her slim fingers glittering with heavy rings, gesturing to accompany her ardent speech. She was speaking to her mother of politics, the Pope, inheritances and marriages. When Adalmode handed over the wine, she planned to sit quietly on a stool with her sewing and hope that her mother would not dismiss her from the conversation, or perhaps she could offer to mind the Duchess' young son. She reached the door of her mother's chambers, bringing her feet together in the cessation of her rapid skip, placing her palm on the door to push, but then drew her hand back as she heard her name pronounced: .'.. to Adalmode?' It was the Duchess' voice. 'Yes, she has grace and beauty.'

Adalmode's mother laughed softly in reply to the Duchess' question, but there was an earnest note in her voice when she spoke. 'Why not?' she said. 'There's only nine years between them. This handsome child will be a handsome man soon enough.'

Adalmode drew back a step from the door in surprise. Baby Guillaume and her! They were talking about betrothing her to the Duchess' little son. She knew her parents were bound to start thinking of her marriage soon and for the last year she had been examining the sons of visitors, expecting her husband to be one of these young men, but a baby! She hadn't considered that. She placed her palm on the door again but still hesitated. It would be a good marriage of course. Baby Guillaume was the heir to the throne of Aquitaine but it meant that she would be twenty-four or more before the marriage could take place and her betrothed husband would not be a strong, exciting man but a small child. Adalmode frowned. She would be Duchess of Aquitaine, but she did not like it. What about Audebert? She had imagined him released and envisaged her marriage to him over and over again.

She pushed open the door and walked in, handing the wine bladder to her mother and giving her an angry glance at the same time. Her mother looked away guiltily from the ferocity of Adalmode's green gaze.

The Duchess, it seemed to Adalmode, was looking her up and down, appraising. Adalmode held her arms out to the boy on the Duchess' knee.

'Thank you child,' his mother said, hefting him into her arms.

Adalmode sat glumly on a stool looking at the fat child, who looked as glumly back to her from large, serious brown eyes. She tried to imagine him as a full-grown man but it was impossible. He had a sour, fruity odour. After some time, the nurse rose to take the child from Adalmode but the boy began to wail piteously as he realised he was being removed, holding a chubby hand out to her.

'He likes you dear,' said her mother and Adalmode suppressed a scowl. Lady Rothilde turned back to her conversation with the Duchess and Lady Blanche: 'What is the news here? Is there still a threat from the north?'

Having fed him some sweetmeats, the nurse deposited the fat child – her husband-to-be! – back on Adalmode's lap.

'Now that Aquitaine has an heir,' the Duchess glanced fondly at young Guillaume, 'our House is secure. My husband's behaviour, however . . .' she said to Rothilde shifting to a more conspiratorial tone.

Adalmode served the ladies wine, knowing that this visit was a good sign and perhaps her brother's ploys were about to pay off after all.

'My, how he likes you,' Duchess Emma said as her son attached himself to Adalmode's skirts and would not let go, even though he was hampering her movements with the wine jug, hanging onto the fragile fabric of her gown with fat little hands. Unable to shake him off without physically injuring him, Adalmode sat down near her mother instead, causing him to sit on the floor beside her, still clutching the fabric of her gown in his fist, his eyes turned adoringly upon her.

'This Doctor Madelme is a man of obscure parentage and such as he should not be elevated to become counsellors of princes,'

Emma said with disgust to Rothilde, who agreed emphatically. Emma said nothing of her husband's open affection for Viscountess Aldearde.

'What do you think of this mooted marriage between your brother and the heiress of Ségur?' Blanche asked Adalmode, but without waiting for her reply, continued, 'My own brother is overbearing. He allowed me no choice in my husband you know and married me off when I was much younger than you are now.'

'Oh,' said Adalmode, but again there was no real chance to engage with either of Blanche's opening conversational gambits, before she launched into several more.

'What do you think of Raymond, the Count of Toulouse? This is the first time I've met him and he seems a very fine man don't you think? Have you heard of this scandal of the Queen?' she barely paused for Adalmode and Rothilde to respond by shaking their heads. 'Her brother-in-law, Duke Charles, has accused her of adultery with Bishop Adalbero of Laon.'

Rothilde expressed shock at the news.

'These scandals do not touch us here,' said Emma with tight lips, 'for the French King does not rule in Aquitaine.' Her implication was plain: that she and her husband ruled in Aquitaine.

'I hear that King Lothaire's only son, Louis, is a simpleton,' stated Blanche, but again, before Rothilde could think how to respond, Blanche rushed on: 'Tell me Lady Rothilde do you have any more beautiful daughters at home? I have two sons.'

Rothilde looked more comfortable now, on ground that she could cope with. 'Why yes, Lady Blanche, I have three more daughters besides Adalmode here, who is my eldest . . .'

Adalmode looked into the supplicant eyes of the small, fat heir to Aquitaine who had managed to squirm his way up her leg and onto her lap, where he was twirling his chubby finger round a hank of her hair which he had dislodged rather roughly from her headdress. She pondered on the three women she had encountered here: Duchess Emma, the powerful wife working in alliance with her equally powerful brother to control her husband; Lady Aldearde, the loved concubine, her honour sold by her brother; and Countess Blanche traded by her brother as a child to an elderly husband. She wondered, if Guy's plea was successful, how would she ever learn to cope with such noble conversations and company.

In the evening Adalmode gave Guy an account of the ladies' visitation and he rolled on the bed laughing at her portrait, concurring with her opinion that it was a very good sign. 'If the Duchess has any sway over her husband . . .'

'I'm sure of that,' interrupted Adalmode.

'Then I think he may grant our request,' finished Guy.

'Have you listened to her?' Adalmode said. 'The Duchess commands anything in her path – the sea, the air, certainly any mere men.'

Guy laughed and agreed with her assessment.

'And will the Duke release Audebert of La Marche at this Assembly?' Adalmode asked.

Guy, knowing his sister's fondness for the prisoner, explained gently: 'When he was alive Count Boso of La Marche was here at the Assembly every year making a plea for the release of Helie and Audebert, but now that he has died and Helie has escaped and is on his way to Rome seeking expiation for his sin, no one is here pleading for Audebert.'

Adalmode looked aghast. 'But if Audebert is reliant on Helie for his release, I think he will die there in that hole in Montignac.'

Guy shrugged but seeing the miserable look on his sister's face thought better of it. 'If father's wish for restoration to Limoges is granted, then he will probably release Audebert.'

Adalmode face brightened. 'Really?'

'Well if Duke Guillaume wishes it so, yes, why not? What does anybody have to gain by keeping him captive now?'

The next morning Adalmode resumed her heavy jewellery, met with the inspection and approbation of her father, and followed him and Guy into the hall to hear the decision on their plea, but there was no sign of Duke Guillaume. Instead Duchess Emma sat next to her husband's empty throne, with her son perched on a stool at her feet. There were nobles and many other people present as usual but in lesser numbers. Adalmode's heart sank. After all Guy's efforts this did not auger a positive outcome.

'My husband is unwell,' said the Duchess and indeed the noise of his carousings had resounded throughout the palace the night before. 'However I will stand in his stead and complete the business before this *mallus*, this court of justice. On the matter of Limoges,' she paused at length to wait for Gerard, Guy and Adalmode to step forward, 'my husband and I decree that, being inspired by divine clemency and the love we bear our vassal, Gerard, the Viscounty of Limoges and all its honours shall be returned to you and your heirs henceforth, on condition that the marriage with Aina of Ségur is contracted as proposed.'

She paused to hear the delighted thanks of Gerard and Guy and inclined her head graciously to them and to Adalmode, whilst little Guillaume held his arms out towards Adalmode and she bent to kiss him, searching for a clean spot on his sticky cheek.

'You and your son will swear your allegiances before us tomorrow on the holy relics and we will have a notice drawn up, read out to the court, and subscribed by us, yourselves and several witnesses.'

Guy and Adalmode led their dazed father from the room and took him up to their mother's room to explain the sudden and wondrous change in their fortunes. Gerard and Rothilde wept and clasped each other, and Adalmode wept too with the relief of it. Please, she wished earnestly, looking at her father's happy face, please let Audebert out.

The following day, Duke Guillaume reappeared, his face slack and grey, his eyes red-rimmed and glazed. He presided over the transfer of power in Limoges from Ademar of Ségur to Adalmode's father, symbolized by the ritual exchange of a staff painted in the colours of the city. When this ceremony was completed they witnessed the formal trothing of Guy to Ademar's ten-year-old daughter Aina, who looked so disgusted with the situation and with the sapphire ring that Guy placed on her little finger, that Adalmode was grateful her brother was unable to see the expressions of his promised bride.

# 7

# Ségur

## Winter 975

I look up from the loom, startled as the door bangs hard against the wall, slammed back as Aina hurtles into the room.

'I know it will be tonight!' she declares. Even in the gloom of twilight I can see the excitement glowing on her pale face and in her wide grey eyes. She tugs her head veil off, leaving her mass of dark red hair dishevelled. Since her tenth birthday we had known that her parents would soon decide about her betrothal. As she is Ademar's only child and heiress, lords from Normandy, Brittany and Barcelona had offered for her, because of the wealth her father amassed from his trading fleet and his custodianship of Limoges, and her father had been considering those offers.

Aina had me assist her in casting book lots to tell which lord would be her future husband. We had to fast and pray for twenty-four hours. I prayed to Freyja that Aina's marriage wishes might be granted, and perhaps that the goddess might see fit one day to give me a good Norse husband too. Then Aina lined up three copies of the bible in front of us and opened each one randomly. 'Hmm . . .' She studied the passages revealed.

'Who told you about this method of divining?' I asked. 'It seems more pagan than Christian.'

'The cook and don't be silly, it's the Bible. Sshh! I'm thinking here.'

I looked at the passages which seemed to me to say nothing at all pertaining to Aina's future husband.

'Barcelona!' she pronounced, turning to me, her face alight.

'How do you make *that* out?' I frowned.

'It's *obvious*, Sigrid,' Aina sighed at me as if I were a half-wit.

But then Aina had been appalled to find herself betrothed to Guy at the Duke's Easter Assembly. 'Just Guy of Limoges!' she exclaimed afterwards in the privacy of the chamber with me.

I looked at my mistress alarmed. 'Lord Guy seems to be a good, kind man, Aina . . . You might like him.'

'Yes, but *him* as my husband, Sigrid! That's not going to happen. He lives five minutes away!' said Aina, as if this were a gross offence.

At the Assembly the betrothal took place so quickly that Aina had no time to protest, but ever since she has protested a great deal. 'Father, I do not wish to marry Guy of Limoges,' she told him as we sat one morning in the hall.

Ademar looked up from his tablet in surprise and set down his stylus. 'Aina?'

Aina looked at me perplexed. I could see that she did not know how to go on.

'Tell me why, Aina,' her father said gently.

'I hoped to marry further afield,' she said. 'Those other offers you have received for me – perhaps one of those would be better and I believe that Guy would not mind too much you know. I am just a child to him. I would see something of the world. I am your daughter, after all. I long for the wind and the salt of a voyage.'

'And haven't Sigrid's stories of the dangers lurking there warned you off travel,' said Ademar, his face turning serious.

Aina was silent for a while, thinking perhaps of my stories of murder and slavery. 'I don't think Guy is right for me,' she said eventually, clearly irritated at her inability to articulate what she longs for.

'Aina,' Ademar said and I heard the firmness in the voice of her usually indulgent father, and knew that the conversation would soon be over, 'I believe that Guy *is* right for you. Give it time and you will see that too.'

'Yes, father,' she said, hanging her head so that he would not see the extreme disappointment washing over her face.

Ademar looked at the shiny red top of his daughter's head and at her tall, willowy figure in her rich green gown. She had been cossetted by his wealth. She had no idea of the dangers that lurked outside the walls of Ségur. 'If I had been blest with more children,' he said, 'with a son, then your future might have been different. You might have had more choice of your husband but I need you to do my bidding in this child.'

'Yes father,' said Aina, 'but please won't you at least *consider* the possibility of breaking this betrothal and arranging another that I would like more?'

Ademar could resist his loved daughter very little. He knew he should not give her hope but her grey eyes looked back at him so earnestly. 'I will consider it, Aina, but the Duke has commanded it. I have given my word and you have given your troth. I will not likely change my mind, or your chart, on this.'

'No, father,' said Aina, trying to keep the intensity of hope out of her voice and face. 'I will wait for your consideration.'

With Aina it was always the way that no matter how unrealistic what she wished for might be, nevertheless she believed with a passion that it would happen. Being sensible is over-rated she liked to tell me.

'Consider those three women we saw at the Poitiers court,' I said to her, 'Duchess Emma – the powerful wife, Aldearde of Aulnay – the loved mistress of the Duke, and Blanche of Anjou, the Count's sister married off to an old man. Which of these three would you like to be?'

'Aldearde!' she responded immediately, raising her eyebrows provocatively at me, knowing that I had meant her to answer Emma.

I scowled. 'But this Aldearde has no power, no rights!' I tried to point out to Aina that her father could not go back on the agreement made before the Duke, that her betrothal was to do with the politics of the men and not with her feelings or even her father's affection for her, but she took not the slightest notice of my advice and instead grew in her own mind the very, very slender hope her father had unfortunately planted there.

'For sure, it's tonight. I heard him say as much.'

'What did you hear exactly?' I ask in a measured voice, deliberately trying to slow down the conversation and bring it to reasonableness.

'He was talking over his shoulder to Mama, as he came out of their chamber. He said, "It's settled then. I will tell her tonight and I believe she will be happy with . . ." and then,' Aina rolls her eyes to the ceiling in exasperation, 'he heard my skirts rustle and turned and saw me there. "Papa," I said innocently. "Darling Aina," he said, "I didn't see you there. Run along and don't be late for supper."' Aina pauses and looks expectantly at me. 'Well, what do you think?'

I look down at my hands holding the weaving batten in my lap, weighing the evidence and then nod slowly. 'Yes that sounds likely then,' I pronounce.

'Come on, Sigrid!' Aina bursts out impatiently. '*Of course* that's what it is. He says I will be pleased. Where do you think I will go?' She pauses only briefly to allow me to respond. My mouth has merely opened, before she hurries on, 'Normandy do you think? Brittany then? But I still think Barcelona.'

'Well my lady, I don't know . . .' I begin.

'Imagine, Sigrid, I could be on a ship, sailing the sea, like you did! I could learn a new language like you.' Aina is breathless with delight and expectation but I swallow hard at the grim memories her words evoke.

'I hope that you will not have to leave everything and everyone you love,' I say.

'Oh Sigrid, I'm sorry.' Aina flops down on the cushioned chest at the foot of her bed, deflated, annoyed with herself for such selfish tactlessness. She leans back against the high mattress and furs piled behind her. 'How thoughtless of me. It's not the same at all, I know. How could I?'

I know that my mistress' remorse is genuine, but it is fleeting, quickly displaced by excitement at her marriage prospects. I watch the emotions fly across her face and bite my lip. 'Don't guess, Aina, don't wish so hard,' I caution. 'Wait and see. All this thinking and hoping. You will make yourself disappointed.'

In truth, I feel some trepidation on my own account. Wherever Aina goes for her marriage, it is likely that I will go too. I think with regret of how much I like living in Ségur, how fond Ademar and Melisende are of me and how they tacitly allow my stubborn resistance to Christianity. I will not find such toleration anywhere else. I still tell myself that Thorgils will find me but I believe it less and less.

The dinner bell sounds in the hall below and I stand and clasp Aina's hands briefly in encouragement. We move towards the door and the stairwell. The hall this night does nothing to meet Aina's relentless expectation. It looks and sounds every inch the same as it always has, day in, day out. Apart from the high feast days of Christmas and Easter and the very occasional visitor, things are always much the same. The cook is good at everything except puddings which are never quite right. Robert the serving boy always trips over one of the dogs and slops the sauce. The fire always crackles and smokes. Old Louis who had polished the horse harnesses for Ademar's father and is now too old for much except poking the fire, always falls asleep half-way through the meal and begins snoring gently and everyone smiles when he does. Merry, the cook's assistant, always tries to get Oliver the stable boy to look at her, smoothing her apron over her stomach and hips, but he won't because he likes Millicent who minds the fishpond. And Ademar always looks fondly on Melisende and Aina, and Aina always heaves a loud sigh by the time they get to the *entremets* because everything is always the same. Despite the steward Renaud's quantity of gossip, beneath the daily surface of minor events, a profound calm lies across the days of Ségur.

Things are so peaceful here that in the summer a duck made her nest in the doorway to the hall, and raised a brood of ducklings. Tonight the snow is laying thick on the ground outside, the ponds are frozen over, and the fire is burning bright red against the frigid white night beyond the hall. Tonight Aina is wearing her best green gown and sitting up very straight and can hardly eat, wearing her excitement visibly like a second over-gown.

'My daughter,' Ademar takes Aina's hand and the moment has come when he will tell my mistress of the betrothal decision. 'As you know, you are my heir, and carry all our hopes and honour of the family.'

'Yes father.'

83

Her mother smiles reassurance to her.

'It is time you were married and that our wealth and long lineage should be allied to a family of stature.'

'Yes father, I would wish to do my duty,' says Aina. 'I know that marriage will take me from home,' she adds in a tone that implies she has no actual problem with that prospect.

'We are in agreement that come the next assembly at Easter, my dear, you will be married to Guy of Limoges.' Her father smiles broadly. 'As you know we have had offers for you from much further afield, carrying such wealth as you do, but you will be happier in a place that you know, with people you know, and we will be close to you.'

Aina's protest dies on her lips. What can she say? She would not wish to disappoint her parents who dote on her – their only child and yet she is bitterly disappointed: that her marriage would take her a few miles away and no more, that everything would continue the same except that she would be a wife. I glance at Aina with compassion, feeling relief for myself. My observations of Guy suggest that he will make her a good husband and be a kind master to me.

Aina and I rise to leave and Ademar holds out a hand to me and says in a low voice, 'I wanted to ask you something too, Sigrid.' We both sit down again. 'You will also soon be of a marriageable age and Melisende and I have been talking of it.'

'Sigrid can't get married, Papa. She has to stay with me.'

'Be quiet for a moment Aina.' He turns back to me. 'We have always thought of you as our child too,' he says smiling, 'our Northchild. As Aina says, you could go with her when she marries Guy and you will be of great assistance to her in running the Limoges household, but we also want to make sure we are considering your happiness. Here in Ségur, Phillippe would be glad to take you as his wife if you prefer to stay. We would free you, of course, and I will provide you with a handsome dowry.'

'Phillippe is an old man, Father!'

Ademar warns Aina to silence again with his eyebrows and takes my hand. 'Phillippe is older than you, Sigrid, but so it is with many husbands. Tell me what *you* would prefer, not what my bossy daughter wishes.'

Aina is frowning, grimacing and rolling her eyes at me, so that I have great difficulty not to laugh. I look down at the table top to consider.

'Ah,' says Aina, 'so now we have a famous long Sigrid think.' I can hear from the tone of her voice that she is confident what choice I will make.

'Aina,' her father warns her again.

I like Phillippe but I think of him more as an uncle or older brother. I am flattered by his interest. He is a comely and friendly man, much respected by Ademar and by the rest of the servants and he will no doubt prosper. I am twelve and he thirty. I look to where he sits on the long table his goblet raised to his bushy beard and do my best to ignore Aina looking at him too and grimacing some more. Ademar will not rush me. It would be two years or more before he would allow a marriage to go ahead. I think sadly of Ademar's illness and that he is trying to take care of Aina and I while he still can. I like Phillippe, I think, but if I were married it would be a kind of chain. I would owe obedience to him. I look at Aina who puffs out her cheeks and then deflates them through the round rosebud of her mouth to show what she thinks of how long I have considered and that I have even considered it at all.

'Thank you, Lord Ademar,' I say, 'but I would rather stay with my Lady Aina and help her.'

'Very well,' he says.

'Well, of course,' says Aina, rising from the table and grabbing my hand. 'Phillippe! How ridiculous!' she exclaims, stomping up the steps ahead of me to her chamber, our breath visible before our faces in the sudden chill of the stone stairway. Thinking of him, I hope that he will not be too disappointed by my refusal.

Aina pulls off her veil and throws herself on the bed, with a sullen face. 'God's teeth! I will just be a fat wife to Guy, Sigrid, breeding children, down the road. Wives are subjugated to husbands. Along with modesty, wives lose freedom. No exotic adventures. What's the point of anything if that is all there is in my future? I want to be free, Sigrid, and to travel the seas and see strange lands.'

'Free!' I say angrily. 'It means a different thing to you than to me.'

Aina takes my hand. 'Oh don't be angry with me,' she says, 'I know, I'm sorry. It was tactless of me. You know that father would set you free in a minute if you just learnt to say the Lord's Prayer and were baptised.'

I shake my head stubbornly. 'I am a Northwoman. A Northwoman slave.'

'Yet, Sigrid,' she says, 'don't you see that it is akin to slavery to give your life over to another, to have to do what you don't want to do day in and day out and only that?'

I touch her cheek by way of reply. I do sympathise with her resistance to the marriage, but I know that things could be so much worse for her. A fire burns hard in the grate here too, with a dull red glow smothering the detail of the room. The window shutters are barred against the snow and hail beyond, but we can hear the wind howling.

The slave and the heiress climb into the big, soft bed together to sleep with our red hair splayed around us like the rays of an intense sunset. Before she closes her eyes, Aina looks up to the yellow fabric draping the top of her bed, and sets her full lips tight and determined against each other, so that they crinkle like a crushed rose, and says, 'I will not marry Guy. That cannot be my future.'

# 8

# Limoges

## Spring 976

Viscount Gerard and Viscountess Rothilde sat at the High Table in the Motte castle of Limoges with their sons and daughters ranged on either side of them, interspersed with the senior household staff and two nursemaids who had charge of the smallest children at the end of the table. Hilduin was visiting from the monastery to make the family group complete. The Viscount's men at arms and household servants were greatly increased in number and seated at the long tables in the hall. There was a din of talk, clattering plates, laughter and a smell of wood smoke and food. Adalmode, as always, sat at Guy's side.

'I have news for you, children,' Gerard pronounced and a hush fell on the talk and joking below the dais, since news for the family of the Viscount was news for all the household.

'As you know,' said Gerard, 'I waited a long time for my birthright and now thanks to the astute advice of my eldest son, Guy, I and all of us are in our rightful place.' Gerard paused dramatically, waiting for the cheers of agreement to die down and the raised drinking horns to be emptied and replaced on the table. 'My sons, you have all waited overlong for your inheritances, but now your mother and I, from our negotiations, have resolved your positions.'

Heads were nodding at this. Everyone knew that so many full-grown sons in a household was over-many.

'Guy is my heir to the Viscounty and betrothed to marry Aina, heiress to Ségur.'

'But she is his second cousin,' interrupted Hildegaire, 'surely this is consanguinous?'

Adalmode saw that Hilduin was nodding his head in agreement and had probably put these words into Hildegaire's mouth.

'Silence . . .' thundered Gerard, appalled to have the drama of his announcements so rudely interrupted before he had barely begun. The family shifted and settled again, recovering from the shock of Gerard's angry volume.

'Lady Aina is the daughter of our neighbour,' said Gerard, struggling to inject calm back into his voice, but the residue of his fury was still audible. 'She brings a great fortune with her and the lands adjoining ours. The marriage is the command of the Duke of Aquitaine,' he said emphatically, staring at Hildegaire, 'and a command that I am more than happy to see realised.'

Hildegaire said nothing more, but Guy could hear him breathing heavily through his nose, suppressing his anger at being publicly reprimanded.

'She is very pretty too,' said Aimery, characteristically lightening the mood and trying to dispel the tension, balancing like a skilled boatman on the treacherous currents in the exchanges between his father and older brothers.

'Indeed, she is,' agreed their mother.

'She has beautiful red hair and grey eyes,' said Adalmode, for Guy's benefit.

'She is young yet,' Guy said to his father.

'Twelve summers,' responded Gerard. 'You can take her soon enough and get us some heirs eh?' he clapped Guy's shoulder and Guy braced himself as soon as he heard the lift in his father's voice indicating that the shoulder slap was coming.

'What of the rest of us?' risked Hildegaire.

'I'm coming to that,' said Gerard shortly, not mollified yet with his second son. 'Aimery, I am giving you the viscounty of Rochechouart.'

'Thank you father!' exclaimed Aimery. It was much more than he had expected as the third son. He was ready to leave the teeming household and make his own and now he could look around for his own bride, as pretty, if not as rich as Guy's.

'These decisions,' said Gerard, 'I will announce at the Easter Assembly next week and when they have been formally ratified, then you may act upon them. Geraud,' he said moving his gaze to his fourth son, who looked up surprised from his soup and a lump of meat fell from his spoon splashing back into the bowl.

'Me, father?' At eighteen Geraud was not expecting promotion from boy to man yet.

'You will be appointed as Lord of Argenton at the Assembly, son. Your mother will travel with you to the hall to help you begin your duties there.'

A look of surprised delight spread slowly across the young man's face. He had feared his father might send him to the Church and he worked hard to show his abilities with weapons and contribute to the overseeing of agriculture and trade in the city, hoping to thwart this possibility. Hilduin was rising in the ranks of the Abbey and the two youngest boys, Geoffrey and Hugh, were already novices at Saint Martial. Secular independence so soon was much more than Geraud had hoped for.

'And you, Hildegaire, you are the strongest-minded of my sons,' said the Viscount raising his voice to stifle the anxious query that Hildegaire was already voicing, and Guy knew that his father was about to say something his brother would not like. 'I have arranged for you to take the Bishopric of Limoges.' Gerard sat back, his arms folded and a smug look on his face. His wife patted his arm, avoiding Hildegaire's eyes.

Adalmode watched Hildegaire, expecting an explosion, but was surprised instead to see him clamp his hand over his mouth and drop his eyes to the table. He was calculating his income as Bishop perhaps, and it would be vast.

'And Tisalga, daughter, you will be betrothed to the son of Lady Blanche of Anjou,' said Gerard.

Adalmode looked reassuringly to her thirteen year old sister who was taken aback by their father's abrupt announcement on her future.

Gerard had to wait so long to reclaim his birthright, living out his own prime years caretaking Montignac, his pleas for reinstatement refused, whilst other men grew rich on the tithes and tolls that should have been his. Now that forgiveness had finally come, he was an old man, but at least he could enjoy seeing his sons' futures unfold. Gerard lent to Guy's ear. 'Aina of Ségur *is* your second cousin. You will need special dispensation to marry her . . . from the Bishop of Limoges.' He raised his eyebrows to Guy.

'Ah,' said Guy, in the impressed tone his father wanted to hear, but this news made him feel even more doubtful regarding Hildegaire. Bullying his brother into taking holy orders, as his father intended to do, would only store up problems for the future and Hildegaire would be a scandalous Bishop. He loved wenching, wine, gambling and fighting, and Guy could not imagine that any holy transformation would overcome him. The words that Bishop Ebles spoke a while back from the pulpit occurred to Guy: 'No priest shall keep a woman at home, or allow one to enter a cellar or secret place for the sake of fornication.'

'Ah and Adalmode,' Gerard said as an afterthought, 'we have received an offer of marriage for you from the Duke of Aquitaine.'

For a moment Adalmode imagined with horror that this offer was from the old Duke himself. His appetite for young women was famous. 'He seeks your hand for his son. You will be betrothed at Easter.'

Adalmode felt panic rising inside her but she knew better than to attempt to argue with her father at table, nevertheless she had no wish to be betrothed to that chubby child and every hope of marrying the man in her father's dungeon. She looked anxiously to Guy who squeezed her hand reassuringly beneath the trestle. Could he help her avoid this?

Hildegaire, however, did not know her caution. 'I have no intention of being a Bishop, father,' he pronounced loudly and resolutely.

Gerard uncrossed his arms and lent forward staring fiercely at his handsome, burly second son. 'You will do as you are bid.'

'I am a soldier, father, not a priest.'

'The Bishopric of Limoges holds as much power and income as the viscounty,' said Gerard, 'perhaps more.' Historically the Bishop ruled the town with its rich merchants and visitors, and

the Viscount ruled the Abbey and Castle. In the recent past there had been conflict between the two over the lucrative trade from the Compostela pilgrims coming through Limoges and over the tolls on the Roman Saint Martial Bridge crossing the river Vienne.
'You and Guy could work together in harmony.'
An unlikely idea, thought Adalmode.
'Let Guy take the Bishopric,' said Hildegaire. 'He is more fit to be a priest.'
'Guy is my heir and that's an end of it,' said Gerard, rising to his feet, so that the entire hall must follow suit.

Guy walked from the hall at his father's side. He decided to bide his time to discuss the matters of Hildegaire and Adalmode with his father in private. Nothing would be gained by countering him in front of his retinue. Hildegaire would not thrive as a Bishop. It would be better to give that to one of his brothers already in orders, Hilduin probably. Perhaps Hildegaire could be given Brosse. Of course it was important not to offend the Duke of Aquitaine who offered for his son for Adalmode, but the Viscount had two other daughters he could give to the child heir, nearer his age. Guy would see what he could do to change his father's decisions, but he was pleased for his own part, with an impending marriage to the heiress of Ségur.
Making his way some time later to his bed, Guy could see from the dimness and the lack of light at the end of the narrow stone passageway that someone stood blocking his way. Hildegaire waited until Guy was almost nose to nose with him. 'You're not competent to be Viscount,' he said.
'Let me pass, Hildegaire.'
'You know you're not and sooner or later Father will see it.' He stepped out of the way and Guy felt Hildegaire's hot breath brush his neck as he squeezed past.
Guy latched the door to his chamber behind him, and fetched his Annals out from where they now lay under his own bed. He and his sister were no longer children, who could roam at will in and out of each other's chambers. He set the magnifying water glass, ink, quill, erasing knife and gathered parchments up on the lectern with a candle to light his work. It was much better to write

in the daylight, but this was a momentous time and he wanted to record it now. As was his habit he read through the previous entries before settling on the composition of the next.

*Annals of Guy of Limoges Book II*

+ **973** In this year Helie of La Marche, escaped from the dungeon of Montignac, aided by a dishonest jailor, who also fled. Otto the Great, Holy Roman Emperor died and was succeeded by his son Otto II.

+ **974** In this year the Viscounty of Limoges was restored to Gerard of Limoges by the Duke and Duchess of Aquitaine and his family rejoiced. His son, Guy of Limoges was betrothed to the heiress, Aina of Ségur.

+ **975** In this year Gerard, Viscount of Limoges was weighed down by sickness and lay ill for almost the whole of the summer. Charles of Lorraine, brother to King Lothaire, accused Queen Emma of adultery with Bishop Adalbero. The accusation was found unjust and the king's brother was banished. Guy of Anjou, brother to Geoffrey Greymantle, was made Bishop of Le Puy and held a Council named The Peace of God to restore order to the conflict-ridden lands of the southern Franks. Blanche of Anjou, sister to Geoffrey Greymantle, left her husband Etienne of Gévaudan, and was repudiated by him and has married Raymond, Count of Toulouse.

The shutters of Guy's window were still open and he looked out for a moment at the still gloom of the evening gathering the final glimmers before dowsing this last pale light of the day into blackness.

+ **976** In this year Guy, son of Gerard, Viscount of Limoges and Rothilde of Brosse, was declared heir to the viscounty of the city and Hildegaire, his brother, was made Bishop of Limoges. Emma of Blois, Duchess of Aquitaine, ablaze with anger at her husband's adultery, left Poitiers with her son and rode to the protection of her brother.

He paused, with his quill above the paper. Nothing else was certain. Adalmode might find a way to evade marriage to Guillaume of Aquitaine. Perhaps even this entry so far was not correct. Perhaps Hildegaire would run away and offer himself as a mercenary to avoid becoming a Bishop. It was too early in the year to be writing its rubric. He blew on the ink to dry it before folding up the parchment and returning it to its hiding place.

The argument with Hildegaire raged for days. Yesterday he had shouted, 'Guy is as blind as a mole, Father, and you would risk our patrimony on that!'

Adalmode watched the doubt spread over the obdurate set of her father's features. Guy was worth all of her other brothers put together. His intelligence, generosity and humour would win anyone who talked with him at any length. He would be a hundred times a better viscount than their father, caring for the people and the city and not only for himself. But his near-sightedness made him awkward and strange in company. He seemed aloof because he did not look in the right place. He seemed judgmental because he screwed up his eyes in an effort to see and it looked like a mighty frown of disapproval.

'Say something,' she muttered to Guy.

'You know that our patrimony will be safe in my hands, Father.' Guy turned his face to where his father sat, hoping that a semblance of eye contact was occurring. 'Was it not my advice that retrieved that patrimony? What you know of statecraft, I know. As you have advised, so I will do. I have been at your side in frays and parlays. The viscounty is rightfully mine and when you bequeath it to me, I will guard it and wield it well for the sake of my mother, my brothers and sisters, and my wife and sons.' He did not mention that he also felt the viscount owed a duty to the people and city of Limoges, as he knew this was in no sense a paramount concern for his father.

Viscount Gerard was reassured, recalling that Guy had given him sound counsel in many negotiations with the Duke of Aquitaine, the Counts of Anjou and La Marche, and other men of the region. Gerard was aware that whilst Guy was an intelligent and skilled strategist, Hildegaire was a self-indulgent hot-head, who might easily lose the family the viscount's throne again.

Audebert tracked the flight of a buzzard, trying to slow down the moment where he could see freedom and imagine himself up there with it, soaring, going somewhere else. He had been dozing in the thin spring sunlight and wiped a trickle of drool from the corner of his mouth. He swotted at the flies that landed on his bare legs, thinking him already a corpse. He held his arms out in front of him and thought yes, they seemed thinner now than before. His skin was closely wrapped around his bones and there was nothing left between the two anymore, no fat, no muscle. The light was suddenly blocked out by a head – not Adalmode's head, and a thick rope snaked down to him. Had Helie come back for him after all? Or was this an invitation to climb to his own execution?

Audebert's hands were tied in front of him and lashed to the pommel of an old plodding horse. He was surrounded by ten armed men, all in armour and bristling with swords, knives, spears. Audebert felt like laughing. How did they think he – in his emaciated, rusted condition, akin to this old horse – could threaten them. The heavy rain fell incessantly and Audebert's pale skin felt as if it might never warm again. His black hair was plastered to his head, neck and the edges of his face. He tried to suppress the fear that gripped his stomach at the image he had conjured of a noose. He looked about him. This was the first time for four years that he had seen any environment other than the close walls of the dungeon and perhaps it was the last. He must drink in every detail that he could see through the rain – the intense green of the grass, the smooth white bark of a tree and the brown-black gnarled trunk of another, the grey bleak sky weighted with loaded clouds.

The ride was short. In less than an hour the castle of Montignac had disappeared from view and the impressive sight of the city of Limoges rose up before him. A public hanging in front of hundreds then? As they approached the walls, Audebert looked with grief as they passed by what he knew to be the road to

Bellac, to home, only an hour away to the north. So Helie had not ransomed him. The party clattered through the gateway into the city and Audebert felt assaulted with noises, smells and the curious faces of many people. He could smell the tanneries and the butchers, stables and compost heaps. He could hear the shouts of shopkeepers in the colonnaded market square and looked up short flights of steps to glimpses through archways of more houses and cobbles beyond. He saw servants scurrying with baskets, sheltering from the heavy rain along covered walkways that fronted the tall, tightly packed brown and black timbered houses. 'All brightness dissolves in the rain,' he thought remembering a song composed here in the city, the lament of a swan, lost above an endless ocean. Awkwardly he used his bound hands to pull himself upright in the saddle. If he was going to die now, he was going to do it with defiance on his face, and at least he had seen the world one more time, and despite the rain, it was as he remembered it, as he had dreamed it for all these years, so beautiful, beautiful beyond bearing.

Audebert sank with a gratitude verging on ecstasy into the warm bathwater but suppressed the urge to let out a great sigh of pleasure. No one including the sullen serving boy who had filled the bath and now stood in the corner, would be witness to Audebert's joy at being out of the hole. Would they bother to allow him to bathe if they were going to hang him? Lulled by the warmth of the blissful water he dozed fitfully, waking to stretch a hand to the wooden beaker of wine perched on the rim of the bath, close to his ear. Wine. They wouldn't give him wine surely? The serving boy was staring at the dense hair that furred Audebert's chest, clinging now in wet black commas, and Audebert closed his eyes, ignoring the boy. He heard the door latch click and opened his eyes to an empty room and the water now grimy and cooling around him. Sighing at both the end of the bath and the feebleness of his arm muscles he pulled himself up out of the water.

Audebert stood before the dais where Adalmode sat with her father, Viscount Gerard of Limoges and her mother, Lady Rothilde. Other nobles were seated there but he did not know them. To be out of the dungeon after four long years . . . He did his best to look insouciant and was grateful that the Viscount had seen fit to allow him a bath, a barber and a clean set of clothes before this audience. Audebert was a tall man with broad shoulders but this accentuated how stick-thin he was, and how his clothes hung from him like a scarecrow. The black hair rising from his chest, feathering his neck above his high, elegant shirt collar, contradicted the boyish air that he still exuded, despite the tortuous passing of time carved into him.

'My Lord Audebert, Count of La Marche and Périgord, I greet you,' a grey-haired man said formally but with a cordial note in his voice. 'I am Geoffrey, Count of Anjou, known as Greymantle, and this is my son, Fulk Nerra.' He patted a small black-haired boy sitting next to him on the head.

'Greetings my Lord,' Audebert inclined his head, trying to conceal the confusion he felt at being endowed with the titles of his brother Helie and his uncle in Périgord. Clearly, despite the fact that this was Gerard's court, this was the man in charge. 'You name me Count sire?'

'Indeed – and we will give you that news in due course. You know your hosts,' said Geoffrey, pausing ironically on the word, 'Gerard, Viscount of Limoges and his wife.'

Audebert inclined his head again and although he longed to look at Adalmode, since he had never before been this close to her, he avoided her eyes. He did not want to be distracted from the undercurrents of whatever might be happening here. Did it mean his freedom, his death, or had they raised him from the pit to gloat and thrust him back in?

'Please, sit and eat with us, Count,' said Rothilde. She indicated a seat between herself and her daughter. So much for his intention not to be distracted, Audebert thought, realising that he would be sharing his trencher with Adalmode. Count Geoffrey had the seat of honour to the right of the Viscount.

'Thank you, Lady.' He moved with as much grace as his stiff limbs allowed to take his seat. For a while, there was no further speech as the servants presented many dishes with different coloured sauces and the people sitting around him spooned food onto their trenchers and ate.

Apart from a brief smile, Audebert avoided looking directly at Adalmode, but he felt her leg alongside his under the trestle and part-way through a rabbit stew, he felt her fingers tracing the back of his hand lightly under cover of the cloth. He shook his head slightly at her and she removed her hand. He was aware of a smile being repressed with great difficulty at the corners of her mouth – constantly threatening to break free of her control. He watched her delicate long fingers peel a pomegranate. She loosened the brilliant jewelled fruit from its pale fleshy clasp and opened her mouth to receive the tiny sweet baubles. Her mouth was another jewel. Whenever his resolve failed him, and he inadvertently glanced at her his swift impression was of green – her green eyes, and honey – the tendrils of her fair hair slipping from their gossamer net.

In a bowl of water when the barber was shearing off the rancid tangle of his hair and beard, he had caught sight of his blurred reflection: his blue eyes huge, his red mouth too big in the gaunt face like an old man's. Adalmode could not possibly be interested in him. He focussed on not allowing himself to feel his humiliation and anger. If he let that out of the box he had trapped it in, he feared the explosion might lay waste to everything and everyone in this hall, including himself. He was conscious of the eyes upon him: everyone wondering what it would be like if they had to spend four years in a pit, wondering how he was feeling, was he a broken man. He struggled not to eat rapidly and not to eat much since his stomach so long accustomed to so little, and only to bread and slops, would revolt at the rich food. He sipped at the good red wine and waited. He was skilled at waiting.

Finally the business arrived. 'Count Audebert, I have to tell you the sad news that your brother Helie, has recently died on pilgrimage to Rome and your uncle has died in Périgord. You, therefore, inherit the counties of La Marche and Périgord,' said Geoffrey.

His brother was dead. To everyone else in this room Helie was reduced to that single egregious act of blinding the priest, but to Audebert Helie was much more. He was the older brother he had played with, practised with, hunted alongside admiring his skill, the brother he had followed blindly into daring escapades intended to rile but also impress their father. His Helie, that boy, was dead. Audebert stared at the table. He, Audebert, was Count of La Marche, unless one of his younger brothers had usurped him? Boson might. Boson was always jealous of the two oldest brothers. He might. But Gausbert and Martin, his youngest brothers would not allow it, would loyally be holding the county, waiting for Audebert's return?

Geoffrey turned in his seat to Gerard. 'It is my opinion, Viscount, that Count Audebert should be released. He is now of age and has already wasted four years of the prime of his life in your dungeon.'

Not death then? They were debating his freedom. Audebert's maternal uncles held Angoulême in the previous generation and the Count of La Marche and Périgord had the potential to be the major force in the region. This was, no doubt, what concerned the Count of Anjou, the undercurrent of what was occurring here. So much had happened whilst Audebert was in the pit: his parents had died and now his brother and uncle dead. He wondered – if he *was* permanently lifted from the pit – along with the recovery of his health and strength, would he be able to regain adequate knowledge and political acumen to deal with men such as this Count of Anjou. He felt like a great gasping fish suddenly landed on the bank, ripped into an alien world where he could not function.

'I am sure he appreciates your concern for him,' said Gerard, and Audebert, trying to process this sudden and significant news, heard the anger beneath his words. 'Have you forgotten so quickly, my lord, that this man and his wolf-pack of brothers offended direly against the Peace of God. They should have hanged for their crime and indeed the Lord has taken the older brother and did not, it seems, hear *his* plea for forgiveness.'

'It is not for us to say what offends God and whether or no he has forgiven,' Geoffrey responded coldly. There was an awkward silence until Geoffrey continued in a more pleasant voice, 'Four years in a dungeon for a count of noble blood is fit punishment for the crime, Gerard, but no more. After all, it was his brother Helie who actually committed the crime against Father Benedict and not Audebert here.'

Audebert's heart began to beat loudly in his ears and he could not refrain from gripping Adalmode's hand beneath the cloth. The Count of Anjou was arguing for him.

'He is *my* prisoner and it is *I* who decide how many years is fit punishment,' said Gerard. 'He may not have held the dagger himself but he is kin to the sinner and crimes must be paid for by kin. They both offended against the Peace of God as your own brother, Bishop Guy of Le Puy, made clear to us all last year.'

For the sake of Adalmode, Audebert felt he must maintain politeness to her father, but he would like to run him through now with the knife he held in his hand, for the years of his life lost in Gerard's dungeon, yet he was so weak his wrist could barely sustain the weight of the knife to eat with it, let alone run it into a man's resisting flesh.

'Of course keeping the Count of La Marche and Périgord penned up like a pig and unable to defend his lands and his birthright is precisely what suits you and the Aquitaine Court and coincides neatly with your conjectures as to God's will,' said Geoffrey smiling, and Audebert gulped at the extent of the insult he intended to the Viscount. Audebert looked around and saw that Anjou had brought a great many armed men with him to Gerard's hall and each one of them now looked alert to the verbal confrontation and ready to act.

'No such thing!' denied Gerard.

'Keeping the Count here any longer stinks to me of an intention to annexe his lands,' declared Geoffrey, 'and that, Viscount, I would regard as an act of war.'

Audebert watched Rothilde's hand trembling as she reached for her glass and he sat up straighter in his seat, looking around again. Nobody it seemed would wish to be at war with this Geoffrey Greymantle. The black-haired boy beside him was smiling smugly and watching everything with avid curiosity.

Gerard's face was white, his hand gripped tightly around his sauce-stained knife. 'I will have to consult with the Duke of Aquitaine on the matter . . .'

'Are you his lackey then?' asked Geoffrey.

Gerard rose angrily, pushing back his chair, and every Anjou man at arms reached to his sword-hilt. Why had Gerard allowed them to bear arms in his hall, Audebert wondered. The man was a fool. What price would Geoffrey of Anjou want to extract from him in payment for his support? He would gladly grant almost anything in exchange for his freedom, as long as it did not involve harm to Adalmode.

'While you think on it, my lord,' said Geoffrey also rising slowly from his seat, allowing the tension to deflate a little with the modulation of his voice, playing the audience assembled in the hall like an expert musician, 'I presume that you will extend your courtesy to Count Audebert?'

Gerard swallowed his fury. 'Of course,' he said, 'my wife will see to the Count's needs.' No longer able to bear the shaming Geoffrey had delivered in front of his household, the Viscount moved to leave the hall, merely nodding abruptly to his guests. To cover his exit, Lady Rothilde rose and Adalmode with her. Rothilde extended her hand towards Audebert. 'Please Count, come, I will show you to your quarters,' she said and though Audebert longed to simply run at high speed down the hall and out into the mountains, still his slow progress to the tower room felt like a marvellous freedom too. He carefully avoided giving Rothilde any impression that he and Adalmode were on familiar terms.

The following morning two guards came for Audebert and he was ashamed to find himself twitching and shaking, his whole body revolting at the idea of returning to the pit.

'Viscount's declared you have to do penance, while he's mulling over your crimes,' one man told him. They took away his shoes and gave him a rough wool tunic to put on in place of the fine linen tunic he had worn to supper in the hall the night before. They led him to the church door, and left him there, his hands manacled together and his ankles similarly chained and attached to a sturdy ring embedded in the ground. As soon as the guards were gone, servants and household members sidled up to ogle and pass comments on his sins. Audebert considered turning his back to them, leaning his head against the door with his eyes closed, but no, he was Count of La Marche and Périgord now and he would face them down. He slouched insouciantly with his back against the church door, his arms crossed, and scowled threateningly at them, so that their chatter began to lose its impetus. Please God, Audebert prayed, do not let Adalmode walk this way and look at me humiliated like this.

Count Geoffrey came and tipped a cup of water to Audebert's mouth. 'Gerard was all for giving you the Punishment of Hide and Hair – a birching and shaving off your hair – but I negotiated him to this church door penance instead.'

'I thank you, and will not forget it.'

'Endure. There is a good end in sight,' Geoffrey encouraged him.

At the end of the day the guards unshackled him and took him back to a meal in the tower room, locking the door behind them.

Two days after his release from the pit, Audebert returned to the hall to hear Gerard's decision. In addition to the Limoges family, Emma Duchess of Aquitaine was now sitting alongside the Viscount. Audebert heard of her arrival last night from his guard. Her son, Guillaume, had come with her, and was playing with the boy, Fulk of Anjou. Guillaume appeared large, round, and slow alongside the brilliant, black intensity of Geoffrey's small son. The Duchess arrived trailing gossip that reached even Audebert's ears. She had left her husband over his blatant affair with Aldearde d'Aulnay and was returning to her brother in Blois.

Gerard cleared his throat and the chattering hall and company on the dais settled slowly to silence. He summoned Audebert to stand before him. 'I am pleased to grant you your freedom Count,' said Gerard.

Audebert looked down momentarily to conceal his intense relief and joy. When he had regained some control of his expression he looked back to Gerard.

'The terms,' Gerard continued, 'are those that Count Geoffrey has negotiated on your behalf and include a heavy fine.'

Audebert hesitated but decided that it would be best to strike now. 'I thank you,' he said graciously, 'and before I leave to return to my lands, I have a request.' He was conscious that Adalmode shifted on the bench at his words and her mother looked at her enquiringly.

'Yes?' said Gerard, his frown increasing.

'There has been enmity between our two houses,' said Aude-bert, 'which I deeply regret. We are neighbours and I would like to move to the future in a new accord with you.'

Gerard inclined his head.

'I ask for your daughter Adalmode to wife,' said Audebert.

There was a stunned silence. Gerard looked taken aback and Rothilde was regarding Audebert with her mouth open. 'We are greatly honoured by your request,' stammered Gerard, frowning, 'but . . .'

'The Viscount will no doubt take your offer under consider-ation,' snapped the Duchess of Aquitaine in her precise clipped voice, 'and he will communicate his decision to you in Bellac in due course.'

Audebert turned to her in surprise. What business was it of hers to make a decision for Gerard? He turned back to the Vis-count. 'Lord Gerard I entreat that you consider my offer yourself and now,' he said.

'Certainly I will,' replied Gerard and Audebert saw that this was not going in his favour. 'You have already been granted the boon of your freedom, Count Audebert, and to make this offer now is,' he reached for a word, 'unfortunate. My decision is that your offer for my daughter Adalmode is not, alas, possible to accept, as I am already in negotiations for her hand elsewhere. Yet I will consider the possibility of an alternative betrothal. I have two daughters who are not promised yet.'

The Duchess sat back, relieved. Adalmode looked desperately at Audebert. The party of people were staring down at him from the dais. There was nothing to gain by continuing argument, but wishing to give Adalmode hope he bowed in farewell, saying, 'It is Adalmode I ask for and only Adalmode and not one of her sis-ters. I hope you will reconsider Viscount since I am your neigh-bour and allegiance between us would benefit us both. I vow here that I will marry no-one but Lady Adalmode, and I will ask you for her again.' He strode out of the hall without looking back, trying to keep his pace swift but sedate, torn between wanting to snatch up Adalmode and ride out with her, and a physical need to put distance between himself and this place of his grim captivity.

Audebert was in the bailey, swiftly preparing the horse that had been handed to him, when Geoffrey of Anjou loped up and took his wasted arm in a firm grip.

'Congratulations Count Audebert. Glad to see you freed.'

The boy, Fulk, was with him and looking curiously at Audebert's horse.

'I owe immense thanks to you, Lord Geoffrey.'

'Yes,' said Geoffrey, grinning voraciously.

Here it comes thought Audebert. What did he want?

'I would ask a favour of you in a few years' time.'

Audebert waited.

'Fulk here,' said Geoffrey, 'is four now but when he reaches the age of training in three or four years, I would like to send him to you as your foster-son.'

Audebert nodded. It seemed innocuous but it was of course Geoffrey's first move in gaining Audebert's allegiance and there would be more to follow. The military aggression and expansionism of the House of Anjou was well known, yet Audebert had little to lose from an alliance with Geoffrey. Aquitaine and Limoges were hardly his allies after what he had suffered at their hands, and one way or another they would have to pay. He placed his hand on Fulk's head. 'I would be glad to take your cub,' he said smiling and offered Geoffrey his hand to seal the bargain.

# 9

## Brioude

### Easter 982

'I thought the accommodations would be more splendid, mother,' says Aina, disappointed at the tiny space with one bed and one pallet on the floor that we have been shown to. Ademar and Melisende have answered a royal summons from King Lothaire and Queen Emma to attend the marriage of their son in Brioude, and Melisende allowed Aina and me to accompany them.

'They have many guests to accommodate, Aina,' says her mother, 'and Brioude is not a royal palace after all.'

Brioude is one of the holdings of Lady Blanche of Anjou who is to marry the King's son, Louis, after the death of her second husband, the Count of Toulouse. Households up and down the region have been buzzing with the news for weeks and this marriage of an older woman, twice widowed, to the fifteen year old heir to the French throne has been dissected again and again, over laundry, over spits, over chopping boards, on horseback and at table, all over the countryside.

Earlier we stood in the courtyard and watched a stream of chariots bearing the royal insignia entering the gate for the great assembly gathering here. In the privacy of our own room, Ademar told us the Carolingian family are desperately trying to shore up their throne. A few years ago King Lothaire's brother Charles accused Queen Emma of adultery hoping to cast doubt on the legitimacy of Louis as the heir, and Charles waged war against his brother. Lothaire prevailed but Charles escaped to Germany and was tainted as a traitor. Prince Louis, then only eleven, had been crowned as Associate King, alongside his father.

'Lady Blanche is more than twice Prince Louis' age!' exclaims Aina, who has been very taken with the glimpse of the royal heir that she saw as we entered the city. A tall, thin boy with brown hair, splendidly dressed, but otherwise unremarkable as far as I could see. 'It's almost like me and Guy,' says Aina.

'Aina!' says Ademar.

'Nothing like you and Guy,' sighs her mother. 'Guy is not twice your age.'

Aina pulls a face. She does not miss any opportunity to express her dismay at her betrothal, still hoping to sway her doting parents, and I wish she would not bait them so, because it is likely that this marriage will take place eventually and her hopes of change are baseless. He lives a mere five miles away and this is his continuing offence in Aina's eyes, together with the lack of any glamour she could discern when she met him on the occasion of her betrothal at Poitiers. Yet, for now, Aina has her way, since the marriage has been delayed by Guy's brother, Bishop Hildegaire, who will not yet give his dispensation.

There is a jaunty knock on the doorjamb and there is the offending groom himself: Guy, long and lean, and ever attentive to Aina and her parents. Aina pulls her veil over her face which is her way of indicating that she is not available for conversation. To soften the insult, I pull my own veil down too, as if it is merely modesty that motivates us both. I hope that Guy has not over-heard Aina's complaints. He greets her politely: 'Lady Aina.' Yet he appears to be looking at me and I hear Aina stifle a giggle.

'Ah, Lord Guy,' says Melisende, 'this is Sigrid, our maid.'

Guy is greatly embarrassed and shifts his gaze to the other veiled young woman in the room. Aina nods perfunctorily and lends an unusual focus to some embroidery in her lap. Guy has blushed a dark red and stutters an apology for his mistake. I feel cross with Aina that she offers him no mitigation for his blunder.

'Come in, Guy,' says Ademar, who holds a real affection for him. They talk of affairs in Limoges. Viscount Gerard has more or less given over the management of the city to Guy. Aina's father, as former custodian, is well placed to discuss Limoges with him.

I take the opportunity of my veil to study Aina's betrothed husband. He has light brown floppy hair, a long thin face with strong planes, a long chin with a slight cleft, a large nose, brown eyes that slant upwards towards brown brows, neat ears, a pale large mouth with a full bottom lip and a bow of a top lip. He is not handsome, but I decide that his looks are interesting.

Bored with the talk of tolls, mills and abbey disputes, Aina asks Guy: 'Do you know who else is here for the marriage?'

'All the main families of the south,' he says. 'The Duke of Aquitaine and his entourage, his estranged Duchess with her son and brother, the Count of Blois. Geoffrey, Count of Anjou, of course. Audebert, Count of La Marche and Périgord. We from Limoges and Ségur and most other nobles hereabouts I'd say. And the grand lords of the north have accompanied the King: Duke Hugh Capet and the Duke of Normandy.'

'What illustrious company,' says Aina. 'The Duke of Normandy is a Viking isn't he, like Sigrid?'

'Aina!' exclaims her father, 'Sigrid is not a Viking. She is a demure young lady.'

I am amused at the idea that I am a Viking and wonder what that might mean in the present company – cutting a swathe through sadistic priests and lascivious lords? Leaping into a longship brandishing an axe?

'And the Duke of Normandy,' continues Ademar, 'whilst his ancesters were from the Northland yes, he is a Christian and hardly a Viking either, although it is said that he gives safe harbour to many of them.'

Aina's mouth curves below the hem of her veil and I know that she is delighted at provoking this reprimand.

Her mother turns to our visitor: 'Guy, do you know why this royal marriage is taking place here in Brioude? It's not the obvious choice.'

Guy shrugs. 'No, it's not. There is much speculation about it. There is some political intent on the part of the King and Duke Hugh Capet no doubt. They are intending to make some point to us southerners but it is not clear what that is yet. Geoffrey of Anjou, having brokered such a royal marriage for his sister and such alliances for himself, looks like the cat that has had the cream.'

106

We all smile at this image. 'Geoffrey of Anjou,' says Ademar in a low voice, 'is more akin to the wolf that has taken a lamb, perhaps.'

Guy nods.

'I wonder how Prince Louis feels being wed to a woman who could be his mother and who has already had two husbands and five children,' says Aina.

'Yes a daunting prospect, perhaps, Lady Aina,' says Guy, 'for a fifteen year old boy. Nevertheless Lady Blanche remains one of the most beautiful women walking the earth.'

I see the sour set of Aina's mouth beneath the edge of her veil. 'Really,' she says coldly.

'Excepting yourself of course,' he says, too late. He leans a little too close to Aina, apparently aiming to decipher her expression, and Aina shifts her stool backwards away from him, with a loud scrape.

'I am looking forward to gazing on this wondrous beautiful ancient bride,' she says.

At dinner in the hall Aina has her wish. Blanche of Anjou sits alongside the young prince on the raised dais, together with her brother Geoffrey, the King and Queen, and the two northern Dukes. Many have quietly remarked on the fact that Duke Guillaume of Aquitaine has not been invited to join them on the High Table. We are seated far down the board. I watch as Duke Hugh Capet stands up from the trestle and turns around to speak with Geoffrey of Anjou. Geoffrey has become even richer, now he has wed the widow of the Count of Chalon and taken control of her lands. Yet Duke Hugh is richer still and earns his Capet name from the splendid capes he wears in his role as Lay Abbot. I look with pleasure at the one he is wearing today. It is a deep rich red embroidered in silver thread and seed pearls with scenes of animals and birds. I imagine the process of making such a beautiful textile: first the underdrawing in lead or silver point, then working on it for many, many weeks and months careful not to make mistakes. Perhaps it would take years to complete, depending on how many women were at work on it. I would like to make such a thing. How enormously satisfying it would be at the end of the labours to stand and marvel at it. My attention is pulled away from the display of clothing and jewels on the High Table to my immediate neighbours.

The Limoges household are ranged across the board from us: Guy's parents and his brothers, Bishop Hildegaire and Lord Aimery, are seated directly opposite us. Guy himself and his sisters Adalmode and Tisalga, are further down the long table, too far away for conversation. The Bishop looks at Aina, who is still veiled, with a mix of lust and distaste as if she has already committed the sin of incest with his brother. Perhaps my mistress will have her way after all and not marry Lord Guy, but I will make sure not to entrust her alone with that burly Bishop.

Lady Rothilde is seated opposite me and leans over the table to speak with Melisende: 'We hoped that Guy and Aina might be wed at this Assembly, but,' she says glancing crossly at her son, 'Bishop Hildegaire is still consulting lawyers and theologians on the matter. He says it will be resolved soon however.'

Melisende smiles. 'We are exceedingly fond of Guy,' she says.

'My daughter Tisalga is to wed Lady Blanche's son this week,' Rothilde announces proudly. Aina and I turn to look at Tisalga whose brown head is bowed in conversation with her golden-haired sister, Adalmode. I guess that Tisalga is about the same age as me – nineteen. Suddenly I wonder, will I ever marry? No Christian man would marry me if I remain a pagan slave. I look towards the Duke of Normandy on the dais and recognize his height, his blond hair and his big, broad face as the marks of my countrymen. The Northmen of Normandy are said to have accepted Christianity and abjured Thor and Odinn, but perhaps a man of his company might take a fancy to me.

Melisende and Rothilde are still talking of marriages in loud voices, to be able to hear above the din of the hall. 'What of Adalmode?' asks Melisende. 'We heard a rumour that she is to wed the Duke of Aquitaine's heir?'

'Yes,' says Rothilde avidly. 'Another marriage that we hoped might take place at this assembly but which also suffers delay.'

'What causes the delay?' asks Melisende.

I see that Adalmode has heard her name and turned her head to hear the conversation.

'The Duchess has been much preoccupied,' says Rothilde, 'with her own marriage troubles and the business of Maillezais Abbey where she is patron. And of course we have to wait a while for young Guillaume to grow from boy to man.' Aina and I look to where Guillaume sits with his mother, Duchess Emma. He is thirteen now but is still carrying a padding of fat on his face and chin. He has a neck so short that his head seems to be simply balanced on top of his barrel-shaped body. He holds a pet squirrel on a leash on his lap and is stroking its red back. Guillaume's gaze is trained on Adalmode who does not look in his direction. 'Adalmode is gorgeous,' Aina whispers in my ear.

'Yes.' She is an unlikely looking sister to Guy. Now twenty-two she is in the prime of her beauty with a profusion of honey-coloured hair and striking green eyes. Her fine red velvet gown has bright blue embroidered edging, and emphasizes the shapeliness and upright carriage of her body. I cannot blame Guillaume for his adoration. She shows no signs of interest in the boy who is her intended husband.

Towards the end of the feasting Ademar is tired and Melisende excuses herself to attend him to our chamber. Aina begs to stay a little longer, feasting her eyes on the rich clothing and manners of the royal court. 'Take care of Aina, please Sigrid.' I nod, gratified at Melisende's confidence in me. Guy too leaves the hall and I tut at Aina when she chooses to throw the veil back from her face, after he has left the company.

'What?' she says in mock innocence.

Music starts up and Prince Louis ceremoniously leads Lady Blanche out to dance. They do, I confess to myself, look a little foolish as partners. Blanche's beauty is the beauty of the matron, not a young girl, and the Prince is clearly more interested in the younger women in the hall. He asks Tisalga to dance when Lady Blanche sits down. 'Ridiculous!' says Aina. 'He will be Tisalga's father-in-law and he is four years younger than her!' but she stills her tongue and holds her breath as she sees that the Prince is now coming in her direction.

Aina is one of the most striking young women in the room with her dark red hair, shining grey eyes and small, perfect pink mouth. Aina accepts Prince Louis' proffered hand. I watch them for a while but decide that she is safe enough. While she dances with Louis and imagines herself a Queen I find that I must go outside in search of the privy. I don't know exactly where it is and linger at the foot of the staircase in the dark, waiting for my eyes to adjust and to discern some landmark. I hear a murmur of voices to my left and think I must ask for directions. I follow the wall with my fingertips round in the direction of the voices. There is no moon and it is very dark out here. I round the corner but then immediately draw back into the shadow of the wall as I see that Lady Adalmode stands with her hand on the cheek of a tall black-haired man. One of her brothers I think at first but then realize that it is the Count of La Marche. I hold myself very still as I watch Adalmode step into the Count's embrace and put her mouth on his. I want to close my eyes and not bear such dangerous witness and yet my curiosity keeps my eyelids pinned open. The kiss they exchange is passionate and lingering. I see that the Count holds his hands away from Adalmode's body, clad in it luscious red velvet, as if contact with her will burn him, and yet it is clear that the kiss burns them both. He steps away, placing his hands on her shoulders. 'God knows, I love you Adalmode,' he says, 'yet this is madness that we indulge.'

'Don't say so,' she says in a voice low with desire. 'Can you not take me?'

I think that I may have to witness more than a kiss, but then realise that she is asking him to abduct her.

He shakes his head. 'That would bring war from Aquitaine and your father onto my people,' he says. 'I am not ready for war yet, but I will be, if I must. I have asked your father four times for your hand, and four times he has refused me. He offers me your little sister, Aldiarde.'

'No Audebert!' Adalmode's anguish is plain in her whispered response.

'No, no,' he says stroking her hair and her cheek with the back of his hand. 'I have vowed to have you and only you to wife.'

'You will not say so, if you are faced with the prospect of no woman and no heir,' says Adalmode. 'You will take my sister.'

'No,' he says.

'It will be too late. They will betroth me soon to the fat Aquitaine.'

He laughs softly. 'No, no,' he says again. 'We have time.'

A door opens above our heads and light and noise spill out. Audebert steps back into the shadows, close to me. 'Go,' he says quietly and I watch the candlelight from the hall glint on Adalmode's golden head as she mounts the staircase. The Count turns and as he does so catches sight of me. I draw in a fearful breath.

'Who are you spying there?' he demands, his hand moving to the hilt of his dagger.

'I did not mean to spy, Lord. I am a serving maid to Ademar of Ségur. I was lost, looking for a privy.'

He laughs shortly.

'I know Lady Adalmode's brother, Lord Guy,' I say. 'I mean no harm to her and will not tell.'

His hand is still on his dagger and his eyes glitter studying my face in the gloom. 'What is your name, maid?'

'Sigrid Thorolfsdottir, sire.' I am shaking now and take a small step backwards away from him. It would be easy for him to stab me here in the dark and protect Lady Adalmode's honour.

'Norse?'

'Yes, sire.'

'Swear on your sign of Thor then,' he says.

I had not realised that I am clutching the hammer at my neck in my fear. 'I do sire. I swear on Thor's hammer that I saw nothing out here but turds in the privy and heard nothing but the thunder of my own piss in the garderobe.'

He laughs heartily at that. 'Alright Sigrid Thorolfsdottir, vivid-speaker. If you break your oath you'll find yourself head down in the piss in the garderobe. Go.'

'I won't break my oath. Thank you sire.' I move off.

'The privy is this way,' he calls softly, gesturing in the other direction. I walk back past him with my head down, my eyes on his fingers touching the dagger and my hand in my pocket on my serpent brooch, the pin opened and clenched between the fingers of my fist. If he makes a sudden lunge at me I will not die without

111

a fight and without drawing his blood to my Viken serpent, but he lets me pass and I find the privy and sit there shaking for a long time before going back to Aina in the hall.

In the doorway my way is barred by young Guillaume of Aquitaine who is standing with a group of other adolescents. He is only a few years younger than Prince Louis, and already his boyness is on the verge of the man he is becoming. 'Well,' he says gripping my upper arm painfully, 'look here, lads, a red-haired beauty.' I am still shaking from my encounter with the Count of La Marche and do not have my wits about me enough to push past quickly. Suddenly he grips the back of my head and kisses me, forcing his tongue into my mouth, and I am struggling, panicking, pushing at his chest, kicking at his shins, hearing the cruel laughter of the boys crowding close around us.

I feel my elbow gripped and I am borne forward out of Guillaume's grasp and through the doorway. 'This young woman is clearly not enjoying your attentions, boy.' I recognise Count Audebert's voice. I rush through, pulled along with the force of his stride until I find myself firmly pushed down onto the trestle next to Aina. 'Your seat, I think,' he says and is gone. I gasp for air and stare with shock at the doorway, where Guillaume is looking furiously at Audebert's receding back.

Aina stares at me. 'Sigrid! Where have you been? You look strange and were gone a long time. You haven't been dallying with one of those Northmen and given him your virginity have you?' she asks suddenly.

'No!' I exclaim crossly. Across the hall I see Lord Audebert looking intently at me, standing alongside Geoffrey of Anjou and his son, Fulk. Audebert is black-haired, blue-eyed, tall, muscled. There is a suppressed and dangerous energy about him. I can see why Adalmode clings to him and does not wish for marriage to the lustful boy-heir to Aquitaine. I look away demurely from the Count's gaze. 'We should go to bed, Aina. Men are getting drunk and careless of courtesy.'

She sighs. 'Oh, I suppose so, but I am enjoying the adventure of tonight.'

Not I so much, I think. We pick our way carefully through drunken guests, holding the hems of our dresses away from the messy rushes, and I feel Count Audebert's blue eyes like heat on my back.

In the morning Ademar is telling Melisende how Guy requested further formal discussion with his brother Hildegaire concerning the necessary dispensation for his marriage to Aina.

'Did you see how Bishop Hildegaire rode into Brioude on a magnificent horse with caparisons decorated in gold and silver, a handsome falcon on his forearm, and accompanied by a large retinue?' says Melisende, disapproval in her tone.

'Yes indeed,' adds Aina. 'He wore a fur cap, a split coat and a sword in a silver scabbard on his belt. His clothes are made from the finest linen.' She giggles and raises her eyebrows at my serious shake of the head.

'Bishop Hildegaire has become a gourmand in the last few years,' Ademar says, referring tactfully to Hildegaire's extreme corpulence.

'He conducted his meeting with Guy lounging in his bed,' Aina says.

'Aina you do not know that. The man is a Bishop,' exclaims her mother, exasperated.

'Yes I do,' Aina argues. 'I heard it directly from his own servants.'

'Well you should not be gossiping with servants,' her father tells her. 'Guy meant to be conciliatory, of course, but he could not resist pointing out the inappropriateness of Hildegaire's lifestyle.'

'That would not help Guy's request for dispensation to marry I fear,' says Melisende.

'No,' Ademar, continues his tale, 'he said that Guy would always have made the better priest and asked him if he wanted to swop places?'

Aina looks at me pointedly. Here is yet more evidence, from her point of view, of Guy's unsuitability as her husband. I ignore her glance and listen to the rest of Ademar's account of the brothers' argument.

'Hildegaire asked Guy if he would have him shaved and tonsured, sacrificing the adornment of his beard and hair, wearing a womanly cassock, spending his days blessing pilgrims' staffs and travel bags.'

'Oh dear,' says Melisende, 'poor Guy only wanted to find a solution to the impasse on this marriage, but I fear he has made matters worse.'

Aina smiles gaily to me.

The following day we rise to witness the royal wedding but the families of the southern counties are taken by surprise when King Lothaire steps forward, and two pages stand behind him, each bearing a crown on a cushion. The King takes the larger crown and places it on Louis' head. 'Bear witness,' he says, 'that this day, in the tradition of my ancestor, Charlemagne, I crown my son Louis, King of Aquitaine.'

There is a collective gasp from those gathered. The French royal family have made no claim to Aquitaine for several generations and if Louis is King of Aquitaine where does that leave Duke Guillaume?

'Mother?' I hear the Duke's young heir begin to question Duchess Emma.

'Silence!' she snarls her command to him. Her hand is gripped like a talon on the head of her staff.

King Lothaire lifts the other crown aloft, declaring, 'And I crown my son's wife, Blanche, Queen of Aquitaine.'

Duchess Emma's face has assumed a look of hatred. The Duke of Aquitaine rises from his seat, and followed by his entourage, he stalks from the hall. With the King's announcement, I feel allegiances swirling, shifting and reforming in the room around me. Duchess Emma stares with loathing at Queen Blanche, who had been her erstwhile friend and I see her bare her teeth, before gripping the arm of her son and following her estranged husband in abandoning the assembly.

On the way home, Ademar explains that the King has not only made claim for the submission of the southern counties with his surprise act, he has also curtailed the ambitions in this region of his powerful ally Duke Hugh Capet. 'Lothaire thinks to gain the submission of the south through this marriage but he has only gained himself the enmity of the Aquitaine family and of Duke Hugh. The Count of Anjou, who no doubt has brokered the whole plan, seeking to bind the King closer to his own house, has also now made himself a serious enemy in Duke Hugh. It is the start of a new round of power plays,' says Ademar wearily, 'and I doubt the wisdom of it for *anyone*!'

I think of Lady Adalmode whose lover Count Audebert is allied with Anjou, and whose mooted fiancé, the Duchess' son, is on the other side of the divide. I hope that Count Audebert knows how grateful I am to him for rescuing me from the unwelcome attentions of young Lord Guillaume. I have not told even Aina any of it. I find myself hoping that Adalmode and Audebert will not be injured in these power plays and that they will gain possession of one another, and I hope that Count Audebert knows how steadfastly I will keep their secret.

# 10

## Angers

### Autumn 987

Audebert stood on the top step above the courtyard of his *domus* looking around at the massive, solid walls of Bellac, the La Marche stronghold. It was eleven years since he had been hauled from the Montignac pit barely able to stand or ride a horse, and there were no visible signs of his ordeal now. His height and the breadth of his shoulders were finally rewarded with the musculature they had been promised in the boy, but cruelly denied in the young man. The invisible signs of the pit, however, were another matter. He could not abide to be in small spaces and even being indoors was something he avoided as much as possible. Returning his body and health to fighting fitness had taken more than a year, eating well, regaining the hard muscles of his arms and legs practising with weapons and horse, engaging in small skirmishes each year to develop both his own skills and the coherent fighting and loyalty of his men. The thought of being captured filled him with utter dread but he found that instead of inducing panic on the battlefield, this secret terror, sparked a ferocity in his fighting. He would not ever be taken alive again.

Each year he asked for Adalmode in marriage and every time he had to wear her father's rebuff. They contrived to meet briefly most years and had agreed that if she were threatened with another marriage, with Aquitaine's heir, then she would get word to him and he would take her regardless of who might stand against them.

'But do not harm my brother, Guy,' Adalmode told him. 'I could never forgive that.'

Looking around at the newly fortified walls of Bellac, thinking of the solid loyalty of his *milites*, he was satisfied. Finally he was ready to seek vengeance for his unjust incarceration and ready to take Adalmode as his bride. He was thirty-two and his wait for her had been overlong. She was twenty-seven this year and they could not wait much longer. Bellac was a predominantly male household with his brothers and his men, a military camp in effect. He wondered how Adalmode would fare here, what he could do to make her at home, when he would finally ride in with her at his side.

It was good to feel confident in the stronghold of Bellac with the unsettling sequence of news from the north. Last year King Lothaire died and the throne passed to his nineteen-year-old son Louis, who imprisoned his mother and resumed charges of adultery and treason against Archbishop Adalbero. Fulk's father Geoffrey, who supported Lothaire and then Louis, had fallen ill in suspicious circumstances. Then Louis also died, falling from his horse during a hunt, which was most likely a polite description for regicide. Since Lothaire's brother, Charles of Lorraine, was accused of treason and excluded from the succession, Louis was the last of the line of Charlemagne, and so the northern nobles elected Hugh Capet, Duke of France as their new King. Charles would undoubtedly contest this. Guillaume of Aquitaine refused to recognise Hugh's crowning and the new king besieged Poitiers but was driven back to the Loire. No one doubted that he would be back to claim the fealty of the southern lords when it suited him. These were uncertain times when it was good to have high solid walls.

Audebert turned his thoughts from these court complexities to reimagine how he had first seen Adalmode, but his picture of her was dispersed by the noise of horses returning at the gate. He shaded his eyes against the sun to watch the black-haired boy ride in alongside Audebert's brothers Gausbert and Boson, and a group of squires. They had been exercising the horses and Fulk was riding Audebert's warhorse.

'He's going really well!' the boy called out.

'Fulk, come in right away. There is news from Anjou. We must prepare to ride north.'

Fulk's cheerful expression was replaced with a frown. He knew it must be news of his father who had been sick for months. He leapt from the huge horse with the ease of an acrobat, tossing the reins to a groom and running up the steps two at a time to follow Audebert into the hall. At the trestle table Audebert pushed a bowl of water towards Fulk to wash his hands and he shunted forward the wine jug and a goblet.

'Is he dead?' Fulk asked.

'Yes, Fulk. I'm sorry. The messenger came from your uncle, Bishop Guy, less than an hour ago whilst you were out riding. Geoffrey Greymantle, Count of Anjou, has died and you must ride north to claim your rights.'

'My father's burial?'

'The funeral and burial have already taken place. The news reached us slowly. He died some weeks ago. We should not delay.'

Audebert admired how Fulk kept the trepidation and excitement that must be rising in him from his face and the set of his body. Fulk had respected his father but spent very little of his life with him. The news of his illness over the last months had prepared him for this death, and now his thoughts were mostly on his future as Count of Anjou and not on the past or familial grief.

'How ready are we do you think?' he asked.

'As ready as we must be.'

Geoffrey had spent hours poring over maps of the Angevin holdings with young Fulk and Audebert, passing on his knowledge, explaining threats from neighbours in Blois, Saumur, Maine, Aquitaine and Thouars, weaknesses in the lines of communication and defences, the importance of gaining and managing loyal followers, the policies he was pursuing. It was good fortune that one of those policies had been to announce Fulk as Associate Count last year and to betroth him to Elisabeth of Vendôme, bringing her father, Count Bourchard, as a powerful ally. This was a good start for enforcing Fulk's claim to his birthright. Yet Fulk's neighbours would waste no time in seeking to undermine the rights of the youthful count. Audebert owed Geoffrey his freedom and his life, but he would support Fulk because he had a genuine affection for the boy, and an admiration for his qualities. He would make a good ruler in Anjou if he could only hold onto it for the next few years. Waiting so long as Audebert had for marriage and children of his own, his affections were invested in the energetic, black-haired boy seated before him.

'Let's go,' Audebert said, with his characteristic forthrightness and urge to constantly move, get out, do. 'The men who ride with us are already assembled, waiting. Our provisions and arms are packed. The servants have loaded everything from your chamber onto the oxen cart. We can waste no time.' Audebert's brothers would hold Bellac in his absence.

Recently arrived for the Assembly in Angers, Guy settled his horse and servants and retired to his room to look through his Annals. There was so much to record now.

*The Annals of Guy of Limoges Book II*

**+ 978** In this year there was war between King Lothaire of the Franks and his brother Charles, who was accused of treason. Across the Narrow Sea in England Athelred became King. A new priory at Chambon has been built to house Saint Valeria's relics. The walls of Saint Martial Abbey in Limoges have been rebuilt and the crypt enlarged and the city swarms with pilgrims.

**+ 979** In this year Geoffrey, Count of Anjou, took Adelais, Dowager of Chalon as his second wife and took the lands of her dead husband. His sister, Blanche, was also widowed and became Regent of Toulouse and of Brioude for her sons by her two dead husbands.

**+ 980** In this year there was a great sickness in the city of Limoges and many died. Viscount Gerard went on a journey to Rome and left his son, Guy, to oversee the affairs of the city.

**+ 981** In this year Duke Guillaume of Aquitaine made peace with the Viscount of Thouars and the Lord of Parthenay after warring.

+ 982 In this year Geoffrey of Anjou wed his widowed sister, Blanche, to the son of King Lothaire. Louis was declared by Lothaire to be King of Aquitaine. The Duke and Duchess of Aquitaine were ablaze with anger at the insult to their power in the south.

+ 983 In this year there was famine in the Limousin and many died. A comet streaked across the skies. Viscount Gerard and his wife, Rothilde, went on pilgrimage to Compostela and left their son, Guy, to oversee the affairs of the city.

+ 984 In this year Blanche of Anjou abandoned her husband, Louis Associate King of the Franks, and she was sheltered in the Abbey of Saint Martial in Limoges. The Duke of Aquitaine took Louis hostage in Poitiers. King Lothaire came with a vast army and Louis was surrendered to him. Lothaire's army besieged Lady Blanche at Limoges but in time the King raised the siege and rode to deal with pressing matters in the north. Guillaume of Provence married Lady Blanche. Otto II, Emperor of the Holy Roman Empire died and his Empress, Theophanu, stood Regent for her young son. A bright star was observed shining in daylight at noon.

+ 985 In this year King Lothaire charged Archbishop Adalbero with treason but Duke Hugh Capet marched with a vast army and rescued the Archbishop.

+ 986 In this year King Lothaire died and Louis became king. He imprisoned his mother and charged Archbishop Adalbero again. In Denmark the king Harald Bluetooth died and was succeeded by his son, Svein Forkbeard. Merchants thronging the port of Limoges say that Norse sailors have discovered a new land far to the northwest that they name Vinland.

+ 987 In this year the marriage of Guy of Limoges to the heiress, Aina of Ségur, suffers delays caused by the ecclesiastical deliberations of Bishop Hildegaire. Duke Guillaume of Aquitaine made war and then peace with Geoffrey of Anjou. Geoffrey of Anjou fell dangerously ill. King Louis of the Franks, the last of the line of Charlemagne, died in a fall from his horse (like the previous King Louis before him) while hunting near Senlis. Hugh Capet was proclaimed the new king by the nobles of the court. Norse raiders made grievous attacks on many coasts again. Duke Guillaume of Aquitaine refused to recognise Hugh Capet as king. Hugh Capet came with a vast army as far as the walls of Poitiers but it was late in the year for warring, the grass was thin for his horses and he was driven back beyond the Loire. Geoffrey Greymantle, Count of Anjou died and his son, Fulk, a young boy, is made Count. The Anglo-Saxon monk Bede calculates that the End of Time will come in the year 1003. Then will be the Second Coming of Christ and Judgement Day for the living and the dead. Many see the end of Charlemagne's line and the turbulent and uncertain times we are in now as portents of this imminent End.

Guy put the quill down, read it through again and frowned. The times were certainly turbulent. In the southern counties and cities, much depended on the strength of the Duke of Aquitaine, and he was not strong. His strength came only from his wife, Emma of Blois, who held the kingdom together through her alliances and the support of her brother. There was no knowing what might happen now that the carrion that had been collecting around the corpse of the Carolingian royal dynasty for a long, long time, were finally starting to feast.

Audebert and Fulk were amongst the last to arrive for the Assembly at Angers after a long ride north from Bellac along the old poplar shaded Roman roads, through the mountains of the Auvergne and along the ridges and limestone plateaux of the Central Massif. From the high roads they could see blue distances and the causses ridging the land like reefs running out to sea. In the mountains they looked down on the forest belt, its greens and browns turning to orange and red. The river wound gleaming like polished metal, swinging from side to side seeking the lowest point. Audebert's horse picked its way carefully, descending into the meandering valley, squelching through boggy lands threaded with small streams, until finally they were crossing the swampy flood plain of the Loire with the imposing walls of Angers before them.

Fulk would need Audebert now as Geoffrey claimed Audebert's debt to him from the grave. The lords to the north, Eudes of Blois and the new King Hugh Capet, and the Duke of Aquitaine to the south would try to take advantage of Fulk's youth and carve out parts of his lands for their own. Audebert must give Fulk counsel and if needs be, his swordarm.

Audebert had finished practising in the bailey with his men. He threw some water over his head from the bucket at the well, washing the sweat from his face and the back of his neck and the grime from his hands. His stomach rumbled and reluctantly he dipped his head under the arched doorway and stepped into the gloom of the hall to find a crust of bread to assuage his hunger until the meal in a few hours time. He could get back out into the bailey as soon as he found something to eat. The hall buzzed with discussion and activity. Men sat in small groups talking over the news. It was a time of great changes and therefore of great anxieties. The last descendent of Charlemagne was dead and now they all stood on the brink of a new era that in its uncertainty felt to some like standing on the edge of an abyss but others saw opportunities they might grasp.

Guy of Limoges was amongst those summoned to this assembly and Audebert, recognising the back of his brown head, swung around the edge of the trestle, gesturing that he would like to take the seat opposite. Despite his antipathy for Viscount Gerard, his erstwhile jailor, Audebert liked Guy for his sister's sake and his own. Contact with Guy felt almost like contact with her.

Guy greeted him warmly and they settled to discuss the drastic developments at the northern court of the Franks. 'Are we in the End Time?' said Audebert.

Guy inclined his head, his mouth temporarily full, chewing on hard bread. He glanced up to assess if Audebert was in earnest and saw a sarcastic expression on his face which he mirrored. 'So the monks say. You heard that Lady Blanche sought refuge with us in Limoges when she abandoned her marriage to Louis? It was said they never shared a bed and did not live under the same roof.'

Audebert knew this since Adalmode had told him, but he feigned surprise.

Guy nodded. 'Yes. She accused the Prince of a violent temper and a dissolute life style. She was in control of her own great wealth from her previous marriages. Louis quickly dissipated the resources King Lothaire left for him, and Blanche had no intention of having her wealth and that of her sons sucked upon.'

'No doubt Geoffrey of Anjou dangled his sister's wealth as bait for the marriage, but the lady had other ideas,' said Audebert. 'This marriage to Lady Blanche, merely rendered Prince Louis miserable and ridiculous.'

'Or perhaps he did that to himself.' Guy raised his eyebrows and Audebert nodded. He cared nothing for any of them and gave no allegiance to anyone except Fulk, but still it was important to know what was going on and how it might touch them. Guy continued: 'Lothaire besieged us in Limoges wanting vengeance against Blanche and we who harboured her, but then other matters prevailed to call him north. Did you hear that Lady Blanche has recently married her fourth husband, Guillaume of Provence?'

Audebert raised his eyebrows and clashed his drinking horn against Guy's. 'A beautiful lady is best wed it seems,' said Audebert. They were both silent, each knowing that it was Adalmode in their thoughts, rather than Blanche. 'Is your sister, well?' Audebert burst out, irritated with himself, since he had planned not to speak of her to Guy.

'She is well.' There was no need for Guy to question which of his sisters Audebert referred to. Audebert looked down at the tabletop, wondering whether or not he should open the question of his marriage to her brother. Her elderly father was set against him hard as adamantine, but it was Guy in effect who ruled Limoges.

'You were at the royal court,' asked Guy, evidently aiming to distract him from the topic of Adalmode, 'when these events of the succession occurred weren't you?'

'Yes. Count Geoffrey called me to him with his son and we were witness to what happened.' Audebert paused to reflect on it. 'The court was a hotbed of intrigue.' Audebert screwed his mouth into an expression of disgust.

Guy nodded and raised his hand to a passing serving boy who poured more wine into their beakers. They paused their conversation until the boy was out of earshot. A shaggy dog that Audebert knew to be one of Fulk's, came in, recognised Audebert and settled itself down on his boot with a happy grunt and a quick glance upwards to see if there might be any chance of food. Audebert threw a hard chunk of bread to the dog who wolfed it down noisily.

'Louis lacked authority and Capet manipulated the situation,' Audebert said.

Guy was eager to hear the story from a first-hand observer. Everyone had heard some version or another of the end of the royal line of Charlemagne, passed through many mouths and diluted, but Audebert had actually been there.

'We are well out of it here in the south.'

They were both silent for a moment and Audebert caught a whiff of the broth being prepared at the hearth and his stomach rumbled again. He looked over to where the fire burned high, tended by the household servants, and the cooks were busy chopping vegetables and dicing meat.

'What was Geoffrey of Anjou's role?' asked Guy.

'Geoffrey was devoted to King Lothaire and upheld the rights of his son Louis, despite the debacle of his sister Blanche's unhappy marriage to him. Conveniently, in June, Geoffrey too fell ill whilst on campaign with Hugh Capet and was rendered incapable.' Audebert lowered his voice and leant forward. 'Perhaps poisoned.' He sat back again and resumed in his usual voice, 'As soon as he fell ill, Geoffrey asked me to return to Bellac with Fulk to safeguard him. I thought the worst, but Fulk didn't realise he was looking on his father for the last time. Then as you know news came in July that Duke Hugh was elected King and Geoffrey was dead, the only man who might have stood in Capet's way, spoken against the election. It was always rumoured that Lothaire was only king in name, and the Capets held the real power.'

Audebert bit into the chunk of bread which he had been soaking in wine. It tasted disgusting and he threw the rest to the dog who was not so particular. 'So now the legacies of Charlemagne are shattered. Northmen overrun the counties above the Seine because these weakened northerners could not defend the land against them, and these Northmen are set up as Dukes and Counts in Normandy. A king, not of Charlemagne's blood, sits on the throne.'

Guy tapped his ring against the rim of his metal beaker. 'Hugh Capet plans to crown his son Robert as Associate King this Christmas. The Capets are claiming rights to Aquitaine and Duke Guillaume is refusing to recognize their royal succession.'

'Where do you stand?' Audebert asked abruptly. Adalmode's father was an old man and this brother seated opposite him would be Viscount before too long. Adalmode had told Audebert that this brother Guy in particular was close and dear to her.

Guy was silent some time considering Audebert's question. 'My family lost Limoges once before taking the wrong side in a dispute over the sovereignty of Aquitaine,' he said eventually. 'I will stand where I see the best interest of my family honours and my citizens.'

Audebert raised his drinking horn again to Guy. 'Aye. Every man for himself when there is no leader worth following.'

Guy changed the topic swiftly to talk of the hunt planned for later that day. Audebert was vassal to no one and it was well known that he was readying for war, whilst Gerard and Guy were vassals to the Duke of Aquitaine and Audebert's words were tantamount to treason.

The following day Fulk was confirmed as the successor to his father in the County of Anjou. Fulk inherited a well-developed military household and had an entourage of loyal young men from neighbouring families. Audebert advised him in taking command of these followers, making the appropriate show of strength and ostentation for the occasion. Fulk had immense organisational acumen already and Audebert was pleased to see that his assistance was more in the nature of listening, concurring, reassuring, rather than *telling* Fulk what he needed to do. The boy exuded a ferocious energy and asserted a confident grip on matters. He confirmed the betrothal of his sister, Gerberga, to the son of the Count of Angoulême. He wed the woman his father had betrothed him to in an astute piece of political alignment, though he did it with a sour expression on his face, for Elisabeth of Vendôme was twenty-nine to Fulk's fifteen. 'She's already looking past child-bearing,' he said to Audebert at the wedding feast.

'Give her a chance, lad!' Audebert laughed. 'She might surprise you.' And Fulk had looked cheerful enough the following day, after the marriage had been consummated and the prospect of an heir might be on the horizon.

Fulk's uncle, the influential Bishop Guy of Le Puy, had not yet arrived in Angers to support his nephew in the transfer of power. The first challenge to Fulk's position came that morning and it was ecclesiastical. Fulk sat on his throne looking only slightly too small for it and listened with an increasingly furious expression as Renaud, Bishop of Angers, and Guntarius, Abbot of Saint Aubin, sought to recover, at Fulk's expense, lands they claimed his father had wrongfully taken from them. Audebert watched with concern as he saw the signs of Fulk's rage developing. A nerve beneath Fulk's left eye began to twitch. His knee jerked impatiently up and down and he gripped the arms of his throne so hard that his knuckles were showing white. It would not do for Fulk to lose his temper in dealing with this. He would look like a child throwing a tantrum. 'Have you finished?' he snapped at the two priests. 'Your request is denied. The lands are rightfully mine and will stay that way.'

'But my lord Count,' said the Bishop, 'we do not find this answer satisfactory and if we must look to the Count of Blois for justice we will do so.'

Fulk stood and Audebert saw that his temper, always like a brooding volcano, was about to blow. He stood too and called out: 'Count Fulk!' and the boy's eyes turned to him, burning with fury. Audebert had no idea what he could say but he must bring Fulk somehow to an awareness of a need to calm down and handle these two politically, not violently. Audebert heard a movement and voices behind him and Fulk's eyes went to the door. Audebert turned to see Bishop Guy entering, wearing a sword and with a great armed entourage at his back. Audebert heaved a sigh of relief and sat down. The Angevin family could sort out their own priests now.

'Bishop Renaud, Abbot Guntarius, can it be true that you so dishonor my nephew and the memory of my revered brother so recently laid in his worthy grave . . .'

Fulk sat, anger washing slowly from his face and a smile spreading in its wake, as he listened with the court to his uncle delivering a swingeing chastisement to the two rebel priests. Fulk looked to Audebert and nodded acknowledgement that he had nearly and inappropriately lost his temper. Bishop Guy's lengthy oration was conclusive. Bishop Renaud retired with the few shreds of dignity he had retained from the tirade and Abbot Guntarius was miserable to find that he must go on pilgrimage in penance for his offence to Count Fulk.

Later in Fulk's private chamber Audebert and Bishop Guy sat down together with the new count to consider his position. 'Your western frontier is insecure,' said Audebert, 'and your holdings in Touraine are endangered.'

'These two today were just the testers,' said the Bishop. 'Abbot Robert of Saint Florent who supports the Count of Blois, is scheming against you with Viscount Renaud of Angers. You need to neutralize these threats.'

Audebert nodded. 'Gelduin of Saumur is another Blois supporter who blocks your access to your lands in the east.'

'Yes,' said Fulk, 'that's noted. First I plan to stabiise my *familia* for the next few weeks, assessing who I can trust, who I will replace, who I need to mollify and win over. I need to establish confidence with my castellans and *fideles*. I already have a core of good men: Aimery of Vihiers, Roger the Devil, Lisoius of Amboise and Roger of Loudun. We will undertake small raids to keep my enemies off-balance.' He grinned at Audebert. 'But then I have a longer term plan.'

'Of course, you do,' said Bishop Guy.

Fulk drew a diamond shape onto the map of Angevin holdings spread on the table before them. It pointed into Aquitaine. He dotted the lines of the diamond here and there. 'I will build small castles at each of these points. They will form lines of communication and defence for my holdings and protect me against a large invasion. Gradually I will reinforce and push forward my frontiers in all directions. In time I will encircle Blois and I will encircle Poitiers. The threatening will become the threatened.'

Audebert took the charcoal stick from Fulk and drew a thick curving corridor on the map starting at Bellac, moving across Gençay and Poitiers and then on north to Tours. 'And this is the swathe of my march to join up with your diamond,' he said.

# 11

## Ségur

### June 988

'We're here!' Aimery and Adalmode chimed together.

Guy listened to the sound of their horses clattering across the Ségur drawbridge. He heaved a sigh of relief. Finally his marriage would take place and his position would be secured. It had been a long wait. At thirty-two he was more than ready to take a wife. He had been forced to point out to his father that it was probably a very large bribe that would persuade Hildegaire to give the necessary dispensation for the two cousins to marry, and he had been right.

'The wrong wife could expose you,' said Adalmode, leaning close to him. 'I could show Aina how to assist you. I need to hand over my duty as your support to someone totally reliable and committed to you.'

Guy was amused at his sister's concept of him as her duty. 'I will do what I can to make her committed to me,' he smiled. 'I'm quite good close up.' He had not confessed his suspicions to his sister that Lady Aina was not pleased at the prospect of taking him as her husband.

Adalmode smiled affectionately. 'No doubt, you will be,' she said. 'I will miss you terribly when the time comes for us to part.'

Guy reflected that Adalmode too was long past the age for a timely marriage since their father had insisted on holding out for an alliance with the Aquitaine heir and had repeatedly rejected the offers that Audebert of La Marche sent each year. Adalmode's younger sisters were likely to be married before her.

'Is that Aina?' said Guy, looking up to a window where a woman stood with tendrils of red hair flying in the breeze.

'I think it's her maid,' Adalmode said.

Guy groaned, his face flushing at his remembered error in Brioude.

I watch as Lord Guy rides into Ségur with his brother, sister and a retinue of twenty knights. At the last Easter Assembly in Poitiers Lord Ademar's sickness gained on him fast, his roundness fell from him and he looked like a skeleton in his bed. The Duke's Italian physician recommended a treatment of doves' dung applied to the soles of his feet, but within a few days Aina's beloved father and my kind master died. Melisende went to the Duke and Duchess to take our leave and in the Great Hall of Poitiers I felt the eyes of the court upon us and heard the gossiping begin: 'Sick for a long time . . . betrothed to Limoges . . . Northwoman . . . slave.' I held my head up and ignored them.

Ademar gave me my freedom when I reached my 21st birthday, despite my continuing refusal of Christian baptism. 'We never thought of you as a slave, Sigrid,' he said, 'and we never could. I understand that you want to adhere to the beliefs of your father, but I hope in time to you will come to love Christ.' He gave me a gift of furs and cloth to mark my freeing. I always wear my silver serpent brooch at my shoulder, fastening my cloak and I hang my keys and thimble from it, and still, around my neck beneath my clothing, is my iron Thor's hammer, the mark of both my slavery and my former life before I came to Ségur.

Lord Ademar's shroud was tied at the top of his head and at the neck to keep it in place and his body was roped to the cart for his last journey home from Poitiers to Ségur. Now there is nothing for it: Aina must marry Guy, and I must prepare to leave this place that I have loved. Perhaps the move to Limoges is the signal for me to leave, to find my way back to Norway, to find my brothers, but I am torn now between hankering for a home I can barely remember and my great love for Aina, who will need me in her disappointment.

I run down the stairs to the kitchen to rejoin the work of preparing for the feast. I am skinning a hare when my name is called. Hurriedly I wipe my hands and stand up to face Melisende expectantly. 'I need you in the solar,' she says and I follow her out and back up the staircase.

In Melisende's chamber Aina is standing in a near-transparent white shift with a flimsy white cloth draped around her shoulders, bunching in piles at her feet.

'Hold this end, Sigrid, and help me,' Melisende says. 'We need to pin it firmly to her head like this. We want Lord Guy to only catch the merest glimpse of his magical future wife.'

Despite the sulky mood that Aina has sustained since Guy's arrival, she laughs at her mother's description. Aina is twenty-three and has grown into a beautiful woman, tall and slender. Her skin flushes easily. Her hair hangs in a long shiny chestnut waterfall, loose down her back underneath the veil which Lady Melisende is pinning in place arranged around a thin gold circlet. The fine opaque cloth cascades from Aina's head to her feet, silkily caressing her curves. The outline of her thinly-clad body is vaguely visible through this white outer covering. When her daughter is suitably arranged, Melisende and I pull our own veils over our faces, and she signals to the servant to admit Guy. I can feel Aina's nervousness emanating from her.

Guy and his sister come into the chamber, accompanied by their priest who will bless the impending marriage. Through the thick veil Aina is looking at the tall, awkward man in front of her.

'Lord Guy,' Melisende says and they bow formally to each other, 'May I present to you my daughter Aina, soon to be your wife.'

He stands a few feet in front of the quivering mass of textile.

'Lady Aina,' he says, bowing, and she inclines her head.

The look on Guy's face is hard to comprehend. His expression seems perhaps contemptuous, his eyes screwed up and lines engraving his forehead. Despite her coverings I realise that Aina must be feeling exposed. I suddenly remember the shame of being purveyed by buyers at the slave market. Aina is a bed-slave in a way. I see her shoulders trembling and the toes of her slippers

131

trilling up and down on the tiles, her breath coming fast through the veil covering her face. Guy clears his throat and Aina startles at the sound. He seems uncertain what to do but eventually steps close and fumbles for her hand, giving her a small box as a gift, whilst the priest intones his blessing.

Guy steps back from Aina. 'Excellent,' he says, nods, turns, and strides from the room. Melisende kisses the top of her daughter's veiled head and follows Guy, Adalmode and the priest from the room.

'Sigrid, I am humiliated!' Aina bursts out as soon as the footsteps can no longer be heard on the stairs, slamming the gift box down hard on a small table that rocks in response to her emotion.

I throw back my veil and give an eloquent sympathetic look to my friend. 'What is it?' I ask, pointing at the gift.

Aina tugs the fine fabric from her face and head, as if it were cobwebs encumbering her, and steps out of it. 'I care not. This is like a shroud.'

'Shall I open the box for you?'

'No.'

I shrug and when it is clear she does not wish to speak further, I hurry back down to the kitchen to tell everybody about the scene I have just participated in.

'Could you see much of her?' Guy asked Adalmode.

'She was heavily veiled so not really,' she said. 'But she has red hair, beautiful red hair,' seeing Guy screw up his nose, 'the colour of a chestnut, shiny and the deepest of reds. It extended beyond the bottom of her veil so I saw that. She has long white fingers.'

'Yes I saw that myself,' he said, having had to peer quite closely to make sure he was putting the box into her hands, with his gift of a green emerald necklace that would look fine with the colour of her hair. He had heard her breathing rapidly. 'Did you see the colour of her eyes?'

'No. But I saw that she was slim and tall and graceful.'

'Grey, I think, as I remember from our betrothal when she was a child,' said Guy, disappointed that this was all he knew of his future wife.

Adalmode strummed the lute for Aina and Sigrid, singing a lyric from Al-Andalus and watching the pleasure on their faces. Aina's cheeks and throat were pink, framed by the heavy red of her hair. Her movements and speech were quick and emphatic. The Norse maid, in comparison was calm, serene even, her graceful neck bent always over her sewing. The maid's skin was ruddy and her hair was a lighter shade of red than Aina's. Adalmode had spent all day in Aina's chamber, sewing, listening, contributing to the conversation. At first they were wary of her but as the day wore on they grew accustomed to her presence and forgot that she might have her own reasons for the visit.

Aina talked guilelessly of her desire to travel, to see exotic places, and she boasted of Sigrid's adventurous early life. 'But now,' she said, 'Sigrid's sewing never leaves her hands without reason.'

Adalmode watched the indulgent way in which the maid received her mistress' description of her. She had the measure of them now. Sigrid was cautious and devoted to Aina. Adalmode knew that as soon as the words, 'my brother' crossed her lips they would draw back so she decided to try a different tack and see what information that might elicit for Guy.

'I am in love with a man who would show me adventure,' she said, 'but my father has refused him my hand many times.'

Aina lent forward and her eyes grew round. Sigrid's incessant needle stilled and she looked up.

'Who is he?' asked Aina.

'Audebert, Count of La Marche and Périgord,' said Adalmode proudly, but as she said his name she began to regret her ploy, that she should bring her pain out into the open before them.

'I have heard of him,' said Aina. 'He is reputed to be a great warrior.'

'He did not commit the crime against Canon Benedict,' Adalmode stated defensively. 'It was his brother's act.'

'Of course,' said Aina.

'He has offered for me over and over again, but my father refuses. Audebert says he will marry no one but me.'

Aina looked even more excited and Sigrid was studying Adalmode's face with interest.

'But why does your father refuse? 'asked Aina.

'Two reasons. There is bad blood between my father and the La Marche household, since my father used his capture of Helie and Audebert to regain the favour of the Duke of Aquitaine and his viscount's throne with it.'

'What was his brother's crime against the Canon?' asked Sigrid.

Adalmode tutted. Of what significance was that now, but she told the story nevertheless. 'Soon after the time when the Counts of Poitou and Toulouse and Duke Capet were all warring for control of Aquitaine, Helie, the son of the Count of La Marche took a warband into the lands of the Count of Poitou, looting in the monasteries left ruined and devastated by the Norse invaders. Excuse me,' she said rapidly to Sigrid, remembering that she was Norse.

'It is simply truth,' Sigrid responded.

Adalmode watched the way that Aina lent forward on the edge of her seat at her story, her hands clasped and her mouth slightly open, showing how interested she was. If her brother could win this passionate woman's heart it would be a great prize, but she was doubtful. She continued, 'By chance they came across the priest who was kin to the Count of Poitou and had an armed escort. Mistaking them at first for a warband like their own, they slew the escort and then Helie, discovering who his captive was, panicked, and blinded the Canon, thinking to save himself from recognition and accusation.'

Aina gasped.

'That was stupid,' said Sigrid.

'Yes. It was a heinous act that gave impetus to the Peace of God Council. My father and my brother Guy hunted down Helie of La Marche for his crime and took him captive, and Audebert with him. My father held them captive for a long time in the dungeon of Montignac stronghold and I grew to know and love Audebert in that time of his misery.' She paused to allow this image to sink in and watched the passionate empathy burning on Aina's face.

'Could you help him?' asked Aina. Every child had looked down into a dungeon and shuddered at the thought of spending even one night there, let alone years.

'He said I helped him by visiting him and talking with him. I gave him blankets, food and wine when I could, a manuscript once or twice. Despite being in that awful, hopeless situation for so long he was kind to me and asked me about the small problems of my life – my lessons, my new gowns, the bullying and jesting I endured from my younger brothers, problems that were as nothing to his.' Adalmode's eyes filled with tears and Sigrid lent forward and clasped her hand.

'He is out now,' Sigrid said, 'and this grief is over.'

Adalmode felt comforted by her solidity and her evident understanding of the suffering Audebert had endured. She struggled to remember that she was telling this story not for her own relief but to help her decipher Aina's character for Guy.

'What is the second reason?' asked Sigrid.

'My father intends to betroth me to the son of the Duke of Aquitaine,' Adalmode said morosely.

'But this is also an excellent marriage,' Aina said.

'Yes, I suppose it is, but Aina I love Audebert and he loves me, whilst Guillaume is still a mewling boy – nine years my junior. I would have a man,' she said defiantly and watched Sigrid mirror her own resistant pose.

Aina did not shift her pose. 'Either marriage will bring you wealth, power, position,' she said and Adalmode knew now that Aina did not love another man and did not know love. 'Aquitaine more so,' Aina continued, thinking it through, 'and they will both be fighting men,' she said brightening at this thought, but then slumping deflated again, 'whilst you will sit at home sewing and making babies either way.'

Adalmode stayed long enough to allow Aina and Sigrid to make their comforting comments on her dilemma and then took her leave and hurried back to Guy to share her insights. 'So.' She pulled him to sit down close to her. 'I've spent the whole day cooing and sewing with your bride.'

'Thank you Addy,' he smiled. 'Does she hate me?'

'She said nothing of you but don't despair.' She watched the droop of his expression. 'I can tell you this about her: she longs for excitement and adventure; she wants to see something of the world; the thought of merely childbearing and homemaking does not make her content. You must let her see how you would involve her in your politicking and rule and how that could be exciting. Tell her you will take her on pilgrimages every year, to Jerusalem and Santiago, everywhere.'

Guy grimaced. 'But I don't want to do that! 'he protested. The challenge of coping with travelling was unappealing: getting on and off boats and horses, negotiating unknown environments. Aside from combat, this was Guy's worst nightmare.

'You don't have to actually do it,' said Adalmode pragmatically, 'just tell her you will. She doesn't love another man so there is no reason why you shouldn't win her heart.'

Guy smiled vaguely at his sister. 'You love me but how can I win Aina's love when I can barely see her features to engage her in conversation?'

'Don't neglect the Norse maid,' said Adalmode. 'She is astute and greatly loved and relied on by Aina.'

'Perhaps she will discern the problem with my vision.'

'Perhaps, but she is not cruel. If you can win her admiration she will bring her mistress with her to you.'

'Thank you Addy as always,' said Guy, buckling his belt and preparing mentally for another social ordeal.

From the window Adalmode watched Aina and Sigrid walking in the enclosed orchard below. She saw the vivid colour of the girls' heads beneath their veils, contrasting with the surrounding greens and blooms. She saw how Aina constantly broke away and ran ahead, whilst Sigrid paced evenly, bending now and then to cut a bloom for her basket.

# 12

# Saint Michel en l'Herm

## June 988

Aina has been sulking for days. I keep my head down and sew.
Guy and Adalmode left two days ago. The marriage must take
place now. There is nothing to be done and best to be stoic,
surely. Aina slams shut the book she has been reading. 'I can't
stand it!,' she says for the tenth time this morning.
'Aina, there is no point,' I begin.
'But I can't bear it, I will go mad if that is all. If my horizon is
the five miles from here to Ségur. Where's that map that Father
Dominic showed to us last year do you know?'
Minutes after consulting the map, Aina is leading me down to
talk with her mother in the hall. 'Mother, I wish to ask a favour of
you in preparation for my wedding.'
'A new gown?' Lady Melisende asks, looking up with a smile.
'No. I wish to go to the monastery of Saint Michel en
l'Herm.'
'Whatever for?'
'To pray for fertility and blessings on my marriage. Can I do
that? The monastery and the feast day of the Apostles – it would
be auspicious. I must get a male heir,' says Aina slyly, knowing full
well that her mother feels her own failure to do that keenly. I look
at Aina in surprise – at the proposal, and at her use of this lever-
age. She is desperate for some last few days of freedom.
'Very well,' her mother says slowly. 'Sigrid and Father Dominic will accompany you and a detail of guards. I will go ahead to
Limoges and wait for you there.'

'Thank you Mother,' Aina says demurely, and turns to beam a secret gleeful expression at me.

Aina and I move around the castle making sure every candle has been blown out and every fire and oven is cold, putting away precious tapestries and carefully folding clothes, closing up parchments and objects in chests to protect them, making sure the spigot is tightly shut off, and the wooden shutters pulled and barred at each window. I think about the rituals of coming and going and imagine us returning and reversing all our actions – throwing open shutters, hanging sheets and quilts from the window to air, but realise that we will not be returning, at least not for some time, and when we do, Aina will be Guy's wife. I have tried to point out to her that the Limoges household and the tensions and competitions between Guy and Adalmode's many siblings (seven brothers and four sisters in all) will surely present her with an interesting challenge, but she remains disappointed in her marriage.

Our summer ride to Niort is pleasant and we break our journey, staying a night at the Abbey Guesthouse, and then travelling on to the island Abbey of Saint Michel en l'Herm, planning to arrive the day before the feast of the Apostles towards the end of June. Saint Michel en l'Herm is not exactly an island, but rather a piece of land between two rivers and a marsh. From the top of a small hill we look down on the monastery and out towards the sea beyond the marsh. 'Oh Sigrid how wonderful it would be to set out on that blue swell.'

'It's not so wonderful,' I say. 'A lot of people puke. Quite a few more fall overboard and drown. Or there's a big storm and the ship breaks in half and everyone drowns.'

Aina tuts and smiles at my pessimism. Despite my words, I too am longing to set sail on that enticing ocean. It is the first view of the sea I have had for many years, since Ségur is far inland. We take deep breaths of the salty air and watch clouds scudding fast, competing with their shadows on the waves. The longing I feel is physical, in my hands, my stomach, my knees, my feet. Every part of me wants to be swaying on a longship, holding a rope, squinting at the sun and wind.

We set our horses downhill towards the salt flats, where rivers and streams wend and glitter. Aina points out to me the bent back of a monk on a donkey ahead of us, crossing the marshes. One of the streams we cross is in spate, brown and muddy from recent rain. The water is full of swift debris: branches ripped from trees, mats of vegetation making small moving islands. As the horses start to ford we are surprised to find how deep and cold the water is for this time of year. The small pack pony flounders and begins to panic, thrashing and whinnying in the water. Two of our leather bags come loose from the pony's pommel and float in the current, bobbing away from us.

'Oh no, Sigrid!' Aina calls out, pointing. 'I think my best gown is in that one!'

Her servants are struggling to calm the pony and set it on a sure footing to complete the crossing. A man reaches out an arm just in time to snatch one of the errant bags from the water. 'I've got one my lady!' he calls out.

'And I've got the other!'

We turn to look downstream towards an unknown voice, and see that the monk who had been travelling ahead of us has snagged the other bag with his staff and is holding it clear from the current. Water is gushing from it and whatever its contents are they are sodden now. Aina is ahead of me, riding towards the monk, and I follow, trying to catch up with her. 'Thank you so much, Brother!' she calls out, dismounting to assist him in hauling in the wet bag and dumping it on the bank.

I arrive and look down on the procedure. 'You nearly lost it, Lady Aina.'

'I'm so grateful,' she tells the monk.

'It's nothing,' he says. 'I am glad to help you.' He speaks with a strange accent – unusual but familiar. I cannot quite put my finger on what it reminds me of. With Aina standing next to him, it is apparent that he is very tall. He is engulfed in a brown monastic robe, but it is a little too short for him, and I look in surprise at his boots – soldier's sturdy boots, but then I suppose that is sensible if he is journeying out and about, crossing this soggy terrain.

Aina smiles up into his face. He is wearing a large cowl but it is just possible to see that he is young and exceedingly handsome, with brilliant pale blue eyes in a sun-browned face, and wisps of white blond hair just visible in the recesses of his hood. A shame he is a celibate monk, I think to myself, admiring his face.

'Where are you going, ladies?' he asks.

'We are going to the monastery,' Aina points to where we can see the monastery walls, perhaps ten more minutes ride away, 'for the feast of the Apostles tomorrow.'

'Of course,' he says. 'A busy feast day for sure.'

'Oh yes,' Aina responds. 'There will be much feasting and many guests arriving for tomorrow's festivities. Are you going there yourself, Brother?'

'No doubt I will be there,' he says.

I hear the thud of one of Aina's servants' horses behind me, approaching us to help his mistress. The other servants have managed to straighten out the bags on the shivering pony and reassemble the party on dry land.

'I must be on my way,' the monk says abruptly, turning away. 'I have a sick old woman to visit before dark falls. Good day.' He swings onto his donkey, his long legs dangling ridiculously from the small beast and the tips of his boots near touching the ground and turns his back, with Aina calling her thanks again to him.

We arrive at the monastery gatehouse at dusk and Aina tells the monk who shows us to the guest dormitory: 'We are chilled to the knees from our journey. We nearly lost some of our baggage crossing a stream on the marsh.'

The gatekeeper tuts and pats her arm. 'We'll have you warmed up soon enough my Lady,' he reassures her.

In the church dozens of candles are burning in preparation for the feast day, and their flickering light ranges across angel corbels and stone carvings of winged lions. Aina and I listen smiling to the monks' beautiful singing. After the service the Abbot welcomes us and asks if we would be kind enough to visit three old men in the hospice. 'They are waiting for death,' he says with calm resignation. At the hospice the monk in charge tells us to find the old men in the warming room instead. They are seated close to the fire and make room for Aina and I and tell us about their former lives with their wives, children and grandchildren. The monks swish around the abbey in a state of excited preparation for the feast tomorrow when they will be able to break their fast. A board outside the refectory gives the list of their duties in the kitchen, garden or on the farm. Young monks move between the cellar in the undercroft and the refectory bringing up bottles of good wine. At the end of their labours they wash their hands in a stone trough in the courtyard with a squeaking handle that forces up a dribble of cold water.

We sit down to dine at the high table with the Abbot on their fasting fare – a good vegetable and bean soup with bread, and Aina answers his enquiries concerning her forthcoming marriage and the news in the Limousin.

'Godfrey thinks he saw a Viking sail near Ré,' Brother Peter interrupts.

'Godfrey thinks so every day,' says the Abbot.

'Where is Ré?' asks Aina.

'It is an island just off the coast here,' says Peter.

'Let's not frighten our guests,' says the Abbot. 'If Godfrey is sure – again – then we will send a lookout to report back to us.'

At the end of the meal, we watch curiously as the monks rise from their seats, each carrying a book or scroll which they place down on the carpet. Then they look around at the documents placed by the other monks and select another text for themselves. 'We change our books each time this year,' the Abbot says, explaining that they read one text each throughout the year. Aina pulls a face at me that he cannot see indicating how amusing she finds this, but then she assumes a serious expression, passing a heavy purse full of silver pennies to aid the poor to the Abbot.

'Bless you, Lady Aina. The monastery's treasure is all safely hidden below,' the Abbot says smiling conspiratorially at her.

'In the cellar?'

'No, we'll wait for the brothers to leave and then I'll show you.' We wait patiently as the monks file out in silence and then the Abbot directs our attention to his chair which is higher than the others, but I had assumed this was because of his seniority. He shows us how the chair can be moved aside to reveal four decorated tiles and how one of these tiles has a loose edge where you can insert your knife and it will lift on a hinge and there is a hole beneath. Inside is a lidded jug, and the jug, he shows us, is filled with silver pennies. He pours the contents of Lady Aina's purse into the jug so that it is filled to the brim. He puts his finger to his lips and replaces the tile and chair, but then looks up with irritation as we hear footsteps running back in our direction.

The monk called Godfrey comes running breathless into the Refectory, tripping over the ragged hem of his habit, 'The stinging hornets, the stinging hornets!' he shouts, saliva spraying with his words. 'They've brought their wave-stallions over the ocean's back.' He is pointing to the door behind him, his eyes wide.

The Abbot reaches out a hand and opens his mouth to calm the man, but before he can speak the bells begin to peal and the Abbot turns to us in consternation. 'It seems Godfrey is right for once. We are indeed being raided by the *esnèque* – the dragon-head ships.'

'We must get Lady Aina to safety, Abbot,' says Father Dominic stumbling in, but the Abbot looks indecisive.

'I will go to see,' I tell my mistress and run outside to see what is happening. As I pass under the gateway I am in time to see a long, slender boat coming on fast. Its oars beat up and down like the wings of an eagle. *Snekkja* – a small warship. I count fifteen pairs of oars – thirty or more men. The ship's elegantly carved stem has a fearsome dragon's head with a flowing golden mane, a googling blue eye and a long curling red tongue. The vertical black, yellow and red stripes of the ship's sail look astonishingly alien against the gentle blue-grey lapping of the sea, and the familiar tolling of the monastery bell behind me. Yet I recognize this too. A sense of home stirs within me. As a small child I must have seen such ships coming home in just such a way, bearing my father and his companions. So entranced am I by the sight that I momentarily forget that now I stand here in the attire of a Frankish woman and I am prey. Gravel and sand crunch as the boat beaches smoothly against the shore. A small boat is set adrift with flames and curls of black smoke rising from it. The fireship floats with a grim inevitability towards the haystacks piled on the monastery's wooden pier. An anchor-stone splashes into the water and men in shaggy skins begin to leap over the sides of the ship, wading the short distance ashore, brandishing axes, spears and swords. I turn and run.

My mistress is standing just in front of the gates and behind her, monks are struggling to close them before the attackers reach it. 'Run, Aina! Get into the monastery! The gates!' There is a confused expression on her face. She sees that I am shouting something to her but cannot hear me over the battle din the warriors are raising. They are howling like wolves and crashing their weapons on their round shields. I break into a sweat at the sound and reach Aina but see from her open mouth and shocked eyes that I am too late. I am hard gripped about my waist and two men, their arms and necks festooned with swirling tattoos, grasp Aina's arms. 'No!' I scream once to the sky with all the force of my lungs. We fight and struggle as the men clasp fetters around our wrists and then metal collars around our necks that trail heavy chains. The chains link us together and we are swiftly and roughly yanked by the neck, through the advancing men, towards the ship. The leader of the men is exhorting them as we pass, pointing his sword in the direction of the monastery: '*Drengr*, flee neither flame nor steel!' His words seem unnecessary since the monks behind us are offering only screams and prayers as their resistance.

Enslaved again! I want to cry, scream, vomit but in my shock I can do nothing but shake. The collar and fetters bite greedily into my flesh and the chain drags painfully at my neck. Two men stand guarding the ship and two more are evidently the human booty managers as our chains are passed to them. 'Kneel down,' one says to us in Norse.

'Kneel,' I say dragging my mistress down. The man nods his satisfaction, grinning and showing filed grey teeth.

'Sigrid,' Aina begins in a small voice but the man yanks forcefully on her chain, making her whimper, and with a fierce expression shows her the whip at his waist. I shake my head at her to be silent. We look back to the monastery where the monks have not succeeded in closing the gates in time. Shouts come from within the walls and fire spews from the roofs and windows.

Monks collared and chained like us are being assembled outside the gates, and forced to their knees. I can see no sign of Father Dominic or any of the men who came with us from

Ségur. It seems likely they have put up some resistance and not survived. I grimace for them and the wives of the men. I never liked Father Dominic and he never liked me naming me 'damned heathen' under his breath when Ademar could not hear, but he did not deserve to die on the end of a spear. The Norsemen move between the monastery and the ship with tapestries laden with silver chalices and plates, golden candlesticks, jewelled book covers, joints of meat from the kitchens that had been intended for tomorrow's feast. They have timed their attack well. We turn our heads to more screams but this time they are animal shrieks rather than human, as the men set about slaughtering the monks' livestock to restock their ship. Two men pass through the gates rolling one of the monks' wine barrels down to the beach and I can see from the cut of some of them, that others have already sampled Saint Michel's cellar. I notice a man carrying the jug full of silver pennies the Abbot had shown to us only a short while before and I wonder what persuasion the raiders used to make him reveal the hiding place beneath his chair.

One man, worse for drink, approaches us and begins to run his hands on my body so that I have to twist away from him. The man with the whip cracks it, shouting 'Pilot!' A tall man with a red beard and pale red hair lightened by the sun, turns to look at us, barks commands in Norse and the lecherous man draws back from me immediately. What had been deteriorating into chaos suddenly becomes a well-ordered loading of the ship with the plunder, wine barrel and slaughtered meat. Even the drunken man who approached me pulls himself together under the eye of the sandy-haired pilot and fulfils his part of the work. A second large barrel of wine is rolled down to the water's edge but the pilot shouts no, the ship will be overloaded, and it is abandoned there with the surf breaking around it. There must be a firebox on the ship because there are wafts of smoke and I smell meat cooking.

The shackled monks are pushed and pulled to join us at the water's edge and my heart turns over to see the trails of blood on their hands and habits, and the tears on their faces. I imagine the pretty church we had so recently sung in, spattered with the blood of priests and despoiled of its gleaming ornaments. Two of the monks seem to have lost control of their bladders for a Norseman throws buckets of water over them, waving his hand under his nose to indicate what he thinks about sharing a boat with such odorous cargo. The pilot comes and looks us over. 'The women wear rich clothing,' he says, and I am glad that I had put on one of Aina's cast-offs for our trip here. I have not heard or spoken Norse for so long. I feel as if old chambers in my mind are slowly creaking open where I had put the memory of my language. 'We will ransom them. Put them in the hold with the silver and goods. Where is the Abbot?'

'Dead,' responds one of the men flatly.

'The rest we'll sell on at Noirmoutier then,' he says. 'Set them to row.' I look with pity on the monks as they are stripped of their habits and loaded on before us in their underclouts and in some cases naked. They are mostly young and hale, the novices and younger monks, so the Norsemen must have already sorted their human booty inside the monastery. There were around thirty monks in all in the monastery and there are twelve monks chained here. I hope they have spared, rather than killed all the old and less able-bodied monks but look back with doubt to the smouldering buildings. I think of the three small boys, the oblates, one of them blind, who I saw at the meal and the old men in the hospice who Aina and I chatted with. Surely they have spared them? None of the monastery's serving women are here. I hope they have hidden themselves in the cellars or escaped to the woods.

We are loaded last and as we are prodded up onto the ship, balancing on the narrow oar held steady for us, one of the Norsemen waiting onboard groans, 'Not all these red-heads and priests, surely! We will be *Naglfar* – the Ship of the Dead.'

'Shut it, Toki,' snaps the pilot crossly. 'Haven't I navigated your ungrateful hide safely all these years?'

I murmur quietly to Aina, explaining that redheads and priests are supposed to be unlucky onboard ship. She murmurs to me that she asked Saint Michel to intercede and save her from a boring marriage and perhaps this is all her fault. Her eyelashes are wet and her face is ashen. I shake my head. 'It's not your fault,' I whisper. We are pushed down to sit in the central, sunken hold with the bundled tapestries, chests of coins and a live goat. There are barrels down here too which from the smell of them hold quantities of dried fish. Our feet dangle wet in the small pool of water gathered in the bottom of the boat. 'Is it leaking?' Aina whispers. I shake my head. I know that the men will bail the water when it becomes necessary. The poor young monks are chained to the cross-beams, and I feel the boat loosen from the bank and get underway.

# Part Two

# HOSTAGES ON THE SWAN ROAD

## 988–996

*'One day I wrote her name upon the strand, but came
the waves and washed it away.'*

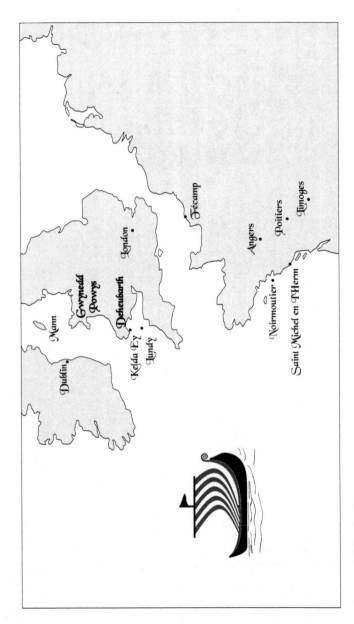

France and Bretland

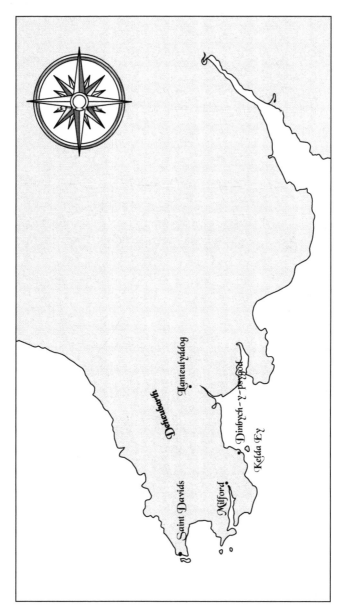

South West Bretland

# 13

# Atlantic Ocean

## June 988

The ropes fizz in the wind. An hour of evening sea breeze and contemplating our situation sucks fifteen years of Ségur summers from my bones. The sides of the longboat are shallow and we cringe and gasp as gouts of frigid water slop over us, with each dip and rise of the boat on the waves. It gets so that I know which dip will result in a dousing. I taste the salt on my lips and the sea washes the fear and sweat from me. Aina and I do not dare exchange words but occasionally we glance at each other, and once I manage to stretch out my fingertips awkwardly with my manacled hands and touch her knee reassuringly.

Aina has only ever been on a river boat before and she is caught somewhere between terror and fascination, looking about herself wildly at the sea, the cruel crew and the ship. For me, I struggle to keep the rational part of my mind swimming in the tidal wave of emotions and memories that assail me. This is different I tell myself emphatically. Different from the time before, when I lost my father. I am not a child now and we are worth a ransom. Our captors have already acknowledged that. It will not do to panic, I tell myself, even as I allow myself to do so in fits and starts, to see how bad it is. But it is very bad. Panic will not help us. Panic is useless I recite in my panicking head.

I note everything around me as a means to calm myself. The crew are well practised, working together and with the ship with great familiarity, and they are well practised too in dealing with their human cargo. They have done this many times before.

They talk excitedly of their success in the raid and who will have what part of the booty and I notice they are on good terms with one another. Several of them have scarred faces or are missing fingers. They are clearly a battled-hardened band. The pilot is silent, apart from the occasional order, concentrating on keeping the ship on course, but I notice how his facial expressions register that he is listening to and occasionally amused by the banter of the crew. Despite my anxiety, I am intrigued to be encountering for the first time in so long, these examples of my countrymen.

Each oar has one monk and one Norseman and if the monks are not pulling well the man with the whip moves to flog them mercilessly. One monk has been whipped more often than the others, weeping that he has great pain in his hands. After a while the man with the whip calls out, 'No, chuck him over. It's useless.' The monk is uncoupled from the cross-beam and his face shows immense relief that quickly turns to terror as he is prodded to the ship's edge and kicked hard so that he falls overboard. His sudden scream is very short. Aina jumps next to me and stares into my face. Fear grips at my stomach. Shock ripples palpably through the captives. Chained as he was the man could not possibly survive and he must drown there on that bottom and his bones in their chains will be swilled back and forth by the sea. Poor man I think. Poor man, but perhaps he has the best of it. The atmosphere shifts in the boat, as now the other monks see they could so easily follow that man to death themselves.

I blink and sniff away sea-spray and the watering of my eyes, wishing my hands were free to wipe at them. The wind is billowing in the great striped sail that is criss-crossed with a network of ropes. The sky is a spectacular expanse of blue and the pink and red streaks of sunset, the sun a blinding red ball low on the water horizon. Aina and I shiver in our damp, thin gowns, and I look with concern at the gooseflesh on her arms. We are making good headway, so that often the monks are ordered to pull in and rest at their oars as the wind does the work for the pilot. I notice, though, that the ship is battered and has seen recent storms. Some of the planks are loose from their lashings and nails. There is a great rip in the sail that has been hastily and imperfectly repaired so it is not holding the wind as well as it ought. The long, slender yard that the sail is suspended from is splintered in two places and held together with rope bindings. The mast shudders even though the wind is not particularly brisk. I hope we will not see bad weather since this ship is no gazelle of the storm. I keep my thoughts to myself, not wanting to worry Aina.

The Norse soldiers' shields hang on rails near the stems at either end of the ship and the setting sun glints on them, turning them from silver to gold. The cook works on the firebox and delicious smells tantalize my stomach. A boy working with the cook passes chunks of meat to the Norsemen, starting with the pilot and then moving around the boat to serve each of the crew. By the way they eat I guess they had been hungering for many days when they landed at Saint Michel en l'Herm. I know there is a limit to how much dried fish anyone can consume. The boy passes round beakers of ale. They offer no food or drink to us or the labouring monks who are sweaty and bloodied from the whip. Their hands seep blood from the blisters of this unaccustomed labour. One crewman is evidently satisfied with the exertions of his monk-slave. He passes him two cloths and indicates he should wrap them around his hands to ease the pain of his blisters. The monk complies gratefully and the other monks look at these rag hand protectors with jealousy for they are offered none and must row on in pain or loose the skin off their backs. So swiftly are all our fortunes changed utterly, when rags seem like riches.

This leg of the journey does not last long. After a few hours the pilot calls commands preparing to beach and Aina's shoulder jolts painfully against my breast as the ship's bottom skims the ledge of the shore. We are pulled up onto the deck where we watch the monks being led off the boat, wading to the shore. Several lose their footing in the water and splutter fearfully, dragged down by their chains, until the laughing Norsemen right them or simply drag them onto the sand like beached whales. It was only a few hours rowing and I know the Norsemen can do a great many more hours at the oars, but the monks, terrified, without water and unaccustomed as they are to this hard physical labour, are exhausted and broken already. The compliance and silence of the captives is strange, but harsh whipping, chains and the sight of one man casually killed has been enough to cow them, and besides only I here understand the Norsemen's speech and only I could make myself understood. Why have I not spoken? Perhaps it is an ingrained response like the first time I was enslaved when I remained mute a long time with Aina's parents. Or perhaps my instincts tell me I must learn the situation first, save that small power I have to understand what they say and to communicate with them if it should become necessary to save myself and my mistress.

There is a small boat lashed to the side on the deck above our heads and opposite, on the other side of the ship, a hide-covered bundle is similarly lashed. This bundle is unrolled by two of the Norse crew and we watch as a large canvas is erected on the deck, slung over the dropped yard arm. One of the men prods Aina and I towards this tent, and before dipping my head to enter, I glance over my shoulder to see the sorry line of naked monks disappear with their cruel guards into dark trees lining the beach.

'Sit!' our guard indicates and I pull Aina down. He gives us a beaker of water which we pass between us, drinking gratefully, our chains clanking and awkward. He lifts the tent flap and calls out: 'Food, Pilot?' I cannot hear the muffled response but am glad when the man passes us two pieces of dried fish. He sits watching us eat, a gleeful expression on his face, his eyes roaming over our bodies and faces.

'Don't make eye contact with him,' I mutter to Aina. From my own sidelong glances I have seen how big the man is. Everything about him is big: his legs and arms are unexpectedly long and covered with thick fair hair contrasting with the dark brown of his skin, and his chest is barrel-like, thrusting out at the top. Even his head is big. After some time the pilot lifts the tent-flap and jerks his head to indicate to the man that he should come out and we are left alone but chained and fettered, helpless to attempt escape.

'Can you understand them?' Aina asks in an urgent whisper.

'Yes, they intend to ransom us, which probably means they will treat us well.'

'Treat us well!' Aina exclaims raising her voice and her shackles.

'Sshh!' I hush her. 'Compared to those poor monks who they are selling into slavery.'

Aina bows her head. 'Yes. Those poor young men and the Abbot dead, Sigrid! And do you think Father Dominic and the men from Ségur too?'

I nod and grimace sympathetically as her face crumples.

'What do they talk of?' she asks.

'Of their success in the raid, the treasure they have taken, the wealth they will have from the sale of the monks. They are predators, Aina,' I say with disgust.

She nods and bites her lip. Outside the familiar sounds of night are beginning. Cicadas, creaking frogs hoping to mate, a man snoring gently somewhere nearby, the sea lapping at the sand. 'We should sleep,' I say. 'We don't know what is coming next and sleep is our best friend to deal with it.'

'I *can't* sleep,' Aina says, but awkwardly with my fettered hands I lay her head on my shoulder and recite my serpent runes softly over and over: 'Leap from the fetters. Escape from the foes. Leap from the fetters. Escape from the foes.' Within minutes Aina's breath comes slow and regular. I close my own eyes, thinking again, we do not know what is coming next.

I sit up, woken abruptly by a loud bark of laughter. Sunlight is streaming through the open tent-flap and standing there, I recognise the comely tall blond-haired 'monk' who helped us retrieve our baggage from the water when we crossed the marsh to the monastery a few days before. The man is staring at us, standing alongside the sandy-haired pilot. He is dressed in the weaponry and armour of a rich soldier, and is clearly no monk. A small crowd of muscled, grimy crewmen are gathered behind them at the tent-flap, craning around each other to be entertained by this encounter, early sun glinting on the swords and axes slung against their hips. Aina is struggling to consciousness more slowly beside me, her headdress awry, and then she is staring with her great grey eyes at the blond man who is finding us hilarious. He is slender but well-built and looks strong. Without the monk's cowl we can see him clearly now: blue eyes, high cheekbones, a straight nose, thin lips and white blond hair that curls and reaches to his shoulders. His even white teeth are revealed by his amusement at us.

'You!' Aina breathes in disbelief.

'Well done, well done, my friend!' he claps the pilot on the shoulder. 'Look at this. You have caught in your net those two red-heads I spoke of.'

'Yes – they are noblewomen. They will bring a ransom,' the pilot says. The blond man approaches us and swiftly pulls off Aina's headdress and then mine. 'Young red-heads!' he exclaims, delighted at the sight of our bare heads.

I look steadfastly into his handsome face. It will not do to show our fear.

'I am noble-born,' Aina says angrily. 'You should treat me with respect.'

'Well, my lady,' he says, bringing his face close to hers, and she holds his eye and does not attempt to shift away from him. I hear the growl of the crew's low laughter behind him, and one man grabs at his own privates suggestively. 'I don't understand all that you say, but I understand your tone. Here's a riddle for you: I grow very erect, tall in a bed, and bring a tear to a maiden's eye?'

'Keep your dog on a lead,' I shout at him in Occitan and a small man standing behind the blond leader, translates my words into Norse.

The man raises his eyebrows gleefully and laughs heartily at me, falling back on a chest behind him, slapping his knee. 'Listen to this brave one!'

'Let the women be,' calls out the pilot. 'They will only be worth something if they come to no harm.'

The blond leader moves away from us for the time being, gripping the pilot's shoulder and turning with him to the opening of the tent, speaking of their plans.

'He's the handsomest man in all Norway,' the small translator whispers to us in Occitan. 'Every female breathing, from the teenagers, to the wives, to the old toothless hags, would go with him if he asked them. He's a hot rabbit. I doubt you'll have your virginities when we next pitch on dry land.' He grins unpleasantly through flaky lips.

Aina looks anxiously to me. 'Take no notice,' I say. 'He is trying to scare you. They won't harm us.' But I feel no certainty of this. These men are a long way from home, a long way from any wives they have. I am conscious of how many of them there are, how large and vicious they are and that all there is standing between them and us is the flimsy promise of a ransom. I pray to Thor to make their venery stronger than their lust.

The blond man returns to stand looking us over. His long sword hangs unscabbarded from his belt and is engraved with words. I read the runes: Hugin and Munin – Odinn's ravens. The man's cloak is pinned with an enormous circular gold brooch with the longest pin I have ever seen. If my hands weren't shackled I could get close and grab that brooch and use that long, sharp pin as a dagger.

'The master wishes to know your names,' says the translator.

'I am Lady Aina of Ségur, betrothed to Lord Guy, heir to the Viscounty of Limoges,' Aina tells him, 'and this is Lady Sigrida, my companion.'

The translator communicates this information to the blond leader whose eyes light up at the words Viscounty and Limoges. 'Ask them will this Lord Guy pay their ransom,' he says.

We wait for the question to be translated.

'Yes,' Aina tells him, 'if no harm comes to us, Lord Guy will pay your ransom demand.'

I am proud of her arrogant assurance as she speaks to him.

'The question is how much to set it at,' I hear the leader say to the pilot as they leave the tent, the translator stepping close behind them.

As soon as they are gone, Aina bursts out: 'It's my fault, Sigrid! All my fault. I prayed for something to halt my marriage. I told that blond man of the feast at the monastery when he was pretending to be a monk and that is why they raided it when they did! All those men dead, those monks enslaved.' Her face is distraught.

I take her hand, shaking my head. 'Sshh! It's not. It's *not* your fault. They probably already knew about the feast. They will have had spies out for days scouting the defences and finding out such things. All that we did in that encounter when he saved our bag-

157

gage, was show him there would be rich visitors, worth stealing away.'

'My mother will be so distraught when the news reaches her.'

'Yes. If word has not been sent from the monastery,' (in my mind's eye I have an image of that ravished place with nothing but dead bodies to tell the tale) 'then Guy will certainly tell and comfort her when he receives the ransom demand. They will waste no time sending the money I am sure.'

'Will they keep us here then, while they wait for Guy to pay?'

'I do not know, Aina. We shall see.'

Soon after we are pulled roughly from the tent, chained again in the hold and watch the tent being taken down, folded tightly and lashed to the side. Only the Norse crew and the small boy are onboard, together with the blond leader. The boat shifts rhythmically in the surf. I breathe in deeply, savouring the salt of the morning sea. On the beach the line of chained monks who have slept in the trees, are being assembled to march to the slave market. Along the shoreline small, green trees lean far over the water's edge. I watch entranced as the light reflects off the water, rippling and shimmering across the green undercroft of branches and leaves. Another day this sight would be an idyll. Today, there is the same beauty, the same water and light, and such grief and pain.

I notice the monk who had wrapped the cloths around his hands as he rowed. He is standing in the shade whilst most of the other monks are near to naked in the burning sun and even from this distance I imagine their sweat and heat exhaustion. Perhaps the monk in the shade will survive his enslavement and humiliation and find his way back to freedom. As the Norsemen bark orders for them to start shuffling off, the monk looks back to Aina and I on the ship and I raise my hand to him.

From the calls between men and the sounds of other oars I can tell we are moving off from Noirmoutier in the company of another ship. The blond man hangs from the rigging yelling across to the pilot of the other boat: 'Brittany, then Syllingar, then Lundy,' he calls out. 'If there is a storm and one of us is blown off-course we will wait for each other at Lundy. We are heading for Kelda Ey.'

Apart from Brittany, I do not recognize any of the names he calls across, but I guess he might be making for the islands route towards Norway threading up between Ireland and the west coast of Bretland. 'I think we are going to Norway,' I tell Aina.

'Really?' She looks excited.

'Aina, how can you look as if this is a pleasure trip after what we witnessed at the monastery and the fate of those poor monks.'

She looks down chagrined.

'And Aina the fact that you are noble and they have sent a ransom note for you, is no guarantee of your safety.'

'We have another card up our sleeves,' she says eagerly. 'They don't know you are Norse and can understand everything they say.'

'Yes, but there is no reason for them to treat us gently just because I am Norse. I have no living kin in Norway or anyone who might offer us protection. Many ransom victims have died in the 'care' of the Norsemen. There is no law or custom that prevents slavers from preying on their own kind.'

She nods but my words do not rob her of an inappropriately blithe expression as she looks out to the vast sea spreading before us, gulls shrieking and wheeling around the mast. I shake my head. 'Aina, I think you should have been born a Norsewoman with your love of venturing.'

'Better a Norseman,' she says, looking with admiration at the blond leader who stands in the bow with his legs apart, bending confidently with the regular lurching of the ship.

# 14

# Brioude

## July 988

It was a bright morning and the sun streamed in through the narrow window slit in Adalmode's chamber in the Motte Castle of Limoges as she sat combing out her hair. She could glimpse the green of the fields below, beyond the city walls. Her father had refused Audebert's request for her last month for the sixth time. She was getting no younger and if this persisted there would come a time when he would no longer want her, when she would be past desiring and he would find himself another wife, or take one of her sisters as her father frequently and stubbornly offered every time.

She and Guy attempted subtle persuasion, and even her mother tried to sway Gerard but Adalmode saw his continuing refusal was double-edged. On the one hand he was flattered by and desirous of the mooted alliance with the Duke of Aquitaine's family, and on the other hand he wanted to affront Audebert, in payment for the affront offered to him by the Count of Anjou over Audebert's release, and there had been no amelioration of his resentment over the years.

Adalmode sighed and held a thick bunch of her hair up to the light, watching the sun dazzle in it. Would she be white-haired before it was resolved. The marital discord between Emma of Blois and her husband had given Adalmode a reprieve from the mooted marriage to Guillaume of Aquitaine when Emma left her husband and returned to Blois, taking her son with her, but Adalmode's father still stubbornly persisted in his resistance to Audebert.

'Adalmode!' her mother called up the staircase. 'Are you coming down? Your father is waiting to speak to you.'

'I'm coming now!' She tied a bow in the laces at the top of her gown and put her ivory comb – a secret gift from Audebert – into the small chest beneath her bed, lifted her skirts with one hand and tripped down the steps to the hall, breathing in the scent of freshly baked bread. Her father was sitting with a scroll in his hand and looking impatiently towards his eldest daughter.

'You're late down,' he said curtly.

'Sorry Papa, I was daydreaming.'

'Well,' he said, mellowing, 'it's unusual enough for you.'

She took her seat and her mother returned to her own. Adalmode smiled across to Guy, but said, 'Morning darling brother,' in case he could not see her smile.

'Good morning darling sister,' Guy responded but Adalmode noticed there was no smile in his voice.

'I've a letter from the Duchess of Aquitaine just come,' her father said. Adalmode's mood plummeted. She stared down at the yellow and white eggs and bread before her with disgust.

'The Duchess has lately returned to the Duke and commands that I bring you to the Poitiers Assembly at the end of this week.'

Adalmode could feel her father's eyes on her but she kept her own downcast, trying to gather herself.

'You know what this means,' said Rothilde, excited. 'We shall have two weddings in the family this Spring!' Guy's marriage to Aina was due to take place in a few weeks' time. They were waiting for her to arrive now from the monastery of Saint Michel en l'Herm and Lady Melisende was on the road to them from Ségur.

'Don't rush ahead of yourself, Rothilde,' Gerard said, 'but one wedding and a betrothal, certainly, seem likely. Well, what do you say Adalmode? The Duke's heir is a man now and that was always your concern before wasn't it? He's full nineteen and a strapping lad.'

Adalmode swallowed. One moment she had been innocently indulging a little vanity looking at her hair and thinking about how much Audebert admired it, and now suddenly her world was focussed down into this moment, into how she could handle, evade this, or else her life would be something other, something she did not want. 'Father, I am not inclined to wed Lord Guillaume, no matter his age. I am inclined to wed the Count of La Marche and Périgord who offers for me and who has equally rich holdings, adjacent to our own lands.' She looked up passionately into her father's face. 'You married the woman you wished to Father, against opinion, against law even.' She would try truth now, for persuasion, cajolement and excuses had yielded her nothing. 'I want to marry Audebert with all my heart Father. I beg you to give your permission and send my sisters to Poitiers instead for the Duchess' choosing.'

Guy nodded his head to her in approprobation. Her mother was nervously knitting her fingers around and around each other. Adalmode's three sisters had finished their own breakfasts and were quietly clearly away plates and glasses, but they stilled their movements and waited for their father's response. An old servant sitting by the fire cleared the phlegm from his throat and spat it sizzling into the fire.

Adalmode lifted her chin and looked her father in the face. It was an ominous face promising her only storm and battle.

'I have refused my permission for your marriage to La Marche and that is final.' He paused and took a gulp of wine, wiped the back of his hand across his mouth. 'You will go to Poitiers and that is final. Guy will escort you there today and he will hear what the Duchess wants with you and if it is a marriage offer to her son he will accept it on my behalf.' He stood up and her mother rose with him.

Adalmode looked desperately to Guy who lifted his shoulders to her, his expression helpless. Her father turned his back and made his way towards the door. Adalmode opened her mouth to beg further but Guy shook his head and told her in a low voice, 'It will do you no good.' She closed her mouth on bitter distress. 'Are you ready to travel, Adalmode?' he asked gently. 'We must go today I'm afraid, if I am to make it back in time for my marriage.'

Adalmode nodded miserably.

Less than an hour later, she and Guy passed through the city gates and out onto the road. Adalmode reined her horse at the crossroads and Guy drew up alongside her, with a querying look on his face. The road north led to Bellac and to Audebert who had been forbidden to her, and beyond him, to Poitiers, where Guillaume waited for her. She had no doubt that if she went to Poitiers now she would return as Guillaume's betrothed bride.

'Help me, Guy. I can't go there. You know what will happen.'

'What then?'

'Countess Blanche writes to me that she is with child and wishes I were with her. Could I not go to her? Make excuse of her sudden need of me with the birth?'

'In Aix-en-Provence! That's an enormous journey, Adalmode. I wouldn't make it back in time for my own wedding!'

'No, not in Aix. She is in Brioude, visiting with her sons and will have the child there. That is not much further than Poitiers itself.' Adalmode reached her hand to Guy's on his horse's pommel. 'Please, Guy. Perhaps you could just convey me part of the way.'

'No, you know I won't do that. I won't leave you to travel unaccompanied. The Duchess will be mightily displeased if we do not arrive in Poitiers. I read her letter to Father and it was not a request.'

'Blanche will smooth it over.'

'Duchess Emma is not so well inclined to Blanche since she got herself proclaimed Queen of Aquitaine for a short time in her place.'

'That is over now and Blanche has great powers of persuasion. The Duchess is not well inclined to anyone in any case.'

Guy regarded Adalmode for some time, sighed a mighty sigh and nodded his consent.

Adalmode broke into smiles. 'Oh Guy thank you. This is the best course. I cannot give myself to Aquitaine. I just cannot.'

'I will have to leave you there to get back for Aina's arrival in Limoges.'

'I know. Blanche's servants will escort me home when the time is right. I will wait for the storm to blow over, with Father, with the Duchess and perhaps when we do not arrive she will cast around and find him another bride at this Assembly.'

'You will miss *my* wedding then?'

'I'm sorry Guy, I so want to be there for you, but not at the cost of incurring such an unwelcome marriage for myself.'

He nodded again and Adalmode could see from the slump of his shoulders and his self-absorbed frown that he was already worrying about how to deal with their father's inevitable fury at this disobedience. They turned their horses east towards Clermont-Ferrand and the road to Brioude.

Adalmode's reception at Brioude was all that she could have hoped for. Blanche was delighted to see them, sorry that Guy could not stay more than one night, greatly relieved to have Adalmode's company for the birth, thrilled to have the task of writing a convincing and soothing letter to Emma and even more pleased to be thwarting the Duchess. 'I know what unwanted marriages are, my darling, through and through, and I'll not have you sold into one if I can help it,' she exclaimed after they had waved Guy goodbye and good wishes for his marriage to Aina.

Adalmode knew Guy was sorely disappointed that she would not be there to support him. 'Aina will become your support now,' Adalmode said, but Guy had grimaced wryly, telling her: 'I don't think that is likely to be Aina's mode.'

'Your brother can take care of himself,' Blanche reassured her. 'All men speak well of him, of his government of Limoges.'

'Yes.'

'How shall we while away the time waiting for this baby?' Blanche said looking down with an indulgent expression at the huge swell of her stomach, swathed in a voluminous pale and dark green silk gown. The child would come this week or the next. Blanche's bump looked impossibly large and round in contrast to the rest of her body which retained its slenderness. She lent back against a pile of brown brocade cushions. Adalmode glanced around the opulent room. The bedcover and drapes were dusky pink. Silver candlesticks and slavers shone on every surface. A large tapestry on one wall was shot through with silver, green and pink thread depicting a scene of musicians and dancers, their faces joyful, their hands outstretched to one another.

'You must tell me the stories of your marriages,' Adalmode said, 'for I only know parts and have not heard it all from you directly.'

Blanche looked delighted at the idea. 'Yes, indeed,' she said, looking ostentatiously over her shoulder to ensure that her sons from her first marriage and none of the servants were in earshot. She lent close to Adalmode who admired again the vivacious beauty of this woman – four times married and coming to her seventh childbed but still a woman who could charm birds from trees and certainly men from high horses or anywhere else.

'My first marriage here in Brioude was terribly unhappy for me,' she began in a conspiratorial whisper. 'I was not lucky in my early childhood. I did not have a warm and loving family and especially a caring brother as you have. My mother died when I was three and my father when I was ten. My brother Geoffrey succeeded as Count of Anjou and he was barely fifteen, but still he had plenty of ideas and plans even then. One of the first things he did was marry me off for an advantageous alliance.'

'At ten?' Adalmode asked. 'You were betrothed?'

'No darling, I was *married* at ten to Etienne of Brioude here, who was a mere fifty years old to my dolls and puppies!'

Adalmode looked down at her hands. Perhaps she was being selfish and self-indulgent in resisting this marriage her parents wanted after all. She looked back to Blanche and saw the child who had been so carelessly disposed of still there, in her eager face. 'Was the marriage consummated at so tender an age?'

'No, no, there was that at least. He waited for a few years but still that just meant we were both a little older. As you can imagine it was not a pleasant thing to be bedded by a man who could have been my grandfather.' Blanche pulled a face of disgust. 'I put up with it then. I thought I had to. I had three children by him when I was still a child myself.'

'And then he died?' Adalmode said.

'Well, yes he did die eventually but that wasn't the reason for the end of our marriage. Didn't you know? I suppose you were too young to know or understand that scandal.'

Adalmode laughed at Blanche in admiration. 'Another scandal? I thought the scandal of King Louis was your only one.'

Blanche laughed, rocking backwards in her chair and helplessly throwing up her slender, white hands. 'No, love. I've been a scandal all my life. It's a wonder *any* man wants to marry me really!'

'What happened?'

'I met the Count of Toulouse – Raymond – and well to cut a long story short he was a handsome, younger man, much more to my liking and I determined that I needed to get out of my marriage to Etienne. Raymond was enamoured with me,' she lifted her chin, tucked a bright strand of hair behind her small ear, raising one eyebrow, and Adalmode had no difficulty in imagining that. Blanche's voice dropped to a whisper: 'I became pregnant by him!'

'What!' said Adalmode. 'What did you . . .?'

'He was avid for me and his wife wasn't producing children so he repudiated her, I left Etienne who repudiated *me* and I married Raymond.'

Adalmode regarded Blanche, astonished. 'Was there not opprobrium? From your brother? From the Church?'

'Of course,' Blanche said carelessly, 'I listened to a few lectures from both. Nobody on the other hand felt the need to lecture Raymond I noticed. Then when I felt I'd listened enough and done enough penances he and I just got on with our lives and took no more notice.'

'Were you happy with him?'

'Yes, happy enough. Happier.'

'And then what?'

'Well I had two children with Raymond, a son and daughter, and after Etienne died I became Regent for my son here too, so I was kept busy running between the two households, taking care of it all.'

Adalmode knew that despite Blanche's frothy façade, she was judged an astute manager and politician and had taken care of it all, as she put it, very well.

'Then Raymond died too. I am a black widow spider, you see. My husbands die shortly after marrying me! So I was twice widowed, still only twenty-nine, with five children and two great estates to manage! I won't lie to you Adalmode. I enjoyed it. I was good at it.'

Adamode nodded and smiled at the enthusiasm of her friend. 'You are still managing them all I think, as well as your newest husband's household.'

'Yes!' Blanche laughed with amusement at her own competence and scandalousness.

'But what induced you to move from being a widow to marrying the royal boy, Louis?'

'Hmm, yes,' said Blanche, switching to a theatrical expression of dissatisfaction. 'That was a complete error on my part, I admit it. It was my brother's idea again, seeking great advancement for himself and our house, but I had no need to do it and I shouldn't have done it. I allowed myself to be swayed by him against my better judgement.'

'Did you want to be Queen?' Adalmode ventured.

'Well, no that wasn't it,' Blanche responded. 'I was already Countess of most of southern France. It was more that Geoffrey represented it to me as my duty to him, to the house of Anjou and to the line of Charlemagne that was in danger of dying out. I told him a fifteen year old boy would not want a wife twice his age but he told me Louis needed managing, and he was right in that. He said I was proven fertile, and King Lothaire was desperate I should agree. Well, I was foolishly persuaded.' She sat back and took a sip of wine, frowning.

'Do you regret not being Queen or the mother of the next Carolingian King? If you had borne a child to Louis, Hugh Capet could not have seized the throne.'

'Not at all! I could not stand that boy Louis in my bed, let alone bear him a child, and I had borne an old man bedding me before as you remember. And who is to say that Hugh Capet would not have murdered me and a child in any case, as he surely murdered my brother and that fool Louis?'

'Hush, Blanche!' Adalmode said in alarm. 'If you are heard . . .'

'What then? I have my husband and sons now to protect me from my own rashnesses.'

Adalmode saw the child emerge in the woman's face again.

'So, as you know, my marriage to Prince Louis was a disaster and I abandoned the boy when he raised his hand to me because I would not give him control of the purse strings, and my purse and money it was. It wasn't my bed or his heir that he was wanting.' She paused again. 'I was grateful for the help your family gave me, so offering you refuge now in your time of need is the least I can do in return.'

Guy had persuaded their father to aid Blanche when she fled from Louis to the Abbey of Saint Martial outside the walls of

Limoges, and there had been a stand-off that lasted long enough to allow Lothaire to find he had more pressing problems in the north and to ride away with his shamed son. Nevertheless Blanche would have been an embarrassment on Gerard and Guy's hands if it were not for the convenient serendipity that Guy's friend, the young Count of Provence who had willingly assisted in opposing Lothaire, had been enthralled by the beleagured Queen and married her himself.

'There is no end to your bewitchments!' Adalmode laughed. 'And are you happy enough with your new husband or will you be leaving him sometime soon for a fifth husband?'

'Sshh!' Blanche rocked with stifled laughter again and wiped a tear from the corner of her eye. 'No,' she said, her expression sobering, 'Adalmode, I have to tell you that I am in love this time! Who would not be. Perhaps you should rethink your rejection of a younger husband. I can recommend it now!'

'In your case perhaps,' said Adalmode, 'but my heart has been set for many years. Every fibre of me is committed and already in imagination married to Audebert. To marry another would be torture and the death of my soul.'

Blanche lent forward and patted her hand. 'We can't have that,' she said. 'If necessary I shall just keep having babies and keep you here until such time as your Count Audebert can come and get you. But why does he not do so? Your father, after all, kidnapped your mother. It's common enough.'

Adalmode nodded. 'I think it may come to that soon, but he tells me he has to build up his forces for the war there will be if he commits such an act, and he does not want to expose his people to the ravages of war until he is ready to defend them fully.'

'This does him great credit,' said Blanche, her face unusually and briefly serious.

'Do you believe that Hugh Capet has stolen the throne and unjustly claims overlordship for himself and his son where he has none?' Adalmode asked in a low voice.

Blanche shook her head and was silent for a while as if she would not answer.

'Well that is certainly the view of Lothaire's brother, Charles of Lorraine, who leads a rebellion against King Hugh.' She paused again, clearly more reluctant to speak on this topic than on the vagaries of her marriages. 'It's true enough that any of the other lords had as much claim to the throne when Louis died – Emma's brother in Blois, my nephew in Anjou, your Duke in Aquitaine. But well Hugh Capet is King.' Blanche closed her mouth deliberately and looked at Adalmode.

'Did you hear that Aldearde d'Aulnay remarried?' Adalmode said, seeing that a change of topic would be best.

'I did,' Blanche responded. 'To the Count of Angoulême but that was a record brief marriage wasn't it, since he took the cowl only a few months later. He was in ill health before the marriage. No doubt the Duke did not want a virile husband for his beloved mistress.'

'She is *still* his mistress?

'Oh yes.'

The following week, Blanche was easily delivered of a healthy girl and named her Constance. She sent word to her husband in Aix-en-Provence and she pushed herself up in bed, to dictate a letter to her clerk to be sent to Duchess Emma in Poitiers:

'Beloved friend, Emma of Blois, Duchess of all Aquitaine, I greet you, Blanche of Anjou, Marquessa of Provence, Dowager Countess of Gévaudan and Toulouse. I heard of your new concord with your husband, the Duke, and of your return to Poitiers, and am glad of it and that you can continue with your plans for the Abbey of Maillezais. I must beg forgiveness from you already as if you were the Mother Abbess of such a great foundation. Forgive me my dear friend. I have just risen from childbed for the seventh time and brought forth a daughter named Constance for my husband at great labours and pains.'

Blanche paused in her dictation and raised her eyebrows expressively in the direction of the midwife and Adalmode who both knew there had been no such thing. 'An easier birth I never witnessed,' muttered the midwife and Blanche's laugh chimed contagiously. She continued her dictation:

'. . . great labours and pains, which I know that you, as the mother of sons, will commiserate with me upon. And here is my trespass. I had great need, in my fearful time, of my dear friend, Lady Adalmode of Limoges but she told me she could not come for you had commanded her presence. Will you forgive me? I wept and wailed and wrung my hands and said I should be dead in childbed if she did not come and so she did. With all felicitations etc etc, fill that part in.'

She waved away the clerk. 'Will that do?' she asked Adalmode, who simply nodded her head for she was laughing helplessly and could not speak.

# 15

## Kelda Ey

### 988

We are at sea for two days, stopping briefly on dry land for only a few hours when the men forage for provisions. Then we are sailing again up and down the slopes of the sea and sleeping on and off in the rocking boat. On calm days the gentle swell licks perpetually at the ship and on other days the crew and the boat fight rough waves. The battered sail is soaked and the ship we are in is slower than its companion. The collars and chains Aina and I wear chafe and pain us. I keep an eye on the blond man. I do not trust his intentions towards my mistress.

'He's a king's son, so they say,' one of the men says to me, attempting a rough approximation at Occitan and misunderstanding my interest in the blond leader.

'What's his name?' I ask.

'Olafr.'

'Olafr . . . whose son?' I am suddenly urgent in my questions and switch to Norse.

He raises his eyebrows in surprise. 'Olafr Tryggvason.'

I sit very still, staring at the blond man and Aina places her hand on my arm. 'What is it?'

I shake her off and stand abruptly, my chains clanking, calling out loudly, 'Olafr Tryggvason!'

'Sigrid?' says Aina at my elbow, alarmed. 'What . . .'

The blond man turns and regards me. 'That is my name and . . .'

'I am Sigrid Thorolfsdottir.' I take a quick breath. 'We were separated at the slave market in Tallinn many years ago.'

Olafr's mouth drops open. 'Sigrid?' then he looks quickly to where the pilot is staring in our direction. 'Sigrid!' he says to the pilot, pointing at me.

'What . . .' Aina tries again.

But now all eyes in the boat turn to the pilot as he sits down abruptly and hard causing the boat to lee precariously and the men to all shift to cope with his sudden movement. He lets go of the steering oar that swings wildly against the ropes lashing it in place and the boat slams a wave suddenly uncertain of its path. One of the men close to the pilot dives to grab the oar and steady the ship. 'Sigrid, Sigrid,' the pilot moans, staring at me. 'Yes, Sigrid, I thought, I knew . . .'

'Ware the boat Thorgils,' shouts one of the men. 'You'll capsize us with your Sigrid, Sigrid.'

Aina opens her mouth to ask 'What?' again but looks with astonishment as the pilot lurches to me and the boat lists dangerously again and the men call out in dismay at this untoward behaviour. Hampered by my shackles, I hurl myself awkwardly against Thorgils' chest and he embraces me like a great bear, flattening my eyelashes and nose against him and taking the breath from my lungs. Then he puts me back from him and we drink in the sight of each other, oblivious to everything around us. He cups my cheek and his eyes are wet. I think of him, still a boy, shouting to me to be brave in the slave market, a great red collar of sores and bruises circling his neck. Now that I know it is him, I see it is him. Tears sluice down my face and drip unregarded from my chin. He unlocks the fetters on my wrists and at my neck. 'No more slavery, Sigrid,' he mutters as he does it. We begin speaking in my old language and we are weeping and smiling. Thorgils is a good head's height taller than me, more than six foot I am guessing. The promised muscles of his boyhood have filled out with his life as a sailor and fighter. I see now the boy I was torn from, in the freckles that still splatter his ruddy skin, in the pale red of his hair and the blue-green of his eyes with white crinkle lines at their edges amidst his sunburned skin. I trace his features with my fingers, shaking my head in wonder.

Olafr swings lithely around the mast and crosses the swaying boat to join our embraces, touching my hair with astonishment and saying, 'It's obvious now. I can't believe I didn't see it before.'

Eventually I turn to Aina. 'Oh Aina,' I say gasping for breath as if I have climbed a mountain, 'it's my brothers. It's Thorgils,' I gesture to the pilot, 'and Olafr,' I pat the arm of the blond leader. 'My brothers!'

'Sigrid,' she exclaims. 'That's wonderful!' She holds up her fettered wrists and I persuade them to remove her chains, after all what could she do if she did wish to escape. The only escape is in the cold depths of the sea.

We camp on shore that night and whilst some men set to building the fire and securing the ships, others slide off silently into the woods to forage. The fire is crackling and warming us when some of the men return, one carrying a sheep carcass slung over his shoulder. 'It's all we could get without waking the shepherds. The flock was well guarded,' he says, throwing it down, where the cook's boy immediately sets about skinning and preparing it for the fire. 'We could get more if we attack them?'

'No this is enough. We need to keep moving,' Thorgils tells him.

Two other men return with their helmets full of rattling seashells. One helmet is a haul of limpets, the firelight catching the brown circle of glistening meat inside the shells. 'I had to sneak up on them, Lady Sigrid,' the man holding this helmet tells me in a theatrical whisper, 'so that they didn't feel the vibrations of me coming for them, because then they clamp down real hard onto the rock and are a bugger to get off, but if you are quiet and creep, you can knock them off easily with a small rock or your foot.'

The other man's helmet is full of the grey snail-like shells of periwinkles and he dumps them into a soapstone bowl of water standing boiling in the hot embers. Thorgils shows Aina and I how to scrape off the black foul-tasting blister at the top of the limpets with a knife and just eat the woodsmoke flavoured meat. He gives us thorns to pluck the periwinkles from their shells. The men pass around a bowl of soured beer and pepper to dip the warmed shellfish into. We feast hungrily on the tiny meat, knowing there will be a long wait before the sheep is cooked and ready.

Sitting around the cracking fire with its light playing on the circle of faces, Thorgils tells us the story of what happened to them since we were last together so long ago.

'When we lost you at the slave market, Sigrid, Olafr and I were bought by a man named Reas, and we stayed in Eistland for six years, working hard and growing to men,' Thorgils begins. 'All the while my heart ached for my little sister and that I did not know what had become of you.'

His men are all looking at me with admiration and finding the likenesses between he and I. It feels strange after all these years of being a slave, a mere servant in the background, to be the centre of such attention. With every minute I feel I am slowly growing back into who I once was, the daughter of a Jarl, the sister now of a Jarl, the old playfriend of a King's son, for Olafr's father who was murdered long ago, had been King of Viken. I sit up straight and do my best to do credit to Thorgils and Olafr, under the curious glances of their crew.

'One day,' Thorgils continues, 'in the marketplace, a grand lord was curious to see Olafr's fairness and asked who he was. Olafr seeing that this was a man of Norway told him proudly that he was Olafr Tryggvason. The man was astonished, telling us he was Sigurd, brother to Olafr's mother, in the service of King Valdamar of Holmgard. Sigurd treated with Reas to free us and took us back with him to Holmgard.

We were chopping wood outside the house, when we were sick to see Klerkon, the Eistland pirate, the man who killed our father and enslaved us Sigrid, strutting down the street towards us. Before I realized what he was about, Olafr strode to Klerkon, called him a murderer and slaver, and buried his hand axe in the man's brain.' Thorgils pauses for the grunts of admiration and agreement with this act to die down. Olafr is sitting with his arms crossed and his face modest.

'*They* are slavers!' Aina whispers in my ear and I frown her to be silent.

'For such a killing without legal permission,' Thorgils tells us solemnly, 'the law of Holmgard decreed Olafr should hang, and a crowd came to take him, but the Queen gave him shelter, paid his blood-fine and he became her favourite.'

I watch Olafr smile slyly at that, his gaze still modestly on the ground.

'We lived there, in the close friendship of brothers laid in the same cradle, until we reached manhood.'

Olafr says, 'I lay my thoughts bare before your brother, Sigrid, and listen to his advice. He has been my shoulder-companion through slavery, misfortunes, storms and battles.'

Aina is agog with excitement, not understanding all the words, although I translate a few for her here and there, but thrilling to the drama of the evening and the men's responses to Thorgils' tale. She stares overmuch at Olafr. He was a handsome boy and he is a handsome man now.

Thorgils continues the tale. 'Of Norway, the lands that are Olafr's patrimony, we heard that King Harald of Denmark sent warriors who killed Harald Greycloak and drove out Gunnhild and her other sons who murdered Olafr's father. The feeder of wolves became food for the ravens.' Thorgils pauses receiving the admiring shouts that greet his epitaph for Harald Greycloak. 'In Holmgard, King Valdemar made Olafr a captain of his warriors and he fought ably for the King.'

'You too!' says Olafr.

Thorgils shrugs smiling. 'But then people muttered that Olafr was becoming over-great and was the Queen's favourite and the King should feel jealousy, so the Queen advised us to leave, saying that wherever we went men would admire Olafr's prowess. So we began viking!' There is a shout of approval from the men who clash their horns of ale together and slap their sword hilts.

Aina laughs nervously beside me and I see both Olafr and Thorgils look at her with admiration. 'You should cover your head,' I tell her, but instead she shakes it and the firelight shines on her glorious hair. 'What then?' I ask Thorgils, to distract them from Aina.

'We gathered our *drengir*,' Thorgils says, looking around at the circle of faces and naming them. 'Toki Barelegs, Leif Hairy Breeks, Sibbi, Geiri, Gormr, Skogi, Eimundr, Asjborn, Erra, Asvaldi. We had just one ship in those days, *The Orm*. We raided Bornholm and took booty, we parted Danes from their war-sarks south of Hedeby, and then we were driven in a gale to seek haven on the coast of Wendland, where Queen Geira heard about us and invited us to her court. She was young and beautiful and in no time at all,' laughs Thorgils, 'she was smitten with Olafr and he took her as his wife!'

Olafr smiles his smile to himself again.

'Halfrod the Troublous Skald, will speak it,' says Thorgils, gesturing to a man who I had noticed did not row the ship and I had wondered if he were a *godi* or a shaman.

Halfrod stands up slowly, arranging his robes around him, clearing his throat and then pronouncing in a loud, melodic voice:

'On the spring tide,
bountiful Queen Geira of the dark forest land
tested Olafr Tryggvason, warrior from the north.

Becoifed in a golden helmet,
he rode the steed of the sea across the billows,
dyed the grass red with the blood of her foes
He gave his Queen the brown blood of Frisans,
the flesh of Walloons.
Hundreds were pressed beneath the claws of the carrion bird.'

Halfrod sits down abruptly, drinks deeply from his replenished horn and the men mutter their approval. Aina, has opened her mouth in amazement at Halfrod and is still staring at him long after he has resumed his seat. I, however, am a little disappointed. I thought there would be more from Halfrod who seems more interested in beer than poetry, but then Thorgils resumes the tale.

'In Denmark, King Harald had seen a Christian priest named Poppo put his hand in a fire.' The group of men scoff loudly. 'King Harald became a Christian and ordered all the people of Denmark and Norway to put aside our Gods and accept Christ.'

The men hiss and Aina is startled, looking around her as I whisper a translation and she remembers she is amongst pagans. Thorgils holds up his hand and I admire what a good storyteller my brother is, like me I think, and dab a finger to the corner of my eye where tears of joy keep gathering.

'War continued in Norway, in the lands that rightly belonged to Olafr, the dead lay in heaps on the battlefield and Odinn took the brave to Valhalla.' There are more mutters of approval from the group of men.

'Alas,' declares Thorgils, 'we were three winters with Queen Geira, when she fell sick and died and Olafr had no more pleasure for living in Wendland.'

The men bow their heads in sorrow at the passing of Olafr's wife and are silent for a moment. Aina turns to me with a questioning expression. 'Olafr's wife died,' I say abruptly, trying to damp down her fascination with Olafr in the disapproval of my tone.

'So,' says Thorgils, slowly, 'we found we must go viking again.' There is another clashing of metal at his words. 'We plundered in Frisland and Saxland and Flanders. We sailed for Engaland and around the coast of Scotland and plundered well there.' The men nod and murmur their agreement. Thorgils' aquamarine eyes glint in the moonlight. 'We were the terror of the islands of the Hebrides and of the Isle of Mann, of Bretland, and now we are famed even unto Frankland.' Thorgils ends with a flourish of his arm and the men stamp their feet and shout their approval, and he looks warmly to me.

I look round at the men, mostly golden haired with gold rings on their muscled arms, mostly long-shanked and broad-shouldered and I remember my childhood and feel at home. Most of all I look at Thorgils and Olafr, my chest heaving up and down, at the strength of emotion I feel, reunited with them, but I am saddened to hear that grief and destruction is their way of life. Like Aina, I could ask Thorgils how could he be a slaver when he has been a slave, but I know the answer. He and Olafr are dispossessed, landless in Norway. The sea is their only homestead and the plunder of its shores, are their crops.

We sight another coast. 'Engaland,' Thorgils tells us. He has threaded his way with expert sea-lore between the coast and the islands scattered alongside it, his eyes creased against the sun and the wind. '*Syllingar* islands,' he gestures to them. He often spends time looking at the shadow cast by the sun at midday and at night he holds out his arm measuring the height of the Pole Star above the horizon with his hand and thumb.

Aina boldly seats herself next to him. 'Ask him: How do you know where to go?' she says to me.

'I can understand you,' he tells her in pigeon Occitan. 'I have spent enough time raiding here and staying at the Norman court. A pilot studies the sun and the stars and the landmarks visible on the coast to keep on the right heading.'

'But now,' says Aina, looking around us, where ocean stretches in every direction.

'Now,' he says, 'I look at the birds and sea-creatures, the cloud formations and the colour and currents of the water, the drift-wood and weed, the feel of the wind.'

Aina laughs, assuming he is joking, but sees his expression is serious, and looks at the water around us anew, straining to see what he sees.

'Don't worry,' he says, seeing her frown, 'I won't take you to *Ragnarok*. The world's end,' he adds guessing that she doesn't know what he means.

'That crewman there,' Aina says pointing at a man with black spots on his bare calves, 'he needs to eat fresh meat or he will sicken and die.'

'Is that so?' says Thorgils looking at her with a mixture of surprise and scepticism.

'It is so,' she says. 'My father was a merchant trading in your lands and those of the English, the Irish and the Rus. He told me about this illness. Has he been having nosebleeds, lost any teeth?'

Thorgils raises his eyebrows some more and regards her from narrowed blue-green eyes. 'He has as a matter of fact.'

'It's urgent then,' she says.

'Thank you healer,' he says with pleasant sarcasm. 'I will see to it. Would you leave me in peace now to steer the ship?'

A few hours later and what had been a sunny, blue sky suddenly darkens like night and rumbles above us. The surface of the water becomes black as charcoal and lightning flashes on the horizon.

Thorgils gives orders and the men lash down loose barrels and show Aina and I two loops of strong leather nailed to the side of the ship, telling us to hold on there.

'A storm is coming?' Aina says unnecessarily so no one answers her.

The clouds open as if slit with a long knife and unburden themselves, watering the sea in great long curtains of rain sweeping vertically in front of us. Aina and I hold on to the straps for dear life and throw our hoods over our heads but we are drenched nonetheless by rain and seawater. There is a great tearing as the sail rips again where it had been patched and it flaps uselessly in the gale. The waves are high enough to swallow the ship and drag us all down to the bottom but the crew calmly wear the storm, trusting to the ship and their pilot. Sibbi and Geiri, following Thorgils' shouted commands, take down the shredded sail. The ship ploughs the sea roughly, rising up and down nauseously on the swollen billows that shake the dragon-headed stem. Thorgils shouts above the wind that the bilgewater is too high and Skogi and Gormr bail furiously, close to our feet, but it seems as fast as they throw the water out, the rain-gorged sea throws it back in at us. My fingers holding the strap are red and frozen and pained with the imprint of the leather. There is a crack above my head and Leif and Geiri jump up swiftly just in time to avoid being brained by part of the yard arm breaking off and dropping with a thump and bounce to the deck, its jagged edges spitting splintered wood. Thorgils shouts to bring down the rest of the precarious yard and mast and when Eimundr and Asbjorn have done this, everyone hunkers down holding onto straps and ropes to ride out the raging storm.

I shiver uncontrollably in the weight of my sodden clothes and look anxiously to Aina who has her eyes shut, her long eyelashes meshed wet together on her pale cheek. 'Aina, it's easing up,' I call to her.

She opens her eyes and tries to smile, her teeth shivering on her bottom lip. 'We are still alive, Sigrid!' she calls, fear shaking her voice despite her bravado.

Thorgils looks to see that I am safe as the calm grows. After the storm it is cool and overcast and the men row the last part of the journey, scoring our path through the sea with a well-practised unison that the poor monks could not achieve.

The ship limps on for one more day and then we join *The Crane* at anchor in a small bay on Lundy Island, a high rock in the sea. The ripped sail is taken down and folded in a heap. *The Crane* has a patched spare sail and the men transfer this to *The Orm*. Thorgils looks at it frowning, 'It will get us to Kelda Ey.'

'Aina will not escape,' I tell Thorgils and he nods and allows us to walk free on the island while the repairs are underway. We walk beneath gnarled branches of rhododendrons growing out of the cliff edge like an enchanted forest. Piping birds fly up before us. Wild ponies are grazing in tall grasses in the distance, and Aina points out to me the sudden black silhouettes of deer leaping on the horizon. The sound of the waves lapping is everywhere.

'Thorgils says we are not going to Norway,' I tell Aina and she looks crestfallen.

'I would like to see the fjords and the midnight sun and the *Nordrljos*, the Northern Lights, and the white bears,' she says and I know that some of this she has heard from Olafr rather than from me. 'Where are we going?'

'Thorgils says he has to lay up this ship to make repairs and he will hold you on Kelda Ey Island, which is off the coast of Bretland, one day's sailing from here, waiting for the ransom to be paid. No point in taking you all the way to Norway if Guy can pay soon. I imagine he will pay fast, so that he can marry you.'

'Don't remind me of that,' says Aina, crossly. 'I hope Olafr has asked for an enormous sum and Guy can't find it. I told him Guy was as rich as Croesus.'

'Don't be ridiculous, Aina.' I am angry now. 'If Guy can't pay the ransom Olafr will sell you on to one of his men and you wouldn't like that at all.'

'He will not sell me on,' says Aina confidently.

I frown at her. 'Be careful, Aina. These are not boys but men who have raped and murdered. You do not know what you are tangling with.'

I see the stubborn set of Aina's mouth that indicates she does not agree with me but will not say so. How often have I seen that in my time with her!

The men reloaded and readied the ship in the bay at Lundy a few hours ago but now we wait, sitting on rocks on the beach watching the seaweed pulled in and out by the waves, and Thorgils studying the water.

'What are we waiting for?' asks Aina.

'Tidal gates and streams,' says Thorgils abruptly, not wanting his concentration disrupted.

'Gates?' Aina shrugs at me.

Thorgils turns to her impatiently. 'I need to concentrate on finding the right moment to set sail,' he says, 'so be quiet woman.' Seeing her face fall he says more gently. 'There is a tidal stream between here and Kelda Ey, our destination. If I judge the time right we'll get there fast with no rowing. The tides will push us swiftly where we want to go, but if I get it wrong and we founder against a foul tide and big seas, this injured ship will take us down with it.'

Aina nods brightly to him but then turns to me with a frown. 'Is it pagan magic?' she asks in a whisper.

I lead her off a little way to stop her disturbing my brother and explain how the sea and tides work to aid the sailor for those who are wise enough and patient enough.

At last Thorgils judges the right moment has come and there is a flurry of activity as we embark and weigh anchors with two ships: Thorgils leading and Olafr in the second one following behind. I thrill at the way the ship rushes with the tide. 'You judged the stream right!' I call to him and he smiles, the breeze blowing his rusty hair from his face and his clothes flattened against the broad, lean front of his body. It takes us only half the day to reach Kelda Ey.

'The island of the spring,' Thorgils announces as the land comes visible on the horizon. 'It will be your home for some months now ladies and then you must decide what to do Sigrid,' he says to me. 'When Lady Aina's ransom is paid and we return her to her husband, we must find a Norse husband for *you*. I will look about me.'

'As will I,' I say crossly, 'if it's a husband for me.'

'Of course,' he says laughing, mollifying me.

Aina stares at me. 'Sigrid, you would leave me?'

'Hush, Aina. I do not know. We both need to see what transpires and think on it. For my brother's honour I cannot return to servitude.' The prospect of regaining my homeland, of finding a Norse husband, my own homestead, children, hovers enticingly in my mind, but I would not abandon Aina until I know she is safe. I cannot make her happy with Guy, but I can ensure that she is safely returned to him and her mother. My spirit sinks suddenly. I cannot imagine being without her. She is the sister of my soul. We have been together now for sixteen years and no one in the world knows me or loves me as well as she does.

She is studying my face and her eyes swim with tears. 'What is the outcome of the long Sigrid think,' she says, trying to make light of things.

'Don't rush on so, with guessing,' I tell her. 'We don't know what is coming.'

Thorgils had told us that Olafr has set Aina's ransom at 3,000 pounds of silver and we had reeled in shock. 'Guy can't find 3,000 pounds of silver!' Aina exclaimed.

'He will try, no doubt, for such a wife,' Thorgils said and Aina looked smug at his compliment.

The *snekkja* forges through the waves and the island before us grows larger and larger. Beyond it are scattered rocks, small islands and then the sweep of the mainland – Bretland – a great swathe of sandy beaches as far as the eye can see, and distant mountains rising far beyond, blurring blue with the sky and clouds.

'Why here?' I ask Thorgils.

'Olafr and I made a base of it two years ago,' he says. 'We saw off the monks. It has a spring of fresh water, good defences, a water mill, good farmland, plentiful resources of food and fuel. We use the old monastery buildings as our longhouses, and look after the old monks' livestock and crops. We keep a garrison of men here when we travel. The Bretar on the mainland have left us be, so it suits well, and if we need something the island cannot give us then we raid that mainland. There are thriving market towns across the way, and not far up the coast is a rich cathedral.'

Soon I have the opportunity to see for myself why they chose this island. The two ships beach in a sheltered bay and we disembark, the men dragging the boats up onto the pale yellow sand.

Their anchors are dropped over the side to the dry land as a precaution against high tides and two men stay with each of the ships at all times. 'A Northman robbed of his boat is worse off than if you robbed him of his trousers or his hair,' Thorgils tells us as we observe these precautions. There are a number of other boats already beached there – one large ship and several small ones, which are in the process of being caulked with animal hair and wool.

A path winds up from the bay through woods on the left and farmland on the right. People are working with scythes in the fields and I spy a few more people in the woodland collecting sticks for the fire. 'Captured slaves,' Thorgils says, seeing me look that way.

'How can you do to others, what was done to us?' I ask, but he only shakes his head in response, not meeting my eyes.

'Where from?' asks Aina.

'Everywhere,' he responds to her, glad to avoid tangling with me. 'Some from Bretland, some from the Frankish lands like you. Others from Frisia and Wendland.'

'Why don't they run away?' she asks.

'How? They would have to be mighty swimmers to make it to the mainland from here. Olafr and I did the swim once, and a few others of the crew can make it, but most of these slaves don't know how to swim and none of them have the courage to attempt it,' he says disdainfully, but then looks away from my angry expression.

Later Aina and I see other reasons why the slaves do not run. The majority are female and many have children with them, who labour alongside them. At night they are chained at the ankle and bedded down in a large barn. The slaves sleep in the loft and the animals and guards are below. They are counted in and out of the barn and accompanied by at least two Norsemen whilst working. They have to work hard but I see no whips or cruelties, beyond enslavement itself, which is more than cruelty enough it seems to me. I am haunted by the eyes of the thousands of slaves who had no one kind to buy them as I did, and the thousands more born to that miserable condition. I know I have been very lucky with Melisende and Ademar and now in finding my brothers. The

Aesir have answered my constant prayers and granted me great luck, but others who are enslaved do not fare so well.

As we climb the path we see two watchtowers on the cliffs to either side, and then a water mill, a series of ponds and a fast stream running downhill to feed the mill. I hear the distinctive hammering of a forge. In every sense it looks like an active homestead, except that most of the people labouring here have been stolen from their own homelands. Through the woods on the left we glimpse a stone building. 'It's one of the Christian chapels,' Thorgils says. At the crest of the hill stands the Priory, with smoke issuing from holes in the roof. 'If you keep going from here,' Thorgils tells us, 'you come to the high beacon point where there are excellent views of this whole island and then the mainland beyond and you can see Lundy where we came from this morning to the south.'

We enter the monk's refectory which has been turned into a longhouse with a fire pit dug in the centre of the room and the smoke curling up. The long open hearth has a flat stone slab across one end where bread and oatcakes are baking and a pot of stew is simmering. A tapestry strip runs the length of one wall telling some of Olafr's heroic adventures. Aina paces slowly along its length discerning the story.

The cooking smells are delicious and I hope we might be able to eat soon. The old monk's tables have been reconfigured as a raised platform down each side of the room to sit and sleep on. Other tables are stacked where they can be placed in front of the platform for feasting, but they are cleared to the sides now to allow the women room to weave and cook. A number of slave-women squat near the fire preparing vegetables and kneading dough. I recognise soapstone basins that must have been brought from Norway. A woman works on an array of knives on the table in front of her, sharpening them with a whetstone. Two more labour with butter churns. From a large upright loom a long trail of woven textile spills onto the floor. They are making cloth for a new sail.

Thorgils introduces us to three Norse women who came with the crew from Norway: Ragnhild and Naerfi, married to two of Thorgils' men, and Tofa Wisdom-Slope, who is the mother of another man in Thorgils' *drengir*. They oversee the running of the household and supervise the work of the slaves. Tofa moves stiffly around the room. Her hips and hands pain her she tells me. I am excited to talk with these women in Norse and keep translating for Aina parts of our conversation. At first they look at her with disdain. She is one of the foreign prisoners, but after a while they see I am fond of her and they show her courtesy for my sake.

A dark, slender girl steps forward to offer Thorgils a bowl of water to wash his hands and a goblet of ale. 'Welcome home, master,' she says. She has lustrous black hair, dark blue eyes and olive skin. Her mouth is large, with full pale pink lips, and her chin is strong and dimpled.

'Morag, this is my sister, Sigrid Thorolfsdottir,' Thorgils tells her with an enormous grin at me. She bows her head politely and pulls Thorgils' heavy cloak from his shoulders to sling it over her arm. 'And this is Lady Aina who is a noble hostage belonging to Lord Olafr. Show these ladies to the best guest chamber.'

Morag beckons us to follow her.

'Are you from here, from Bretland, Morag?' Aina asks her kindly, but the girl looks nonplussed at her language. I try Aina's question in Norse which she seemed to understand when Thorgils spoke to her.

'Yes, lady,' the girl replies in passable Norse. 'I was taken by Lord Olafr when he raided the cathedral up the coast at Saint Davids. I was a nun,' she says and when I translate for Aina she looks aghast.

'I'm so sorry.'

Morag looks down. 'Jarl Thorgils is a kind master. I am glad that Olafr gave me to him and not to one of the other men.'

'Can you tell us something of the island?' I ask.

'In my language we call it *Ynys Byr*, Lady. It means Pyro's Island, after an Abbot who fell in the well drunk long ago and drowned.'

I am surprised again to find myself being addressed as Lady, and when I translate for Aina she bends over, clapping her hands to her knees and laughing loudly at the Abbot's mishap. Morag looks confused at Aina's hilarity at first, but then joins with her infectious humour.

Morag pours water into a large bowl for us to wash ourselves. Our clothes are soiled from the violent abduction at Saint Michel en l'Herm and from the sea voyage so Ragnhild takes us to look through a chest for replacements. I find us each a white linen shift with sleeves and pleating at the neck and strapped woollen overdresses that look as if they will fit. Aina exclaims at the strangeness of the Norse clothing and laughs happily looking down at herself in this new attire, but I pin two oval shoulder brooches onto my dress straps and in a rush feel suddenly and entirely at home. Just so had I learnt to dress myself as a small child. The memories and feelings of those days flood back to me, when I had my father and a sure place in my world in Viken. I wish then that I had the colourful glass beads that Lord Ademar gave me in Hedeby long ago to string between my brooches, but for now this will do and in time I will acquire more decorations for my clothing.

A bell sounds in the hall below and Morag says we are called to feast and should not delay for Olafr will be angry if we are late to take our seats. 'His anger is swift and harsh,' she says anxiously, obviously having witnessed or felt it herself at first hand.

'The first meal on dry land for many months,' Olafr calls out enthusiastically, raising his drinking horn to the company. There is plenty of meat and metheglin – a drink made from honey and herbs that I find tastes very well. As men grow drunk I feel anxious again for my mistress but I know that Thorgils will protect us and I hope Olafr will protect his investment.

Each of the crew members seems to have at least two personal female slaves – one for their bed and one to see to their needs – food, bathing, clothes and errands. Thorgils and Olafr's personal slaves are more numerous. Olafr continues to look with lustful eyes to my mistress. I warn him off with my own eyes and he laughs at me. 'Alright, alright, Sigrid. What fear you set in me with your furious glances!' he says sarcastically. Then in a relenting tone of voice he tells me, 'For our shared childhood and the love I bear your brother, I promise to bring no battering ram to your friend's virginity!' I see Aina swallow at that. It does not help that she is clearly fascinated by him and observes with interest which slave he intends to take to his bed each night.

'Perhaps your Lady Aina would like to assist me in the bath-house, Sigrid,' Olafr says, half-teasing, half-serious.

'You have slave girls for that Olafr,' I respond sternly and he chuckles, while Aina raises her eyebrows in query to me. 'The men wash in the bathhouse with water poured on hot stones, cleansing in the steam,' I say quietly to her, 'and sometimes other things go on there, so you stay away.'

I am intrigued to see that Thorgils does not bed down with Morag or any of the other slaves at night. 'Are you married, Thorgils?'

'No,' he says shortly in a way that brooks no further conversation.

'Why do you harry beyond your own lands?' Aina challenges Olafr at our next evening meal.

'It was your race that started it,' Olafr responds, 'when your Charlemagne cut down our holy tree Jormunr and Christian missionaries set out to plague us from Lindisfarne. That's when we began our attacks.'

Aina says nothing for a short while. 'I knew nothing of that first provocation. We have always been told that you Northmen raid because you are ravenous by nature.'

'Oh we are,' Olafr laughs, his eyes roaming across her face and breasts, following every curve of her body, until Aina reddens and I bang my spoon down hard on the table, deciding it is time we excused ourselves to sleep. Next morning I wake to find Aina's pallet empty. It is unusual for her to wake before me. In the hall I find her staring into the fire, a crust of warm bread in her hand.

'Come do not be a charcoal-chewer,' I tell her.

'A what?'

'Someone who hangs around the hearth lazily when everyone else is out working. Let's go and look at the view from beacon hill.'

We climb the hill in the direction Thorgils indicated. As we move up the path we alarm plump brown curlews with long curving beaks like darning needles that are nesting in the brilliant green bracken. Large dragon-flies fly towards us swerving at the last minute. Above us falcons and crows circle, watching our progress, on the lookout for voles and other prey. We pass several heaps of feathers around tangles of tiny bones and guts. From the top of the hill we can discern the rough diamond shape of the island, cliffs spearing out erratically into the blue sea on all sides and ravines full of white flowers. Our eyes crease against the brightness of the light reflecting from the surrounding water. There is an overwhelming sense of space. The grey cliffs are dotted with short bright green grass and yellow lichen. To the left comes the regular boom of the sea in a rocky blow-hole. The white foam of waves studded with black boulders looks like a thin necklace slung around the coast. Thick green and yellow seaweed rolls back and forth on the strand. The irregular patchwork of fields established by the monks where the thralls now labour, blanket the rocks and undulations of the island. Planes of colour are visible in the sea – greens, dark blues, grey-blues, grey-greens and blacks. Strings of other islands in the distance look as if they have been dropped out of the sky from a giant's hand.

The island is teeming with life. Raucous seabirds wheel around us, sit on nests on the narrow ledges of the guano-streaked cliffs like a great shrieking city, skid across the surface of the ocean carrying flapping fish in their beaks, plunge-dive at dark clouds of mackerel. Aina and I lay on our bellies on the edge of the cliff, watching the birds. There are fat black and white birds with striped beaks and long talons like the fingers of a lute player. Aina laughs pointing at some birds that have no nests and balance their eggs on their toes instead.

The hazy blue-green view of sea, sky, islands, distant mountains, yellow beaches and just discernible settlements on the mainland stretches all around us. Aina stands and turns round and round with her arms flung out until she falls over dizzy, watching the swoop of screeching gulls from her back on the grass. 'If this is captivity, Sigrid, it's not too bad at all.'

'No,' I agree, 'although I would not be one of the slaves on this island for anything. Commanded to any man's bed, with no control of the fate of any child I bore, worked hard through all the hours of daylight.'

'Yes,' Aina says, sobering.

A ship passing from Norway docks for two nights to take on

fresh water and Olafr and Thorgils entertain the pilot and crew with two days of feasting, drinking bouts and entertainments. A huge cauldron of ale sits in the middle of the hall and Morag and the other slaves hurry back and forth dipping drinking horns into the liquid and handing them back to the thirsty men. Late in the evening, Thorgils has to diplomatically intervene to prevent one of the visiting crewmen forcing Morag to his bed.

In the morning when the headaches have cleared a little, the visitors engage in contests with Thorgils' men – wrestling and horse racing. The crews practise 'swine-array,' marching in a tight wedge formation, clashing together harmlessly, or more or less harmlessly. Olafr shows off his ability to cast two spears at the same time. Thorgils shows his skill in casting a twisting spear with a cord looped about the shaft so that it spins in flight. They are both stripped to their breeches, gold rings gleaming on their upper arms: Thorgils, large like a bear, his muscled arms and chest clad in light red hair, dense freckles dusted across his shoulders; Olafr is as tall and well-muscled as my brother, but slighter, his sinews sleek beneath his golden skin, like a lynx. Practising together they show how they can fight with either hand to bewilder their opponent or in case one arm is wounded. Aina sits on the grass, at the front of the spectators, elbows on her knees, chin in her hands, her eyes wide and avid.

'Let's see the spear, trick, Thorgils,' calls Olafr. Thorgils stands at one end of the field and Olafr at the other holding an unblunted spear. He hurls it accurately at Thorgils who dodges to one side, catches the spear back-handed in mid-air, swings his arm back up, and flings the spear at Olafr who ducks to the side, rolling on the ground. Other men try this trick unsuccessfully and Morag has to bind several wounds as a result.

On the second evening there are board games and then as the drinking gets underway again, humorous exchanges of insults.

'You are a hot rabbit!' a crewman shouts at Olafr, imitating the mating movements of a male rabbit.

'But your trouser-snake is too cold to emerge from its hole,' Olafr yells back.

'You mince around like a woman,' Toki shouts to Gunnulf Flatnose who does not take this particular insult in good humour, instead lunging across the table to grip Toki's throat in his huge hand, so that Thorgils has to hammer on the table with his fist to get them to break apart.

The second morning after the visiting ships docked I enter the hall from fetching water to be greeted by an extraordinary sight. A person covered in different coloured shaggy furs, wearing a great many strands of threaded beads and stones and holding a long wooden staff is seated high and precariously on five feather cushions. Several women of the house, including Aina, stand around this raised up person chanting. A small bowl on the ground has a few smouldering leaves in it that are giving off a dizzying pungency. It is impossible to see the person's face because it is enveloped in a furry hood but I can see the mouth below the edge of the hood chewing or mumbling. That mouth seems to be rolling its tongue around and around. It begins to babble – incomprehensible mutterings in a low, inhuman voice.

Morag stands at the back not joining in the chanting.

'What is it?' I whisper.

'She is named a *völva*,' Morag says. 'She came with the ship and can tell us the future they say.' Morag crosses herself and I wonder how Lady Melisende would feel to see Aina chanting there of Odinn and Freyja.

The hooded woman stamps her staff once and the chanting stops. Aina sneaks an amused look over her shoulder to me and I frown at her. She should not participate and scoff if that is what she is doing. The *völva* pronounces that the harvest will be good, the milk will flow in the goats' udders, next winter will be mild and then the women begin to ask her questions.

'Will I carry this child to term?'

'Yes, it is a boy.'

'Will my master marry me?'

'No. He has a wife in Norway and will sell you to the next slaver passing this way if you pester him.'

'Will I marry the man I love or the man I should?' I hear Aina ask in her clear voice and halting Norse.

The hooded head turns in her direction. It is impossible to see anything of the *völva*, so shrouded is she in her strange clothes and decorations, that she seems more a thing than a person. 'You will marry the man you love,' she pronounces, 'if you tie my runes to your wrist for three days and nights and pray to Freyja naked under the moon. Aallatti!' One of the assistants with the *völva* passes a rune stick to Aina who looks at it curiously.

I frown. The seer's answers are sowing much mischief it seems to me. I watch Aina tie the rune stick to her wrist and when the ceremony is over and the *völva* lifted down from her cushions, I follow Aina outside. 'Aina, what *are* you doing, chanting with pagans? *What* man do you love? You're not really going to pray to Freyja naked under the moon are you? Show me those runes now. You don't even know what they say.'

'No thank you Sigrid. It's my business not yours,' she tells me tartly and skips away.

She could not think that Olafr will marry her, surely? I know her head is stuffed with romantic longings but that would be ridiculous. Thorgils told me that Olafr is preparing to reclaim his birthright to the throne of Norway. Aina's ransom would help him in that but his wife will not be the heiress of a minor Frankish Viscount. She will be a Queen or a Princess and bring him military allegiance. I run after Aina and catch up with her. 'There's a big difference between being a prized concubine and being a legal wife,' I tell her, 'It's not worth it, and what happens if you are ransomed and returned to Guy without your honour? He will not take you then.'

She frowns at me. 'I don't know what you are talking about Sigrid.'

The following morning I look for Aina in the hall and cannot find her, as often happens now. I know that she will be down at the beach, watching the men working on the ships, pestering my brother and Olafr with a million questions about Norway and seafaring. I walk down swiftly to ensure that she is safe and am relieved to see that she has at least had the good sense to take Morag with her. Olafr and Thorgils are looking over the ships. Thorgils has worked on the less battered ship, *The Crane*, and it shines now as if readying for its maiden voyage; its planks repaired, lashed with new ropes and nails, freshly tarred, newly carved stems at either end resembling the beak of a crane. The ship that we travelled in, however, *The Orm*, is still a sorry sight.

Thorgils has used axes to prop it up on the beach and the gaps between the warped planks and the damage at the front of the hull, where it has repeatedly beached and scraped across gravel and rocks, is clear to see. The broken yard and the torn sail have been removed and will have to be replaced. The dragon's head has been taken down and carefully wrapped.

'Is it done for, Thorgils?' asks Olafr, 'just a ridicule-ship after all our adventures in it? It was my first ship,' he says to me, turning at the crunch of my feet on the sand. Aina takes advantage of my presence to move up close to listen to the men's conversation and grabs my hand, and both men take advantage of her approach to stare openly at her. I frown at Thorgils sternly and he resumes his work. The fraying thong that binds the *völva*'s rune bracelet to Aina's narrow wrist tickles the side of my hand.

'No, not done for,' Thorgils says, walking around the ship, considering it from every angle. 'I can repair *The Orm*, but it will be months of labour, making a new yard, replacing the planking, but she could be seaworthy, fit for you again in three or four months time. It will take a fair time for the women to weave enough cloth to stitch together for a new sail too.'

Olafr nods. 'Well, make the repairs then, Thorgils, and I must sail without you this time.'

Olafr has decided to sail to Dublin where the King's sister, Gyda, has become a rich widow and invited suitors to woo her at the Thing – the Norse Assembly. Since Olafr needs both a wife and money he intends to try his luck. Looking at him – lean, lithe, blond, fearless, the great-grandson of King Harald Finehair and his wife Swanhild, the only survivor of the royal race of Norway – I think it likely that when we next see him he will be a husband alright.

'If Lady Gyda will have me, I'll sail to England with her, for I have business there. When you hear news of the ransom, send word,' he tells Thorgils. 'Will you come with me, Sigrid?' he says, surprising me. 'Leif Hairy Breeks has a liking to take you to wife.' Aina gasps and clutches at my arm, shaking her head. 'His chest is filled to the brim with gold and silver, and I can vouch that he would make you a fine husband, foster-sister,' Olafr goes on, frowning at Aina.

'I thank you, Olafr,' I say formally, 'and I thank Leif, but I am not inclined to marry at present. I wish to stay with my brother for a while, since I have newly found him.'

Olafr looks regretful at my reply but nods his acknowledgement of my decision. 'Take this then, little Sigrid,' he says, removing a thick gold ring from his finger and placing it in my palm, 'we three are rich indeed in our reunion and I will be richer still when your friend's ransom arrives!'

At dinner that evening I surreptitiously look at Leif's gleaming yellow hair and long moustache which he keeps well washed and combed, and I look at his bulging arm muscles, clinched with gold rings, and hope I have made the right decision. Despite my desire to stay with Aina and with Thorgils for now, I do not wish to be an old maid. I am not a young girl and I cannot turn down too many husbands.

Before bed I look at myself in a burnished plate and wind my loosened hair around my fingers. I have never thought of myself in this way before: as a woman that a man might ask for.

In the morning we stand on the beach and watch as the cover is thrown off *The Crane* and it slides on its rollers, thundering into the water, looking splendid there after Thorgils' hard work. Aina is standing some way off from me laughing with Ragnhild and I suspect, that despite my attempts at disapproving surveillance she waited for me to be fast asleep last night to creep out and danced naked as the *völva* told her to. Leif is one of the men standing on the beach, waiting to board. I step to his side and touch his sleeve to gain his attention.

'Lady?'

'May Thor protect your journey, Leif,' I say shyly. 'I thank you for the honour you did me . . . asking for me.' I look down, faltering. Perhaps I should have said nothing. 'But I need to spend time now being a sister, before I can think of being a wife.' I look up at him now and there is a silence between us before he speaks.

'Then in time I may ask for you again,' he says.

I give him a small smile and move towards Aina. Olafr reaches her before me and with irony in his voice, he wishes Aina happiness in her future marriage, tells her that she is a maiden for kissing and suddenly takes her in his arms, pressing a long kiss to her mouth. Aina struggles in his embrace, pushing at his shoulders and I move towards them, planning to intercede but Olafr releases her just before I reach them. She is breathless and flustered, her mouth puffy and reddened. She raises a hand to slap him and I catch her elbow and tuck her hand firmly under my arm. 'Fare well, Olafr,' I say to him, and he laughs loudly at both of us as he balances up the oar, boarding the ship. We watch *The Crane*'s hull slice smoothly through the sea and Olafr, and Leif with him, sail from view.

I am relieved to see over the next few days that Aina does not seem to pine at Olafr's absence. At dinner, Thorgils mentions her betrothal.

'I do *not* wish to marry Guy,' Aina says sulkily. 'I hope he doesn't pay the stupid ransom.'

'No you don't,' Thorgils tells her bluntly. 'If your Lord Guy does not pay then Olafr will get his price for you another way and you'll like it even less.' I see fear creep over her face then, and no doubt she is remembering my tale of how Olafr's own mother had been sold as a bed-slave, even though she was a queen. Thorgils studies her face for some time. 'In Norway we do not marry off our women against their wishes and if a marriage does not work we divorce.'

'Well, that is very sensible,' she says, raising her eyebrows defiantly to me, as if it were my fault that she is betrothed to Guy. All I have done is try to get her to see reason, to accept the inevitable with dignity instead of petulance.

In the morning I wake to a glorious sunrise over the sea and mist coming off the surface of the water. I offered to Thorgils and Ragnhild that I would assist with the weaving of the new sail but Aina screwed her nose up hearing my suggestion. She has no patience for hours of weaving and will aim to avoid it. I walk down to the landing beach and she is there at the water's edge skipping stones. She points at dense underwater kelp wafting in the shallow waters and the bobbing heads of seals, out in the swell. Some days on the island we see porpoises and dolphins leaping the waves in graceful arcs or white dangling jellyfish and pink lobsters in the water, crabs climbing rocks on the beach. Yellowheaded gannets swoop and black choughs stroke the thermals with broad fingered wings. 'I love my prison!' Aina shouts to me above the wind, her arms flung wide.

'I need to worship my God,' Aina says to Thorgils this morning. 'May I have your permission to pray at the altar in the small chapel in the woods?'

He considers and then nods. 'You're not Christian, are you Sigrid?' he asks.

'No, brother,' I say. 'I refused to abandon Thor and Odinn, but I will accompany Aina for her devotions.'

'To stand by Thor and Odinn in these late days is to be a dog howling in the wilderness, it seems,' says Thorgils.

The small chapel amongst the trees is still mostly intact. We sit near the altar in the dark wood pews looking at the colourful stained glass windows and Aina bows her head in prayer for some time. 'I prayed that God will comfort my mother,' she tells me. Outside in the graveyard, generations of monks' graves are starkly marked with rows of brown wooden crosses. Aina walks around looking at the names and dates scratched there. 'Hundreds of Christian men worshipped and lived here before the coming of your countrymen,' she says. There are inscribed stones set along the paths to the chapel but I cannot divine the meaning and see that these are not runes put here by the current occupants but come from the earlier Christian inhabitants. 'I think some is Latin,' Aina tells me and reads out: 'All you who walk past, pray for the soul of Cadwagn. But I can't decipher most of it.'

We walk back past the beach and stop to watch Thorgils at work, standing astride an oak log, swinging an adze skilfully to shape a new stem for *The Orm*. Beside him, his tool chest is open, and curious, we admire the array of saws, rasps, axes, gouges, chisels and hammers, neatly arranged within it. 'I can make you anything in wood, sister,' Thorgils tells me, pausing to wipe the sweat from his eyes, 'from a spoon to a house.'

'Let's start with a spoon, then,' Aina laughs. 'Sigrid loves porridge.'

That evening when Thorgils and I are alone together, staring into the fire, he tells me he was married a few years back to a young woman in Viken named Hildr. 'I am haunted by one mistake, Sigrid. I knew Hildr was with child at the beginning of the summer but I chose to follow Olafr viking to increase our wealth. My homestead was remote and we had no thralls or slaves then to keep her company. She was alone when she tried to birth our child and alone when she died. I dug her grave near the cliff's edge and buried her with her wool combs and loom weights. I put her beads and a filigree gold pin I gave her on our wedding day beside her on the cold earth on a square of blue cloth. She was only twenty, Sigrid, and our daughter never saw the sky or the sea. The child was so tiny I could hold her cold body with her head nestled in one hand and her perfect toes in the bend of my arm.' He holds out his big hand, cupped, to show me where the baby's head had fitted and draws a finger to mark at his elbow where the child's feet had rested. 'I was sorrow-clenched Sigrid. I laid the baby gently in the grave, in the crook of Hildr's arm.'

'I'm so sorry Thorgils.' I sniff and wipe my eyes, reaching up a hand to wipe a tear from his cheek too as it trickles towards his sandy beard.

'Hildr made this tunic for me while I was away and she nurtured our child in her womb. I found it folded neatly at the foot of the bed where she and the child lay pale and dead.' He tugs at the garment, seeming to notice for the first time that it is threadbare and has a hole at one elbow.

'Did you name the child?' I ask. He shakes his head. 'Perhaps you should and carve both their names on a rune stick?'

He looks at me with interest. 'You give her a name, Sigrid. You are her aunt.'

I think carefully. 'We should call her Ingemar Thorgilsdottir.' It had been the name of our mother who I never knew.

'Hildr and Ingemar. I will carve the runes. You're right, always right, little Sigrid. You used to irritate me in our childhood with your precocious wisdom and unwelcome advice to your much bigger brother! Like an old scold in the body of a five year old.' I laugh with him but see the pain still trying to pretend it is past in his eyes. 'Sigrid the Deep-Minded,' he says affectionately and the name sticks to me even more so because Aina finds it amusing to call me that, especially at times when I am trying to give her good advice that she intends to ignore.

'We hold deep-minded women in great esteem,' Tofa scolds when Aina teases me with the name, 'unlike flightly Frankish princesses.'

Thorgils and his *drengir* set sail to raid on the mainland, burning the great cathedral up the coast at Saint Davids, bringing back more gold and silver booty and towing oak beams to mend the ships, but no more slaves as there are enough. 'Our way is wolfish. We need to keep our sword-arms in use,' he says, giving Aina and I each a gift of jewellery from his haul.

One morning Toki Barelegs comes at a run into the hall and shouts up its length to Thorgils, 'Lookout's sighted an enemy boat!'

Thorgils runs out and we rise and follow him, watching his swift progress up the hill to stand beside the lookout, shielding his eyes. 'It's just one small craft, bearing a white flag. A parlay,' he tells us, striding down again past us and moving towards the beach where a boat is approaching, still small on the horizon. There are just four men on board, short in stature and dark-haired. They look around them nervously at the tall Norse, their hands on their dagger hilts. Two stay with the boat and two come on to the longhouse to speak with Thorgils, one leading a donkey loaded with beautifully carved wooden chests, which we glance at curiously under our eyelashes.

As we wend in procession up the path, one of the slave girls working in the woods suddenly breaks away from the work party with a joyful yelp and comes running towards the dark-haired Bretar who is leading the donkey. Toki draws his whip and looks ready to berate her but I see that the two know each other, and stay his arm. At first Toki looks down at my hand fiercely but then remembers himself, that I am his *drottinn*'s honoured sister and he nods to me and puts his whip back in his belt. The girl has her arms laced around the man's neck and is sobbing and speaking fast in the Bretland tongue. The man looks around him fearful and unsure what to do.

'Allow her to come with us,' I say to Thorgils who nods his agreement. I hold out my hand and the Bretar man gently unlaces the girls' arms and she takes my hand. I hear her swift breathing and feel the fast pulse of her blood in my palm.

In the hall when they have been offered ale, and Thorgils is seated on the high seat with the two visitors before him, the man who had been greeted so ecstatically by the slave girl speaks. 'I bring greetings from King Maredudd ab Owain of Gwynedd, Deheubarth and Dyfed.' His Norse is terrible but we have the general idea of what he is saying. 'King Maredudd offers you silver not to raid his kingdom.'

'How much silver?'

The man gestures and the second man brings forward the chests and opens them. They are both filled to the brim with silver coins.

Thorgils raises his eyebrows.

'This is one silver penny from every person in the kingdom,' the man tells him, 'as tribute to you, Jarl Thorgils.'

'Kind gift,' Thorgils says, 'but I have many mouths to feed here and ships to repair.'

The man nods. 'King Maredudd asks if you will come to him when his court rests at Milford, the haven at the mouth of the Cleddau, and there will be more to discuss to your advantage if you will live alongside us in peace and not raid and burn our towns and churches more.'

Thorgils is silent considering and then pronounces his agreement to this bargain. Toki and Gormr remove the chests and Thorgils confirms that he will accept King Maredudd's invitation to a parlay at Milford soon and bids the two men farewell. I see the man's eyes go in grief to the slave girl.

'Brother,' I say softly. I do not wish to undermine him in front of his men or these visitors, but he knows what I am thinking.

He puts a hand up to stay the two men who are preparing to leave and beckons to the girl to come forward. 'What is your name?'

'Elen, Lord.'

'Do you know this man?'

She nods, and then speaks up. 'I was betrothed to him before I was taken and came here two years ago, master.'

Thorgils considers them both and for a longer time, considers me. 'Do you hold to this betrothal?' he asks the man.

'I do, Jarl, yes,' the man speaks fast, looking wildly back and forth between the girl and Thorgils.

'Take her then. I free you Elen. Take care of her,' Thorgils says and looks to me.

I smile broadly at him and then at the girl who has seen that it was me who interceded for her. She throws herself to her knees embracing my legs, sobbing. 'Thank you.'

I raise her up and give her hand to the Bretar man, who looks shocked and happy and we accompany them down to the boat.

'I can always change my mind about raiding again, next year,' Thorgils tells me as we watch the Bretar boat sail out of the bay, and I wave to Elen and her man. 'And I can't free too many slaves, Sigrid.'

'You should free them all,' I say, uncompromising, my mouth a tight line.

'Tell me about Norway,' Aina begs Thorgils at night in the hall. She asks many questions but she is learning Norse rapidly.

'There are many thousands of islands off the coast of the mainland and the waters squirm with fish, large and small, jostling each other. Tall, thin pine trees curve their skirts just above the ground and line the long, slender waters of the fjords. Silver rivers run straight in deep ravines. Norway is a landscape of wolves and sea-eagles,' Thorgils says and Aina's eyes glint silver-grey in the candlelight. 'The sea-eagles create a mound of shit at the edge of the sea before they set off into the void so that it will be a marker to them on their return, to guide them home.'

'I hope you don't do the same!' says Aina and he laughs long with her, slapping the table, his eyes watering.

When he has recovered from laughing, Thorgils tells her, 'In the summer, the light does not fade from the sky and the sun and the moon stand together in full view.' Aina shakes her head in wonder. 'But as winter comes on the sunrays brood low near the horizon and we see little light for many months, snow and ice grip the land and our lungs, our thighs are red and chapped with the freezing winds.'

'Is that horrible, so dark?'

'No,' Thorgils says insouciantly. 'You can see to move about by the light of a million stars and moonlight. Many babies are made during the winter.'

Aina smiles, her eyes cast down at the table.

The following morning I find Thorgils has been teaching Aina *fupark* – our runic alphabet, and he is trying to tell her how to make a kenning in *drottkvaett* poetry. 'What's this one? River-bone,' he asks her.

'An animal's bone in the river?'

'No, no. It's a stone. River-bone, stone. See? How about corpse dew?'

'Blood?'

'Yes! You're getting the hang of it. Necklace support?'

Aina shrugs and shakes her head.

'Woman,' says Thorgils, as if it were obvious. 'One more: foe of boughs.'

Aina frowns and then exclaims: 'Fire!'

'*Right.*' Thorgils is nodding enthusiastically. 'You try one for me.'

Aina screws up her nose and one eye, pondering hard. 'Hawks' stand?'

'Arm!' She is laughing and nodding. 'That's good, very good, Lady Aina. Poetry is Odinn's mead.'

'And blood-thirsty is best,' says Aina, who drank in all of Half-rod's poetic performances at the feasts while Olafr was still here, 'and verses should be about war, sailing or gold.' She stands and holds her arms to her side, looking up at the ceiling, her cheeks and neck are flushed pink, her wine-red hair swings loose behind her. She draws a great breath and pitches her clear voice to resound the length of the hall:

> 'The song of the spears
> Brings the ravens to feast.
> Snake sword bites down on skin.
> The shields smash into faces.
> Corpse liquid drips from hair bowls.
> The eaglets sup on eyes.
> Wolves wade red there,
> Where corpses pile the field.'

'Hmm,' Thorgils raises one sandy eyebrow comically, 'well perhaps we will make a skald-maiden of you.'

At dusk the seabirds gather in great rafts off the coast waiting to come back to their nests under cover of darkness to conceal their secret entrances from the predators. Other birds whirl feeding on late insects. The puffins gossip on the cliff tops tapping their orange, yellow and blue bills together and making strange groaning sounds. As the sun falls below the cliff edge, the night island begins to emerge: a rush of wings, birds crying out like lost souls in the pitch darkness of moonless nights, brilliant tracks of glow worms in the air and an owl's yellow eyes in a tree. If it has been raining a sliver of moon shows the path covered in big olive-coloured toads that we have to step around carefully. On clear nights the vast expanse of black sky is freckled with stars and you can twist around and around, and crane your neck and not manage to see it all. And always there is the perpetual shifting of the sea.

# 16

# Charroux

## June, 989

'Guy, I know you cannot undertake it now, but I want you to know that I earnestly wish to accept Audebert's offer of marriage if he should make it to you again during your visit to Charroux.'

Guy nodded but Adalmode knew he was distracted by a great many other cares and preparations for his journey and did not press her point further. He knew her heart and that was enough. Guy had been summoned by Archbishop Gunbaldus of Bordeaux to be in attendance whilst a special council of bishops met to discuss peace at Charroux Abbey, in Audebert's lands. She and Guy had never been forced to encounter their father's wrath at their disobedience when Adalmode went to Brioude. Guy came to fetch Adalmode back with the news that their father lay dangerously ill. Gerard died a few days after her return at midwinter, before the beginning of the Christmas feasting and Guy took on the Viscounty, along with the terrible news of the kidnap of his betrothed wife by Viking raiders at Saint Michel en l'Herm.

With her father recently dead, and Guy weighed down with so many new responsibilities, she knew it was too soon for her brother to think of arranging her marriage. No ransom demand had come for Aina. Guy in Limoges, and Lady Melisende in Ségur, waited in great anxiety, hoping that the riders Guy sent to the Norman court might bring them some comforting news of her. Although Adalmode dearly wanted the opportunity to see

Audebert, she had agreed to stay in Limoges to manage Guy's household in his absence, during this visit to Charroux.

The narrow road into Charroux was lined either side with high stone walls and the entry arch was topped with a high square tower looming above his head. Guy looked up and squinted at the sun glinting on a cockerel weather vane. The Archbishop had called this Peace Council in Charroux probably because it was one of the principal seats of Audebert of La Marche and everyone knew the main threat of war and violence might well be coming from that direction.

The Benedictine monks at the Abbey bustled around greeting their visitors, finding room for them in the guest house and for their horses in the stables. This Abbey, with its cloisters set around neatly laid out herb gardens, had been built by Guy's ancestor, Roger of Limoges, two hundred years before, a fact that he should record in his Annals. Guy intended to go and look at the wonderful relic that Charlemagne himself had bestowed on the Abbey: the foreskin of Christ. Charroux and its Abbey had become part of the holdings of the Count of La Marche only sixty years ago when the Capetian king Rudolph created that county. Guy's father had regarded the Counts of La Marche as upstarts who had leached yet more property rightly belonging to Limoges, but despite the enmity there had been between the two families, Guy found himself liking Audebert. In any case, now he was Viscount, he intended to deal with how things were at present and not with how things had been. Audebert was a major force in the region. It would be a good alliance for Adalmode to marry him, and it would bring closure to the feud between the families since Helie's attack on Brosse and the blinding of Benedict.

Guy moved through the Abbey Refectory, greeting people he knew and being introduced to others as the new Viscount. He strained to remember their voices, listen to news, feeling vulnerable without Adalmode at his side. All the lords of the Poitou were gathered there and many others besides. The bishops: Gilbert of Poitiers, Frotarius of Périgueux, Abbo of Saintes, Hugh of Angoulême and Guy's brother, Hildegaire Bishop of Limoges – they were all gathered for the Council and there was much talk of the End of Time and the need for all to purge themselves of sin in readiness. There were other clergymen from monasteries in the region. Many had brought the relics of their patron saints to the Council and these were reverently given temporary housing in the Abbey Church.

Cadelon, Viscount Aulnay, brother to the Duke's mistress, Aldearde, greeted Guy. 'What do you think of it?' he said. 'It strikes me that it is not the business of priests to be dispensing laws and justice, interfering with our traditional and long-held rights. They think to cow us by rattling saints' bones at us!'

'Perhaps some have abused these rights too greatly for too long,' Guy said.

Cadelon frowned, not getting the response he wanted and moved on. Guy's brother Hildegaire approached. He had put on more weight and was a hulking presence in a splendid red silk robe. 'What do you think of the Duke's son?' he asked. 'He looks to be as weak as his father, both of them ruled by the iron fist of a woman, Duchess Emma.' Hildegaire kept his voice low, jerking his head slightly towards the Duchess' party who stood with Archbishop Gunbaldus. 'It's not what we need here at a time like this with a Capetian newly on the throne, one who looks towards Aquitaine and the Limousin as new spoils for himself, eh?'

Guy shrugged. 'We must hope that the Duke's son is more like his mother and that King Hugh Capet is kept busy in the north with the fractious lords there,' he said diplomatically. Now that he was here, he sorely wished he had brought Adalmode. It was a struggle to ensure his eyesight did not betray him into some grave error. He heaved a sigh of relief, blooming into a smile, recognising the shout, and eventually the face of his brother, Aimery. Hildegaire lifted a hand in benediction and moved off to more important conversation. Guy and Aimery clasped each other with real affection and Aimery cheerfully gave Guy a commentary on their neighbours milling around them.

'Viscount Acfred of Châtellerault is standing there, see, with the Viscount of Maillezais and his brother, Odalric who are rumoured to be in great dispute with their younger brother,

Alduin. No doubt the dispute has something to do with the vast sums of money exchanging hands for the building of the Duchess' great Abbey in their vicinity.'

Aimery raised his eyebrows in query and Guy nodded agreement that this seemed likely. He looked in the direction that his brother was indicating but aside from Aimery himself, standing close to him, the Refectory held a sea of indistinguishable faces, clothes and noise for Guy.

'That's the new Viscount of Thouars,' Aimery said, indicating a different direction and Guy shifted his head and gaze as indicated. 'Aldearde's son you know,' Aimery said, a quizzical note in his voice. Guy wondered along with many others there, whether the Viscount of Thouars was in fact the son of the Duke of Aquitaine rather than her first long-suffering husband Arbert.

'And,' said Aimery, hurriedly, under his breath, 'Here is Hugh, Sire of Lusignan, bearing down upon us, who has built a great castle fit for a king on his lands, much to the irritation of the Duchess.'

The brothers exchanged polite greetings with Hugh. 'These priests are more interested in protecting their lands and treasure chests than in peace,' he said, but getting only diplomatic responses from Guy, he too moved off to accost the Duchess herself.

Guy listened carefully to Aimery's sketches of the Poitou nobility and to the conversations around him. Many men were sceptical of the Council and the intentions of the bishops. The new Count of Angoulême was there. His father, Lady Aldearde's second husband, was gravely sick and ceding his title to his son, had entered the monastery of Saint Cybard's.

'The news is that the old Count of Angoulême will die at Saint Cybard's soon,' said Aimery. 'His son has taken Fulk of Anjou's sister, Gerberga, as his wife.'

'Yes,' Guy said. 'I was at Angers for Fulk's coronation when that betrothal was announced.' The brothers raised their eyebrows together but said nothing. The match had made many of the Poitou lords uneasy. The Anjou-La Marche alliance now seemed to corral them within a long, curving flank from Angers in the north through La Marche, Périgord and now Angoulême.

Only the Touraine and Tours interrupted the noose of Fulk and Audebert's allegiances around Poitiers, and Limoges too was in the path of that curve. The recent Viking raid on the Poitou coast which Aina had been so grievously caught up in, had shown the backs of the Poitevins were also still exposed at the Atlantic seaboard.

The Duke of Aquitaine's heir, shouldered through the throng of men, his shortness and stoutness compared to many of them noticeable as they made way for him. 'I'll see you later,' Aimery said hastily, moving off. Guillaume stepped to Guy's side. The bray of voices raised in greetings and exclamations around them was so loud they had to stand close to hear each other and Guy at a gangling height above Guillaume had to bend to his voice. 'Congratulations Viscount on your accession.'

'Thank you Lord Guillaume.'

'I hope it is clear to you, Viscount,' said Guillaume, 'that I am strongly opposed to any marriage between your sister Adalmode and Count Audebert.' Guy inclined his head, not looking at the youth. Damn! He had hoped to evade this subject altogether and it was the only thing the Duke's son had to say to him. All he could do was buy time, let the topic march in one spot for a while, and hope he could resolve it according to Adalmode's wishes. He said nothing in response to Guillaume's statement, and politely made an excuse to move away, saying that he must give greeting to their host, Abbot Adalbald.

Audebert smiled wryly to himself, surveying the visitors to this 'Peace' council. It was a copy of another such council called by Fulk's uncle, Bishop Guy, in the Auvergne. Bishop Guy was up to his neck himself in Fulk's military intentions and these meetings merely provided opportunities to discuss strategy. Audebert had left his brothers in charge of his holdings, Boson at Roccamolten and Gausbert at Bellac. Since he had inherited two counties his lands were extensive and the business of managing them, dispensing justice, improving his fortifications, building up his army kept him busy, moving back and forth between his castles. He installed his youngest brother, Martin, as aide to the Bishop in Périgueux, and he was as much a soldier as the rest of the siblings. Audebert knew he could rely on his brothers to keep his men training and his network of information active. He noticed Adalmode's brother Guy as the crowd moved and opened for a moment but could not see her there. He moved towards Guy but there was no sign of her.

'Might I speak with you on the matter of your sister?' asked Audebert.

'It is too soon now, after our father's death, to discuss such a matter.'

'Of course,' Audebert said graciously, although he could not keep his disappointment from his face. 'May I visit Limoges in a month's time?'

'Please do,' Guy said vaguely and moved off. Audebert had assumed her brother would be supportive of their marriage and looked after him perplexed. War was coming and he needed to get his marriage concluded before that happened. He would wait a few weeks, rather than a month, before he rode to Limoges.

Guillaume sat silent, listening to the men at the table and his mother arguing, with Archbishop Gunbaldus making the occasional interjection to calm the discussion or decide on the order of who should speak when. His mother had insisted on representing his father who was sick again, and she had no difficulty at all in contending with these men and making her views known, and so he, Guillaume, was effectively muted.

The discussions began stormy with Audebert of La Marche vexed that the measures seemed aimed at him. 'You forget, that it was my brother, who was wont to blind priests and plunder churches, and not I,' he shouted angrily. 'Do you see me committing any such crimes?'

The Archbishop held up a pacifying hand and mollified the Count so that discussion could continue calmly. At the end of a long day, with scant provision of wine Guillaume thought, the bishops reached agreement that non-combatants who could not defend themselves, that is the peasants and the clergy, would be granted immunity from violence and that excommunication would be the punishment for anyone attacking or robbing a church, robbing peasants, or robbing, striking or seizing a priest or clergyman. Audebert insisted on an addition to the terms so that they read 'a priest or clergyman who was not bearing arms.' The clerks scratched out the copies of the agreement and Guillaume listened, his teeth on edge, to the unpleasant and prolonged noise of the scribing.

Archbishop Gunbaldus lifted the document to read it to the assembly in a resounding voice. 'Splendid is the name of peace!' he began, 'as the venerated Bishop Hilary of Poitiers himself declared many generations before us. My lords we must consider the Court of Heaven! The evils that have fouled the fair countenance of the holy church of God will be struck down by anathemas!'

Guillaume considered that this part could turn out to be long-winded and hoped the rumbling of his stomach could not be heard by his neighbours over the Bishop's words.

The hubbub of agreement died down and the Bishop continued. 'We have assembled to root out the criminal actions – the *noxia* – that have sprouted up through evil habit in our dioceses. We have reached an historic concord that we shall all swear to uphold on our knees before the marvellous relic of Charroux Abbey – the Holy Prepuce.'

Guillaume suppressed a smirk. Christ's foreskin was rumoured to be in several other places too. There was no knowing whose foreskin it was that they were bowing and scraping to in this Abbey. The churchmen and nobles filed past, signing their names and making their marks on the parchment. His name should have been there too, but his mother preempted him again.

Still at last the feast could get under way and Guillaume's stomach would be filled and perhaps the wine would flow more now that peace had been reached. Guillaume was seated at the trestle below the High Table on the dais where Audebert presided. Guillaume should have been allowed to handle this important Council meeting on behalf of his father now that he was twenty, but his mother insisted she would represent the Duke. She, instead of Guillaume, sat at the High Table in the place of honour, next to the Archbishop, surrounded by the splendidly dressed bishops.

Guillaume rose from the feasting and walked unsteadily towards his bedchamber late that night. He was a little the worse for wine perhaps. His costly purple and blue robes did not conceal his rotund figure. In the bedchamber a girl was waiting for him, his latest attempt to find a serving wench with at least some semblance of Adalmode about her. She was seated on his bed, wearing a white shift, one naked foot swinging above the floor. The swinging stopped when she looked up and saw him in the doorway and she faked a smile in his direction. Yes, from here there was something of Adalmode about her – blonde hair, green eyes, but she was too young, too skinny, her skin too pale he realised, as he came closer. He scowled and saw a flash of fear on the girl's face. Well that was something at least.

'Wine!' he said, and she stood quickly to pour him wine from a jug on the small table next to the bed. As she bent to her task her skinny shanks were visible through the thin covering of her shift. Nothing at all like Adalmode. Guillaume sat on the bed, on the warm patch where the girl had been sitting and took the wine goblet from her. 'Shoes.' She knelt and took off his shoes, looking up for her next instruction. 'More wine.' He felt bored with her already. She refilled the goblet and Guillaume saw her hand was shaking as she held the jug, from its weight or from fear of him? She put the jug down and stepped back.

Guillaume thought of his mother this evening, speaking with the Bishop and the other nobles as if *she* were the Duke, embarrassing him with her disagreements. He stated his opposition to the continuing acceptance of Hugh Capet as King, since the man was an upstart, but his mother reminded him, in front of everyone gathered there, that Hugh's wife, Queen Adelaide was his aunt, his father's sister, and was he not proud of that, she asked him loudly. Why should he be? What had a woman to do with the matter? She was merely a breeding ground for a man's heirs.

He had been slowly and carefully unfolding his thoughts to Count Fulk of Anjou on methods of building in stone, and the Count he thought was listening with a fascinated expression when his mother suddenly retorted, 'Oh for goodness sake, Guillaume! Get to the point. If we all have to listen to you meandering forever these new stone buildings you speak of will be lying in ruins, overgrown with grass and weeds like the monuments of the Romans!'

He watched, silently furious, as Fulk suppressed a smile. The Count of Anjou was a boy, younger than he, and his mother shamed him before this youth. Oblivious to the serving girl standing in front of him, Guillaume clenched his teeth and screwed up his face imagining himself forcing a gag into his mother's wrinkled mouth.

'Lord?' the girl said in a quavering voice, thinking the anger on his face was a response to her.

He could take it out on her. He had done it on a few occasions before with other serving wenches. This one might be a virgin like the others, found for him by his steward. He could hurt her. Make her cry and send her back to her father soiled and dishevelled with silver coins in her palm, but Guillaume suddenly felt deflated. He would be Duke soon! He would be all powerful and yet his mother and other men laughed at him and he had nothing he wanted.

He had a sudden idea. He could go on pilgrimages – often, long ones. His mother would not wish to accompany him due to the pain she suffered in her joints. The idea grew on him. It was genius. He could be rid of her and he could appear then before other men as a Duke's heir, rather than as his mother's mewling son which was always the effect of her presence. He would plan a journey right away to Rome and begin creating his own allegiances along the way, unencumbered by her.

'Just get out,' he said, waving a hand at the girl. 'Get out.'

'Lord?' Her expression was bewildered.

'Get out before I change my mind.'

She was out the door faster than a frightened hind leaping from its cover in the thicket, and as she disappeared in a flurry of white shift and blonde hair, Guillaume imagined that he glimpsed Adalmode fleeing from him.

# 17

## Poitiers

### Easter 990

It was over a year since Guy had received the terrible news of Aina's kidnap by Vikings and continued to suffer the disappointment of his long thwarted marriage. They heard rumours of a lady held hostage by Vikings who had raided an Aquitainian monastery which might be Aina, but still there was no definite news that she lived or a ransom demand. Adalmode sat next to Guy at the trestle, watching the bustle of the morning hall. Their mother and unwed sisters, Aldiarde and Calva, had gone to live in Aimery's household and for now, Adalmode did service as the lady of Guy's household. 'We are a sorry old maid and an old bachelor, Guy.' She and Guy had been expecting a visit from Audebert for some months now, since her brother's encounter with him at Charroux, but he had not arrived and they received no news of him. 'But Aina will be returned to you soon, I know she will.'

Guy smiled tightly. He was thirty-five and kept a mistress in a fine house in the city. There was a real affection between them and it could get difficult in that quarter if his betrothed wife were ever to be returned. Adalmode, on the other hand, was nearing thirty and had no means of the consolation that Guy was able to take.

'We must go to this Easter Assembly in Poitiers, Adalmode. We should set out tomorrow if we are to take the journey at a pleasant pace and stay a night in Ségur with Lady Melisende.'

Guy needed to gain confirmation of his succession to the Viscounty and to give his fealty to the Duke.

'I can't go with you Guy. What about the Duke's son Guillaume and this mooted marriage?'

'We won't let that happen,' he said, 'but I need your assistance in this visit. It will be our opportunity to gloss over any slight the Duchess has felt at your earlier failure to answer her summons, but we will stop short at agreeing to any marriage for you. I promise you this. If her son must have a Limoges girl to wife then it will have to be Aldiarde or Calva and not you.'

She nodded her agreement reluctantly.

The ride to Ségur took less than two hours but they stopped overnight so that Guy could do his best to comfort Aina's mother and assure Melisende her daughter was too precious a prize for the marauders to harm her. 'As soon as I receive the ransom demand I will pay it in a blink of an eye,' he said, 'and I *will* retrieve her.'

They found the Aquitaine court in turmoil, following the recent return of the Duchess. Anxious for his succession and the state of his health, the Duke had brought about another reconciliation with his wife. Emma had been in high dudgeon at her husband's debauchery and abandoned his court, but now Aldearde was wed to the Count of Angoulême and safely out of the way, the Duchess had deigned to return. The effect of her presence was felt by everyone. Her iron hand was on the tiller. She dismissed her husband's drunken doctor, Madelme, and retrieved back lands her husband had given to his friends. She formalised peace with several of the lords of Poitou whom her husband had been unable to quell. After the Peace Council at Charroux, her new Abbey at Mallezais was consecrated by the assembled bishops and the Duke gave Emma a very substantial gift of land to bestow on the new foundation. Now she had started to build another new abbey at Bourgeuil.

Adalmode watched Emma's face as she sat on the dais with the Duke, waiting for his pronouncement on Guy's request for the confirmation of his title. Adalmode remembered the vivacious, brown-haired young woman who had first spoken with her mother of betrothing her to the baby heir, sixteen years ago, and was shocked to see the tracks that time had left on

Emma's face. Or perhaps time was not the culprit. Guy always said the worst thing about being an unpleasant person, must be having to live with yourself. The Duchess' bitterness and anger were living on and under the seamed skin of her forehead and cheeks.

The Duke's heir, Guillaume, was transformed from the chubby, sticky boy Adalmode remembered into a strongly-built, well-padded, blond twenty year old who stared at length at her. He cannot want me still surely, she thought, I am an old woman to him now, nine years his senior. She felt discomfited by his stare and regretted coming to Poitiers.

'I will confirm your title to Limoges provisionally,' the Duke told Guy, 'but it was granted back to your family on condition that you marry Ademar's heiress and that condition still stands. If the girl is not returned by the pagans and the marriage does not take place I will have to reconsider.'

Guy bowed his head and they withdrew, talking as soon as they were out of earshot. 'We must be satisfied with this, Guy,' Adalmode told him as they walked from the hall, 'and we have to ensure that your marriage to Aina does take place.'

'We don't have a ransom letter from her abductors yet,' Guy said. 'We don't know who her abductors are even. Where she is. If she is still alive.'

'We will soon know all this and I'm sure she is alive.' Adalmode injected certainty into her voice to reassure her brother.

Lady Blanche had been reconciled with the Duke and Duchess, and was attending the Assembly and Adalmode gladly went to visit her friend in her chamber. Blanche's reception was warmly affectionate. 'But darling twenty-nine years old and the sun shines out of your beautiful face still, and yet you remain unmarried? How is this?'

'I am happy to keep company with my brother.' This was Adalmode's stock response to such enquiries but then looking into Blanche's affectionate face, she felt an urge to elaborate. 'You know that I love a man and he me, but my father would not countenance the marriage.'

Blanche leant forward avidly. 'Darling! *Still* the Count of La Marche?'

Adalmode hesitated but was there any need to be secret now? Wouldn't Guy agree to the marriage next time Audebert asked for her which he had every year for the last thirteen years. Adalmode sighed. When she first looked with desire at Audebert as a thirteen year old girl she had no idea she would wait the same number of years longing for him. 'Yes, still Audebert of La Marche and Périgord,' she told Blanche who clapped her hands together in delight.

'Darling, yes. He is gorgeous. I heard that he asked for you long ago and was refused. But *still*? He is still asking for you?' Blanche sounded doubtful and her expression had fallen. Adalmode knew what she was thinking. Why would Audebert not take a younger wife now.

'He . . .,' Adalmode faltered, suddenly uncertain herself. 'He asked for me last year, yes.'

'But darling,' Blanche said, 'surely now that he is aware your father has died?' Then seeing the distress on Adalmode's face she went on rapidly, 'Yes, of course, he is giving you time to grieve before he asks again. Will your brother agree?'

'I think so. We haven't spoken of it lately as he has had a lot of his own concerns with the kidnapping.'

'How lucky you are in your brother,' said Blanche. 'Mine cared nothing for my feelings in the marriages he traded me into. But tell me about the kidnapping, about these cruel Northmen.' She was avid again for the new topic.

After a while Adalmode took her leave and returned to the chamber she shared with Guy who was pacing up and down. 'I was waiting for you,' he began.

'What is it? Have you news of Aina?'

'No. Duchess Emma and her son, Guillaume, were here. You just missed them.'

'Good,' said Adalmode sitting on the edge of the bed.

'Adalmode, Guillaume is offering for you.'

She looked up at him blankly.

'In marriage,' Guy added. 'I didn't know what to say. I thanked them . . .'

'Guy, no,' Adalmode suddenly burst in realising what he was saying. 'You did not agree? You must not agree. You promised me.'

'No, I just thanked them and said I would discuss the proposal with you.'

'We must leave immediately.'

'What? We can't do that. The Duke will be greatly offended. They might take away the Viscounty, Adalmode. We *can't* do that.'

'Guy, as you love me, we must leave now. We must avoid it. Leave word that I am taken very ill.'

He raised his eyebrows.

'Guy you know how I feel about Audebert. You might give your permission now. You must!' Adalmode's voice was desperate.

He frowned but agreed to leave surreptitiously. They packed hurriedly and instructed the servants to discreetly bring the horses out into the courtyard. Night was falling and they could leave just before the city gates were closed and perhaps no one would know of it until the morning. Guy left an apologetic note for the Duke, to be delivered at noon the following day.

Adalmode walked swiftly from the doorway towards her horse, her hood raised over her hair. In her peripheral vision she saw two figures in the courtyard standing by the well: a man and a woman, but she kept her head down and her face concealed. She stepped into the stirrup and rose easily into the saddle, her motion inadvertently dislodging her hood. In the instant the hood fell back from her fair hair, the man and woman at the well turned and caught sight of her: Lady Blanche and young Lord Guillaume. Adalmode pulled her hood back into place and kicked her horse towards the gate but Guillaume stepped out and grasped her bridle.

'My Lady, you are riding out so late?' he asked, but addressed his question to Guy. Blanche approached, curious, and smiled up at Adalmode.

'My sister is unwell and I have decided to take her home,' Guy said staunchly. Blanche, who had seen Adalmode shortly before in the best of health, studied her with query in her eyes.

'I am sorry to hear that,' Guillaume said. 'Then will you give me an answer now?' he asked Guy.

Guy glanced at Adalmode. 'I cannot at present.'

Adalmode looked desperately to Blanche.

'Dear Adalmode is as a daughter to me, Lord Guillaume,' she said suddenly. 'Tell me of your question and perhaps I can help but do not delay her. You might injure her health.'

'I would not do that for anything,' he bowed gallantly to Adalmode, smiling. 'I would expand the waters of the Rhine to marry your beautiful "daughter," Lady Blanche,' the young man declared dramatically.

Adalmode's heart sank. She was trapped.

Blanche looked in surprise to Adalmode and saw in an instant the distress on her face and knew why. 'Ah but you must let the lady go now Lord Guillaume,' she said gently.

'Of course,' he said. 'I must obey the commands of two beautiful ladies.' His smile had become close to an angry sneer and his tone was petulant.

Adalmode and Guy rode out of Poitiers and Adalmode hoped fervently never to return or at least to return as the Countess of La Marche.

The ransom demand arrived soon after their return to Limoges and came by way of a messenger from the Duke of Normandy, who gave the hand of friendship to the pagans. Guy ripped open the letter. 'She lives!' he exclaimed, but then Adalmode watched a horrified expression develop on his face as he read on. '3,000 pounds of silver! Where am I to get such a sum?'

'Send word back quickly that you mean to pay a ransom for the lady, that you can only pay 1,000 pounds, but you can pay it now,' Adalmode said. 'They will rather have the coin quickly.'

'But even 1,000 pounds?'

'You send the reply and I will find the silver.'

The messenger set off with Guy's reply and Adalmode set a clerk to concentrate on the task of amassing the ransom. He emptied Guy's coffers and weighed that pile of silver. Melisende sent 500 pounds and Adalmode diverted all silver from the tolls and markets to this clerk. She combed through her chests and boxes and gave over to the clerk all of her own silver ornaments and coins too for weighing.

'A total of 992 pounds,' the clerk pronounced to Guy and Adalmode the following week.

Adalmode smiled brightly to Guy. 'So if they will negotiate we can send this very soon and regain her.'

The following week, the messenger returned with a refusal of the offer of 1,000 pounds and a restatement of the original 3,000 pounds of silver for Aina's release. The letter was signed Olafr Tryggvason. The Duke of Normandy enclosed a note of reassurance to Guy telling him this Olafr was a member of a Norwegian royal clan, he would treat Lady Aina well, but Guy should not delay in paying the ransom.

'No wife and no heir, Guy,' Hildegaire said to him, over dinner. 'You should draw up a testament making me your heir as a safeguard. To be sure that the viscounty stays with our family, after father fought so hard to regain it.'

'No need for that at present,' Guy said irritated.

'The clerk and I will start working on what we can sell of lands and rights,' said Adalmode, 'and I will send requests to all the Abbots and Lords hereabouts for donations to help us.'

Their sales were more profitable than the requests and now the coffer weighed out at 2,000 pounds of silver. Guy kept it under his bed and set two guards on his door day and night. He sent a fast messenger to the Duke of Normandy asking that Olafr Tryggvason accept 2,000 pounds for the return of his betrothed wife.

No word had come from Audebert and Adalmode decided she had to act. 'Lord Audebert,' she wrote, 'my father has died and my brother would look kindly on a match between us, but Guillaume, heir to Aquitaine has offered for me. I beg you to renew your offer now and quickly if you still mean it. If you are long past wanting me to wife, tell me so and I intend, in that case, to take a nun's veil.'

Adalmode set down her stylus and read back her words. She had not seen him for so long. Perhaps their marriage was just a fantasy of youth now to him. Perhaps he never thought about her anymore. He could be negotiating for another bride somewhere.

217

Guillaume rode through the sun-streaked forest, staring morosely at the ram-rod straight back of his mother riding ahead of him. The woman was impossible. The first time she left his father over his affair with Aldearde, and took him away from Poitiers with her, he had been too young to offer resistance. His mother ruled all around her with an imperious presence and her certainty of a God-given rightness in her decisions and actions. She had screamed at his father, 'You gulp down sin like vintage wine! Your head is whit-ening as you sit upon a throne stained from top to bottom with adultery!' They had only been returned to the court of Aquitaine for two weeks when his mother discovered her husband was still sneaking away to consort with his mistress and so here they were, leaving again, on the way to his uncle's holdings in Blois.

'I am the political glue connecting the two great houses of Blois and Poitiers, who have oftentimes been in conflict in the past,' Emma told her son. 'I adopted and accepted that role through a negotiated agreement, which involved both parties contracting into marriage as it is understood by the Church, in order to foster peace and reconciliation and to strengthen both our kin. Your father, despite my entreaties to him and my tears, has not upheld his side of the contract and that sacred duty and has therefore weakened and well-nigh eradicated my ability to continue to be that glue. I must do as God bids me. I have prayed and he bids me take the path that I am taking.'

Guillaume resisted this time. 'I am sorry for your pain, mother,' he told her, 'but I will remain here at court with my father. I need to learn my business for the future and perhaps I can prevail upon Father to obey his marriage vows in your absence.'

'You will *not* remain here,' his mother retorted. 'I will not leave you amongst debauchery at your impressionable age. Your saddle bags are packed and you will accompany me now.'

He attempted further remonstrance but the maids sat in the corner tittering behind their hands at his mother's tongue-lash-ing and in the end it seemed he would save more face if he did as he was told. Now as he rode behind her, which was after all not correct – she should ride behind him, he wished he had simply dug in his heels or appealed to his father that he might stay at court. His mother both impressed and repulsed him. When he was small, he tried to love her but she turned his love away, telling him not to be girlish. Since she kept him in her retinue with no entourage of his own he had few male compatriots. Guillaume resolved to change the situation. He was the heir to Aquitaine. He was twenty-one! Of age! It was ridiculous really.

The group of riders were heavily guarded with a troop of his mother's ten best fighters, mercenaries recruited from the Northmen in Normandy. They were all huge and Guillaume felt inadequate in their presence, a good six inches shorter than all of them. They joked with him good-humouredly: 'You're well rounded, Lord Guillaume,' 'You're wearing your dinner well, Lord Guillaume,' but their jokes cut him to the quick. He wanted to be tall, hard and spare as they were. He was encumbered and embarrassed by the rolls of fat around his waist. His mother told him it would fall away as he grew older, but she was wrong.

Then there was the matter of Adalmode of Limoges rankling in his mind. Guillaume's mouth turned down at the corners thinking of it. When he succeeded his father he would be the richest and most powerful man in Aquitaine and such a chit had defied and so far evaded accepting his offer of marriage. He knew the stories of the Count of La Marche's repeated requests for Adalmode and her father's repeated denials. Could that be the reason? That renegade count, who his father said was the biggest threat to the coherence of the Duchy. All the other lords in Aquitaine gave his father their allegiance, some a little reluctantly and skimpily perhaps, but still all, except this Audebert, did so. Since he was a child Guillaume had looked on Adalmode as his betrothed wife and relished the thought of entering manhood, taking her to his bed and breast. He imagined it over and over. She would have to accept him. He and his mother were at least in agreement in that, but why had Adalmode not been more grateful for his attentions? She had not looked ill when she had ridden out of Poitiers evading his proposal. Indeed she looked splendid as usual. Guillaume's cock began to harden at the thought of her golden hair and her golden limbs in his bed, her pride and disinterest subsumed to his pleasure.

There was a shout up ahead and Guillaume tore himself away from his developing fantasy of Adalmode to see what was going on. The front horsemen had halted to make way for a small party of riders coming in the opposite direction and needing to pass them on the narrow road. Guillaume rode forward to have a look at them and heard his mother's voice raised in anger. 'You will halt and make way for *me*!'

The riders were three women, a noblewoman and two maids from the look of their clothing. Perhaps the women were good-looking. He moved closer to see. The noblewoman threw back her hood and revealed herself as Aldearde d'Aulnay. She was fifty-one, an ageing lady with fine cheekbones and still beautiful eyes, but her once brown hair was threaded with grey. Guillaume rather admired the affection between her and his father. That he had stuck to her so long, and as she aged, spoke of more than a sexual liaison. It suggested love and perhaps that was why his mother had such an unquenchable hatred for the woman. It was unusual for a lady of her stature to be riding without a male armed escort and then Guillaume realised why she was moving so secretly on this road. She must be on her way to meet with his father. Perhaps at the hunting lodge not far back on the road. His mother had also jumped to this surmise.

'You must rub my face in your sin!' his mother shouted.

Aldearde looked at Emma of Blois calmly. 'There is no call for this anger and abuse,' she said. 'I will be on my way in peace.'

'Abuse!' screamed his mother, standing in her stirrups, her face red, the cords of her neck taut and ugly. 'This is not abuse enough for your crimes, but I will see that you do receive the punishment you merit as a great whore.'

Guillaume swallowed. His father would convulse with anger at his mother for this display. Why could she just not let it go. Many noblemen had mistresses. Even Aldearde's husbands had taken her long affair with his father in good part.

'Mother,' he thought to intervene, 'let us . . .'

'Take her!' his mother commanded the mercenary leader. 'Take her and her maids and show them what it is to be a whore.' The man grinned.

Aldearde knitted her brow and then gasped, astonished, as two men hauled her from the saddle and others were giving her maids similar treatment.

'Mother!' Guillaume exclaimed, appalled. 'You cannot! Mother!'

His mother turned a face to him that he did not recognise, so distorted was it with fury and a horrible joy. 'Watch me,' she said. 'Watch or join in if you like, if you are man enough.'

Guillaume gulped on his shock. The mercenaries were dragging the screaming women into the woods. Briefly he considered the possibility of following them and at least taking one of the maids, but Lady Aldearde would tell his father of it. Controlling the nervous prancing of his horse, he heard their screams increase and then die out, leaving a disquieting silence, ruptured only by the occasional bird twitter.

'Mother, father will never forgive you for this.'

'I do not need his forgiveness. It is *he* who will go to hell for his fornications. My anger is virtuous, my zeal is righteous for I am fighting against evil.'

'And what of the Count of Angoulême? Aldearde's step-son. How will he react to such appalling treatment of her?'

'I care not,' she said. 'She has been punished for her crimes. Her husband should have burnt her for adultery.' There was a rustling of leaves ahead and Guillaume watched the Northmen emerge from the trees, brushing aside leafy branches, adjusting their hose and slapping each other on the back. 'Be quick, about it,' Emma called to them. 'Ride on,' she said to Guillaume.

Guillaume considered going to Lady Aldearde's aid but would his father see him as complicit with this terrible punishment meted out to his concubine? He was caught between his parents as usual and shrugged his shoulders. He kicked his horse, determining that his own marriage to Adalmode would be of a very different calibre. She would love him and bear him sons, and he would honour her with his fidelity. He restarted his fantasy, conjuring Adalmode with her golden hair and her green eyes before him again, telling him how dear he was to her.

# 18

# Limoges

## 990

Two weeks and Adalmode had received no reply from Audebert, nor had Guy received any offer for her. She was nearly thirty years old and Audebert thirty-five. He had to wait one year too many perhaps she said to herself, and grief welled up inside her at the thought that she would never have him as her husband. A messenger strode into the hall and Adalmode's heart beat fast as she watched Guy reading the letter. Was it from Audebert?

'It's from Paris,' Guy said, looking at her with a shocked face. Adalmode raised her eyebrows in query. She knew their brother Hildegaire had gone to Paris to a Council of Bishops there. It had been a scandal because Hildegaire had stripped Saint Martial Abbey of many fine gold and silver ornaments that he had taken with him to enhance the ostentation of his entourage, and the monks were in high anxiety whether they would ever see them again. 'Hildegaire has died,' Guy told her in a flat voice.

'Hildegaire? So young, so suddenly?' Adalmode reached for Guy's hand. They sat for some time in silence, remembering their brother, hunting through their memories of childhood and recent years amongst the bad for the few shards of good.

'The Abbey's treasure?' she asked.

'Hildegaire bequeathed it to Saint Denis in Paris, as intercession for his soul, as he lay dying.' Adalmode frowned at the image of her brother's desperation at the prospect of God's judgement, and at the consternation there would doubtless be at Saint Martial's at the news that their treasure was lost.

'Our brother, Hilduin, should be his successor,' Adalmode said eventually and Guy nodded. He rose to call for a clerk, but paused at the clatter of more hooves in the courtyard as new messengers or visitors arrived.

Adalmode rises slowly to her feet as Audebert strides up the hall, with his brothers, Gausbert and Boson, and ten of his men behind him. All of them wear partial armour, black leather jerkins and swords. They have clearly ridden hard and fast. Audebert's thick black hair is cut close to his head and his beard too is trimmed short. He stops at the edge of the dais looking up at her. She realises her mouth is open and slowly presses her lips together in a welcoming smile. Audebert's face is smeared here and there with dust from the road and amongst the grime his blue gaze is intense.

'Viscount Guy,' he nods briefly to her brother before turning his eyes back to her face. 'My lady.' His voice gentles after the momentum with which he entered the hall. 'May I speak with your sister?' Audebert asks Guy, without taking his eyes from Adalmode's own, and she hears Guy give his agreement.

He is going to tell me he cannot marry me, Adalmode thinks. If he had come to ask for me as his wife, he would just ask Guy now. Audebert reaches out a gauntleted hand to her and she places her slender white fingers on the gritty black leather and steps down to him. His men bow politely as she passes. They are all observing that I am an old woman, Adalmode thinks. She is conscious she is wearing her shabbiest gown, her faded red velvet, since today is wash day and all her best dresses are with the laundress.

Audebert leads her outside to the courtyard where servants and grooms are running around taking care of his horses, and as she had guessed, the sweat and foam on their flanks show the signs of a hard ride. 'My lord,' she says recovering her manners, 'I apologise. I have offered you no sustenance.' The grooms have the care of the horses well in hand and she does not doubt that Guy will see to the needs of Audebert's brothers and men. 'You have ridden hard and far?' She raises her eyebrows in query. 'Some wine?'

Audebert grips the shoulder of a boy passing with a pitcher of water for the horses, stopping him in his tracks. He takes the pitcher with both hands and drinks several gulps from it before handing it back and sending the boy on his way. She can feel Audebert's damaged, dangerous energy, cracking the air around them.

'Wine in a while, thank you, but I must have speech with you first.'

Adalmode's heart sinks again. Why else? He must be here to break off all hopes of marriage. I will have to take the veil she thinks, and that idea is swiftly displaced by grief engulfing her at the loss of this man.

'Is there a quiet place we can talk?'

'Yes,' she leads him towards the staircase to the battlements, desperately wondering how she can change his mind. She is not past childbearing yet, she will tell him. The sky is clear blue with a cool breeze. It will be pleasant on the ramparts. She goes ahead, emerging into the sunshine and the wind whips off her head veil. From the top step behind her, he laughs and leaps, trying to catch at the flimsy veil waving tantalisingly at them in the slight wind, but it slips through his gloved fingers and is gone. Adalmode stands with her hands gripping the battlements watching it fly and feels Audebert approach close behind her.

He turns her around to face him, his knee pressed to hers, and she smells the acrid sweat on him. He pulls off his gloves and lets them drop to the ground. He places both his hands on her head, slowly stroking down the length of her hair. 'Thread of gold,' he murmurs, and he leans to kiss the top of her head. She is suddenly a shy girl again, embarrassed by his admiration and by her own desire. He takes her hand and kisses it, holds her face in his hands. 'My love,' he says and Adalmode feels the years and the anxieties drop from her.

She smiles up at him. Their kiss is long and begins tentative and then becomes avid. His hands move on her breasts and hips. She pulls away from the kiss and sets to the difficult task of unlacing the sweat-hardened thongs of his jerkin.

'You have dust on your nose,' he says, wiping at it with his thumb.

'And you, my lord,' she says laughing, 'are covered in the stuff!'

He reaches into a pocket inside his jerkin and produces a crumpled but fine linen handkerchief. She takes it from him and wipes the smears from his cheeks and forehead, while he smiles at her.

'I was on campaign in the north with Fulk and your brother put me off at Charroux when I asked him about you. Your letter went first to Bellac and then came forward to me at a snail's pace,' he says. 'I came as soon as I read it. I am sorry, Adalmode, that I did not know and did not come sooner.'

She nods, making slow headway unlacing his jerkin.

Audebert sniffs. 'I need a bath.'

'I will arrange a bath for you later, Audebert.' She hesitates, but wants no pitying duty from him. She lays her hands flat on the leather jerkin, leaning into him. 'I would be an old wife to you now.'

'No!' he says, cupping her chin again. 'I love you Adalmode now, and since I first saw you. You kept me alive in that hole, looking at you, talking with you, gave me the strength to survive and now you are still so beautiful you take my breath away. Every time you came and looked down at me with these beautiful green eyes,' his finger gently traces her cheekbone, beneath her eye, 'you conjured visions of a rope hung down for me to climb out of there.'

'I lacked the courage to help you escape,' she confesses. 'I thought about it often, how I might take a rope long and strong enough from the stable and find a way to steal the key to the grate from the jailor's belt. But I was afraid that if you were caught escaping they would kill you.'

'No,' he said, 'you did not lack courage. If you had not given me hope and kindnesses, I might have taken a jagged rock one bitterly cold winter night and carved my own throat in my despair.'

Swiftly she placed her fingers on his mouth. 'No! Do not say such things. Here you are now. You survived that awful misery. Here *we* are.'

'Yes, and yet I do confess myself angry. Angry for our lost years together and for the lost years of my life. Someone will have to pay for this anger.'

'Think of anger another time,' Adalmode says, loosening the last loop of the jerkin's thong, so that it falls open. He is wearing no shirt beneath it. She places her hands on his exposed chest, traces the contours of his collar bones, twirls her fingertips through the swirls of thick black hair. His skin is brown from the sun and she imagines him moving around in the mornings amongst his war tents, bare-chested. She will ensure that Audebert never knows that his capture was Guy's idea. She softly bites her bottom lip looking at him. She is breathless as if she has run up the battlement staircase. She traces his hard stomach with the flat of her hand, and sweeps her fingertips lower towards the top of his breeches where a thin stripe of black hair rises towards his belly.

'Adalmode, will you marry me? I wanted to ask *you* and not your father or your brother.'

'Yes,' she smiles into the astonishing blue of his eyes. 'Yes, Lord Audebert of La Marche. I will marry you and no other. And Audebert, will you take me now?' She watches him digest this.

'Here? Now?' He looks around him.

She nods and forces herself to keep her eyes on his, despite her embarrassment. 'We have waited far too long already.' She catches her breath as he unlaces the front of her red gown, pulls the gown and loose chemise below her breasts and bends to suck hard at her nipple, one hand grasping her buttock. Washes of desire flicker and shiver on her skin and she grips her fingers into his hair. 'Wait,' she says, and points to where a guard stands with his back to them on the opposite side of the battlements. She holds her gown up against her breasts and pulls him towards the tower room at one corner of the battlements. The guards do not venture in here. It is where she used to come and dream of him as a girl when he was a prisoner, where she composed the contents of the baskets she dropped into the hole for him, and where she thought about what speeches she might make to give him hope and perhaps grow to like her, as she liked him.

Audebert looks around at the high stone room. There are streaks and dollops of bird shit here and there and feathers in the empty fire grate. 'Palatial!' he grins and then his face suddenly becomes serious and intent again. He unpins his cloak and lays it on the cleanest patch of ground, unbuckles his sword belt and wraps it around the scabbard neatly, leaning it against the wall.

She lets her gown fall again, exposing her breasts. He drinks in the sight of her, kisses her cheek and eyelids, picks her up, one hand flat against her back and the other hand beneath her buttocks, swinging her legs to either side of his hips. Still kissing her, he sinks to his knees and lays her head back gently on the cloak. Adalmode's legs are raised and parted and he kneels between them. She feels cool air as he pushes up the heavy layers of her skirts to expose her. She feels the palm of his hand run slowly over her stomach and then his mouth is on her skin. She grips his head with both her hands and draws short gasping breaths as his kisses rove over her. He sits back on his heels and looks in her face. She watches him hastily unlacing the thong of his breeches.

'Are you sure?' he asks.

'Yes, yes.'

Adalmode stood with Audebert and Guy at the door of the Abbey of Saint Martial. It was two weeks since Audebert's arrival in Limoges, and they had not repeated their physical union although Adalmode felt the desire gnawing at her whenever he was in her vicinity, and whenever he was not in her vicinity too. 'I give my consent that you take my sister, Adalmode of Limoges to wife,' Guy said formally. 'Do you consent to the marriage Lord Audebert?'

'Yes, I consent, and most gladly,' Audebert responded smiling warmly at Adalmode.

'Do you consent Adalmode?' Guy asked.

'Yes, I consent.' Overwhelmed, Adalmode wondered if life would ever feel mundane again.

Audebert looped her arm through his and pushed open the Abbey door. Inside the static air was cool and smelt of incense. She took a deep breath. Thirteen years. Thirteen years to wait to be wed to him. She looked sidelong at Audebert, her husband, and he smiled too, without turning his face fully to her. Every time she looked at him she was surprised by the blueness of his eyes, the look of him that she could not put into words but simply knew as a bodily response, an emotional thump. They walked towards the altar where Adalmode's brother Hilduin, who would soon be ordained as Bishop, waited to bless the marriage.

The wedding feast went on for two days. Guy had given Adalmode a quarter of the Limoges city tolls and tithes as her very generous wedding gift. On the third day when the guests rose from their beds, jaded from drinking and eating, a messenger from Poitiers was waiting in the hall with a declaration of war against La Marche and Limoges, ostensibly because the marriage had not been sanctioned by the Duke and Duchess of Aquitaine, but no doubt it was the affront to the heir of Aquitaine's pride that really provoked the challenge.

'I ask their sanction for no act of mine,' said Audebert, 'and I was intending to declare war on them in any case, so now we are all happy.' He smiled at Adalmode. No, she thought, no now we are not all happy. Not if I should have you so briefly after waiting so long and then see you ride away to war and danger, but she has always known this is who he is: not a lord to sit at home counting his money or discussing the progress of the crops. Bellac has always been a military household. She must take her happiness as she finds it. Perhaps it was inevitable since Audebert had spent half his early adulthood in a deep pit in the ground. Being enclosed and static at home could not hold much appeal for him.

'Ride to Bellac,' Audebert said to his brother Boson, 'and take charge of the garrison there. Send on the rest of the men to me at Roccamolten and we shall see if the Poitevins will enact their words.'

Adalmode watched Guy knit his brows and his brown eyes stare off into nothing in the centre of the hall. 'My wife kidnapped by Vikings and the Poitevins declaring war against me! This is not an auspicious beginning to my rule,' he said and shrugged his shoulders. 'Well, but my dearest sister is happy,' he smiled in the general direction of her anxious face.

The reply to Guy's last negotiation for Aina over the amount of the ransom had been negative. 'What else can I do? I don't know what to do.'

'The Abbey of Saint Martial has 1,000 pounds in silver,' Adalmode told him.

'But you have already asked them and they gave you only 30 pounds.'

'Yes so you must take it from them.'

Guy looked at her aghast. 'But I can't do that.'

'Yes you can, and you must. Since Hildegaire has died and Hilduin has yet to get his feet under the table as the new Bishop you can do this. Do it Guy.'

'I can help you, brother,' Audebert said. 'Before we ride to Gençay to engage the Poitevins, I and my men will accompany you to cow the Abbey Treasurer, and we will escort the last part of Lady Aina's ransom back to Limoges.'

# 19

# Kelda Ey

## 991

I watch the seasons wheel on the island as the clouds fly across the skies and the tides slap back and forth against the rocks. In May a purple blanket of bluebells smothers the ground in the woodlands and in June the island changes its garb to pink with Red Campion blooms. In the summer the green bracken is full of nesting birds and in our second summer here Thorgils took Aina to his bed and whilst I am glad for their happiness, my heart weighs heavy with fear at their recklessness. I had been wrong in my suspicions concerning Olafr. It had been Thorgils all along that Aina wanted.

Aina and I join the slave women gleaning after the harvest, bending over and over to pick up stalks and kernels to fill our baskets. In Autumn the bracken rusts and dresses the island in copper hues; whiskery seals haul themselves out of the sea and birth white pups in the caves. In winter storm clouds gather low and grey or a rainbow leads the black edge of clouds loaded with rain. There might be a dusting of snow somedays but mostly harsh gales blow the breath from my body when I venture out, the wind whips my hair against my rime-cold face, and the sea batters the cliffs relentlessly. Thorgils makes skis for Aina and me, and shows Aina how to use them, but the snow is not really deep enough on the ground. No boats can sail to or from the island so that our world retracts small and cosy around the hearth. No visitors arrive with news of the outside world so we tell each other stories instead from our memory hoards.

Aina and I add a third layer to our clothing: tunics decorated with bands of woven braid which we wear between our shifts and overdresses for added warmth. Ragnhild generously lets me look through her pile of clothes to find one for myself and Thorgils presents Aina with a luxurious tunic from his stock, hemmed with a woven band of silver metal weft. We have warm cloaks for when we must go outside. Thorgils wanted to give us each a cloak brooch from his hoard. Aina's is a trefoil design, but I tell him I don't need one and pin my silver serpent to my cloak. 'Father's,' he says, tracing its complex curves with his finger and meeting my sad smile.

'The pirates did not find it and Aina's father, Ademar, discovered it but let me keep it when he bought me as a slave. He was a very kind man.'

'I'm glad of it, Sigrid. I thought of your little tear-streaked face often with great sorrow in my heart as Olafr and I grew tall, not knowing what had become of you. I took care of Olafr because I could not take care of you. I felt I had failed you. Always underlying every expedition I undertook was the thought that Thor might see fit to let me find you. I knew the chances were so very slim, but here you are.'

'This serpent helped me to survive my separation from you, and to survive my slavery. It was my secret badge of who I really was: the child of Jarl Thorolf, the sister of Thorgils and Olafr, a free Viken girl of noble blood, a pagan.'

Tofa died last week in the cold winter weather that gave her so many aches and hardships and we mourn her, even though her nickname Tofa the Spiteful was well-earned. 'It was her pains that made her spiteful,' I tell Aina. Thorgils made a slab-lined grave for Tofa and we break her antler comb and shears and put them in the grave with her before he seals it up with a stone lid. Thorgils asks me if I will take charge of the household in Tofa's stead but I shake my head and suggest Ragnhild.

'Why not, Sigrid?' Aina asks me and Thorgils is looking the question to me too.

I look down and suppress a smile at Aina's inevitable: 'Here we go, Thorgils! It's a long Sigrid think. You may want to call for bread and cheese to sustain us through the hours.'

'Not hours, just a few minutes,' I say, looking up. 'I don't know, Thorgils. Perhaps I feel that I might wish to make a household of my own somewhere soon and I don't want to get tied down, enmeshed here.'

'Is there a man in view?' Thorgils asks me raising his eyebrow.

'No. Just a need for freedom. The possibility that I can and might pick up and go if the whim takes me.'

'Whim, Sigrid!' Aina scoffs. 'You never acted on a whim yet! We would not ever have you leave us,' she says more seriously.

'There's no likelihood of that right now,' I say and decide they have to be satisfied with that. Indeed I cannot explain it to myself. I just feel a need to be potentially free of all responsibilities, in case.

A passing ship mostly of Danes comes with news that Olafr has won a great victory in England in allegiance with the Danish King Svein at a place named Maldon and that they will attack England again soon.

Now the spring floods are over and Thorgils has made a few short voyages 'to test the waters.' I wake up with a thick head from too much bad wine that Aina urged on me last night. I drift back to sleep again and wake two hours later with the sun shining into my eyes, high in the sky. Cross with myself, I dress hurriedly and go down to the hall which seems unusually empty. No Thorgils. No Aina. No men, I suddenly realise.

'Where are they Ragnhild? I'm sorry I had a headache and slept late.'

'Thorgils has gone raiding up the coast. He said we needed to replenish our supplies of silver to trade with passing ships and more oak that he needed for the ship repairs.'

I pick up a mug of water to clear the taste of old wine from my mouth. 'Is Aina out?'

'Yes,' Ragnhild says in a quiet voice with her eyes down on the sewing in her lap.

'Ragnhild?' She doesn't raise her head. 'Ragnhild, where is she?'

Finally she looks at me with an anxious expression. 'She went with the ship. With Thorgils. I told her not to and that you would advise against it, but you know what she . . .'

'Yes,' I say, jumping to my feet, but then I sit down again with a thump. What can I do? 'Oh Odinn preserve her,' I say fervently and Ragnhild nods. 'Ragnhild give me something to do, something difficult that needs concentration.'

She hands me the weaving batten on the table in front of her. 'The pattern now is very difficult.' She gestures to the half-woven tapestry on the large upright loom behind her.

They were gone for two days and I could not sleep or sit still at any task for long. I ran up to the beacon hill and shielded my eyes against the sun to look out for their return for many hours. I tried the watchtowers in case they might come from an unexpected direction. 'Would he usually be gone this long on a raid?' I ask Naerfi.

'Sometimes they are back before nightfall, but I've known them to be gone for a week or more. It depends.'

I look around me and realise that I am not the only one suffering during this absence. Ragnhild and Naerfi's husbands are with Thorgils and several of the slave women are very attached to their masters. I am surrounded by anxiety and strangely this recognition calms me.

It is four days since they went when I hear: 'Sail!' passing from mouth to mouth, from distant whisper to proximate shout. I am running to the landing bay to see them come. After ten minutes of straining my eyes I am sure it is Thorgils' longboat. Five more minutes and I think I can see him on the deck. He would not let harm come to her I keep telling myself. A few minutes more and I can see everything as Thorgils' ship makes its approach to the beach and there is Aina waving and laughing at me hanging off the stem, one arm cuddled around the mane of the fearsome dragon-head. I sit down on a large boulder behind me holding my hands to my cheeks, saying, 'Thank you Odinn, thank you Thor, thank you Freyja.'

In the hall, Aina, her grey eyes wide with excitement, recounts their adventures. Thorgils picks her up by her slender waist and swings her around in a circle in the air. Her hair is uncovered and loose and flies out behind her like the deep red silk tassel of a great bell rope. 'My red maiden, my skald-maiden,' he says, and putting her down dizzy, he kisses her so passionately that we all have to look to the ground and clear our throats to remind him that we are there.

'Won't the Bretar King seek reprisal,' I ask Thorgils in the hall that night, 'since you took his silver not to raid.'

Thorgils smiles at me. 'Sigrid the Deep-Minded. Yes. I have sent a messenger to him asking for a parlay and to establish a lasting truce. I've decided that's my last raid on the mainland and that I will take advantage of the hill fort at Tenby that he has offered to me and of the land around and have some of my men establish homesteads, start farming here. It's good soil, lashed with plenty of rain.'

'This makes good sense, Thorgils.'

'I killed no one and took no slaves on this raid,' Thorgils says. 'But I wanted to remind Maredudd what could continue to happen if I am not satisfied with the terms he offers me. I have been an earth-stepper wandering the seas for a long time but now I have sent word to Olafr asking if he will release me from my fighting oath to him, so that I can settle and farm this land – make my own real homestead here.'

I keep thinking my long think. Perhaps there is a life for me, a life of my choosing. A man of my choosing, a homestead here or over the narrow water on the mainland so that I would be close to Thorgils and Aina. I look down the long table at Thorgils' *drengir*. Toki is a nice man but he is Ragnhild's husband. Naerfi's husband, Gormr, I don't like much. He is given to moods and sometimes acts as if he has never grown from a child to a man. Skogi is a good-looking hot rabbit like Olafr, often flirting and teasing me about my 'bonny hair,' but I don't want such a man, who would soon turn those attentions to another woman. Asbjorn perhaps, or Erra, might suit me. They are both large blond men and seem dependable; Asbjorn is the taller; Erra a little older. I know very little of either man and determine to observe them and seek out conversation with them, see how I think they would behave to a wife if they had one. Or perhaps Leif will return one day.

'Thinking again, Sigrid?' Thorgils asks and I snap out of it realising that I have been staring off into space for five minutes or more.

'What has brought about your change in policy?' I ask.

Thorgils looks to Aina and she leans to whisper in my ear that she thinks she is with child. 'You will be an aunt Sigrid!'

'But Aina . . .' I begin.

'Don't scold me, Sigrid. It's done. I am Thorgils' handfast wife.'

Some days after they have returned from the raid I decide to open a topic I have been thinking of for some time. 'Thorgils, I heard tell of a farmer who has a scheme to motivate his slaves and stop them sabotaging his yields.'

Thorgils looks at me sceptically, knowing that freeing slaves is in my mind, beneath my words.

'No,' I answer his look. 'It's a good scheme. It works. He tells the slaves that if they work well and hard for three years he will free them at the end of those years. It gives them hope. There are always more slaves to replace them and anyway many decide to stay but as free peasants instead.'

He nods. 'We can try that Sigrid, if that is what you wish for. I wished to find you and here you are, so now I can grant your wishes too.'

Aina and I are astonished to enter the hall this morning to find a messenger standing gagging in front of Thorgils, attempting to eat a large lump of sealing wax and shreds of ripped parchment.

'What on earth is going on?' Aina exclaims.

'He is eating his message,' says Thorgils, furious, his freckles standing out against his red face.

'Stop it! Thorgils, you'll kill the man.'

Thorgils turns his back and faces the wall, his arms crossed and his shoulders vibrating with anger. Aina helps the man extract the undigested mess from his mouth and I usher him quietly to the door. Aina steps up and places her arms around my brother, leaning her cheek between his shoulderblades. 'What's gotten into you?'

'It is a letter from Olafr,' Thorgils says and his voice is a groan.

Aina pulls him around to face her. 'Yes?'

'I am sorrow-clenched, Aina.' He hesitates. 'He commands me to give you back to your betrothed husband.' Aina blanches. 'Guy of Limoges has raked together the sum asked for and Olafr needs the money for his next invasion of England.'

'Well you must go to Olafr and tell him no, despite the money,' says Aina. 'He won't argue with you, surely. No man could have been as loyal to him as you. He is your brother, a knee-set child of your father. He has been a ring-giver to you and rightly so . . .'

Thorgils holds up his finger to her lips. 'Alas, I know Olafr much better than you and I assure you that my loyalty will weigh nothing with him against this money, but I will not give you up,' he says, 'not ever. The waves will cover the mountains before I do it.' He engulfs her in a tight embrace and with his chin on her silky head, looks over at me with eyes full of grief and hopelessness.

Olafr arrives ten days later with four ships loaded with warriors. He is here to oversee the conclusion of his orders regarding Aina. Thorgils attempts persuasion with him at first but Olafr holds steadfast and uninterested, and so Thorgils moves to defiance.

'I am your leader,' says Olafr coldly, 'and you will obey me.'

'Yes,' shouts Thorgils angrily, 'and the Danes had the little dog Rakkae as their king for a while!'

There are muted sniggers amongst the men and Olafr looks around himself furious and back to Thorgils. 'You can obey me and convey the girl to Fécamp or I will take her myself tomorrow and I will sample her too, as you have done.'

'I will take her,' Thorgils says, with a face like thunder, his fists clenched.

'No!' Aina cries against my shoulder. 'Oh no, Sigrid.'

'And you will collect the silver from the Duke of Normandy,' Olafr tells Thorgils, 'and bring it to me at Benfleet. Duke Richard will not hand over the coin to you unless he is sure Viscount Guy will be satisfied with his restored bride.' Olafr looks suspiciously at Aina. 'Is there any reason why he shouldn't be satisfied?'

'No, Olafr,' I say, before either Thorgils or Aina can answer. 'I know Lord Guy and he will be well-satisfied with Aina and give you your 3,000 pounds of silver. He hankers greatly for her.'

Olafr nods to me, and I see new lines of anxiety and tension in his handsome face that were not there before. 'Thank you Sigrid. Look to your sister, Thorgils, and give me the duty you owe me.'

Aina looks at each of us in turn, her face pale and distraught, her hand held out, palm up, in disbelief. 'Why did you say that, Sigrid? We have to tell Olafr I am pregnant and then he will call this off. I will be huge with your child by the time I reach Fécamp if you ship me there now, Thorgils.'

Thorgils and I exchange anxious glances. 'Telling Olafr of our dilemma is not any solution,' Thorgils says. 'When his sister refused a marriage he had arranged for her, he plucked all the feathers from her favourite hawk and sent the naked bird to her. She took his meaning and married the man the next day. His fury would break brutally against you, me, and our unborn child if I defy him. We must find a way to delay so that the child is born before I have to deliver you to the Norman court. Then I will have to expose the child,' he ends miserably.

Aina looks at him in shock. 'Then you give me up?' she says, 'and you require me to give up my child and my true husband also? Is this always your way with your wives?'

Thorgils winces at her angry words. He looks at her, his expression bleak and pleading. 'I know no other solution, my heart.'

Aina stares at him as if she has never known him. She sets her mouth, lifts her chin and stalks from the room. For sure she will not accept Thorgils' suggested course of action and I fear what she will do – try to talk with Olafr probably, which will do her and Thorgils no good.

In the night I think long on many things: my love for Aina, and for her parents who had been so good to me, my joy at being reunited with my brother, my hopes for a life and family in Norway or at least amongst the Norse, the restoration of my status as a free woman. I rise and creep to where my brother lies, his eyes open and Aina curled asleep in the crook of his arm. I gesture to him that we must speak and he gently untangles himself from her lithe limbs without waking her. We look down at her sleeping there. Around her neck is the lucky amulet carved in the shape of two duck's feet that Thorgils made for her when he first heard she was carrying his child. In her nightshift it is plain to see the gentle round of her belly.

Thorgils and I pad out in bare feet to a corner of the hall where we can talk without being overheard. 'Sigrid?'

'You stare unsleeping at the ceiling, brother.'

He shakes his head desperately. 'She is like the young green leek to other grasses, Sigrid. My heart is fettered to her with the breath of fishes. I cannot think of a solution or a way to change Olafr's mind in this.'

'Take me in Aina's stead to the Norman court and I will marry Guy.'

Thorgils stares at me. 'How could that happen? You speak nonsense.'

'Aina and I are of an age, of a similar build and height and we both have red hair. Aina was heavily veiled when she was betrothed and Guy has never seen her face as a woman. He only knew her and me as children, many years ago. Besides he has bad eyesight. No man will know the difference between us.'

'That's ridiculous.'

'It will work. I have been speaking the Occitan tongue since I was nine.'

'No, I don't want this, Sigrid. You would be marrying a man you don't want. Committing an act of deception that could be discovered and if that happened the consequences would be dire for you. Even if you were not exposed, you would be returning to another kind of servitude.'

'I will not be discovered, and I have three reasons for doing it: you, Aina and my unborn niece or nephew.'

'No Sigrid, you cannot. Perhaps someone else.'

'No. I know Ségur and Limoges. I know everything that Aina knows. This can work.' I look at Thorgils and think how, if he accepts, I must part with him again and never see him or Aina anymore. I will not have the Norse husband, homestead, children that I have been dreaming of; instead I will return to the land of my slavery, to a dangerous and uncertain future, but I keep my expression confident and clear of these thoughts.

'There is one, apart from my mother, who has seen our faces and would tell us apart,' says Aina the following day when we moot the idea to her. 'Adalmode. Guy's sister.'

'She is wed herself now most likely,' I say, 'and will not be at the court to see me. If there is an Assembly and she is present I

238

will feign illness and avoid her gaze. I will adjust to what I find. I'm resourceful,' I say, boasting in a confident way that I do not feel inside.

'I can't lose you, Sigrid,' Aina says. 'I love you and I need you when my child is born.'

'You will have Thorgils and he will have you.'

'But what of you? Married to this Viscount Guy that Aina has disdained?' Thorgils asks.

'I may grow to like him.'

'Yes,' Aina turns to Thorgils, who is still shaking his head.

'There is no other way, Thorgils,' I tell him.

Olafr is leaving with his ships this morning, confident that Thorgils will enact his orders. The hall is chaotic with dogs, men and slaves – looking for food, packing up equipment, saying goodbyes. I am sitting at the trestle, my porridge untouched before me, lost in a vacant daze at my own temerity, trying not to think of what will happen now. The trestle creaks and rocks as Leif sits down next to me. 'Lady Sigrid.'

I realise that the expression on my face is akin to horror and quickly change it to an anxious frown.

'I was thinking to ask you again, lady . . .'

'Don't.'

I glance up at the consternation on his face and look away.

'I'm sorry Leif, truly, but don't.'

I can feel him silently studying my bowed head for some time, and then he pushes himself up swiftly from the bench, looks at me again, but when I say nothing and will not meet his gaze, he makes a low angry sound and moves towards the door. I watch his back and he does not turn to look again in my direction.

Aina and I rummage through a great pile of stolen clothing that Thorgils has dumped onto the table, looking for Frankish clothing that Aina would wear if she were being returned to Guy and also for good, thick veils. 'Will I see you again?' she asks tears running down her face.

'Yes, of course,' I say although I know I probably speak a lie. 'We will write news to each other but always be careful to disguise what you say so that our writing can never be used as evidence against us. You must address me as Lady Aina and I will address you as Sigrid.'

She laughs mirthlessly and shakes her head.

The following day I stand onboard Thorgils' long ship, looking back at Aina on the shore in the embrace of Ragnhild, trying not to weep. Aina has written my name on the beach in huge letters: Sigrid. Thorgils has freed twenty slaves as a gift to me, including Morag, but she decided to stay with him and Aina, and I am very glad of that.

Thorgils gives the order; the oars splash and the ship begins to move. I raise my hand to her, looking and looking until my dear Aina and the Island of the Spring have disappeared from view. I wipe my face and walk forward to the prow of the ship to look in the direction we are going. At least it feels good and right to be on the water again. As the island recedes behind me, we pass huge walls of water lashing the cliffs of the outlying rocks. The swell of the dark water calls to me and I think briefly of how it might be to drown. I feel a perverse desire to join with the water, as water drops desire to join one with each other. Trying to keep my mind from Aina behind me and the risk I am going to, I admire the water's ability to be so diverse: glassily smooth or choppy and churning, light bouncing on its surface or beaming into its depths. As night comes on I watch the moon reflected in minature a hundred times on the bend of the waves like myriad drowned stars.

Standing in the rich green gown Aina and I picked out together, I try to get used to masquerading as her. You are Viscountess Aina of Ségur, betrothed to Viscount Guy of Limoges I keep telling myself in my head, holding out my hand before me to look at the moonlight reflecting on the sapphire betrothal ring on my little finger that Guy gave to Aina and she to me.

# 20

# Fécamp

## September 991

Thorgils took *The Orm* into the Narrow Sea that runs between the lands of the English King and the lands of the Bretons, Normans and Franks. As we approach the Norman settlement at Fécamp I look at the land rising up in a sheer wall of tall white cliffs topped with vivid green grass. There is a long slick of beach and then a narrow entrance to the harbour. The town is built on the steep hill rising up behind the beach and harbour. My stomach churns as *The Orm* slices towards the U-shaped structure in the harbour. The anchoring point is on the west side, and alongside that is the Duke's palace. We approach the jetty under oars, Thorgils with a grim expression at the rudder, his sandy hair whipping up from his face in the wind. We have agreed that he will not come ashore with me, in case he inadvertantly gives me away, 'Or in case I *cannot* give you away when the time comes,' he said. So when the ropes are thrown and the boat steadied at the stone steps, it is Gormr and Eimundr who step out to escort me, who hold my elbow to help me off the ship. I take one last look at Thorgils and we raise our hands to each other. His eyes are wet, his expression an agony. I try to fix the sight of him in my mind: the sea-green of his eyes, the pale red of his hair, the boyish freckles on the man's lined face. I turn away quickly before my own eyes fill and I betray myself by expressing a surprising affection for my Norse 'kidnapper.' The faces of many people crowding the jetty are turned upon me in eager curiosity and I have to carry off my role.

'Lady Aina!' The richly dressed man who steps forward to greet me who I recognise as the Duke of Normandy, is enormously tall, perhaps seven foot with the longest shanks I have ever seen. I trust that he will not recognise me from Brioude years ago, or at least that he paid scant attention to which red-haired girl was Lady Aina of Ségur, and which was her Norse maid.

'My lord,' I say, taking his offered arm although I have to reach up uncomfortably high to do so. Duke Richard is an elderly man but strong and upright, with a long white beard and thick white hair standing up from a tanned face.

'Return to your ship and wait at anchor,' he commands Gormr and Eimundr. 'My wife and I will speak with Lady Aina, here. If we are satisfied we will bring the ransom down to the jetty in the morning.'

Gormr and Eimundr glance to me, and I nod to tell them to comply. I force myself not to turn for one more look at my brother's face. The Duke leads me to the end of the jetty and the steps up to the palace where a party of finely dressed women are waiting. 'My wife, Lady Gunnora,' he says, passing my hand to a blonde haired woman, and I greet the lady.

They lead me to a chapel newly built from white limestone, standing high at the very top of the hill. Inside they are gratified by my exclamations at the fresco covering the walls and the gold and gems gleaming everywhere. Huge golden lampstands tower over us. At the altar stands a Christian priest, as splendidly attired as his church, in a purple silk robe shot with gold thread and littered with green emeralds. He blesses me, giving thanks to their God for my safe return. I pray silently in my head to Thor to protect me from their Christian magic, to give luck to my endeavour and safety to my brother. After the blessing the Duchess takes my hand again and we walk to the ducal residence where a feast is in preparation.

'Make a hole, Lady Aina! You are on your way home now and delivered from barbarians,' the Duke shouts down the table to me, raising his glass, and meaning that I should drink down the small glass of burning alcohol in my hand, to make a hole in the substantial amount of food already consumed, so that I can eat some more. The drink is made by the monks here, a mix of brandy and herbs. It smells good but is no doubt exceedingly strong. I smile back to the Duke and put the drink to my lips but do not drink it. I need to keep my wits about me. The reference to barbarians is a joke since the Duke and his entourage all come from Scandinavian stock.

Thorgils told me he could kidnap 'Aina' again when the time was right and everyone was satisfied – the Duke, Olafr, Guy . . . and not return her this time. I have a sudden rush of the same terrified bereftness I felt at the slave market in Tallinn, separated from Thorgils' reassuring presence, but this will not do. I am a woman now, not a traumatised child and I can do this. I look around at the hall which is sooty with constant feasting on pork and goose, and at the guests who have come to gawp at me.

First I have to give a convincing performance as Aina of Ségur to the Duke of Normandy and his household so that he will confirm the handover of the hostage and pay Olafr his pounds of silver. Then I need to find a way to convince Aina's mother to support my deception. I have no ideas on this for the moment, but trust that something will come to me or at least that Melisende will see it is the best way to protect her daughter and her unborn grandchild. Aina has written a passionate letter to her mother, explaining our actions and asking her to help me. The small rolled letter is hidden inside the hem of my cloak. Then I will have to convince Guy that I am Aina, and avoid his sister, Adalmode. Would Guy know the difference I wonder. How would it be to marry him, to be his wife, if things should get that far. My wonderings on that second subject are not entirely unpleasant, but then my face falls, as I remember I will have to live a lie my whole life or until Thorgils comes to get me. I will have to lie in my every dealings with people, including my most intimate dealings with my husband. If it gets that far, is the refrain in my head.

Duke Richard sits alongside Gunnora and their sons and daughters, Richard the heir, Emma and Matilda, Robert who is Archbishop of Rouen and their youngest son, Mauger. The whole court teems with their kin. Gunnora's brother Herfast, the Duke's brother Rodolf, and the Duke's very many illegitimate sons all hold important positions in the household. I feel alone and vulnerable amidst this horde.

A cleric, Dean Dudo is seated next to me and tells me he is visiting from the Vermandois court. Whispering close to my ear, he recounts the story of how the Duke first took Gunnora as his concubine. 'Night had fallen whilst he was out hunting and he took refuge in the home of one of his foresters. Conquered by the needling frailty of pleasure-seeking humanity he lusted for the man's wife, Sainsfrida. But Sainsfrida wished to be faithful to her husband so, in the darkness of the night she sent her unwed sister, Gunnora, to the Duke's bed in her place.' Seeing my interest in his tale, Father Dudo explains he is writing a history of the Duke's family. 'Duke Richard was first married to the sister of Hugh Capet, Emma, but she is long dead in childbed and gave him no living heir, so for the sake of the succession, the Duke married Gunnora and legitimized their children.'

I nod and let him continue. The less I say the less opportunity for error.

'As you see, the Duke is blessed in his wife. She was the most beautiful of all Norman maidens and now as Duchess she is the most circumspect concerning public and civil affairs. She is well versed in the talents of feminine artistry, discreetly strong in richly fertile eloquence and profusely endowed with the treasure of a capacious memory. She is descended from the domineering Danish race,' he says, nodding towards her, 'prudent in her deliberations, devout, gentle, diligent and wise in every matter.'

I hope that his rosy portrait of the Duchess has some truth, as I suspect she will play a significant role in deciding whether or not to accept me and pay the ransom. The Duke is nicknamed The Fearless and this is a household where the master is respected by all around him.

'A mountain would sooner withdraw or depart than the Duke's words be fruitless,' Dean Dudo tells me, passing a small silver bowl of salt to me. 'You do not need to fear now, Lady Aina. Whatever the Duke promises he will abide, true. Whatever he offers will endure, unbroken.'

Richard's oldest son is also enormously tall. Every time one of them stands up I find myself having to lift my chin higher than expected to follow the progress of their heads on their shoulders, thrust up so high they are on legs that seem impossibly long. This tallness, Dean Dudo says, was inherited from their ancestor Rollo who came from Norway and won the kingdom of Normandy in France from King Charles the Simple. Among the French the rumour is that the *Nordmanni* of Normandy are converted to Christianity but I see more evidence of continuing pagan practices around me than I see Christian worship. It is said that Rollo sacrificed one hundred Christians when he was on his death-bed to appease Odinn for his disloyalty in praying occasionally to the Franks' Christ-god.

For now my masquerade is progressing well. My clothes are fine enough and everyone knows the *pagani* who held me hostage would have taken my jewels before returning me. I keep my serpent brooch carefully hidden inside the fold of my belt. Duchess Gunnora was expecting a red-headed girl and so I seem to do. The Duchess speaks with me of Ségur, of Lady Melisende and of Guy and is satisfied that I am indeed Aina. She whispers to me: had I been violated, and I tell her no, I am still a virgin.

The Duchess has me taken to her chamber and tells her two maids to strip me. 'It will be alright, dear,' she reassures me, seeing how embarrassed I am. The maids first remove my headdress and admire my hair. They unlace my gown and pull it down and ask me to step out of the encumbering layers of cloth, folding it carefully and laying it on the bed. I stand in my shift and hope they might stop there but they pull the shift from me and I am naked whilst the Duchess looks me over.

One of the maids seems to have no control of her mouth. 'She has orange hair round her privates,' she says. 'She's brown and spotty and white.'

'Tut, Birgitta! You speak rudely. Please take no notice, Lady Aina,' the Duchess tells me. 'Birgitta is not altogether right in the head but she works hard.' I look down at myself and the girl is right that my face, neck and arms are brown and freckled from the sun on the island and the sea voyage, whilst the skin of my belly and thighs are as white as a nun's wimple.

'Your red hair is glorious, Lady Aina,' Gunnora says. 'I heard it was so.'

'Tis lovely, lovely hair,' Birgitta grins at me, standing a little too close for my comfort. As the maids redress me, Birgitta giggles all the while like a small child, and I have to make an effort to stay my fingers from helping the maids with their task, since I am a lady now.

We return to the Duke sitting in the hall, and the Duchess tells him in a loud voice that everyone in the hall can hear: 'Her breasts are well-sized, but the girl has borne no child. You can see that from the pinkness of her nipples.' The Duke nods, and I drop my eyes, feeling the intense heat of my face.

They ask me about my kidnappers. 'Did Olafr Tryggvason offer you no rudeness,' asks the Duke in a sceptical voice, one eyebrow raised.

'No sire,' I say not having to feign how abashed I am. 'He kissed me goodbye once with too much liberty, and I thought at first he might take me to his bed, but for the most part I was treated with respect and honoured.'

'My son, Richard, will convey you to your husband tomorrow, Lady Aina, with an escort of my best men,' the Duke says.

'Thank you, my Lord. I will be overjoyed to see my mother and Lord Guy after all this time.'

'I'll authorize the shipment of the Viscount's silver to Olafr's man, Jarl Thorgils, who is waiting off-shore,' the Duke tells the Duchess, and I feel an emptiness through to my core at his words.

I lie down on the best soft bed in the castle, staring at the canopy above my head and thinking I will never be able to sleep, but I wake the following morning – the beginning of my new life as Aina – having slept soundly for hours and hours. I realise that by now, Thorgils is gone and Aina is far away.

# 21

# Bellac

# 991

Adalmode sat on the top step leading down to the courtyard to observe the training. Watching her husband and his men was a far cry from her early experiences of anxiously witnessing Guy's inept fumblings as a boy at Montignac. Audebert and his household *milites* presented a well-drilled unit, expert in all their weapons, expert as individuals and as a combined force acting as one to orders. It was a pleasure to watch such competence, but a fear as well. Landless men flocked to Audebert's courts, seeking his service as he moved between Périgueux, Bellac and Roccamolten. There were strong rumours of war and where there was war such men could prosper. The news from the north was that Fulk of Anjou's castle building progressed well and he achieved small military successes against both Blois and Poitiers.

Adalmode felt a kick in her side and stroked her palm around the curve of her belly. Her child would come in a few months. Audebert would go to Roccamolten tomorrow, leaving her ruling Bellac in his stead. She knew his brother Boson resented this and resolved to ask Audebert to take Boson with him to Roccamolten and leave Gausbert here to keep her company. He was more polite and companionable. She was well aware that every parting from Audebert could be the last time she saw him, but it would not help or be seemly to show her fears for him. Instead she must try to live life every day with a vehemence that matched his.

A peddlar came yesterday and brought them news of the northern court. Bishop Adalbero of Laon had betrayed the Carolingian

Charles of Lorraine to King Hugh Capet. Charles was imprisoned now with his three-year-old son. Many lords were grieved at King Hugh's treatment of Charles, who was the last living branch of the line of Charlemagne. Duke Guillaume in Aquitaine briefly took arms against King Hugh in protest but he had been easily defeated and forced to make peace. Hugh's son, Robert was rumoured to be desirous of repudiating his wife Rozala and marrying his cousin Berthe but his father opposed it. These events seemed distant from them and yet Adalmode knew their ripples could reach to touch both Audebert and Guy. Fulk was closer to the politicking in the north and whatever impacted on Fulk was likely to impact also on Audebert. She envisaged them all like a line of precariously balanced dominoes.

That night Adalmode watched Audebert undressing before coming to her bed. She focussed her gaze on his mouth. It was a large mouth with a thick bottom lip and a pronounced bow in the top lip. If she could somehow close his startling eyes out of her view, all of his features offered her some interest: his mouth, his long straight nose slightly bulbed at its end, the black hair that feathered at his neck rising above his collar. But his eyes always dominated his face and one's view of him. Only when his eyes were shut was it really possible to see the rest of him. He sat on the edge of the bed to unlace his boots. In her thin nightgown she knelt up behind him as close as her large belly allowed and put her hands over his eyes. She turned his head towards her and lent around to study him as he laughed at her. The dimple in one cheek when he laughed was still there. 'What are you up to?'

'Nothing. Nothing. Just looking at you.' She took her hands away and watched him fold his clothes and place everything neatly in order on the chest. He was always ordered, everything in its place.

'So Fulk is gearing up for war, building more castles,' she said.

He nodded but did not look at her.

'It's not your fight, Audebert.'

Now he did cease his concentrated preparations for bed and looked into her eyes. 'Yes it is.'

'You just need a fight, any fight.'

'Perhaps you are right.' He looked down again winding his sword belt around his sword.

'Am I to wait all these years to marry you then and be widowed?'

'Have more confidence in me, Adalmode, do!' he laughed, flipping the quilt to one side and climbing in beside her, silencing her with a kiss, curving his hand on the rise of her stomach.

She often tried to speak with him about his imprisonment, about its effects on him now but it was a subject he spoke of with great reluctance, only tolerating the topic for a short time before breaking off. Both his parents died whilst he was in the dungeon, robbing him of the opportunity to be received back by them, to be reassured they did not believe him guilty of Helie's crime. So much of his life had been taken from him. The sense of the stolen years of his imprisonment, when his life was on hold, was buried deep but still there. She felt it all the time. He would never simply return to normality. The huge cost in physical suffering had been assuaged, replaced in time by the luxuries and health of his life now, but the emotional trauma scarred his mind and his heart, and could sing in his sinews at any time and at any unexpected trigger. It was there in his vast sense of injustice, in his need to be always moving, never confined in a small space, in his need for vengeance, but against who? Helie whose crime had put him in the pit and who had abandoned him there, was dead. Her father Gerard who had put him in the pit and kept him there was dead. The old Duke of Aquitaine, Guillaume IV who had ordered his captivity and refused his father's entreaties for mercy had entered a monastery and was likely to die soon. Audebert needed an enemy, he needed to escape whatever situation he was in. He needed, always, out.

# 22

# Limoges

## 991

My ride with Richard, the Duke's son, and his men, took four days. We stopped at monastery guest houses or the homes of ally lords along the way. We rose daily at dawn and our horses swished quietly through wet grass. From high hills we watched the morning mists wreathing the valleys, slowly dissipating to reveal rivers, and woods laced with laburnum. 'They say a squirrel could cross the country by swinging from branch to branch and never have to touch the ground,' Richard told me. As the sun climbed the sky, the ochre rocks began to reverberate with heat. We rode past the dark wrinkled trunks of chestnut groves and on a mountain summit looked down on an abyss of air. Our horses rocked carefully from knee to knee down the steep paths and occasionally one hoof would slide on loose stones, causing the horse to have to save itself, and the rider's heart to thump at the risk of tumbling over the edge. In the valley we had to wait for shepherds passing up country with their flocks. A goat stood on its hind legs to chew at the tender lower leaves of a beech tree and was prodded on with the goatherd's long stick.

Now as we approach the city of Limoges there is a dust cloud on the road ahead of us and soon we see that a great procession of people has come out to meet us, carrying tall wands, festooned with flowers and little bells. Guy and his household are riding at the head of the crowd. He reins his horse alongside mine. He is a tall, thin man with brown hair and brown eyes, richly dressed in dark brown brocade and grey fur. The planes of his face are sharply angled. It is a face that looks as if it has collided together rather than being softly sculpted, yet I find myself interested by it, tracing its unlikely tilts and slants.

'Lady Aina!' he exclaims. 'Welcome home at last!' His glance slides over me but does not linger. I murmur my thanks in a quiet voice. Have I passed this test?

Riding through the city gates, all the church bells are pealing for my return and people come out of shops and houses to wave and cheer at us. 'Felicitations on your marriage, Viscount!' one woman yells from the crowd and he smiles in her direction. 'God-speed Viscount! Viscountess!' There are kindly shouts all around us and it seems Guy is well-liked by his citizenry. They are pleased to see his betrothed wife returned to him at last. I feel glad and sick at the same time, a monstrous imposter.

We clatter into the courtyard of the Motte where Richard hands me from my horse and up the steps and ceremoniously transfers my hand to Guy's. I will be discovered now for sure. Guy kisses me formally on my cheeks three times. He is a little taller than I am and I am taller than Aina, so beneath my skirts I bend my knees slightly to mask any difference he might perceive. 'Thank you for your deliverance of me Lord Guy,' I murmur.

'You must be very tired from your ride,' he says. 'My sister Adalmode wanted to be here to greet you but she is in the travails of birth now at Bellac.' I hear the anxiety he feels for her in his voice.

'She is wed to Lord Audebert, then?' I ask, remembering their desperate passion in the dark in Brioude.

'Yes,' Guy says and there is warm affection for his sister in his tone whenever he speaks of her. 'My younger sister Calva is here to take care of you, before our wedding.'

'Thank you.' I keep the relief from my face. Calva has never met me. She will not know that I am a great liar.

'I fear we are a small wedding party. My mother too was unable to come to Limoges. She is unwell and my other sisters are caring for her. Archimbaud of Comborn and his wife, Lady Sulplice, have agreed to stand witnesses for us.'

'Never mind it, my lord,' I tell him, again relieved that I do not know Archimbaud and his wife. 'The main parties are here finally.'

He laughs and I realise that he too is feeling nervous. 'My mother?' I ask.

'She will be here on the morrow. You must be very anxious to see her and I know she is coming with all haste to clasp you in her arms in joy. I thought we would wed tomorrow? When she is arrived and you are rested?'

'Yes, thank you.' What would Aina do now I am thinking – but then realise with a suppressed smile, that Aina would probably do something she ought not to do, and it would be best not to follow that model too closely! I turn to Richard. 'Thank you for your great kindness in conveying me here safely. Will you stay for the wedding my lord?'

'Indeed, I will,' he tells us. Guy's steward is waiting to make arrangements for Richard's horses and to give refreshments to the road-weary men.

In the hall I sit with Guy and take a glass of wine to clear the dust from my throat. He is smiling but his expression seems vague and disconnected. Perhaps he is starting to doubt me. I cannot look him full in the face. He asks me: 'No Sigrid?'

My heart leaps at his words as at first I misunderstand his meaning and then slowly calming myself, I say: 'No she decided to stay with her countrymen. I miss her terribly.' I feel the truth threaded through my lies, thinking of Aina and hoping she is well with her swelling belly without me.

'Of course, you do,' Guy says, briefly placing wide brown fingers across the back of my hand, but then he quickly lifts his hand away, as if he is unsure how I might welcome it. 'We must find you a new maid but I know Sigrid was more than that to you. Perhaps I might fill a little of the gulf of lost friendship you are feeling?'

I begin to smile at him, but remember that Aina would not respond so warmly to him and perhaps he will become suspicious to find a wife suddenly warm who before was so cold.

'Thank you,' I say injecting as much cool disinterest into my tone as I can, and am sorry to see his expression alter. I soon excuse myself to rest. The less opportunity anyone has to observe me or I to make a mistake the better.

I am a barnyard hen that sits on an eagle's nest. Tomorrow my further trials will begin: persuading Lady Melisende to be complicit with the deception, consummating my marriage with Guy and assuming the duties of the Viscountess of Limoges – if I get that far. They are all daunting prospects, but I linger on the last. I watched Melisende training Aina. I know what to do, but knowing is different from actually doing it, from commanding many servants, making decisions, playing hostess to great lords and ladies, advising my husband on the eddies of jealousies and resentments swirling around him. I study Guy at dinner and feel sure I am right in my surmise that his eyesight is very poor. I notice the way he cocks his head to listen carefully to conversations, to music and poetry; how he feels for things: his knife on the table, seeming to caress it before picking it up, the stem of his green glass, the top of his chair. He steadies himself against table edges, the wall, the doorways. I cannot imagine how he has survived thus far, especially in military training and skirmishes. Perhaps he and I will speak of it one day. In the meantime I will help him, aid him to the best of my abilities. Perhaps I need only maintain Aina's coolness towards him for a short time.

I lie awake worrying about Lady Melisende. She will arrive just before noon from Ségur with a train of servants, many of whom might know me: Phillippe perhaps, Renaud. I will have to greet them in the courtyard with Guy and Calva, in full view of the Limoges household and the men of Normandy. Of course Melisende will exclaim: 'But this is not my daughter! This is my slave Sigrid!' I roll in the bed, groaning. What can I do? Waylay her on the road before she gets here? Try to persuade her in the forest? And if she will not participate in the lie – and why would she? An honest Christian woman who is fond of Guy. If she will not, then I must run away and make my way to the coast and get a message to Thorgils to come to get me or try to make my own way back to Kelda Ey on a boat, and hope that Olafr will not wreak vengeance on Thorgils. Perhaps he will be satisfied to have the silver. But a woman travelling alone? I would not last in safety one night. I would have to steal some men's clothing from a laundry basket and travel as a boy. Even then . . .

I wake to the clangour of the breakfast bells. Too late then to ride out and speak with Melisende on the road. I put on the best blue gown I have in my chest, my betrothal ring and some other rings that Guy presented to me as gifts yesterday, and I wear a large silver cross at my neck that Aina had taken from her own neck and given to me, kissing it and crying tears upon it. More lies regarding my beliefs. My Thor's hammer and serpent brooch are hidden in a locked box inside my chest. A red-gold circlet holds my thick veil in place over my head and face, showing only the tip of my nose, my mouth and chin, and the veil lifts up slightly with every breath. Perhaps Lady Melisende has aged in the three years of our absence and her own sight might be as poor as Guy's. I am clutching at straws.

Guy is waiting for me in the hall. 'Good morning, Lord Guy, soon to be my husband!' I smile to him, concealing the anxieties welling within me.

He smiles widely in response. 'You look very fine in that blue gown, Lady Aina, soon to be my wife. Your mother has been sighted from the walls and will be here in minutes. We'll go out and await them.'

In that instant I know I cannot do this. Cannot allow the extreme risk of exposure in front of everyone. I grip my side. 'Oh Lord Guy,' I say, 'I have a terrible and sudden pain. I must retire again. I am so sorry. Please, please,' I call over my shoulder, moving swiftly to the stairs, 'will you send my mother to me?'

He is bewildered. 'Yes, of course, Aina?' but I flee before he can ask more.

I hear the horses and look out of the window to see Melisende handed down from her mount and greeting Guy. I am so pleased to see her, and pleased too that I do not recognise any of the attendants with her. My heart begins to thump at the thought of the conversation coming between us now and how disappointed she will be not to see Aina here but instead to find just me. Guy is speaking to her and she looks up suddenly to the window with an anxious expression on her dear face and I step back that she should not see me. I hear her come running up the steps and know she is on the way to me, but at least alone. I stand close to the door and take a deep breath. The door opens and I catch it in my hand.

'Aina? My love . . .'

Swiftly I take her arm pulling her into the room, close and latch the door so that it cannot be opened from outside.

'Sigrid!' An enormous smile of relief spreads across her face. She embraces me and I feel the thinness of her arms and close up, see the grey in her hair, breathing in her familiar citrus scent. She is more frail since Ademar died and since we have been gone. 'So it is true, you are both here and safely returned to me, my two dear daughters. Aina?' she asks, spinning around, looking confused at the empty bed and the empty room.

'My Lady, I hardly know where to begin but I must tell you a tale. Aina is safe and well,' I reassure her, placing a comfortable stool for her to sit on.

She frowns. 'Where is she? Lord Guy said she was taken with a pain in her side.'

I tell my story in a rush. How Aina is not here but with my brother Thorgils on an island off the coast of Bretland. How Aina loves my brother and carries his child and how I have come in her stead because she could not come. I give her Aina's letter and watch anxiously as she reads it slowly.

Melisende shakes her head, her expression amazed. 'What does my child mean?' she says to herself, running her eyes over the words in the letter, and then touching them as if she were touching Aina. She looks up at me. 'What do you mean Sigrid? This is not possible. She never wanted to marry Guy, did she! What a stubborn girl I have.' She asks me questions about Thorgils' status and wealth and I tell her that he is a great Jarl in Bretland.

'He is the lord of the prosperous island of Kelda Ey. He owns vast tracts of land, islands and many chests of silver,' I say exaggerating a little but trying not to stray too far from the truth.

'Stolen from monasteries, like my daughter,' Melisende says, compressing her mouth in disapproval.

'He is a very good man.' I know she and Ademar worked hard to accumulate wealth to pass onto their only child and grandchildren, and that now she competently carries on Ademar's trading business as his widow. If she agrees to this deception she will be allowing her family's wealth and name to pass instead to me and to my children. I tell her that I have deceived the Duke and

Duchess of Normandy and now Guy too. 'It was the only way to protect my brother and Aina and their child, to give Aina what she so dearly wanted, Lady Melisende!'

Melisende looks at me sombrely for several minutes. 'And what of what you want and need, Sigrid, my Northchild?' She reaches to stroke my cheek with the back of her fingers and raises her brows to me. I lean my face to her gentle touch and remember how she saved me in the Tallinn Slave Market so long ago with her compassion and kindness. I shake my head and can hardly speak more. 'I want them to be safe. I love them and I love you, Lady Melisende.'

'My brave Sigrid,' she says, her voice warm with emotion. 'My brave little Northchild in the Tallinn slave-market ripped from your brother, and now you have lost him – given him up, again.'

We are silent and I look down at our hands clasped together in her lap. I dare not look at her. With my free hand I swipe at a tear crawling down my cheek at her mention of Thorgils.

'Sigrid, have you converted?'

'No.'

'I cannot allow you to marry Guy if you are still a pagan, Sigrid. I couldn't have that on my conscience.'

'I will . . . I will convert.' No other response comes to me, but I know as I say the words, that now I am lying to her too.

Melisende regards me steadily for some time.

'Ademar built up a large fortune and has substantial holdings in Ségur. He wished to pass this on to his daughter . . . I just don't know what to say, Sigrid.'

'You could still pass your wealth to Aina.'

'How? Guy is expecting you to come with Ségur and all its holdings as your dowry.' I don't have an answer for this and Melisende is silent again, thinking. 'You would have to bring Ségur to Guy as your dowry,' she says slowly, 'but perhaps it would be possible to ensure that Ademar's moveable wealth goes to Aina and her children.'

'Oh yes,' I say, 'if we can find a way to do this, that would be wonderful. I do not want what is not mine.'

'Oh Sigrid, I, and Ademar if he were alive, do not resent giving part of our fortune to you. You are also our daughter, and now you have made this great sacrifice for Aina.'

'What about you, Lady Melisende?'

'Ademar left me a very substantial bequest and the holdings of Ségur for my lifetime, which should then pass to our daughter.' She looked keenly at me suddenly. 'Yes I think I can see a way to arrange this, Sigrid, which will be fair to all of us and not obvious to Guy.' She pauses to think at length again. 'Well, Sigrid,' she says eventually placing her hands neatly folded in her lap, 'or I mean, well, Aina.' Her eyes sparkle at me and I know that I am safe, we are all safe.

'Oh Melisende forgive me. Is it so terrible a thing that I am doing? I promise to be a good wife to Guy – if it should get that far.'

'Well perhaps we could spirit you away now, say that your terror with the Vikings was so great that you have decided to become a nun.' I shake my head, pulling a face Aina herself would have been proud of. 'But I can see how Aina and your brother's safety and that of my grandchild is best served by your pretence. I can see that. But Guy? He must know it is you?'

I shake my head. 'I don't think he does. He seems to have simply accepted that I am Aina. He is short-sighted you know.'

'Yes, I always thought he was, but not to recognise you?'

'Very short-sighted,' I say with certainty. 'And he only saw Aina and I veiled when we were women.'

Melisende nods slowly. 'Sigrid I believe that you will make Guy a good wife and you have always been a good daughter to me.' Her eyes fill with tears. 'But am I never to see my child again? Tell me of her, and tell me about your brother. Is he good to her? Does he look like you? And, then, my love, my Northchild, we must prepare ourselves for your marriage, my daughter's marriage, and your new position as Viscountess.'

The noises of the wedding feast are still audible in the hall, but Guy has persuaded the last of those who accompanied us to the bridal bed to leave the chamber. He closes the door with a quiet click of the latch and the noises and shouts are instantly muffled. He turns back to me, seated in my nightdress on the bed, my hair loose down my back. I notice again that although he is looking in my direction, his eyes do not connect with mine. He walks with one hand held in front of him as if he might bang into furniture, though there is none in his path. Compared to the heavy trials I have already endured: convincing everyone I am Aina, gaining Melisende's complicity and marrying this man under a false name in a solemn Christian ceremony that means nothing to me and everything to him; the mere act of consummating our marriage now should seem trivial, yet I feel a thrill of nerves in my stomach, mixed with something more pleasant. I am twenty-eight and I have never lain with a man, although I have kissed a few. The idea is not without its appeal and this man – he has reached me now and sits down next to me – he seems gentle and intelligent. He is not ugly. He too wears a thin nightgown and his knees and calves are visible. He is not striking in any way, yet I feel comfortable with him.

He raises his hand to my cheek and runs the back of his finger gently down my jaw, turning my face to him and looking closely at me. He strokes the fall of my loose hair, and smiling, curls a red strand around his finger. 'Your hair is the most splendid thing I have ever seen. A great flame that I can see from any distance. You are so beautiful,' he says, 'and I am very glad you are here, returned at last and we are wed.'

I smile back. 'I too am glad.'

'Well, Aina,' he says, looking quizzically at me, 'we are married and we should do something about it.' He leans towards me and his mouth touches mine, his hand cupping my breast through the thin fabric of my nightgown.

# 23

# Milford

## 992

*The Orm* slid with smooth precision alongside the wooden jetty at Milford. Toki leapt onto the planking and Thorgils slung a rope to him, then turned to grin at Aina sitting amidships, cradling their one year old son, Ulf, to her breast. It had been a while since King Maredudd issued his invitation to come to a parlay, and now Thorgils, curious to see what the King might offer, had arrived to talk. He tugged uncomfortably at the richly embroidered tunic Aina had insisted he should wear. He would rather have come in his everyday clothes and armour, but Aina assured him he needed to make a great show of status and wealth in this audience with the Bretar king. 'Lordly display is important,' she said, 'in turbulent times and uncertain company.'

He handed Aina and the baby from the ship with care. Asbjorn and Gormr stayed to guard *The Orm* and the rest of the party, armed to the teeth, formed closely around their leader and his auburn-haired woman as they strode towards the marketplace. The heads of men and women, young and old, turned as they progressed, some with alarmed expressions, others snarling with hatred. 'Llychlynwyr.' Thorgils heard them voice one of their names for his kind. People of the fjords. Well that was true enough and no insult.

Viking ships had been overwintering at Milford and other places along the coast of Cymry for two hundred years and the Gentiles, as the local people called the Northmen, were a familiar enough sight by now, as traders, mercenaries, allies, settlers, as well as raiders. Many Norsemen had married local women or bred children with their Bretar slaves. Many had learnt the language from their women and children. Some of Thorgils' men, such as Rhodi, were shorter and black-haired and could pass for Bretar. Yet despite the partial integrations and the degree of peaceful encounters, these predominantly big, blond or red Northmen were still mostly distinct. Many Northmen had not given over raiding as a necessary part of their repertoire. Their specialism of taking and trading slaves was not easily forgiven or soon forgotten and most families hereabouts had someone who had been ripped from home and hearts: a wife, a daughter, a young son, an aunt.

Thorgils and his men took no notice whatsoever of the response to their progress through the thronging harbour with its stench of fish and its crab pots, coiled ropes, piles of nets. 'Don't respond, Aina,' Thorgils warned her in a low voice. He did not want his delightfully mercurial wife getting them all into armed combat before he had even had speech with the King, and he also did not want to find himself fighting when he had his woman and child at his side. Perhaps he should have left them behind but Aina was not given to such ideas, and Thorgils generally found it easier to give way to her. That fight would have been worse by far, he thought wryly, beaming at her, much worse than anything these local men and women might visit on him.

At the marketplace the sale of slaves was in full swing and no knowing where these ones would have been taken from or whether they were enslaved following crimes or destitution, or whether they were the children and grandchildren of slaves. Thorgils overheard one merchant telling another that he was insulted by the offer of toothless, old, feeble merchandise on offer. Another man was haggling with a slaver, wanting to return a sick slave and get his money back. 'But the goods are faulty,' the man was saying, 'and it's just not satisfactory.' Above a crowd of craning dark heads, Thorgils saw three young women standing in thin shifts at the front of the platform, whilst a slaver called out descriptions and encouraged the crowd. One brown-haired girl had a completely blank expression, as if she were dead inside.

Another was shaking and crying, tears streaming down her pink face and snot gleaming on her upper lip. The third had the dark skin and hair of a foreigner and stood staring at the crowd, angry and proud.

'Whenever I see a slave now, Thorgils, I think of Sigrid,' Aina said, 'and her views about it.'

'Yes,' he said, turning his gaze away from the unfortunate three women and the platform where he had once stood himself and been separated from Sigrid. He surveyed the marketplace for signs of danger as well as signs for where he should head. 'This way,' he said, seeing a group of highly armed men outside one of the large houses. He saw how Aina took her eyes and her mind away from the slave women reluctantly, to follow him towards the house. Seeing Thorgils and his small band of huge, fair-haired men advancing on them, the guards crossed their spears with a loud clang.

'I am come at King Maredudd's invitation,' Thorgils said. 'Is he here?'

'Who asks?' a soldier said.

'Tell him Jarl Thorgils of Kelda Ey.' A man at the back of the melee near the door, disappeared into the darkness inside the house and they waited, the soldiers noting the weapons of Thorgils' group.

'Stand back a bit,' the man at the front told them and Thorgils grinning took a tiny step backwards. After a few minutes there was a shifting amongst the soldiers and they cleared a channel towards the door. 'Only you go in,' the soldier told Thorgils, 'and you remove your weapons here.'

Thorgils passed his gleaming sword in its scabbard to Toki behind him and hauled several knives from his belt and passed them back too. He had at least four more knives concealed elsewhere and Aina had one strapped under her long skirts high on her thigh. 'I'll bring my wife and child visiting,' he said, 'and I'll bring three of my men, all unarmed too. I'm a Jarl and not inclined to go about naked with no entourage. The King wouldn't expect it of me.'

The soldier stared at Thorgils for some time and then nodded. The four big men with Aina and Ulf in the midst of them sidled their way through the slim passage allowed by the Bretar guards, in through the doorway. If there was any trouble inside and they needed Toki's assistance Thorgils knew they had only to issue a whistling signal and Toki would have all that crowd of soldiery flattened and laid out for him to run over in an instant.

There was a long, dark staircase ahead of them and Thorgils took the small uneven steps two at a time. The dark hallway and narrow staircase issued into a surprisingly large, light room on the first floor, where a fire crackled, wooden floorboards glistened and sun streamed in through long arched window openings that reached from ceiling to floor. At the far end of the long room, a thick-set grey haired man sat on a carved wooden throne raised up on a dais. A slight fair-haired girl stood behind him, her hand resting on his shoulder, watching them approach with frank interest.

Thorgils inclined his head briefly and then lifted his gaze to the King.

'Welcome Jarl Thorgils and to the men and lady of your party,' Maredudd said, speaking in Bretar. Rhodi stepped up to whisper a translation at Thorgils' shoulder, and to translate the Jarl's words to the King.

'Greetings King Maredudd,' Thorgils said cheerfully.

'You come to petition me?' the King asked.

'No!' Thorgils smiled. 'You invited me a few years back, but I've been overbusy. Now here I am.'

The King smiled back at Thorgils' blithe frankness, responding to the translation. 'Well, I thank you. I had not looked for it after all this time but your coming now is welcome and timely again.'

He exchanged a few words over his shoulder with the girl, who stepped down, moving shyly past Thorgils and speaking to a servant waiting at the door. Wine and bread were brought for the King's visitors and then Maredudd resumed their conversation. 'As you know when last we had dealings my kingdom was much ravaged by your countryman, Godfrey Haraldsson, late of Mann and now squatting on my land on the Isle of Anglesey. He ravaged my holdings and enslaved many of my people, made Cymry into a sword-land laced with fires and screams.'

'Not my countryman,' said Thorgils. 'My country is the sea and its islands.'

Maredudd inclined his head. 'Your base is on Kelda Ey, I understand, off the coast near Dinbych-y-psygod?'

Thorgils nodded.

'I know that not all you Northmen are the same or all in league together, though doubtless you are all inclined one to the other if the wind is fair. I would like to suggest that the wind might be fair with you in *my* direction instead.'

Thorgils grinned at the king's nautical flattery and waited.

'What is it that you want here Jarl Thorgils, in my *gwlad*, my domains?'

'Land, silver, peace,' Thorgils said. 'Here is my wife and child,' he gestured to Aina and the king inclined his head with great politeness to her. 'I and my men look to live in peace with enough to sustain us.'

Maredudd's expression indicated that he took Thorgils' meaning. He needed *more* to sustain them than he already had. 'You have annexed my island of Kelda Ey,' he said, 'and you are welcome to it if you live there in peace, Jarl.'

Thorgils waited. He did not need this old man to 'give' him Kelda Ey or any other island.

'I would strike a bargain with you Jarl, for I know of your strength and wisdom.'

Aina suppressed the frustration that ached to grimace on her face or issue out in loud sighs. This King was long-winded and Thorgils, she thought, is not in need of your flattery, Maredudd. Feeling a twinge in her back, she hefted Ulf's bonny weight to her other hip.

'I need good men like you and yours in my army for this summer's campaigning in Morgannwg,' Maredudd declared.

Aina watched Thorgils raise his eyebrows. 'And why would I sacrifice my peace and leave my land and let my men face down the raven and wolf time again?' he asked.

'If you will give me your allegiance, swear to aid me and not those other Northmen ravaging my coasts, support me in campaign, I'll gift to you the tolls and tithes of the market in the hill fort of Dinbych-y-pysgod, and some good parcels of farmland close to the fort.'

'I'll be needing ten such parcels,' Thorgils said, with barely a pause for thinking it through. He knew how many of his men were in want of land that could not be found for them on Kelda Ey.

Maredudd considered him. 'How many men can you bring me, including yourself Jarl?'

'I'll be bringing you forty men and each one of them worth three of anything Godfrey Haraldsson can muster.'

The King's eyes gleamed and he nodded. 'We have a bargain, my friend, and you may do homage to me in this case.'

'Homage is not our way, King,' Thorgils said. 'Have you not heard the story of how Rollo, the Norse chieftain, received the lands of Normandy from the Frankish King Charles?'

Maredudd shook his head and Aina shifted Ulf back up higher on her hip, irritated at this doubtless apocryphal story that she had heard tell before to the chagrin of her own countrymen, but perhaps Maredudd would find it amusing.

'When King Charles gave Normandy to Rollo, who was the first Duke of that line, the king's servants said that Rollo should kiss the king's foot in thanks which Rollo refused to do but he ordered one of his men to do it. The man stepped forward, lifted the king's foot, threw him on his back, and kissed it.' Thorgils' men and the Bretar standing around laughed loudly at the story, and Maredudd, Aina saw with relief, was grinning broadly. Another man's misfortune, it seemed, could always be enjoyed.

'I will give you my oath of loyalty instead King Maredudd, that I swear on behalf of my household, all that are living, and also all that are yet unborn,' said Thorgils, and again Aina felt a concern at his words. After all the yet unborn would be forming in her womb and she had a say over that. She would be sure to remind Thorgils of that salient fact later, in private.

There was an uneasy truce at the feasting table that night with Maredudd's men who at first cast suspicious glances at Thorgils' blond and ruddy giants, but grew more sloppy friendly as the night wore on, the beer flowed and they heard these men would be fighting with them, rather than ranged against them.

Aina sat alongside Maredudd's young daughter, Angharad, who was delighted by Ulf and took him from Aina at intervals so that she might eat and drink with more ease. 'Do you have a brother?' Aina asked. 'Does your father have an heir?'

The girl's face fell. 'Not anymore,' she said and Aina waited for her to regain her composure. 'My brother, Cadwallon, he died last year, so no.'

'So you are your father's heir?'

The girl frowned perplexed at her. 'No. It's my cousins, of course: Edwin, Tewdwr and Einon.'

Now it was Aina's turn to frown, not understanding. 'Not you?'

'A girl is not an heir here,' Angharad said.

'Oh I see,' said Aina. 'Where I come from, in the Limousin, she is.'

'In England too,' said Angharad, 'but I am glad of it. They would all be fighting over me like dogs with a bone, if I were the heir.'

Aina grimaced. 'Ah yes,' she said. 'So it is.' She looked up as she heard the notes of Thorgils' strong and stirring singing voice and then his men joining one at a time and then in harmony. Maredudd wiped a tear from the corner of one eye, and the friendly atmosphere increased several more notches. Maredudd signalled to one of his captains who stood with a group of his men to reciprocate with their own harmonious and moving song. After the singing Maredudd's bard stepped up and told them tales of the king's valour and wisdom.

'This place Maredudd gives me,' Thorgils told Aina the next morning, 'its name means little fortress of the fishes.' He grinned. 'I like that.'

'You should put a man of this country, a Bretar, in charge of your new rights at the hill fort,' Aina told Thorgils. 'A man you can trust absolutely but who can talk easy with these people and knows their ways.'

Thorgils nodded at her sagacity, knowing she drew on a fund

of knowledge from her father who had been a very successful merchant and ruler in the great Frank city of Limoges where his sister Sigrid was now Viscountess. It was often trying but also often downright useful to have taken this Frankish woman as his concubine, and always so very delightful, he thought, looking into her grey eyes with their fringing of long black lashes.

# 24

# Limoges
## 994

I swallow my anxiety watching the maids filling the tub with hot water and sweet smelling herbs. It is one thing to consummate my marriage with Guy in the dark of our bed, but I am not yet used to him, to being his wife. My husband has returned from hunting and it is my duty to bathe him. I roll up my sleeves and knot the straps of my apron behind me, smoothing it to ensure it covers every inch of my green brocade dress. Perhaps I should have worn something less expensive but I recall that Melisende always wore the same rich clothing when she bathed Ademar, especially in the last days of his declining health. I am startled from my thoughts of how Ademar suffered, by the squeak of the door as Guy comes in wearing a long brown embroidered robe with a cord holding it closed at his waist. His feet are bare and the robe is open on the pale skin of his chest. The maids grin at each other, at me and then scuttle from the room.

Guy clears his throat. 'I could do this myself, wife, if you would rather,' he says.

I look him in the face. 'I would rather do it for you, husband,' I say firmly and reach out a hand to him, leading him to the bath that steams and fills our nostrils with the scent of lavender. Guy clears his throat again and I sense his uncertainty and embarrassment. I step close to him and unloop the cord at his waist so that the robe falls slightly open. My eyes skim over his white belly, the dark bush of pubic hair, the white and red flesh of his penis and testicles. I smile boldly into his face and slip the fabric of the robe across his shoulders, off onto the floor. His skin is very pale and seems to slink around the knobs and bumps of his rangy skeleton with little fat or muscle apparent anywhere. 'I'm sorry, I forgot to test the water,' I say, suddenly flustered. It would have been so much easier if I could have helped him step smoothly into the tub now, but instead I have to leave him standing there exposed whilst I fiddle around getting the water temperature right.

'Ah . . .' he says.

I dip my hand swiftly into the water pulling it out with a yelp at the scalding heat. 'Far too hot!' My face is burning red as my fingertips. I reach for the heavy jug of cold water.

'Let me,' he says, taking its weight from me and tipping the water in. He tests the water again. 'Perfect. You have it perfect Aina,' he says calmly, laying a hand on my arm. 'Don't worry.' So many times I have had to stop myself looking over my shoulder for her, when he calls me by her name.

I smile nervously and watch him step into the water and lower himself in. He closes his eyes and grins like a smug cat at the pleasure of the water assuaging his muscles after a day in the saddle. It is a relief to have him at least covered by, if still visible in, the water. The maids have placed a thick cushion at the side of the bath and I lift my skirts and apron and kneel down on it. 'May I wash you, my lord?' I say.

'Well, Aina, it's really not . . .'

'I will,' I say interrupting him. The bar of soap is in my hand but I am uncertain where to begin – at his head, his shoulders, his feet? I decide to begin with his feet, for then I do not have to look in his face. Clumsily I touch his calf indicating that he should lift his foot. He does so and I wash first one foot, calf and knee and then the other. I decide that his thighs and genitals should be self-washing, immersed as they are in the water and so I progress to sliding my soapy hands over his shoulders and chest. 'Lean forward,' I say and he does so while I soap his back and then I see that his shoulders are shaking with suppressed laughter. I push one shoulder back against the padded wood of the tub and ask offended, 'Why do you laugh at me, Guy?'

'You are handling me like a child,' he says, laughing openly now and I let go of my anxiety and laugh with him. He places a wet hand on my splendid brocade and pulls me unresisting towards him and kisses me.

I pull out of his embrace. 'My dress!' I say in distress.

'Hmm,' he says, standing, so that the water pours down from him, vestiges of soap on his chest where I have washed him so badly, 'best take it off I think.'

I look over my shoulder to see that the door is latched and reach behind me to the knot of my apron.

I arrived in Limoges with the threat of war hanging over the city. After Adalmode wed Audebert against the wishes of the Aquitaine family and without their permission, Guy told me, they threatened war. Young Guillaume, the Duke's son was gathering and training soldiers.

'Could you seek reconciliation?' I ask him, 'instead of war. The marriage is done now and time will have soothed his anger and perhaps you can avert conflict with reassurances of your remorse and loyalty? Gifts?'

'Yes, this is good advice, Aina.'

He went to the Easter Assembly in Poitiers and came back with a pardon from Guillaume for his offence. 'Audebert has not asked for pardon.'

'Count Audebert and Count Fulk are readying for war and seek it,' I say, 'but we should avoid it for the people of Limoges if we can.'

He nods. 'Audebert says he has no need of my troops, so I'll stay out of it, but I'll not take the field against him and my sister, on behalf of the Duke.'

Guy schools me on the political situation that he is contending with, so that I might help him in discussing it. The Duchess of Aquitaine, he tells me, who had been estranged from her husband and left him, returned two years ago. He had to make many concessions to get her back, including a hugely increased dowry that has allowed her foundations of the abbeys of Bourgeuil and Maillezais. All say that the reconciliation of the Duke and Duchess is a façade. The collapse of Lady Blanche's marriage to King Louis and then the end of Charlemagne's line with his death, should have enabled the Duke to fully reclaim his title to control in Aquitaine, but the Duke had fallen into an enfeebled condition during Emma's absence so she immediately took charge of affairs, antagonising many of the sycophants at court. She was skilled in reinforcing alliances with the local nobility: Thouars, Châtellerault, Aulnay, Angoulême, Marcillac.

'It's hard – well impossible – to like her,' Guy said, 'but you do have to admire her and as vassals we have to be grateful for her forceful effectiveness.'

'What about her son, Guillaume? Isn't he of age?' I ask.

'Yes, but they say his mother continues as if he were still a child. She cuts him out of Council meetings and justice hearings. She commands everything and he is not allowed.

Last year the old Duke of Aquitaine entered the monastery of Saint Cyprien during a serious illness and on the advice of his wife, Emma, was tonsured on what he thought was his deathbed. Emma, now took control of the Duchy as Regent for young Guillaume. However the old Duke rallied and is in health again but finds himself confined as a monk and his wife sitting on his throne and conducting the affairs of Aquitaine in consultation with her brother, the Count of Blois. The times continue uncertain as King Hugh Capet is aging and the lords are unsure of the strength and character of his son Robert who will soon take the crown in his stead.

The old Duke yet does battle with his wife,' Guy told me, 'seeking to influence the affairs of the world despite his monk's cowl. He subjected her Abbey of Maillezais to the control of Saint Cyprien and ejected the monks that she bought from her homeland in Tours, and now he threatens the same at her Abbey of Bourgeuil. The Regent Duchess is ablaze with anger at these acts and seeks the support of her brother. The old Duke has reneged on his agreement at Charroux – that was made on his behalf by his wife – and has appointed himself the Abbot of Nouaillé. It is said that he is in conflict with his own Abbot in Saint Cyprien.'

That men in monks' cowls are hypocritical and behave like warring lords does not surprise me, but I keep my opinion to myself.

Archbishop Gunbaldus of Bordeaux, who called an earlier Peace Council in Charroux whilst I was away a 'Viking hostage', has approached Guy and Hilduin asking to organise another Peace Council here in Limoges later this year – in November. 'In the five years since Charroux,' he wrote to Guy, 'there is still much violence abroad.' Guy of course has accepted this request and now I am busy preparing for the influx of clergy, lords, pilgrims, travelling merchants and visitors who will descend on Limoges for the event.

I enjoy the challenge of managing the Limoges household and supporting my husband in his work as Viscount. In the autumn nuts and berries were plenteous and we could add those to our feasts: bowls sat on the trestle in the hall filled with walnuts, almonds, hazelnuts, chestnuts, elderberry, blackberry and rose hips. In the winter, after the Christmas feasting, we were uncertain whether the supplies of salted, smoked and fat-stored meat would last beyond March and into the next growing season. I instructed the cook on making a tasty soup with what the stores or the ground could give us in the lean months: parsley, celery, turnips, leeks, garlic, shallots, onions or cabbages. Like dried fish, however, there is a limit to how many bean suppers anyone can happily eat. When we were starting to suffer from the men's flatulence and an excessive thronging in the privies I knew we had to reduce beans and find more meat for our meals. I sent the kitchen boys scavenging for mushrooms and wild greens but sometimes those also had an unfortunate effect on our bowels. Guy is not enamoured with gruel no matter how hard I try to convince him of its virtues. Now, in the summer, there is an abundance of fruit: pears, apples, quinces, plums and cherries.

The first days and nights of our marriage were good. I was surprised to find how much I liked Guy, liked being his wife and the mistress of his household. Yet I remembered Aina had treated him with contempt and felt I should not show too differently or he would notice. In my ridiculous attempt to ape Aina's disdain I drove a wedge of misunderstanding between us, and now I have to work hard to remove this and make him see, or feel I should say, because I know now he cannot see, feel how much I like him and want to assist him. Yet whatever I do or say he mirrors my first coolnesses to him and disbelieves

271

the sincerity of my affection. The gossip that he had a mistress in the city before our marriage reaches me and I wonder if he might seek her out again. This is the harvest of my lies. I know he feels his near-sightedness as a great vulnerability and wants a place of safety from that constant defence, a safety that Adalmode gave him before her marriage and which I would like to supply, if only I could win his trust. I confuse him with the way I blow hot one week and cold the next. Sometimes my coldness comes from my very real melancholy, and is not mere playacting. When I found Thorgils, I did not think to lose him again. When I achieved my status as a free Norsewoman I did not think to exchange it for lies and guilt.

'What is wrong with you this week, this month, Aina? You have been cold to me, wife, when you owe me a duty of affection.' Guy does not shout. He never shouts at me. Instead I hear pain in his quiet voice.

'Do you mean to repudiate me?' I shout. Part of me is thinking that if he did so, I could return to Thorgils and Aina, I could marry a Norseman, but another, a larger part of me, is fearful that his answer will be yes.

He brings his face close up to mine, and I know by now for sure that he cannot see me otherwise. 'No!' he says, aghast. 'How can you even think that? You are my wife. My greatly loved wife. Unfortunately I must go now. There are visitors waiting in the hall for me and I regret that I cannot continue our discussion. I am sorry that we have argued.'

I feel terrible shame then, for it is all my fault. 'It is I who should say sorry. Stay a moment!' I hang onto his hand. 'I have to tell you . . . I am with child.'

He clasps me gently by the shoulders, his face full of joy and I realise at that moment that I love him, utterly love him, but he does not even know who I am. 'Well, that explains it!' he says. 'That explains your moodiness, my poor darling.' And I feel even worse at those words, because it does not.

I listen to my husband's judgements in the hall, I watch how he behaves to the members of his household and especially to those who are lowly servants and each day I see a man I can admire more and more. One night as we are preparing for bed, I ask him: 'Can I help you?'

'You already do,' he says, glancing towards the bed.

'No!' I laugh. 'I mean with your eyes. Is there something I can do?'

'Well, Adalmode used to help me before she left to marry. You could read correspondence for me when we are private together perhaps? Warn me if I am about to make a fool of myself?'

I nod, eager that I might find ways to atone for my crimes against him.

Who am I? To my husband and all the people around me I am Aina, a Christian noblewoman. My real self is buried and smothered more than it ever was when I was a slave. At least then I could still say my name. I am Sigrid Thorolfsdottir and I am a pagan. I am not a Christian. Now every word I speak is a lie. Every action, from my hand on my husband's cheek to my instructions to the steward for the day, and my attendance at Christian masses. All lies. Now my silver serpent brooch is an image of my own fork-tongue, my mouth full of poisonous untruths, I am a serpent in my husband's breast. Amidst the lies I am losing contact with myself. When I get these morose moods I think of Thorgils and Aina and their child on the island and persuade myself they are happy and I had no choice.

Should I tell Guy? The fact that he is kind and loving towards me makes my deception all the harder. And now to compound it I have to lie to my child, my first-born son, whom we have named Ademar after Aina's father and who will grow up thinking like his father that I am Aina, a Christian noblewoman. When I was enslaved it was important to retain myself, to find my secret rituals for the expression of my identity, to resist the pressures to integrate and comply, to continue in my difference. Now I wonder should I let her go – that Sigrid Thorolfsdottir, just lay her in the surf like an empty nightgown and let her drift away on the ebb tide. Forget her entirely and *be* Viscountess Aina without compromise. I don't know how to exist otherwise. I cannot continue in perpetual misery at my deception, perpetual confusion at who I am.

My child came fast and Guy's anxieties about the birth proved unnecessary. Though I laboured for only a few hours, the vice-like pains were intense but I was not afraid, knowing that I was achieving something wonderful. Our baby son is a delight to us. We bathe him together in a small tub in front of the fire. Guy holds out the cloth to dry him and takes the baby from me, who is giggling and slippery wet like a pink fish. We gaze with wonder into his clear eyes and watch his discoveries of the world, dimly remembering our own.

'He is perfect, Aina, he has your nose, see.'

'And the colour of your eyes,' I say, and see in his frown his fervent hope that his son has not inherited the weakness of his eyes.

I wish I had not tried to ape Aina's disdain for Guy in the early days of our marriage. I have tried to replace that since with affection but he is still wary even though I tell him often that I love him, and that is one sincere thing in my life. Yet he does not believe me. He feels himself to be unlovable and yet he is so dear. I bring to him both the inconsequential and the important from each of my days and share them with him at night before we fall asleep entwined. I stroke his cheek and yet always there is this mammoth weight of lies and he knows there is something, but he does not know what it is.

I am constantly surprised at his small kindnesses. He is always thinking of me, of what I might need, how I might feel – as far as that is possible given the concealment of so much of my inner life. He looks around my chamber one day and the next I have a new tapestry on the wall where the draught had been coming in through a crack. He leafs through the small collection of books on my table and two weeks later a large case of books, to my taste, appear in the centre of the room. His gifts are based on his observations of me. I begin to see that I can be someone clearly reflected in his eyes, I can be the me that he knows and empathises with, but I have to let go of my guilt and I have to let go of Sigrid Thorolfsdottir. I mourn her – she has died too young and I am reborn as this new creature – me as Aina, as Guy's wife, Ademar's mother, the Viscountess of Limoges, managing a large household, advising my husband.

Supervising the bailiff in his collection of rents from my husband's tenants, hiring servants and then keeping a check on them are amongst the tasks that I perform for my husband. If a servant is talking or drinking too much it is my job to tell them so and see they take heed of my warning or I have no choice but to dismiss them. Sometimes I have to prevent quarrels and bad language amongst the servants or to check a man who is too free with his hands or attentions to the maids. I must take care of those who are foolish and young or those who are old and sick. I surprise myself with an avid interest in bee-keeping and viniculture.

As the chatelaine I am expected to wear silks and brocades rather than to make them, but I am loathe to set aside the sewing that I enjoyed for so long. I begin to embroider mine and Aina's story into a great length of linen and it is only me and my serpent who know that the Aina stepping off the boat in Normandy is me and that the Sigrid writing her friend's name on the beach on Kelda Ey is truly Aina and I have transposed the name that is written there.

I have a dark grey gown furred with marten and a violet gown edged with grey fur which is Guy's favourite and so I wear it often. I run the household budget deciding what we will spend on alms, the household expenses, payments of staff, gifts, jewels and clothes. I oversee the accounts each month and my staff confer with me on the daily business of the castle: making candles, curing bacon, salting meat, baking bread. I send the maids shopping in the market for fish, wine, spices. I am responsible for ensuring that our beds do not need repairing or replacing, that the hangings, plate, furniture, vestments and linen of the house are all in good order. When I am uncertain I write to Lady Melisende for advice, or I store my questions up for her frequent visits.

My time now, when I am not busy organising the household or discussing the political problems of Limoges with Guy, is spent hawking, playing chess, reading a book that is the latest fashion with all noble ladies that I might play my part with aplomb as his wife, especially when we have visitors. When there are no visitors he is happy to live simply. I am still known for my skill in telling stories, and he loves to listen to me. Walking on a high cliff edge with him one day, looking down on the steep abyss below, I suddenly feel terribly afraid, like a vertigo, at the ferocity of my love for him.

In March I take my falx, my pruning knife, and join the workers as they set about pruning and manuring the vines. Guy laughs at me: 'You are the only Viscountess between here and Barcelona I believe who is labouring in the garden with the gardeners.'

'Do you mind it much? I enjoy it.'

'Of course not Aina. You look like the goddess Flora.'

In the spring the air is strongly scented with the aroma of the grape blossoms and we all imagine ahead to the gathering and trampling of the grapes. The bees to and fro to the rope skeps or baskets that are their buzzing cities placed on alcoves in the garden wall, with little lip platforms for them to land on. I am fascinated by the rustling, wing-lit hives and draw sketches of the bees for Guy, showing him how they have three eyes. He studies my drawings with a magnifying glass that I ordered from a Jewish merchant who does business with Melisende. It seems so strange that these fierce insects work both in dazzling sunshine and in the scented darkness of the hive, diving for an instant into flower-filled space and then plunging back into crowded blackness. Like the vineyard, the bee hives measure the passing of the year. In early spring the hives start to come alive, shaking off the torpor of winter and the bees begin to search out early violets and anemones. By April the hives are crowded with their tireless workers, arriving with their loads of pollen slung between their thighs, grateful to the generous flowers. On long summer days, the humming and flitting of the bees in their palaces of honey are as much an essential part of my surroundings as the rays of the sun, the balm of the air, the tall poplars calmly guarding the peaceful waters of the brook, my happiness with Guy and my boys. My second son, Geraud, was born this spring.

I watch the bees circle dancing and the servants tell me they call this beating to arms. When the bee-man needs to manage the hives he plunges his arms into cold water beforehand as a precaution against the stings. I watch and listen for the moment when the bees decide to swarm, pouring out of the hive in a black jet and clustering in the nearest tree in a great pendant glob, waiting for their scouts to tell them where to go, and then they are off in an impetuous flight to their new home.

When the time comes to harvest the honey and we must kill the bees with sulphur smoke and shake out their thousands of dead bodies to the ground, I feel grief at their ardent, disinterested work and the exposure of their golden corridors. On long winter nights, I try always to be frugal with candles for the bees' sakes and I savour the smell of honey and wax, remembering the dozy days of summer.

As summer draws to an end, the cooper begins the work of cleaning and repairing the big barrels in readiness for the wine. In September we savour the smell of the grape juice as every man, woman and child comes to help cut the grapes and the vineyards are humming like my beehives with their chatter. The grapes are cut and gathered into panniers and then transferred to wooden vats and trampled. I tuck my skirts into my belt and Guy hands me to step barefoot into the vat with the peasants. 'Ooh, it feels so strange between my toes,' I giggle to him, wiggling them up and down and lifting one foot gingerly, still gripping his hand, afraid that I might slip and fall into the ooze which would not be a decorous display for the lady of the castle.

Guy is attuned to my moods. He can tell from the tone of my voice in just a few words how I am feeling, and then he does something about what he hears. If it is joy, he shares it with me. If sadness, then he enquires what is concerning me, looks for ways to help or take a brighter view. He is my daily touchstone. When I first married I thought I had made a sacrifice of myself for the sake of Aina and my brother, but as I grow to know Guy, I have developed a deep affection for him.

On my birthday each year (or at least the date of Aina's birthday), he grants freedom to two families of serfs on his land. His commands are read out in the hall: 'Piers freed for God's sake and for the soul of my dear wife, Damon the smith and his wife and all their children, who bent their heads for food in the evil days of hunger, freed.'

I hope I reciprocate adequately, doing my best to understand his disappointments and anxieties, talking them through with him, trying to mitigate his problems, celebrate his triumphs. I try to support him with sympathy and advice when he tells me: 'Every side I turn there are complaints. The churchmen complain the castellans take liberties and that religious offices should not go to noble families. The peasants complain of the *albergum* tax to provide food for the *milites*, the dues laid against their livestock and the banalities for their use of my mills and ovens. No one is ever happy.' Little by little, as the years have gone by, I know that I can never be without Guy, will never send word to Thorgils to come to get me, will never see Aina again.

Guy keeps annals like a monk, writing a note in his book in the library every evening on the day's doing. I watch him hunched in a small yellow pool of candle light, his nose almost touching the parchment on the table. He records the big and the small news, as he puts it. There is grim news from the north that Charles of Lorraine, the old king's brother, has died in Hugh Capet's prison, and Guy makes a note of this. Sometimes Guy reads a few passages to me from these annals at breakfast, especially when he has found something amusing to record, and sometimes he flicks through several pages saying, 'Oh no, can't read that one, or that one, or that one. They are about you!' He looks up impishly at me and I lunge laughing for the book, but he snatches it aloft, safe from my grasp. 'All good, all good, of course!' he says airily and smiling.

This morning his mood is not so playful. The city bells are tolling and Guy is sitting with his head in his hands when I come down to the hall with Ademar, who is two years old, holding my skirts, and Geraud in my arms.

'How many cases now?' I ask. Unease and discontent have spread amongst the people. A young girl disappeared from a crowd in the cathedral and despite searches organised by Guy and his men, she was never found. In the panic when she was taken, angry fights broke out in the church and several people were killed. A storm came and destroyed a vineyard and some claimed the destruction was the work of ghost horses' hooves. A wolf entered the cathedral and Bishop Hilduin has declared this is a judgement from God that the city is the habitation of wild beasts rather than Christian people and he is withholding the sacraments from whole communities arguing that treating them all as pagans will flush out the wicked, whereas it merely increases the distress of many innocent people.

The harvest was poor and the people began to starve, to send some of their sons and daughters out on the road since they could no longer feed all of their family members, or to sell themselves into serfdom. The monasteries' granaries were opened to the poor but it was not enough to see off the threat of famine. And now finally the Firesickness has come, giving men, women and children terrible burning sensations in their limbs and fearful hallucinations. The people beg Saint Martial and the clergy to intercede and help them in their suffering. And the bishops will begin to arrive in a few days time for the start of the Peace of God Council.

'More than a hundred cases of Firesickness,' Guy says. 'They are sweaty and fevered and pale and see horrors that are not there. They run around and fall down in exhaustion, still talking of what they see.'

'But they do not die?'

'No, none have died so far, but they are helpless and no work can be done and more fall ill to the sickness every day.'

Guy's brother, Bishop Hilduin, whom I dislike, has arrived early this morning and is sitting on the dais with a look of satisfaction on his face. 'Do not despair, Brother,' he says, nodding a curt greeting to me. 'I will preach a sermon today in the city square and I have ordered a three day fast. This sickness has been brought upon them by their own sins and I will chastise them. Fornications, adulteries and incest are poured over the land, even by some nuns. Avarice, robberies and violence are abroad. They must beg God's forgiveness, mend their ways, undertake pilgrimages, buy prayers and intercessions for the wickedness that has brought the sickness upon them. The wolf in the cathedral was a sign that God has forsaken those who have forsaken him, but I will bring them back to the fold, Brother.'

It occurs to me that a wolf in the cathedral might be interpreted as a sign of a different nature, relating more to the behaviour of these Christian priests and monks, but I say nothing. I must observe the Christian rituals whilst continuing a pagan in my heart – Christmas, Easter, Palm Sunday, but many of their feasts are not so dissimilar from my own I notice – celebrating the first plowing after winter, the rites of May, the summer solstice after the sheep shearing, but I guard my tongue against speaking of Midgard – the world of men, and Asgard – the home of *my* gods, the Aesir.

Guy frowns, regarding Hilduin. 'You believe the people are to blame for their own suffering?'

'Of course.' Hilduin helps himself to a glass of wine and a chunk of warm bread. 'And then there is the matter of the treasure that you took from the Abbey to pay for your wife's ransom which is still outstanding.'

'Why do you think it is only the poor people who suffer and not any of the nobles?' I ask, looking meaningfully to my husband.

'Because they are steeped in sin,' he says in an exasperated tone as if I am a school child who has not learnt her lessons well. 'Fornication, lust, venery, pride.'

Guy shakes his head. 'I think there is another explanation for this sickness and we must find it.'

'The explanation is plain, staring you in the face. A large group of pilgrims are setting off from the square on pilgrimage to Compostela at noon today. Will you come to see them off and witness my blessing?'

'Yes, if you think this will help.'

'Look to the bread, Guy,' I say. 'I saw this sickness once before in Ségur. Not so many people were ill then and we managed to control it quickly, but we found that the flour had rotted or been mixed with some toxic material and this was the cause.'

'Yes,' says Guy slowly, 'but how can we trace it?'

'We need to talk with those who suffer, or their families and find out what they have in common. Are they served by the same miller or granary.'

Guy looks brightly at me. 'You are right.' He calls his steward to him and instructs him to carry out this enquiry, whilst Hilduin tuts at the idea that the problem can be seen in a granary, as opposed to being a spiritual failing of the people.

The following day the steward comes to report that the most likely source of the sickness is the granary at the Abbey of Saint Martial. All the families who are suffering the sickness are getting their grain from there. Guy calls his brother, Geoffrey, Abbot of Saint Martial to him. 'You must close down your granary, brother Abbot. Issue no more flour or bread from it.'

'This is ridiculous, Guy. As Hilduin has told you the reason for the sickness is the people's sin, not the bread. None of the monks and priests of the abbey are suffering, because of our holiness.'

When he has left, I shake my head. 'No, Guy. There is more to uncover here.'

'I don't know what to do next,' he admits. The sickness continues to spread and more people fall ill, more cluster in the city square preparing to depart on pilgrimages. Some of the pilgrims fall ill before they have cleared the city gates and lie on the ground, frothing at the mouth and shouting obscenities as their fellows step over them, crossing themselves. I went amongst the afflicted advising them to fast and avoid bread and flour, but it is all many of them have to fill their empty bellies.

'We have to go and look at the granary,' I tell Guy. 'It has been the common connection between all those who are ill. There is something there despite what Geoffrey and Hilduin say. It is too easy to explain everything as an act of God, when so many things are really acts of men.'

He calls for our horses. 'We will go and question there discreetly then. If there is any hope that we can do something we must before the city is depleted of people who are able to function.'

'We will bring Fulayh, with us,' I say and Guy nods. Fulayh is a Moor and a doctor who has been valued in my household for some years now, after my son's illness where he coughed blood and I was scared witless that he would die until Fulayh took charge of his care and saved him.

At the Abbey gates the Gatekeeper looks unhappy to open up for the Viscount and Viscountess and stares at Fulayh's black face, crossing himself. 'The Abbot is away dining with the Bishop, my lord, perhaps you would like to return later,' he stammers.

'No,' says Guy. 'I do not need to speak with Abbot Geoffrey but with the monk who has charge of the granary. Where will I find him?'

When Guy and Fulayh question the victualler it becomes clear that the abbey has two separate supplies of flour – one for the monks and their noble visitors, and another inferior supply which is the part of the granary the Abbey has opened to the poor. The doctor examines samples of flour from the two supplies. 'There is ergot mixed in the poorer supply,' he tells us. 'This is the cause of the people's sickness and hallucinations. It is not mixed in with the grain that goes to make the monks' bread.'

Guy heaves a sigh of relief that we have found the answer. 'Close this granary supply down right away,' he orders, 'and destroy this grain.'

'Destroy it!' blusters the monk. 'But my lord the people will starve then instead.'

'No, give to them from your good supply.'

The monk's eyes bulge at the thought of how the Abbot will react and we hear his loud plaints behind us for some time after we have turned our horses and started back towards the Motte.

The following day our visitors begin to assemble for the Peace Council. First come the clerics: Archbishop Gunbaldus of Bordeaux and the bishops, Abbo of Saintes, Frotarius of Périgueux, Grimoard of Angoulême, Dagbert of Bourges, Stephen of Le Puy, Gilbert of Poitiers, Bego of Clermont. Hilduin is in his element, bustling around with great self-importance. And then come our noble visitors including Duchess Emma and her son, young Guillaume of Aquitaine. It is the first time I have seen them since I was a girl at Brioude. I am shocked at how aged the Duchess looks: her knuckles gnarled, her face furrowed as if a fork had been dragged down her skin. The young heir to the throne of Aquitaine is fat. He has a small coin-shaped bald patch at the back of his brown head, although he is only twenty-four. I keep my veil down and avoid their company as much as possible in case anyone should recognise me. I am so busy organising the household for these many guests that it is not so difficult to stay out of the way most of the time, although I have to sit next to Guy at the meals. Guillaume keeps close company with the young Count of Angoulême. They seem to love each other like one soul and all their speech is mutual flattery. I overhear them speaking of the Count of La Marche. 'The man is a hair on my tongue,' Guillaume says.

'The portents of the End Time are dire indeed,' Hilduin whispers loudly in the ear of the Archbishop and recounts the catalogue of crises we have weathered here: the stolen child in the cathedral, the people trampled to death, the wolf, the fire sickness. The Archbishop is nodding and frowning. 'I have a suggestion,' Hilduin says. 'I suggest that we elevate the body of our saint, Saint Martial, from the Abbey Crypt and take him in procession to the hill of Montjovy and beg for the saint's intercession and assistance with our important work in this Peace Council.'

The Archbishop nods his head again. 'Excellent idea, Bishop Hilduin. Yes, please organise this.'

The following morning a great crowd of people swarm towards the foot of the hill of Montjovy where I stand on the summit with Guy, my children and Hilduin. The people begin to climb up, excited men, women and children in motley colours, monks in brown and black. Small bells ching and incense wafts. The people are singing *sotto voce*. Above their heads the startled wooden faces of the saints move jerkily as they are carried on litters on the shoulders of the people, Saint Martial keeping close company with The Virgin at the head of the procession. The statues are wreathed with flowers. Behind the procession of saints come a group of monks swathed in purple silk, their heads covered, carrying small whips with which they rhythmically flog themselves across alternate shoulders. When the throng reaches the summit they stand back leaving a clear space for the saints to be carefully set down before us. Hilduin mutters benedictions and makes the sign of the cross, repeatedly. Two oblates stand on either side of him swinging incense burners. On Saint Martial's litter, along with his statue and reliquary, is his actual shrouded body that has been raised up from the crypt. I look with distaste at the wrapped body-shape, the once fine white linen spotted with soil and dark stains. This body of the saint, Hilduin told us, would help the people in their dark hour as the End of Time approaches us. It seems evil magic to me but I keep my face respectful.

'Rejoice!' shouts Hilduin suddenly, making me jump beside him. 'The End Time is coming upon you fast when you will be judged every last one of you. The portents gather to give you final warning to set the accounts of your souls in order. If you repent your sins now, give your wealth and your sons and daughters to the church, then you may purchase your place in heaven, but if you continue as you are, steeped in sin, you will meet Satan in the fiery bowels of hell.'

Looking around myself I see more anxiety at his words than rejoicing. Only the grimmest beggars and those who are mortally ill look pleased. The people groan and weep.

# 25

# Fortress of the Fishes

## June 996

Jarl Thorgils' warriors revived their skills as farmers and his settlement, clustered along the coast and islands around Dinbych-y-psygod, was flourishing. Thorgils' fame as a shipbuilder and pilot had become so great that young men came to learn with him from the Isle of Mann, from Dublin, Orkney and even from Norway. The peace was kept between Norse settlers and Bretar, and urged on by his wife, Thorgils acquired his own skald and large household.

Today the market in the hill fort where Thorgils and Aina took tithes was crowded with people, impatiently jostling the elbows of others in their hurry or sauntering agog at the crowds. They had left Ulf at home on the island with Morag because there were rumours of a coughing contagion spreading in the settlement attacking the lungs and killing especially children and the old.

Each street in the small town houses a particular type of trader – one street of saddlers, another all bakers, and a third vintners. When they visited Dinbych-y-psygod Aina went to church and she kept the chapel on the island in good repair and prayed there, but she allowed no priests onto the island. The priest in the hill-fort told her: 'Lady, as a good Christian woman you should bring your husband and your household to Christ.'

'Thank you for your advice, Father,' Aina said politely, but she had no intention of making Thorgils and his men give up their own beliefs. Each to their own was her view.

Thorgils and his men helped King Maredudd win victory in battle against the king's nephew, despite Edwin having aid from the English king Athelred. Edwin had been forced back to the borderlands where Athelred gifted him lands in Herefordshire, intending a buffer between the English kingdom and the might of Maredudd. Yet there was never much peace, or ever like to be, for Maredudd. His other kin, the sons of Meurig, were now readying to threaten his kingdom.

A merchant *knorr* from Norway, trading in hides and whale oil, was moored up at Dinbych-y-psygod for the market and Thorgils invited the owner to dine with him that he might hear news of his homeland. Aina watched impatiently as the fat merchant chewed slowly through a large pile of food and refilled his goblet three times before speaking. Then Aina and Thorgils both sat back from the table in amazement, exchanging surprised looks with each other at the merchant's first piece of news: Olafr had become King of Norway. Thorgils beamed, listening to the tale of how Olafr sailed the previous year with just five ships against Jarl Hakon who was hated by his subjects for his lascivious treatment of other men's wives. Olafr sailed from the Orkneys and landed at Moster, moving north fast against Hakon. When Olafr was proclaimed King at The Thing in Nidaros, he repeated the actions of his legendary great-grandfather Harald Finehair, allowing his hair and beard to grow ungroomed during the months of campaigning, and then having it ceremoniously cut, washed and combed at the crowning.

Aina exclaimed, 'He looked a beautiful king I don't doubt.'

The merchant had more good news: Olafr was reunited with his mother, Astrid, who had been bought at the slave market in Tallinn, freed and married to a Norwegian named Lodin. Olafr and King Svein gained mountains of silver from their joint attack on London the year before, and Olafr had been able to make good use of this wealth in his first year as King.

'I should be with Olafr,' Thorgils said to Aina and saw her face cloud over, 'but . . . I should be here too, and so here I will stay.' The sun broke out on her face again. Her moods were as swift-changing as the weather and just as Thorgils was an expert weather-watcher so he was an expert in what he thought of as Aina weather.

Thorgils shook his head over the merchant's final piece of information: Olafr had become a Christian, 'Baptised by Elfheah,

Bishop of Winchester and aiming to make Christians of all Norway, and even sending missionaries to Iceland and Greenland.'

'Olafr Crowbone! I don't believe it at all!' said Thorgils.

'Why do you call him that?' Aina asked.

'Olafr is nicknamed Crowbone for his skill with the lots, with divining, seeing omens in the birds and bones. He is half *godi* and Odinn's man. I cannot imagine him Christian. There is a large pile of silver and politicking behind this somewhere, for sure.'

After Aina retired to bed the merchant told Thorgils how Olafr's Christian mission was being enacted: 'maimings, exiles, bribing orators, threatening to sacrifice chieftains, smashing a statue of Odinn, burning pagan magicians in a feast hall.'

'He always had a brutal temper,' said Thorgils, remembering how, when still a boy, Olafr had buried his axe in the head of Klerkon, who sold them into slavery.

'Despite his Christianity he keeps to the old ways when it comes to wives,' the merchant said. Olafr had Gyda in Ireland but that was far away when he was in Norway so he took as a second wife, Gudrun, the daughter of a chieftain he had murdered. 'She tried to kill him as he slept on their wedding night, so that didn't work out. Then he courted the haughty Queen of Sweden, but offended her by giving her a brass bracelet instead of a gold one. Now he is married to King Svein of Denmark's sister, Thyra, who ran away from her old husband the King of Wendland.'

'No doubt, she finds Olafr better in her bed,' Thorgils said, laughing.

The day after their return to Kelda Ey, Aina sat at the trestle in the monks' old refectory slicing easily through the hunk of raw chicken in front of her with a sharp knife and thinking of Sigrid. What was she doing now? Soon after Sigrid had been handed over at Fécamp, posing as Aina, she had written to say that all had gone well and Thorgils heaved a huge sigh of relief as Aina read Sigrid's letter to him. Aina's mother, after some reluctance and anxiety, had agreed to help with the deception and was supporting Sigrid in her new role. Guy accepted Sigrid as Aina and they were married – quite happily married, wrote Sigrid, and Aina grinned to herself thinking of that. Good. Thank goodness. She hated to think of Sigrid making herself unhappy in order that she and Thorgils alone could be happy. The chicken was sliced and Aina turned to the carrots and onions. There were plenty of slaves to do the work of cooking and cleaning around the household but Aina enjoyed preparing food. It gave her privacy and time for thinking to herself. It reminded her of times in Ségur with Sigrid and was the closest she could get to recreating those times.

Ragnhild approached rattling a large bowl and showed her the small white and grey frilled shells inside. 'Do you want to do these cockles or shall I give them to Morag. It's a smelly job,' she smiled.

'No, here,' said Aina reaching out her hands to the bowl. The cockles had been soaked in a bucket of seawater overnight and Ragnhild had already drained and washed them. Aina picked through the shells discarding the ones that had opened and were dead. The sound of them knocking against each other reminded her of dice or of Olafr showing her how to shake and cast small bones to see the future.

Aina splashed apple cider into a hot pan on the embers and put the shells in, placing a lid on the top. They were steamed open in a few minutes. Then she sorted through the shells again, this time discarding those that had not opened. When they had cooled sufficiently she picked the cockle meat out of each shell and placed them in a bowl with a little vinegar made from soured beer and the pepper she bought in Tenby market.

She set the bowl on the table as she heard Thorgils approaching, whistling. He stooped to come through the doorway and she admired the muscled skin of his arms and chest, brown and shiny from dousing at the well. She smiled at him, wiping her salty, wet hands on her apron. He was cleaning his teeth with a hazel shoot and had his antler comb in his hand. He dumped a pile of his clothes down on the bench and sat down next to Aina, bare-chested and bare-foot, wearing only his breeches. She took the comb and began the long process of combing through his hair and beard. She kissed the back of his neck and the rise of his collarbone, laughing at his complaints that she should comb and not kiss, and at his exaggerated yelps when the comb snagged and tugged, and then she enjoyed the way the comb slid through the silky dusky orange of his hair as the combing progressed. 'Done,' she said and Ulf clambered up between them, giggling as Thorgils tickled him in the ribs, and she began her ministrations on her son's small head. Despite Thorgils' hair colour and the dark red wine pigment of her own hair, Ulf's was thick and blond.

She snatched a quick kiss on the top of Ulf's head as he began to grow impatient and fidget, and was soon down from the bench and off to play with the dogs and other children. From the doorway she watched him giggling hysterically as he and two other boys rolled down the small slope with their bodies held straight, their arms pinioned at their sides. When he reached the bottom he leapt to his feet, waved to her and ran up fast to roll down again. Aina suddenly ran out, laid herself down at the top of the slope and to the astonished amusement of the boys, Thorgils and the watching women, rolypolyed herself down to the dip, and then stood, strands of her wine-red hair tangled across her pink face, dust and grass stains on her clean white apron. Thorgils shook his head at her laughing, shrugged on his marten skin jerkin, wiggled his feet into old boots that waited for him on the threshold, and strode off towards the ships on the beach. Aina, dusted herself down, washed her hands in a bowl of water and returned, smiling, to preparing the food.

'Mad!' said Ragnhild in admiration.

After eating the midday meal, Thorgils was back at the beach working again, and Aina sat with Ulf drawing pictures of boats and dragons. Aina heard the sound of boots running and looked up to see Thorgils bursting in. 'Aina, hide yourself quickly! A sail's sighted and I know that ship. It's *The Crane*. It's Olafr.'

'Olafr . . .' It had been so long, that Aina had almost forgotten their deception and their danger.

'Now woman! The boy will be safe but hide yourself now!'

Aina ran down to the beach and crouched behind the large boulder. Carefully she craned her neck around the edge of the rock and saw the sail of *The Crane* fast approaching. The sun was glinting on the blond head of the man standing on the foredeck. She looked around her wildly and then crept under the upturned hull of one of the boats. Carefully she pulled her skirts in ensuring that every part of her gown was concealed and worked to slow the sound of her breathing. Thin slivers of light knifed down through the darkness, between the planks of the boat, pinning her to the ground. She could smell the sea in here and hear its muffled rhythm. Before long she heard the crunch of the boat beaching and the voices of men, Thorgils' shout of greeting and Olafr's reply. If someone thought to overturn this boat she would be exposed, lying there like a woodlouse under a lifted stone.

When the voices receded Aina crept out cautiously, saw no one and sprinted to the woods, moving under the cover of the trees away from the Priory Longhouse. There were many places to hide and she knew every inch of the island. She would conceal herself with the puffins and the seals in their caves on the furthest point of the island and she would watch the boats on the beach from the high point and see when Olafr left.

'I need you by my side now, Thorgils, now I am crowned King in Norway,' Olafr said, seated at the head of the loaded feasting table. Thorgils had instructed the household to behave normally and they had bustled around preparing an extravagant meal, making Olafr and his men welcome and comfortable. Yet there was a suppressed anxiety in the air. Thorgils could sense it. Could Olafr? A maid at the end of the table dropped a precious goblet, smashing it. Olafr looked briefly in her direction and turned back to Thorgils. 'And Leif here means to ask for your sister's hand again, if she's not wed yet. Where is she?'

'She . . . is away,' Thorgils replied, reaching for elaboration of his lie and not finding any. After the meal he gave his bed up to Olafr and as he rolled into his blanket on the hall floor, near the fire, he wondered where Aina was and if she was warm enough. She had run from the hall in only her gown, but he knew she could take care of herself. As he fell asleep he pictured her curled into a ball in a small cave, covered in leaves, her red hair loose and cladding her shoulders and back, like a beautiful magical fox in its lair.

The next morning he went out for a run with the dogs as usual and saw no sign of Aina. Returning to the hall his heart sank as he saw chaos and panic around him, and Olafr pacing in a state of fury that he knew well.

'Brother!' Olafr spat at him and Thorgils watched Olafr's hand go to his sword hilt. 'You lie and lie to me. You betray me. Your brother and your king.'

Thorgils said nothing and waited.

'Leif here sought for news of Sigrid and heard the sorry tale of your betrayal from one of the slave-girls.'

Thorgils looked around him. Who had betrayed them? One of the girls Aina had offended in some way perhaps, or just someone jealous of their happiness, or someone hoping for advantage or freedom.

'Where is she? The hostage. Aina of Ségur. Where is she? I mean to return her as I promised to her husband in Limoges. You dishonour my word.' Suddenly Olafr sat down hard, exhausted by his own anger. 'Thorgils,' he said in a voice of great grief. 'My dearest companion.'

Tears were swelling in Thorgils' eyes and he sat down near to Olafr, but not too near. 'Forgive me,' he said. 'I love her.'

Olafr looked up and the fury was rekindling in his blue eyes, 'And you do not love and honour me! They will find her,' he said, gesturing at the men strapping on shields and cloaks, forming into search parties. Thorgils looked on anxiously at their preparations. 'They will find her and when they find her I will teach her a lesson and I will send her to Limoges, as I promised with my word.'

Thorgils swallowed, wondering how Olafr meant to teach Aina a lesson. 'And you, brother, I will have vengeance against you for your deception. You sell our sister back to the Franks for the sake of your lust . . .'

'No,' Thorgils broke in. 'No, I would not do that. Sigrid made the offer, for my sake, for Aina's. She was . . .' Thorgils stopped. He did not want Olafr seeking out his son and wreaking vengeance on him. 'I was in great agony to deceive you, my *drottinn*, but I had already lost my woman once before, you know that, and I could not lose my woman again.'

291

Olafr looked at Thorgils with contempt, unmoved by his words. 'Take him,' Olafr commanded and two men gripped Thorgils' arms. 'Bind him. Odinn will have a hanging man on his tree tomorrow morning and perhaps I will hang her there too, your Frankish whore.'

'Olafr!' Thorgils shouted at his foster-brother's turned back, as the men dragged him from the hall.

Aina listened to the sounds of the waves, the puffins groaning, the blow hole's regular thump followed by the hiss of the spray on the rocks. She kept moving and laying in places of conceal-ment, observing the parties of men searching for her. She saw men crouching in the low branches of trees hanging over the water's edge, poking the rushes with their swords. From the cor-ner of her eye Aina watched a green and yellow dragonfly hover-ing above the surface of the water at an angle, blunt-nosed, aimed at its prey, like a school master's angry pointer at a slate.

The following morning Thorgils was dragged from his confine-ment in the dank cellar back into the hall fearing that he would see Aina there in chains but there was no sign of her. Ulf sat uncomprehending and unknown on Morag's knee in a corner of the hall, and she nodded imperceptibly to Thorgils. She would keep the child safe.

'Where is she?' Olafr demanded.

'I do not know, brother.'

'Name me brother no more. I gave you gold, arms-amber, and this is what you give back to me. *Drengspell! Vela!* Disloyalty! Deceit! You are *Nidingr!* Betrayer!'

The words fell like axe-blows against Thorgils' face.

'I will strap you to a rock at the sea-edge that you and your betrayal might be covered at high tide!' Olafr shouted.

Thorgils hung his head and every man, woman and child in the hall stilled their activities and drew in a breath at Olafr's words. The only sounds Thorgils could hear were the crackling of the fire, the caws of birds outside, a dog scratching harshly at its fleas.

Olafr's silence persisted until finally he pronounced: 'I cannot find the woman. I cannot find it in my heart to kill you after our close adventures together.'

Thorgils kept his head down and waited. He knew Olafr was not forgiving and would not rest with frustrated vengeance.

'I have written to the Duke of Normandy,' he said and Thorgils looked up at Olafr's face now. 'Soon he and the Viscount of Limoges will know of the deception you have enacted upon me and upon them and they will take their vengeance on the person to hand,' Olafr finished.

'Sigrid . . . but Olafr you cannot punish Sigrid for my crime . . .' Thorgils rose to his feet, holding out his hands in supplication.

'She too has betrayed me. It's done,' Olafr said, standing, 'and so are we.' He gestured to the men and they began to file out of the hall and down towards the ships, many who had been Thorgils' close friends and battle companions for years, avoiding his eyes.

'Olafr . . .'

'Don't speak to me Thorgils. My resolve on your death is feeble. Don't speak.'

Without words of farewell, he swung around and left. Thorgils slapped back down onto the bench. What would happen to Sigrid when the letter arrived in Limoges? How could he bear to break so with his brother who he had been bound to all his life in blood and adventure? Thorgils let out a sob.

Morag put Ulf down from her knee and rushed to comfort Thorgils, holding his shaking shoulders, looking into his anguished face. 'He let you live. She lives,' she said over and over, but Thorgils wept loudly and long for Sigrid and for Olafr, tears sliding down his face, soaking into his beard.

Olafr's ships and men were gone and Aina came running down the hill and into Thorgils' arms and heard the awful news. 'We will be exposed now, Thorgils, and Sigrid too.'

'I will write to warn Sigrid. She will have to run away. I grieve that I cannot help her but she is strong and I vow that I will find her again as I did once before.'

'Yes she is strong.' Aina bit her lip anxiously thinking of how Sigrid would fare, if her deception was exposed: a pagan slave purporting to be the Viscountess. Many men would burn a wife for such falseness, but Guy, would he? 'Can't we go to get Sigrid?'

'No. We would all be at risk then. Once the deception is revealed they will set a trap expecting a rescue. I will send word to her to make her escape, conceal herself and tell me where she is.'

Aina looked anxiously into Thorgils' face, holding his hand.

'Our life here is over, Aina,' Thorgils said. 'We will sail to Greenland with our son and escape Olafr's wrath.' He thought for a while longer. 'If there if no free land for us on Greenland we will sail on to Vinland. I will make us a *knorr*, an ocean-going ship for the journey.'

At night Thorgils and Aina walked hand in hand to the remote cave where she had hidden, leading a donkey laden with a chest. The full moon turned the sky yellow and grey, silvered the water and made the land black.

'Here,' Aina said, indicating a spot between the cliff and the gorse bushes. Thorgils hefted the spade and began to dig a hole while Aina sat on the chest, watching him. When the hole was deep they lowered the chest down between them on ropes. Thorgils jumped down into the hole and gestured to Aina to join him. He helped her half-jump, half-stagger down the mud and roots and they stood in the hole. Thorgils lifted the lid of the chest. Moonlight bounced off the jumble of silver objects inside that were embossed and punched with intricate patterns: belt buckles, coins, rings, bracelets, chains, balls, pins, brooches, clasps and various pieces of silver that had been sheared off, or bent, or broken from other objects. Aina dug her fingers deep into the silver up to her wrist and raised her arm clutching a handful of their wealth and letting the pieces drop back from her hand, thudding and spangling down into the chest, like silver rain.

'We are in a grave, Thorgils,' Aina said miserably, 'a silvered grave of our life here. This shiny metal is but ashes now to me.'

She looked up at the high mud walls around them and smelt the musk of the earth.

'No,' Thorgils said, gazing down at the silver in the moonlight, 'this is a dragon's bed, Aina, and we will come to reclaim it when we are safe.' He closed the lid on their hoard and secured the hasp, pulling himself up out of the hole and reaching down a hand to hoist Aina, her weight nothing on the corded muscles of his arm. He began to shovel the damp earth over the chest.

'I don't want to leave the island, Thorgils.'

'I thought you wanted adventure.'

'I've had adventure and I lost Sigrid because of it.'

'Vinland is a wondrous place,' Thorgils told her, 'and the voyage will be a great adventure,' but he saw that Aina weather did not improve with his words.

# Part Three

# TRUTH

# 997–1009

*'Only the mind knows what lives near the heart.'*

# 26

# Limoges

## 997

Since the elevation of the body of Saint Martial and the Peace Council pilgrims flock here in ever greater numbers. They start to come at Lent and the streets, churches and market stalls become more crowded and slower to navigate, until by Easter our visitors are a veritable tidal wave upon us and Bishop Hilduin at the Cathedral and Abbot Geoffrey at the Abbey have introduced *custodes* who manage the crowds at their nocturnal vigils and tell them the stories of our saints. The pilgrim ranks swell again around 20th June for Saint Martial's Feast and yet again on 12th November when the priests commemorate the elevation of the saint's body. For a short time between late November till early February the city seems emptied as if these wanderers have all been sucked out by a great wind and we can walk the streets recognising the majority of the people again.

I am in the early stages of carrying our fourth child and crave the warm comfort of our hall. Fulayh and I sit talking together and I ask him about slaves in his homeland, thinking how I could have been bought in Tallinn by one of the Moor traders instead of by Melisende, and how different my life would have been then.

'Slaves are given new names,' he tells me, 'that are different from the names of free men and women. They are named for flowers, gemstones or other objects. The women in the harem are given very special names.'

'Like what?' I glance briefly away from Fulayh's face, to look to the door where a messenger is entering, wet and muddy, and a servant goes to assist in divesting him of his sodden clothes.

'*Daw' al-Sabāh* which means light of the morning, *Muntaha al-Muna*, that is object of desires, *Uns al-Qulub*, solace of hearts.'

'Those names are entrancing,' I say, 'but are those women's lives entrancing?'

He lowers his eyes. 'I cannot say, Lady.'

'What would I be called?'

'You, Lady? In a harem!' He shakes his head with a smile.

'Yes, if I were, what would I be called?' I insist.

'Perhaps, *al-Zarqā*, the blue-eyed woman, or *Qatr al-Nada*, drop of dew.'

'My Lady,' the steward interrupts us and I turn reluctantly to him, 'the messenger brings a letter for you.' He is holding it out to me.

I take it and recognise Aina's writing. 'Thank you,' I tell the steward, 'and thank you,' I say to Fulayh, standing to go and read the letter in the privacy of my chamber.

*The Annals of Guy of Limoges*

**+ 996** In this year Charles of Lorraine, brother to old King Lothaire and uncle to the last Carolingian king Louis, died in a Capetian prison. The sons he left lack the wealth or backing to challenge for the return of the throne. Pope John XV died and Gregory V was elected as the new Pope. Otto III became Emperor in the east. Bourchard of Vendôme allied with King Robert Capet and broke with his son-in-law, Fulk of Anjou. The old Duke of Aquitaine, Guillaume IV, died. My brother-in-law, Count Audebert of La Marche leads a triumphant rebellion against the new young Duke of Aquitaine. Audebert attacked Gençay and defeated Guillaume's forces outside Poitiers. He joined Fulk of Anjou, who was besieged at Langeais by Eudes of Blois. Eudes fell ill and was carried to a nearby monastery where he died. Fulk and Audebert haven taken Tours, the King's city and King Robert and Duke Guillaume struggle now trying to take Tours back again. Guy of Limoges and Aina were blessed with the safe birth of a third son, Pierre.

Guy set down his quill and looked with anxiety at the words he had written. Audebert and Fulk had been unbelievably successful in their campaign but where would it end and how might it impact on his sister and on his own family and citizens in Limoges. Fulk, with his holdings further to the north, could only gain from these military incursions but Audebert must in time, come back to his own lands on the edge of Aquitaine and would he be able to negotiate a peace that served him well? Guy heard a noise at the gatehouse below and moved to peer out of the window. He could discern a small party of horses arriving in the courtyard. The flash of a red robe suggested that it was his brother, Bishop Hilduin. He packed away his writing implements and moved to the staircase to find Aina and greet his brother.

In my room I reach my locked casket from under my bed and place it on the blanket. Kneeling beside the bed I turn a key in the small lock and lift the lid on my treasures: my Thor's hammer, my great silver serpent, and my cache of letters from Aina, with news of her life with my brother on Kelda Ey. I insert my finger into a gap at the top of her new letter and start to open it.

'Aina!' Guy pokes his head around the door and is coming towards me. I drop the unopened letter into the box and close the lid. 'Bishop Hilduin is below and wanting to speak with us.' I grimace. 'I know, I know,' he groans into my hair, where he is nuzzling the top of my head. 'A letter from Sigrid?'

'Yes.'

'Is she well?'

'Yes she is very well. We should not keep your brother waiting, Guy.' As I rise to my feet I turn him affectionately around to face in the direction of the door. 'I'm just coming.' I turn the key in the casket and follow him to the door, feeling the coils of the serpent swirling cold around my limbs and neck, entrammelling me in lies.

I try to keep my face neutral as I listen with impatience to Bishop Hilduin, who is blaming the problems of Limoges on sin as usual.

'It is near a thousand years since Christ was born and died for us,' says Hilduin. 'The End Time approaches. The earth is worn out and overcrowded. The world is saturated with people and nature has grown old. The cosmos is senile and the world will soon end. The dead and the quick will be judged. Many are not ready to meet their maker, steeped as they are in sin.'

Hilduin speaks of Hugh Capet's death last year and how his son Robert has been crowned as King. 'The new King Robert repudiated his first wife, Rozala and has illegally married his cousin, Berthe, widow of the Count of Blois and mother of the child heir to Blois.' Hilduin's voice is laced with disapproval.

'Yes,' says Guy. 'What of it? Rozala was his father's choice and too old for Robert. Berthe is a beauty and fertile. Besides Robert now has control of the rich county of Blois too. It was an astute marriage.'

'She is his *cousin*,' Hilduin says with heavy disgust. 'The Pope intends to excommunicate the King and Queen for it. And this is your own sin, also brother, and that of your wife.'

Guy looks at Hilduin in surprise and I turn to concentrate on Hilduin's words, having previously only listened to his rant with half an ear.

'The Pope has instructed King Robert to set aside his wife, Queen Berthe, who is his second cousin, since this is offensive to God,' Hilduin says with satisfaction.

The hall goes suddenly still as everyone else stops their gossip or what they are doing to listen to Hilduin's words. I look at Hilduin with distaste. He pours vinegar on my husband's troubles, instead of balm and only I know how ridiculous his implication is and cannot say so.

'My marriage to Aina . . .,' Guy begins.

'Your second cousin,' interrupts Hilduin, with a pained look at me.

'Was sanctioned by Bishop Hildegaire, as you know, and we'll not discuss this further.'

Hilduin frowns at the mention of his brother and predecessor's name. The memory of Hildegaire's impieties are still fresh in the minds of the Limoges clergy. Hilduin himself, given to the church as an oblate at a young age, is a conservative and a purist in all his views and actions, but he will not go so far as to pronounce a former Bishop's ruling as wrong.

'Guy, we need some fresh air,' I say, when Hilduin has departed and taken his self-righteous atmosphere with him. We ride out of the city for some distance and draw rein to look down together on the countryside which is just waking from the long cold winter. I describe the splashes of colour to Guy, where new growth and early flowers are beginning to bloom.

'The Romans named this land Aquitainia,' he says to me, 'because it is threaded with so many great rivers and tumbling streams.'

I smile at his words.

'I read in a book,' he says, 'that the spring in Aquitaine comes flying from the west in a swirl of flowers, with summer hard on its heels, pursuing it by the rivers and catching up with it on the ridges. Thank you for letting me see that with your vivid descriptions, Aina, my drop of dew,' he says playfully, referring to the tale I have told him of my conversation with Fulayh earlier. 'And know wife, that whatever Hilduin says, or even the Pope, I will never repudiate you.'

It is a busy day and night has fallen when I get a chance to return to my chamber and read Aina's letter in privacy. I light the candles in the room and by their glow and the flickering firelight I lift the lid of my casket again, tracing my finger on the glint of the serpent and remembering, thinking of Thorgils' face and Aina's. I open the letter and read the words.

No, oh no. After all this, after I have convinced Guy of my love, borne him three sons: Ademar, Geraud, Pierre and another child coming, managed this household, now after all this, I will be exposed, shamed, rejected when Olafr's letter arrives to tell my husband of my great deceit. I retrieve the warning letter from Aina from the floor where I have dropped it in my distress, and read it through one more time to be sure I have fully understood and then I throw it on the fire. If I can intercept Olafr's letter I can burn his words also. Should I burn all of Aina's letters, destroy my hammer and my serpent so that there is no material proof, but I cannot bear to part with the serpent. I am grieved to hear of

Olafr's fury breaking against my brother, but know we have been lucky he did not take a greater vengeance.

The Duke of Normandy might write to tell my husband of my shame or he might visit in person, or his Duchess perhaps. If a letter I may be able to see it before my husband and deal with it, but if a visit there will be nothing I can do. Should I confess? I am so afraid now to lose my husband and my children. Aina writes that Thorgils tells me to run away and he will come to find me in time, but how can I do that? How can I abandon my life? In the morning I will give orders to the steward to bring all letters to me first and to give me notice of any approaching visitors. What if the communication slips by me? Guy's words to me this afternoon haunt me: know wife, that I will never repudiate you. Even when you discover the truth I ask him in my head. When you know that I am not Aina but a Norse slave who has deceived you for many years?

# 27

# Gençay
## July 997

'*Il pleut comme un vache qui pisse* – it's raining as hard as a pissing cow,' Audebert said to Fulk, peering out of the tent flap. Rain was not good for war. Audebert preferred sweat to mud.

The old Duke died in the monastery of Saint Maixent last year, Duchess Emma was aging and her son responded slowly and ineffectually to challenges from castellans such as Hugh of Lusignan and Jordan of Chabannais. Whilst Fulk imposed order with his fist and the stone castles he built in his lands, Guillaume appeared impotent. Audebert and Fulk chose that moment to strike.

Audebert had swept all before him in the swathe he drew on Fulk's map years before. Gençay fell easily and then Poitiers itself, as Audebert proved himself to be a captain who could take any town, no matter how well fortified or defended it might be. Audebert had camped two miles outside the solid walls of Poitiers to wait for reinforcements. Those walls, built by the Romans, were ten metres high and six metres wide, spiked with seventy towers, and the new Duke Guillaume was safe behind them, but foolishly he had thought to take the advantage whilst Audebert waited without a full force. Guillaume rashly sent his troops sallying out and they were roundly defeated by Audebert, who then laid siege to the city. Guillaume had been compelled to flee for his life as his garrison, appalled at the extreme loss of life, had surrendered. It was a paltry victory, thought Audebert, when the opponent was such a cowardly fool.

Whilst Abo Drutus, Audebert's castellan at Bellac, held it against Guillaume's attempt to attack him behind his back, and kept Adalmode and their small son, Bernard, safe, Audebert marched his men north to join with Fulk and take Tours. That siege was harder. The defenders knew their business and stripped the countryside of forage so that Audebert struggled to keep his soldiers and horses fed. The city's catapult thumped continuously throwing crushing boulders as his men crossed the killing ground between their tents and the castle walls. Audebert kept up a relentless process of sapping the walls, storming the defences. His own catapult crews worked day and night without let, hearing the dull thud of the massive missiles and screams inside the city. He varied his tactics daily: some days they threw a great battering ram repeatedly at the gates, their shields held aloft to protect them from rocks and scalding tar thrown from the walls; some days twelve men rushed with fifteen-foot scaling ladders and threatened the walls, reaching the parapets in places before Audebert sounded a retreat unwilling to lose too many men in each effort. He ordered the construction of mobile siege towers so that his soldiers and their ladders could approach the walls with less loss of life. The crossbowmen in the Tours belfries were good and punched holes in the attackers' line, but the swarm of Audebert's army far outnumbered the defenders and there was no one like him for keeping men disciplined and motivated. Fulk's men feared their Count's brutal temper and admired his intelligent tactics, whilst Audebert, always fighting in the front and the thick of battle, was loved and followed blindly by his warriors. Together they made an unstoppable combination, even though Guillaume of Aquitaine and Eudes of Blois had gained help from King Robert Capet himself.

Audebert met the newly crowned king on the battlefield. He came briefly to contest with Audebert and Fulk outside Tours but his troop of untried young men in their polished armour were no match for Audebert's seasoned warriors. As the king's men fell around him, Audebert hauled on the reins of Robert's horse and the king rolled in the dust avoiding the crushing weight of his falling mount. Quickly he found his feet, drew his sword to face Audebert. His bright blue shield with its golden fleur de lys rolled uselessly beyond his reach. The king was twenty-five, the same age as Fulk, and should have had the advantage of youth over Audebert. A thick gold band encrusted with jewels surmounted his conical helmet. The helmet grazed Robert's eyebrows and had one of the new-fangled nose protectors, and light metal flaps protecting his neck. The king was encased in a long chainmail dress reaching from his shoulders to below his knees, where the rich red fabric of his tunic was just visible beneath. His silver forearm shields shone in the sunlight. His leather upper-arm protectors clustered in well wrought tongues like dense feathers. 'Who made *you* Count?' he snarled at Audebert, remembering Guillaume's tale of how Audebert acknowledged no overlord and had not bent his knee in homage for his counties as custom demanded, but then the king's face showed surprise as Audebert broke into a hearty laugh.

'Who made *you* King?' Audebert demanded, striking the sword easily from Robert's hand, knocking his shoulder with the flat of his weapon so that the king fell once more to his knees in the dirt. The armour looked as if it had just arrived from the craftsmen. The red and green jewelled crown tilted precariously and the king glared. 'Get him away from here!' Audebert yelled to three of the king's men who were approaching cautiously. It was beneath Audebert to kill such incompetence.

Celebrating their day in the command tent that evening, and hearing Audebert's tale, Fulk growled, 'You should have struck his head from his lily neck, then we could have taken the crown along with their cities and their lands.'

Audebert shrugged. 'We don't want crowns!' He assumed that Fulk was joking, but saw by his friend's grim expression that there was some truth in Fulk's comment.

Fulk, seeing perplexity on Audebert's face, rallied to the humour of the story, raised his brimming goblet, shouting over and over to the laughing, triumphant men, 'Who made *you* King!' 'Who made *you* King!'

No food entered Tours for weeks and the water supply was dammed or poisoned, and so eventually Audebert's blockade outlasted the garrison and the city surrendered to them. Now they were riding back to secure Poitiers and made camp near Gençay.

Looking out at the rain, Fulk nodded. 'Tomorrow, we will discuss a division of the conquered territories between us.' Fulk would take Tours, vastly increasing his territory around Anjou, and if they were successful now, Audebert would take Poitiers and with it rule of all Aquitaine.

Audebert pointed to where the red flag of Aquitaine with its golden lion flew again over the ruins of Gençay. 'He's sneaked back while we were busy in the north and retaken it. We'll make it clear who owns this ground.'

The constant rain was turning the ground to a mud bath. Soldiers were wading, their ankles slowed in the thick mire, leading war-horses similarly slavered in muck and shivering with cold. Men struggled to erect tents in the slime and to hammer posts securely into the liquid ground to tether the beasts. A messenger sloshed through the mud, and made his way to Audebert's tent to deliver grave news from his brother Boson, from Bellac. Guillaume had captured their brother Gausbert and blinded him in retribution for Helie's crime against the priest Benedict.

'God's teeth,' Audebert swore, throwing the letter away from him.

'What is it?' Fulk asked.

'Read it,' Audebert said disgusted, and watched Fulk's face as he bent to pick up the discarded letter and read the words.

'The vindictive, cowardly little shite!' Fulk exclaimed. 'He makes no headway with the real enemy, us, and so he attacks the more vulnerable to make himself a mean victory.'

'Yes.' Audebert sat, morose for some time with the awful news. 'Gausbert did not deserve this.' If Helie were still alive, Audebert would kill him himself for the griefs he had visited upon his brothers.

'Gausbert will have to go into a monastery.'

Audebert nodded. 'Guillaume takes vengeance for the crime that Helie committed more than twenty years ago. Unbelievable!'

'That's not the reason,' Fulk stated, and he and Audebert exchanged a glance of understanding.

'No,' Audebert said. 'It's Adalmode. Well, I will show him no mercy now.'

Taking Gençay a second time posed no difficulties since its defences had not been fully rebuilt. The huge door, the wooden staircase and great beams supporting the five storeys of the thirty foot stone tower had burnt out in Audebert's first attack and the tower still stood but now it was a useless husk, perched on the summit of the hill known to the locals as Roc. Why did that bastard Guillaume hang out his pennant on the tower of the Tour de Moncabie if he could not be bothered to at least make some useful defences there. He had not even cleared away the debris from Audebert's first attack. It was typical of his military inability and petty behaviour.

Audebert strides to his tent and shrugs off his sweaty armour and grimy gambeson, calling to the squire for wine. The arrow comes from the trees. Audebert turns to the sound of its flight, raises his hand to shield his eyes and catches a glimpse of sunlight on a polished bow, is not sure if he feels or simply hears the thud of the arrow in his side, that knocks his breath from him and drops him to his knees. He looks at the arrow protruding from his body in disbelief. Blood wells around the buried shaft. He hears shouts as his men realise what has happened, some running towards him, others running in the direction of the assassin.

'Audebert, Audebert,' Fulk is crying, 'no!' He reaches Audebert and holds him, his head resting on Fulk's knee.

Audebert looks up at a grey sky and breathes shallowly against the searing pain in his chest, the vivid blue of his eyes growing dull.

'No!' Fulk says again in anguish, wiping his hand across his face, leaving a smear of Audebert's blood there. 'Oh no!' Others are running and crowding. 'He needs air! He needs a surgeon! Bring the litter! We will make for Charroux.'

Fulk is organising well as usual, Audebert thinks with satisfaction, but then ignores the panic happening around him and concentrates instead on the mirage of Adalmode's beautiful face bending over him, her golden hair tickling his forehead, strands softly caressing his mouth like whispers. 'Take care of my son, Fulk, as I took care of you,' he gasps hoarsely, 'and take care of Adalmode.'

# 28

## Fécamp

### September, 997

In the palace of Fécamp, Richard I, Duke of Normandy, experienced relief from the pains he had felt for many weeks. His vision blurred and he fought for his last few breaths. He had been failing in strength for some time and had withdrawn from Bayeux, to his favourite residence here on the coast, looking out to the sea. He had named his successor, a splendid stone sarcophagus waited for him in the neighbouring shrine, and he had ordered his affairs. The priest droned the words of the last rites, thumbed a cross onto his clammy forehead in oil. Perhaps he should have sacrificed to Odinn as his Christianised ancestor, Rollo, did on his deathbed. Was it the wings of ravens that he could hear, or the rustling skirts of the valkyrie?

Richard's great sword lay on the quilt at his side and Gunnora gently held her husband's hand to the hilt. The sword's hard brightness belied the passing of time and the battles it had witnessed, contrasting sadly with the wasted muscles of Richard's long arm.

Bjarni, a young servant in the household newly arrived from Denmark, dithered on the threshold of the room, watching the Duke spasm and begin a gurgling death rattle, which ceased abruptly, was followed by a moment's silence and then by a high-pitched keening from the Duchess and the cries and wailing of the Duke's sons and daughters who stood around the bed. Bjarni backed out of the room quietly. This was not the time to bother the family with delivery of the letter in his hand. He set the let-

310

ter down on the chest that stood outside the door to the Duke's chamber. He would find a better time, later, to bring it to the attention of the Duchess or the new Duke.

The following morning Bjarni was sent with three other servants to wash and lay out the Duke's body. He had never seen or handled a lifeless corpse before. The look of it, the heavy cold feel of it, would stay with him forever he thought, like handling a gleaming dead fish newly caught from the sea, that seemed as if it might suddenly swirm back to life again if you poured water over it, and yet so surprisingly inanimate at the same time. Bjarni shook his wet hands above the bowl and reached for a towel, staring again at the body on the bed. A few weeks ago this long, cold husk had been the enormous and powerful Duke of Normandy, guffawing at bawdy jokes, swilling ale, eyeing young women, but Bjarni could not see it as a person at all any more. It was a thing, no longer housing the Duke. Where was the Duke's spirit now then? In the Christian Heaven or fiery Hell, or in Odinn's Feasting Hall, in the depths of Niflheim the cold underworld, or just nowhere? Bjarni swallowed on the thought that he too would come to this one day. He moved out to the chest by the door where he meant to collect the letter and complete his duty, but the letter was gone. The Duchess or the new Duke had already collected it.

Bjarni was nicknamed The Lucky. He always had good luck everyone said when he was offered this place in the Duke's household. His luck was there again the following week when it was his duty to clean and prepare the dead Duke's chambers so that his son, the new Duke, could move in. It was Bjarni, luckily, who moved the old chest out a little to dust behind it and saw that the letter had slipped down out of sight, blown by a gust of wind as a door opened or flicked by a trailing cloak perhaps. Bjarni heaved a sigh of relief, reached down until his fingertips grazed the letter and pulled it out, but looking at it with its seal of the royal house of Norway, he suddenly thought that perhaps his luck had failed him after all. It was over a week late now. He was hoping for preferment from the new Duke, promotion to a new position was likely. Quickly he stuffed the letter inside his jerkin, looking around. Nobody had seen.

Later that day the Duchess sent Bjarni to trim the candles in the library and tidy in there. Perhaps there would be a good hiding place for the letter here. Or perhaps it was safest to destroy it. A fire burned well in the library hearth. Bjarni could not read, so he had no way to tell how important the letter might or might not be, and whether his failure to deliver it would ever come into question. Bjarni dithered again, staring into the cracking fire, his fingers sliding slowly along the top of the letter inside his jerkin. A shaft of winter sun slipped between the half-closed shutters and lit the blue gems on the cover of a small book lying at the side of the chair where the old Duke had often sat. Perhaps he might need to retrieve this letter at some point. Best to hedge his bets. Quickly Bjarni reached for the Duke's letter knife on the library table and slit open the letter. Then he placed the opened letter inside the cover of the small book. If anyone asked he could say that he had delivered it to the old man, seen him read it and put it there inside the book, and there the letter would be as proof if he ever needed to evidence his account. He tidied the blue jewelled book away with the rest of the pile the Duke had been reading, placing them on a high shelf. Pleased with himself, he walked out and down the corridor: Bjarni the Lucky, he would go far, he thought.

# 29

# Roccamolten

## 998

Adalmode looked down at her widow's weeds. She would give anything to undo death. Only the needs of her son kept her breathing and moving around, going through the motions of life. Fulk told her the details of Audebert's death: how he suspected the assassin had come from Guillaume of Aquitaine. How her husband had lasted in pain for several hours, lost to fever, talking of her, or to her, Fulk thought. The doctor removed the arrow and bandaged the deep wound but Audebert was unconscious by then and did not open his eyes again.

She had loved Audebert all her life but she had been his wife for a mere seven years and seen little enough of him as he campaigned with Fulk to the north and west most summers, only coming home to her in the winters when the fighting season was over. One evening as they lay in bed together she told him she hated the night because darkness fell and there was no longer enough light for her to look at him, but he rolled towards her in the bed, cupping her hip, and said, 'No, sweet Adalmode, we cannot hate the night, for we have this, and we can trace with our fingertips what we can no longer see.' Yes, he was right, she had loved the days *and* the nights with him, and the early mornings, watching him rise from their bed to open the shutters, seeing him in the new sun, turning to her with such happiness in his face.

Adalmode cried for days when the news came and yet she had expected it almost from the first day of their married life together. She rode to Saint Sauveur Abbey in Charroux to kiss his face one last time and to give a large donation for prayers for Audebert's soul. Looking on his cold corpse made her grief worse, seeing that truly he had gone from her. The scenes of their life played through her mind. Their first encounter when he was in the dungeon pit with Helie and both she and he were still so young. She felt the anger that he had spoken of. If only her father had allowed her to marry him when he was first released, when he was nineteen. They could have had twenty years together before this and maybe twenty years would have slaked her thirst for him, twenty years might have gentled the beating of her heart every time he turned his blue gaze on her or placed his hand on her hair. But no, she shook her head. Twenty years, forty years, she would have loved him as hard no matter how long they had together. Now she would wake bleak every morning that he was not beside her. Adalmode buried her face in her hands and wept inconsolably, the tears running over and between her fingers, her face as sodden as her husband's last morning.

Audebert's brother, Boson, had accompanied her to the burial and he touched her shoulder, as she knelt beside Audebert's grave, close to the Abbey's altar. 'Sister, we must return to Roccamolten. Guillaume of Aquitaine and King Robert Capet ride against us. We must get behind our walls at the fortress.'

She ran her fingertips one last time around the letters of his name carved in the stone: Audebert, Comte de La Marche et Périgord. Their little son, Bernard, was in Roccamolten and she must go there, leave her husband here. She rose and swallowed on the taste of salt. Her eyes were hot, itchy, blurred from days of crying. She would return to Audebert's grave, to be with him, as soon as she had the chance. Perhaps she could talk to him when no one was by, as she had talked to him in the dungeon, but it was she who needed words of comfort now and he would not reply, except perhaps in her dreams. 'I will be buried here next to you, my love,' she murmured, 'to lie waiting with you for Judgement Day and then we will find each other in the next life.'

'Come, sister, now,' Boson urged her.

She looked at Boson dazed, pulled back from the grief and memories of her husband, to action that must be taken in the here and now. Boson, the third of the old Count's five sons,

looked nothing like Audebert. He was considerably shorter and
his brown hair lay flat on his head and swiped across his forehead
in an overlong fringe. His frame was slender as a young girl's. He
would hold the counties of La Marche and Périgord now, until
Audebert's son was of age.

Two months had gone by since she buried Audebert. Duke Guillaume, King Robert and the Duke of Angoulême besieged the
two La Marche strongholds, swarming like uncovered ant nests
around Bellac and Roccamolten, swirling uselessly around the
great stone curtains of the fortresses. Fulk and Guy harried the
attacking forces from behind their encampments. Audebert's
walls would never fall and their supplies inside the citidels held
out. Only the wind had ever forced its way into Audebert's
strongholds. The walls of Roccamolten held Guillaume from her,
but Adalmode was under attack from within too. Boson, puffed
up with his new power, sent his wife and sons to her family for
safety, and alone with Adalmode, he flirted relentlessly with her.
During the early months of her marriage and her assumption of
duties in the Audebert's household, she had observed how Boson
ached with irrational jealousies of Audebert and Gausbert, how
he resented his siblings.

'Brother,' she told him, exasperated, removing his hand for the
third time from her thigh, 'why do you behave so. You know how
well I loved your brother. I have no intention of taking a second
husband – ever.'

Boson laughed unpleasantly. 'I already have a wife, sweet sister,' he put his hand back again but higher than before so that
his fingertips pushed where they should not be, and she shifted
angrily away from him, 'but I intend to take you as my concubine,
darling. You are wasted as a widow.'

Adalmode drew an angry breath. She was not afraid of Boson.
If necessary, she would run him through. It was what Audebert
would want her to do. 'I am a Princess of Limoges,' she said,
her voice laden with disgust at him, 'and dowager Countess of
La Marche and Périgord. I have protectors – my brothers, the

315

Count of Anjou, even Duke Guillaume, would be appalled at your behavior and will chastise you for it.'

'They, my love, are not here, inside these impregnable walls.'

'Boson, touch me again and I will put on the valour of my husband and slice your ugly head from your neck.'

He looked askance at her and Adalmode took advantage of his surprise to rise and stalk quickly from the hall. In her chamber she hugged Bernard to her in distress until he wriggled away uncomprehending. She moved around the chamber searching for Audebert's daggers and found three. She hung one, with an elaborate brown embossed scabbard, from her belt; a second with a slender blade and a grip that fitted well to her hand, she concealed beneath her skirts, strapped high on her calf just below her knee. The third, a plain, long dagger, she placed unsheathed under her pillow. 'Oh Audebert,' she whispered, 'I need you.'

Guillaume stared with loathing at the walls of Roccamolten, perched precariously, but evidently not precariously enough, above his head. The fortress appeared to be growing directly out of the rock spur, its ragged, erratic walls and crenellations blending with the weathered granite and straggles of green vegetation clinging to vertiginous slopes.

King Robert reined his horse alongside Guillaume. 'No good, Duke, winter is coming fast upon us and we will have to withdraw. Perhaps we will make another attempt at the Mayfield muster next year eh? Or perhaps there is another way to win your bride?'

Guillaume shrugged his shoulders, made a grunt of affirmation and assumed a stoic expression but inside his fury festered. First there had been the insult of Audebert's marriage to his woman, to Adalmode, then the humiliation of Audebert's rout of him at Poitiers and now this, even with the King's help he could not broach the walls of one simple castle and get at what was his – Adalmode and with her, her son's rights to La Marche and Périgord. Guillaume blamed his mother for all of it, for keeping him away from his father's court where he might have

learnt more of war and women and less of piety and righteous-
ness, for undermining his youthful attempts at authority at
every turn.

Guillaume and Robert besieged the walls for three months and
Boson besieged Adalmode but she held on, and so did the walls.
It was not only her own virtue that had to be defended from
Boson, for given the opportunity he would harm her little son,
that he might keep hold of Audebert's inheritance rather than
merely act as Bernard's Regent. Boson insinuated that her compliance would purchase Bernard's safety.

Pale morning sunlight streamed into the hall and Boson joined
her and Bernard at the trestle. 'They're gone,' he announced,
'withdrawn, given up. So now you and I can really discuss our
future together,' he placed his hand on hers.

Adalmode extracted her hand angrily. 'I've told you before,
and I meant it . . .' but then she looked up as the steward cleared
his throat and bowed before them.

'My lord,' he said, 'Viscount Guy of Limoges and Count Fulk
of Anjou are at the gate and ask leave to enter.'

Adalmode tried to contain her relief but it would not be suppressed, and she beamed a smile of triumph on Boson as she
answered the steward. 'I command the gates be opened to them,'
she said, rising, flicking her wrist rudely to dismiss Boson's pro-
tests that she should usurp his authority.

She walked outside swiftly, calling Bernard to come stand
beside her, smoothing her gown, tucking tendrils of hair behind
her ears, and stood straight to receive her brother and Audebert's friend. They would protect her and Bernard from Boson,
she could go to live with Guy and Aina in Limoges now, where
she would have the peace she craved to focus on her loss of
Audebert.

Adalmode was feeding the birds at her bedroom window as she
did every morning. She whispered to Bernard who had clambered
onto the window seat beside her to be very still and quiet. She put

a finger to her lips, smiling at him. He nodded, his blue eyes large and round, thick black tufts of hair standing awry on his small head. She put crumbs and seeds on the ledge and sat back, pulling her shawl closer around her shoulders, and watched them come: tiny green finches, bluetits and a blackbird. Today there was a robin too. Audebert always laughed at her when she fed the birds, telling her she was like a forest hermit. Bernard was grinning with his teeth gently biting on his bottom lip to ensure that he made no sound and sent them flurrying away. Adalmode glanced over to the bed and imagined Audebert there. There was a tap at the door and Guy came in.

'Uncle Guy,' exclaimed Bernard, 'you've scared away the birds!'

'I'm so sorry,' Guy said throwing wide his arms in exaggeratedly comic remorse.

'They will come again tomorrow,' Adalmode told her son. 'Come in Guy. Sit by me. I cannot tell you how glad I was yesterday to see you arrive in this sad hall.'

'Sister,' Guy said, approaching her, and bringing a stool to sit close to her at the window. She saw that something serious was clouding his expression. 'I must speak with you Adalmode. It would be best if we were alone.'

Bernard frowned and began to protest. 'No, Bernard,' Adalmode said firmly. 'Go to find your nurse. She will give you breakfast.'

He pouted but climbed down from the window seat to do as she told him, Guy ruffling his black hair as he passed.

Guy sat and took Adalmode's hands in his, his vague brown eyes peering into her face, their knees touching as they had often sat together in their childhood, and he began to speak. He told her that Boson had come to terms with Duke Guilliaume, agreeing to found a monastery at Moutier d'Ahun and to go on a penitential pilgrimage to Rome, and he told her that she must marry Duke Guillaume.

Adalmode looked at her brother in shocked horror. 'No, Guy, I won't. I can't. Don't you understand that I can still feel Audebert's warmth in the bed beside me. I can still feel his hands on my face.'

318

Guy's expression was deeply sad but resolute. 'There is no other way, sister. I'm sorry for it and I understand, as I know how you loved him, but if you stay here, Boson will make you his concubine and usurp Bernard's rights, and I cannot protect you from that. If I take you with me to Limoges it would only be a short time before Guillaume came in force to demand you. It is his right, as my overlord, to dispose of you, a widow. If I refuse then he will war with me again and I do not have the limitless resources that he and the King can command. Limoges is exhausted by this war and I must make peace with him now. He is hungering for you and always has. He will not let go. If Audebert had lived . . . but Fulk and I between us cannot hold off Aquitaine when Guillaume, Boson, King Robert are all against us. Fulk needs to return to his holdings in the north.'

'Holdings won and kept for him by Audebert,' Adalmode said bitterly.

Fulk walked in on her words. 'You are right, Lady Adalmode,' he said softly, 'I owe Audebert so much and I loved him, as you did, but this is the best way forward for your safety, for your son. Guillaume has sworn to give Bernard Audebert's lands and titles when he is of age and to protect you both in the meantime.'

'Aina and I will take Bernard as our foster-son, Adalmode. We will love him dearly in your stead and Audebert's,' Guy said.

Adalmode swallowed at the thought of being separated from her little son who looked so like Audebert, and being left bereft and alone with Guillaume. 'I cannot take the Duke to husband,' Adalmode said. 'I will not.' But she knew that she must and she would.

# 30

# Llanteulyddog

## 999

Thorgils made Aina a splendid ocean-going vessel with a stem in the shape of Sigrid's serpent brooch and they named the ship *Sigrid*. It furnished them with the means to escape to Vinland if Olafr's wrath threatened them. They laid up provisions for the voyage and waited for news. 'Perhaps we don't need to go,' Aina begged, but Thorgils shook his head. He would not risk Olafr's anger, yet it seemed Olafr was busy in Norway and had no time for fury with them. Their preparations for departure from Kelda Ey were interrupted by an urgent summons from King Maredudd.

'I'll only be gone a few days,' Thorgils told Aina. 'We will leave on my return.'

'Watch out for Myrddin the wild man! Ask him when I shall see Sigrid,' she called out, and he laughed and waved to her from the boat as the anchor was hefted up and he left the island. Myrddin was a former warrior who was rumoured to be living wild in the forest near Llanteulyddog, talking to apple trees and pigs and foretelling the future, but Thorgils saw no sign of him and got no news of his sister on this journey.

Thorgils rode fast along the old Roman road, the Via Julia, towards the town, and news of the king's health along the way grew more and more alarming. The king was dying and his nephews Edwin and Cadell were gathering an army to secure their inheritance. When Maredudd first asked for Thorgils' support they had been victorious, beating back Edwin with his English forces to the borderlands, but the aging king had little respite. The following year he was attacked by the sons of Meurig ab Idwal in Gwynedd and had been unable to send word to Thorgils in time. Maredudd lost that battle, his kingdom of Gwynedd, and his nephew Tewdwr killed into the bargain. Still Thorgils would do what he could to support the old man now.

Thorgils screwed his eyes against the sun to look ahead to Llanteulyddog set on the flatlands of the river Towy that cut its deep, meandering route through the surrounding meadows, hurrying on its final twist to the sea. The ruins of the ramparts and earthworks of the old Roman fort and amphitheatre were visible, against the blue sky. Thorgils turned his horse's head towards a steep path that led down to the river bank where he could ford across a shallow stretch. Emerging from the river, he urged the horse up the far bank with his knees and twitched the reins in the direction of the Clas, the Priory building, guessing that the king was being cared for there.

Shown into the king's bedchamber, Thorgils recoiled at the smell of sickness that greeted him at the door.

'Jarl Thorgils!' Maredudd, propped in the great bed, reached out a wasted hand and Thorgils did his best not to show his own fear of such a death. 'Leave, everyone,' Maredudd croaked. With reluctance and slowly everyone left the room, excepting one serving woman who was wringing out a soiled cloth in a bowl of water. 'And you!' the king groaned. The woman looked up alarmed and scurried from the room, lifting her skirts, too unnerved to think to close the door behind her. Thorgils took two steps from the bed to the door and closed it softly, returning to the bedside and looking down on a man he had grown to respect.

'I have a last mission for you, my friend,' Maredudd said, his voice barely more than a whisper, 'if you will.'

'Name it, Lord,' Thorgils responded without hesitation.

'My daughter Angharad,' Maredudd said, and then could say no more for some time as he struggled for breath, his chest heaving, and Thorgils wondered whether this signified the end before he could voice his request, but eventually Maredudd regained calmer breaths. 'My daughter needs to be got to a place of safety and I would entrust her to you.'

'I will undertake this, King.' Thorgils' compliance was immediate.

Maredudd stared up at him with watery, fading eyes. 'Take her to Powys. She will be safe there.'

'I will go now to perform this,' Thorgils told him, increasingly uncomfortable in the presence and odours of fast approaching death. 'To steal a march on those who might prevent it,' he excused himself.

Maredudd nodded slightly. 'Thank you, Jarl.' His words were expelled softly, painfully, with his breath.

'Don't speak anymore. I will call your family and servants back about you.'

In the hallway the slender girl, Angharad, hovered anxiously with the crowd of ejected servants and doctors. 'You can go back in to your king, now,' Thorgils said, imperceptibly taking hold of the crook of Angharad's elbow as she passed him and preventing her from going in, bearing her with him down the passage instead and whispering to her. 'Your father commands me to take you to safety, to Powys.'

'I cannot leave him now,' she said looking up at him with distressed brown eyes.

'I am sorry,' he said, 'but you must. If you wait it will be too late. There will be those who will come to try to claim you and with you the loyalty of the nobility here. The sons of Meurig in Gwynedd, those jumped up nobles here who want your father's crown for themselves, even your cousins.'

'No!' Angharad said in horror at his last suggestion.

'Come, princess, please. It is your father's wish.'

Her mouth crumpled. Tears rolled down her face but she nodded her agreement. She collected a long warm cloak from her room, threw the hood up to conceal her hair and face, and stood looking into the room, indecisive on the threshold.

'Nothing else princess. I am sorry,' he said, 'but your most valuable possession is your life and yourself now.'

Again she nodded and followed him to his waiting horse.

'My wife is waiting for us at Kelda Ey,' he said, 'with a ship readied, and we will travel together and she will give you comfort.

# 31

# Limoges

## 1000

I am puzzled but overwhelmed with gratitude to Freyja that there has been no sign of the threatened letter from Olafr or the Duke of Normandy coming to expose me. I have resolved that I will not run until I am sure that I must. A sudden evening breeze bangs the shutters and doors that have stood open all day cooling the chamber. I lean out to take a last look at the river before closing up. The slight wind blows a scatter of tiny yellow leaves along the surface of the water. Swifts and bats swoop and circle. I think of Aina and Thorgils at this time of the day, wondering about their life. Is Aina doing just this herself – closing the shutters against the cold and the dark? I think too of Lord Audebert dead and Guy's poor sister, Adalmode, wed against her will to the Duke.

'Couldn't that have been avoided!' I asked Guy flabbergasted when he returned from Roccamolten with news of Adalmode's profoundly reluctant marriage to Guillaume. 'I thought you loved her dearly.' I wished back my words as soon as I saw the pain on his face.

'I do . . . it was the only way to safeguard her . . .'

'Oh I'm sorry Guy, forgive my barbed tongue. I know you will have done what you could for Adalmode.'

I grieved for Audebert, the dynamic but kind man I met long ago in Brioude, and in the weeks that followed I thought often of how deeply Adalmode must feel his loss, and then to be forced to this marriage with Duke Guillaume . . . Perhaps she would grow to love him as I had grown to greatly love my own husband, but I doubted it.

In the morning when I open the shutters, trees have shed piles of white fluffy seeds into the river and they collect in crevices and catch on sunken branches. I watch two large brown rats swimming flat to the water's surface, along the edge of the bank, one eye each above water watching out for predators or food. There is a small heron that fishes on the weir every morning and I take his unwavering presence as a sign that all will be well that day.

Our eldest son Ademar has had his seventh birthday and is ready to go to train in another household. I am thinking of a way I might aid Adalmode, although at some risk to myself. Adalmode's and Audebert's son, Bernard, has arrived in our household as our foster-son. He is a sweet-tempered boy with the open, frank expression of his father. I love him dearly for their sakes and his own, and I write often to Adalmode of his progress.

'Guy, why don't we send Ademar to Poitiers, to Adalmode as a foster son.'

'Clever Aina!' he says his face alight with his sudden smile. 'Yes, this will please my sister well and be a good place for our son too. It would give her the opportunity to come and visit Bernard here.'

'Yes,' I say smugly, since this was my intention. I smile at Guy's agreement but begin to think of the excuses I will have to concoct to be absent when she visits.

Hilduin is a fly in our ointment, regaling us with with his gloomy ideas and prognostications. 'Brother I *beg* you to consider on your consanguinity,' he says one morning, when Guy and I had been feeling particularly cheerful. I put down the fresh bread that had been touching my lips.

'Hilduin, Bishop,' Guy says for Hilduin has objected in the past to Guy talking to him as simply a brother, without ceremony, 'I have told you before that I wish you to desist in speaking on this subject. My marriage has been blest by the Church and I am blest in my marriage.' He smiles warmly at me.

'Alas, brother, you are complacent. As you know King Robert himself has been excommunicated for this very sin of consanguinity with his Queen Berthe and now there is fresh news,' he says lugubriously.

'And what is that?' Guy asks reluctantly.

'The excommunicate royal couple have reaped their reward. The Queen has delivered a still-born son.'

'That is a disgusting imputation . . .' I begin, sorry for the woman, although I do not know her, that she must suffer not only the loss of a child but this ridiculous prating on the subject also. By all accounts the King and Queen are unusually fond of one other.

Guy holds up a hand to still me. 'Aina!'

I clamp my mouth shut. He is right. Past experience has taught us that to argue with Hilduin only prolongs the great irritation of having to listen to the man.

'Sin surrounds us, brother. We are swimming in its filth. There is news of more adultery.'

'There is no adultery here!' Guy says, getting irate himself now.

'No, no,' says Hilduin in a placatory tone, 'but close at hand and contamination seeps into the soil.'

'Hilduin speak plain,' Guy groans.

'The Count of Anjou has burnt his wife for her adultery with a goatherd,' he says bluntly, and adds, looking at me, 'in her wedding dress.'

'Fulk of Anjou?' I say astonished, thinking of the boy I had seen with Audebert.

'This does not concern us,' Guy says and leads his brother out through the doorway with a gentle but firm hand in the small of his back. 'Thank you for your thoughts. Goodbye!' he says slamming the door, that is usually always open, except when the wind blows cold.

'What does he mean Guy about Fulk?'

'Unfortunately it is true, that he has burnt her at least. Whether she committed adultery – well we do not know the truth or no of that.'

'What happened?' I say horrified.

'She was near twenty years Fulk's senior you know, Elisabeth of Vendôme, poor woman. And their marriage has produced only one child living in seven years, a daughter. This is more likely the reason.'

I shake my head, distressed.

'He has taken a second wife, Hildegarde, and there are rumours that she was pregnant before the marriage, so there is another reason for you. And both Elisabeth and her father had taken arms about Fulk, so there's a final reason. There is no mercy in the man. We are blessed with our four sons, Aina, more than we could think.'

'To take life so horribly for these reasons is wrong,' I say.

Guy looks at me and says simply, 'Yes.'

'And every word that Hilduin speaks is wrong,' I say.

'Well,' Guy smiles anxiously, 'I'm not sure I can go that far with you, wife. Sometimes you make me a little alarmed for your soul but I know that it is a generous one.'

# 32

# Kelda Ey
## 1000

The times were uncertain with Maredudd dead and the struggle over who would succeed to his throne beginning. Bishop Morgeneu had been killed up the coast at Saint Davids Cathedral by Irish Vikings, and resentments against the Norse settlers were freshly kindled. Aina argued for many days with Thorgils that they prospered here and no further threat against them came from Olafr. They should stay and not trust themselves to unknown waters and lands. 'Besides,' she said, 'if Sigrid should be exposed and need our help what help could we be on the other side of the ocean?'

Thorgils looked thoughtful at her final argument, but he could waste no time now. They needed to be on the water where he felt most in control. They had heard from Sigrid that there was no sign of Olafr's letter and she was for now safe from exposure. Perhaps Olafr relented and did not send the letter, Sigrid wrote, but Thorgils frowned at this and shook his head. If Olafr said he would do something, then he did. It was a mystery why the letter had not arrived.

'Perhaps it did arrive,' said Aina, 'but Guy loves Sigrid so much he doesn't care and threw it away?'

Thorgils shook his head again, his face a picture of astonished disbelief. 'I fear the real world is not as romantic as the world in your head, my Aina.'

Two days after Thorgils' return to Kelda Ey with Angharad, the family embarked and set sail from the beach, with Thorgils' two main ships. *The Sigrid* was broader in the beam than *The Orm*, not so sleek and fast, but it would cope with a long distance sea voyage better and gave them room to stow their provisions. Aina looked back to the crowd of friends on the beach waving and wondered if she would ever return. She had disguised Angharad as one of her maids and only she and Thorgils knew her identity.

Thorgils took them up the Bretland coast as far as Abermaw and then they entered the estuary of the river Mawddach, sandy beaches and blue-green mountains rising on either side. Part-way up the river the ships were anchored well away from the villages at the head of the estuary. Two of Thorgils' Bretar-speaking men ventured inland to buy horses. When they returned Thorgils, these two men and Angharad, took to the saddle and Thorgils commanded that nobody should leave the boats whilst he conveyed the princess safely to the Powys court of Seisyll further inland at the fort of Mathrafal. He was gone four days and then they were on the sea again. With his duty to Maredudd and Angharad completed, Thorgils set a course to Mann from where he planned to sail to Lewis and then to Greenland. He spent time making measurements and watching the sea. Aina thought of their silver hoard buried under the earth, with curlews nesting above it, waiting for them to return to their life on Kelda Ey and feel safe again.

Aina watched the island of Mann loom on the horizon. They rounded its southern tip, sailing up the western coast to the river Neb and the port of Holmtown, where a wooden castle was under construction on the tip of a causeway. Some buildings in the town itself were made from a deep red sandstone. The port was thronged with fisherman and with many Norsemen who carried news that Olafr was preparing a great fleet to confront King Svein and Jarl Erikr.

Thorgils went very quiet when he heard this news and hardly spoke a word to Aina for two days whilst he oversaw minor repairs to the ship, but eventually he came to her, knelt and put his two big hands on the sides of her knees and spoke in great anguish. 'I cannot bear Olafr's hatred of me, his brother, his sworn *drengr*,' he said. 'I cannot bear that he should sail into the greatest battle of his life without me. I must go to him Aina and ask for the return of his love, offer him my swordarm.' He stopped.

Aina knew this was a long and heartfelt speech for Thorgils. She did not want him to go and feared that Olafr would not forgive her husband and would execute him. The stories of Olafr's brutality were ringing around them, tripping off every tongue. Why should he not treat Thorgils in the same fashion, and beyond that fear, Aina was thinking of a great sea battle where he was like to lose his life in defence of Olafr's. Yet she knew that Thorgils had grieved every day since Olafr spurned him and told him he was *nidingr*. She knew his agony over the deceit of his foster-brother and lord, so she tugged gently on his beard, drawing his face closer to hers, and said, 'I know you must go, my love, but come back to me,' and then she tried so hard not to cry, but the tears would gather in her eyes and they would trickle down her face and drip on the top of his red head where she was leaning and after a while she stopped trying to fight them.

'Go back to Kelda Ey,' he told her when she was calmer, 'in *The Sigrid* and I will take *The Orm* and the best fighting men onto Olafr. I will return to you if Odinn wills it.'

'Do not be food for the eagle,' Aina sobbed loudly against his chest as he held her. She remembered the stories he told her in winter nights and she reached out to the cloth covering the table, scrunched up a corner, blew her nose, wiped her face, stood drawing herself up tall and straight, and said, 'You *must* go, man, to your king and fight bravely at his side and not flee, and do not return to me until you have gorged the raven.'

Aina could see that Thorgils was in two minds whether or not to laugh at her but he remembered it was not a laughing moment and grew solemn, thanking her for her strength and for being his true wife.

As soon as *The Orm* was out of sight and Thorgils gone, Aina wept and wailed, screamed and cried like a small child, and Ragnhild and Naerfi held her to stop her from falling against the barrels and harming herself.

# 33

# Poitiers

## 1000

Adalmode watched the bustle around her listlessly. She looked down at the blood between her legs staining the sheets, at her own poor pale body, clammy with sweat, as if it belonged to another person. This was Adalmode's second miscarriage and she had been married less than a year as yet. She turned her head away towards the window and the shouts coming from the courtyard or the marketplace beyond. Poitiers was a busy populous city that was growing familiar. She could glimpse parts of the ruined vineyard through the narrow window in the chamber. A hailstorm, with ice shards the size of Adalmode's fist, had recently devastated the field and vines.

She had contrived to delay her marriage to Guillaume, first claiming a widow's right to grieving time although the law gave her a mere month for that, then prolonging negotiations over the fostering of her son with Guy and Aina and the regency of his birthright with Boson, then negotiating back and forth regarding her dowry, but eventually it had come to it and there was no more delaying. The delay had won Adalmode precious time to find strategies to calm her mind distraught with the loss of Audebert, but the delay had also inflamed the desire and the resentment of her new husband. He knew full well that she married him unwillingly and that she did not bring him love.

She looked around her chamber. Guillaume showered her with lavish gifts and admiring speeches in the early days of the marriage, but the golden rings and brooches in the carved chest at the foot of her bed and the piles of expensive gowns laid on top of it meant nothing to her. He hoped in time she would grow to at least like him he said, but Adalmode doubted even that would ever be in her gift.

The man irritated her. Physically, he was not attactive. He was short, round, fleshy and prematurely old for his age. He had no notion of how to romance or seduce a woman, and when his softnesses failed to warm her, he could only fall back on harsh commands. Observing him with his mother, Adalmode saw, that Emma had engendered in him both a fear and a dislike for other women. He spoke in a soft-voiced and unbelievably slow manner that Adalmode found perhaps more unbearable than his hands upon her. It was almost impossible to hold a sensible conversation with him because his long drawn out mode of speech meant that whenever Adalmode tried to interject a comment or response, she discovered that Guillaume was still developing his thought and was not to be interrupted. The man thought, spoke, moved at the slimy pace of a damaged snail.

His jealous possessiveness isolated Adalmode since he resented any contact she had with another person, and he made this clearly known to everyone. He cared overmuch for his appearance, unimpressive though it was, and he cared even more for his status. He evinced piety but Adalmode saw only his own appetites excused and concealed there, rather than any true love for God or humility. He was insecure around all other men and paid others for his insecurities in petty cruelties. Adalmode found some common ground with him in their mutual love of the books and scrolls lining the Poitiers library shelves and trestles, but it was not near enough to balance out the rest, by God, it was not near enough.

Last week she brought a physician into the castle to look to Guillaume who was suffering from intense pains in the upper-right side of his abdomen and had been vomiting for several hours. He had been drinking heavily and feasting on venison and other meats from the hunt. The doctor prescribed that everyday he must drink four glasses of pure apple juice and have applesauce on his food prepared with five more apples. This excess of apples had to be consumed in this way for five days, then Guillaume had fasted briefly, and finally he had to drink large quantities of lemon juice mixed with olive oil before he went to bed. The next morning, he passed a number of small green and brown pebbles into his piss pot and the pains had ceased. Nevertheless the fuss he was still making about this illness eclipsed any care for Adalmode as she felt her womb grip with a vice-like pain and discovered the red stain spreading rapidly in her lap. Two of the men in the hall had lifted her swiftly and carried her, weeping and writhing to the bedchamber, but now it was over.

She carried this child for three months and it was impossible not to grieve for it, yet part of her was also glad at the loss of the baby. She did not want his child. He had taken everything from her – Audebert and Bernard gone, her independence and the joy of her life, gone. There was no proof to support Fulk's guess, that Guillaume had sent the assassin to seek out Audebert, but Adalmode found proof enough in the characters of this man and his mother as she grew to know more of them. His mother, at least, vented her angry aggression on the surface, whereas Guillaume's was surreptitious and sly. She found the proof also in some secret guilt he always carried, unable to look her in the eye, planning ambitious annual pilgrimages to atone for what sin?

Adalmode looked up towards a commotion in the doorway. Please God, don't let me have to deal with him just yet. But it was his mother instead. The maidservants were parting and bowing before her like rushes before a new river cleaving its path.

'Clean this mess up, quickly,' Emma commanded the midwife with her usual lack of softness. 'You have not eaten properly during this pregnancy,' she told Adalmode. 'You cannot fast and at the same time give the Duke an heir as is your duty.' She stopped short of accusing Adalmode of deliberately causing the miscarriage. 'Or perhaps you are simply too old for childbearing.'

Part of Adalmode wanted to argue, but she was exhausted and weakened and instead she turned her face away, refusing any discussion. In a few days time when she had recovered her strength, she could return to her ongoing battle with her mother-in-law. Adalmode had left the running of the ducal household itself to Emma, along with all matters ecclesiastical, but she had insisted firmly from the first day that she, as the new Duchess, would manage all civic matters, along with her husband. Adalmode had years of experience as first Guy's, and then Audebert's chatelaine. Guillaume had looked trepidatious at first at Adalmode's defiance of his mother, but then seeing that Adalmode did not mean to give way, he bolstered her position, at last able to claim some of his authority himself from his mother. Emma, for her part, was aging and knew that she must cede something to her son's new wife, and so they had found an uneasy compromise.

Next week was the anniversary of Audebert's death and Adalmode was determined that she would be recovered enough to ride to Charroux. Nothing would stop her – not Guillaume and not his mother. She determined that she would persuade Guillaume that he needed to go on another pilgrimage, that her failures to give him an heir were the fault of his crimes, his actions had induced such grief in her that she was barren, and she would suggest that he repudiate her. Then she could return to Guy and Bernard in Limoges, even if it meant declaring herself a house-nun, and she was sure from her kind letters that Aina would make her welcome.

Adalmode recovered quickly and was able to take her seat again in the hall with Guillaume to receive the messages of the day. 'I am glad to see you recovered,' she told him politely.

'Oh! And also you,' he stumbled, looking with concern at the paleness of her face. 'Yet, we must hope that you will do better next time with your marriage debt to me,' he said, not looking at her now. 'I had hoped you would carry that child. My mother tells me it was a boy.'

Adalmode suppressed her anger at his callousness and her disgust at the knowledge that her poor body must take him again and again until she produced an heir. She gripped her hand tightly around her fist beneath the table.

'Grim news from Anjou,' Guillaume told her.

Adalmode looked at him with interest and saw him scowl. She knew that he resented her continuing concerns with anything that was not him or his: her interest in Audebert's compatriot, Fulk, in her brother Guy, in Guy's son Ademar who they were fostering here in Poitiers.

'Count Fulk's wife, Elisabeth of Vendôme, has committed treason against her husband. She attacked his holdings in Bourges in league with her father, Bouchard and Eudes of Blois.'

Would she have undertaken such a drastic betrayal if it had been a happy marriage, Adalmode wondered.

'Fulk has burnt Elisabeth at the stake,' Guillaume continued in a neutral tone, studying Adalmode's face, 'and he has declared their eleven-year-old daughter Adela illegitimate.'

Adalmode blanched. Burnt her and disowned her daughter. Since Audebert's death Fulk had hardened. He was a successful ruler and commander, but any mercy seemed shocked out of him.

'Fulk is already in negotiations for a new wife who might bear him an heir,' Guillaume said meaningfully.

Adalmode ignored Guillaume's implication and resolved that she would write to Fulk, asking him on Audebert's memory, to send his disinherited daughter, Adela, to her. Along with Guy's son, Ademar, her household could at least be filled with other people's children. She was torn between the strong desire to leave Guillaume or to remain in the world where she could do more good for her son, her brother and others that she cared for.

If it had not been for Adalmode's recent intercessions over the matter of Brantôme for instance, Guy would have suffered a great deal more difficulty. Guy had been at war with Boson of La Marche, disputing the rights to Brantôme. Adalmode accompanied Guy to the battle camp to act as his eyes, since his wife Aina was encumbered with their small sons. Guy suffered a minor wound in the fighting but he had prevailed. She was pleased to watch Boson surrender to her brother and Guy took Bishop Grimoard of Angoulême, who had supported Boson in arms attacking Brosse, as a hostage, against future behaviour. Brosse had been their mother's holding and indisputably belonged to Guy but the Bishop had attempted to annexe it. Guy imprisoned the Bishop in the dungeon at Montignac where Audebert spent four years of his life. It had all gone well for Guy until her husband, Guillaume decided to join the dispute, siding with Boson and besieging Guy's castle of La Brosse and the monastery of Le Sault.

Then complaints by other clerics had been made against Guy to the Pope, protesting the Bishop's incarceration. Guy had been summoned to Rome and found guilty in his actions against the Bishop and obliged to do penance and free Grimoard in exchange for his oldest son Ademar as a hostage. Since Adalmode had already agreed to take Ademar as her foster-son, and had reassured Guy and Aina that he would be treated well in Poitiers, this was neither here nor there. A pact of forced friendship was made between Guy and Grimoard and Guy would go on pilgrimage to the Holy Land, accompanied by his brother Hilduin in a few months time. Guy had needed Adalmode's intercessions in these events and she held on in her unhappiness with her husband for the sake of those she loved.

At the beginning of this year Guillaume had called another Peace Council in Poitiers and hosting the occasion had kept Adalmode busy. Bishops Siguinus of Bordeaux, Gilbert of Poitiers, Islo of Saintes and twelve Abbots with their saints' relics had come. In addition to the peace they had condemned priests cohabitating with women and taking remuneration for penance. All Guillaume's vassal lords attended, the lords of Aulnay, Châtellerault, Maillezais, Thouars, Lastours, Lusignan, Parthenay and Vivonne and swore oaths to uphold the peace. Her brother Guy did not attend from Limoges because he was still on the way back from Rome with Hilduin, where he wrote to her, they met with the new Pope Sylvester.

At the Aquitaine Peace Council the purported End of Time was on everyone's lips and religious fervour gripped both the clergy and many lay people. Abbo of Fleury detected an error in Bede's calculations of the End of Time, claiming it would be 1004, but others claimed it was 1033 on the basis that it would be a thousand years after the Passion of Christ, rather than the Nativity. Adalmode and Guillaume heard the story that at Pentecost, Emperor Otto had opened Charlemagne's tomb and found the body of the great king uncorrupted, seated in his armour on a great throne. 'Many have taken this as a sign of much significance,' Guillaume told Adalmode earnestly.

If it *was* the End of Time she considered, she could join Audebert, and if not, an end at least would come soon enough for them all.

# 34

# Kelda Ey
## 1001

When the news came to Aina on Kelda Ey it was bleak. Olafr had lost the battle at Svold and all his ships, including *The Orm*, were captured by Jarl Erikr. Norway had dropped from Olafr's hand. He would not be taken alive and had leapt overboard to his death. There was no news of Thorgils, but Aina knew it was unlikely he would have survived Olafr. He would have fought to the end to defend him. When Aina heard out what news there was she sat unmoving on Thorgils' throne in the long hall on Kelda Ey for six days and nights.

'Aina, you cannot continue like this,' Ragnhild told her gently. 'You will take ill. You are ill. Look at you: pale as snow, thin as a whip. You must decide what we should do now. Shall we put on black mourning and make a pyre and service for Thorgils, proclaim Ulf our new Jarl?' Ulf was eight but confident. He could step into Thorgils' shoes with Aina's support.

'Not yet,' Aina said, and sat for three days more, taking only bread and a little wine to sustain her and thinking all the while through her memories of her husband, longing for Sigrid to be there and comfort her, to grieve together. Not yet, she said, every time Ragnhild, Morag, or her son tried to remonstrate with her.

On the tenth day a messenger came over the sea from Din-bych-y-psygod in a small boat and Aina had him brought to her. She wanted to run down to the beach herself to hear it from his lips there on the sand where she had lost Sigrid also, there where Thorgils had laboured so long and often on the boats. She wanted to be able to fall with her face in the sand when the news cut into her mind like the sharpest chisel, but she could not rise from the carved chair on the dais, his chair. She had eaten and drunk so little for so long, there was no power left in her legs and arms. She could not raise herself. So Ulf brought the messenger into her and he knelt now before her. 'Speak quickly and true,' she said.

'Lady, Lord Thorgils commands me to tell you he is arrived safely at the court of Powys and will return to you here as soon as he is able.'

Aina tried to speak but found her mouth and tongue would not obey her will. She gaped at the messenger.

'He lives?' asked Ulf in disbelief.

The messenger looked around him in surprise, only belatedly aware of the import of this news on his audience. Understanding now, he looked back brightly to the ill-looking lady sitting before him.

'Jarl Thorgils lives Lady, for sure! He sent me with this letter to you with his own hand and seal.'

Ulf took the letter and carried it to his mother. She read it quickly and it told her no more than the messenger already had himself, and yet she saw that it was indeed Thorgils' seal. He told her only that he was uninjured and would be with her soon. Aina let out a great cry and fell against her son sobbing.

'Come, mother,' Ulf said gently, wreathed with smiles at this news of his father. 'You need to be looking yourself when he arrives. Father will not want to see you so wan and unwell. Fetch food and wine for my mother and this excellent messenger here!' he called out to the waiting people who thronged the hall, pushing and shoving at each other to get closer to the front and know for sure the news of their Jarl.

Aina took many days to recover from her grieving but she was looking better, in her finest clothes, as she stood on the beach watching the ship approach. Not *The Orm*. That was gone with

Olafr, but another small ship that her husband must have loaned or bought on his way home. Aina heard the groans and shrieks of dismay of several women behind her when they saw that Thorgils jumped down from the ship alone. None of the warriors he had set sail with stood on the beach alongside him. Reunited with Thorgils, Aina did not know whether to cry, kiss, or hit him in her relief and fear for him, and he laughed at her confusion, whilst also looking anxiously at how thin and pale her face looked against the abundance of wine-dark hair.

As soon as Thorgils was refreshed and a feast was preparing about them, Aina would have the telling of Thorgils' story but he made her wait until the meal was before them and all the household were seated in anticipation. Amidst the eating and drinking Thorgils began the tale: 'I found Olafr at the head of a *breidr floti*, a broad fleet, on his huge new ship, *The Long Serpent*, south off the mouth of the Svoldr. As I approached I admired how high the ship sat in the water, how her stems were loaded with gold decoration and fine carvings, and her sides slung with many fine war-moons – the warriors' shields, how such a display would intimidate the enemy; but I also worried that such a large ship was not so nimble to maneuver, not so flexible in the water. I stood on the front deck of *The Orm* and drew my ship up alongside until I could see Olafr there, looking down on me. He said nothing.'

Thorgils paused and every face in the hall was turned to him expectantly. Would Olafr reject Thorgils' remorse and send him away? A thin black cat with mange marring its fur took advantage of the still hush to venture to leap onto the table in front of Ulf and lick at a half-finished dish. 'Off!' Aina flapped her hand and the cat leapt back down, racing for the doorway before the hounds could raise themselves to go after her.

'I opened my mouth and spoke to my friend,' Thorgils pronounced. '"Olafr, my *drottinn*, my lord, I come to deliver you back your ship, the little *Orm*, if you will have it, and your *drengir* here upon it." There was silence and Olafr continued to look down on me and then he turned his gaze one at a time upon each of the men who had sailed with him since he was a boy and finally looked back to me. If his mood was still unforgiving, these men would pay as well as I.'

338

There were groans and cries from the people in the hall and especially from the widows and lovers of the men who had not returned with Thorgils.

'Then he took us by surprise, leaping down into *The Orm* and into my overwhelmed embrace. "Thorgils!" Olafr cried. "You do not desert me in my greatest battle! My *heimpegi*, Thorgils, always my closest friend and my greatest warrior and helmsmen. I will take back *The Orm* and I will take back Thorgils and Toki and Gormr and all of you."' Toki and Gormr's widows smiled at Thorgils through their tears. 'He swept his arms around to include all the crew in his gesture and then each of us approached him one by one to receive his renewed kiss of friendship. I was shocked to see, close up, how Olafr had aged in the few years of our separation. His long blond curls were whitening and thinning at the back of his head. There were lines on his handsome face.

"It is hard to be a king, Thorgils," he told me. "When I was just a leader of our small war-band, now *that* was fun." The old Olafr flashed briefly in his face.

"Why do you stand battle *here*?" I asked him.

"It was the advice of Jarl Sigvaldi Strut-Haraldsson."

"That bent-nosed Jomsviking! You trust him!"'

Thorgils' listeners exploded with laughter at his assessment and Thorgils paused, waiting for the laughter to die down, swigging from his goblet and setting it down on the table with a bang, for their resumed attention and hush.

"'No, perhaps not," Olafr told me.

As we rounded the headland we saw a vast fleet before us. The ships of Jarl Eirikr, King Sveinn and the Swedes greatly outnumbered Olafr's ships. "The bastard! He has lured us into a trap, Olafr!"

Olafr nodded his head and I saw a muscle work briefly in his jaw. He drew his sword and set his face to the enemy. Leif and I exchanged glances. Outnumbered in this way we should have turned and fought another day, but Olafr never ran from a fight and his enemies had connived to take advantage of that virtue.'

Aina watched the people in the hall bow their heads. They knew what was coming.

Thorgils continued: 'We rowed to bring the ships close to the enemy, broadside on, side by side, clashing shields on the shield rails, they were trying to encircle and isolate *The Long Serpent*. We lashed the ships together to provide a fighting platform, tying the stems of the three ships. The enemy boarded, hundreds attacking and coming over the sides howling, trying to empty the ships. Olafr shouted to us that each of us should fall one across the other rather than give way, and so that is what we did.'

Thorgils paused solemnly and took a long draught from his drinking horn and then spoke rapidly: 'We slashed with swords, chopped with axes, shot with arrows, parried with shields, tried to kill and not to be killed, reddening our weapons and piling up enemy corpses for the delectation of the three beasts of battle. We were forced to retreat the length of the ship, stumbling over the thwarts, with many a well-loved warrior sinking under the blades. Whilst we had weapons we fought on. The *drengir* fell one by one on the deck – Leif, Toki, Skogi, all.'

Aina's heart ached as she thought of those men that she knew well and listened to the soft weeping of their women.

'The dead lay tightly packed and the planks were slippery with their life's blood. Some men went over the sides, dead or wounded. My arms were greatly wearied and I could no longer lift my weapon with any speed. I saw an enemy warrior raise his hammer axe before my eyes and knew nothing more.'

Again Thorgils paused to stab his knife into the meat before him, take it from the knife and chew. Again the people in the hall waited.

Eventually Thorgils had eaten enough and washed it down with enough wine that he could continue. 'But that axe-blow only stunned me and when I came to, corpses lay across and on top of me and I could no longer hear the screams and shouts of battle. I began to push the dead limbs away that I might emerge and was in time to see Olafr standing on the rim of the ship, his red cloak whipping out behind out like a sail just filling with the wind, and I watched in anguish as he jumped overboard.'

The listeners gasped at the image of golden Olafr leaping from the ship. 'He could not survive, weighed down with the silver of his great armour. I swallowed the shout that was on my lips, for I saw through the tangle of limbs still piled on me that Jarl Erikr was stepping aboard *The Long Serpent*. The enemy had carried the battle and Olafr jumped because he thought he was the last man standing. I pulled the corpses back around me and closed my eyes. Olafr's sixty ships including *The Crane*, *The Orm* and *The Long Serpent* were all lost, floating empty and bloody. King Svein, Erik the son of Jarl Hakon, and the Swedish king, had joined forces against Olafr, and Sigvaldi, chief of the Jomsvikings had betrayed him.'

The men in the hall shouted angrily and the women wept louder. Thorgils eyes brimmed with tears and Aina's stroked his arm, gentling his grief. 'Tell us the rest of the tale, husband. How did you come to return back to us?'

Thorgils nodded and resumed. 'After some time the corpses were lifted from me and I heard splashes as they were thrown and rolled overboard. Then I was limp in the arms of the enemy and tried not to gasp as I hit the cold water. I swam down, with the pale arms and faces of my companions waving around me. While I could hold my breath, I looked for Olafr's red cloak but could see little in the murk. I dropped my own armour on the sea floor and watching the shadow of the ship above me, I rose slowly into that shadow. I could hear the enemy shouting above, celebrating their win, boasting their victory. Corpses floated past. I grabbed onto a tangle of dead arms and legs, closed my eyes again, and waited for the tide to take me into the shore.

I felt my toes hit gravel and cautiously opened my eyes, avoiding looking too closely at the dead faces I swam with. The yellow sand of the beach was before me and I saw there were hundreds of corpses swilling back and forth in the red surf and at the edge grey wolves slavered and fought over their rich feast, pulling bodies out of the water, tearing at bellies. Ravens gathered shrieking in the trees and eagles sat on the faces of men and pecked at their eyes.'

Aina glanced around at the murmurs of distress and saw that Ulf's face showed him enthralled by the images of Thorgils' tale.

'I stood quickly and ran for the trees, before one of those beasts should try to make a meal of me and I heard no shouts from the boats behind me. As I ran stealthily through the woods, I saw at some distance, a group of men and women poorly dressed, making their way down to the shore, intending to share the corpse plunder with the beasts. I sorrowed for all my friends and Olafr who had fallen there. *The Orm* gone and all the *drengir* gone. Olafr, the hawk-minded, the benchmate of his *drengir*, the deed-strong, the flight-shunning, Olafr was gone into the depths.' Thorgils leapt to his feet, raising his goblet. 'Olafr!'

Benches scrapped, swords clanged, dogs howled as they failed to move out of the way quickly enough as every man, woman and child in the place, leapt up, their own beakers raised, roaring, 'Olafr!'

Thorgils subsided and all fell back to their seats again and each picked over the meal before them in silence, until Thorgils spoke again. 'My golden friend is drear-cheeked now. I was covered in sand and blood and stopped to wash my wounds in a small waterfall. I found a hole under an earthbank and crept in, pulling a bush to conceal me, for I was dead tired and needing sleep. When I woke, darkness had fallen and I moved on until I came to a hamlet and a tavern where I offered myself as an armed guard to any merchant going on the Swan Road and I came home that way.'

Alone later in their chamber, Thorgils told Aina: 'Olafr told me quietly when we stood shoulder to shoulder waiting for the battle to begin that he had lost his way as king without me.'

'It was good that you went and were with him, Thorgils.'

'He said he had to rule by force alone when he should have remembered how well he ruled by consensus, with the unwavering love of his men before he was king, when he and I rode the sea together in little *Orm*.'

Aina looked silently and gratefully into Thorgils' face until he spoke again: 'In valour Olafr was a lion, but in wit and resource he was a squirrel on the ground. Still,' he added doubtfully, 'he was a wondrous swimmer.'

Aina wrote to Sigrid to tell her of Thorgils' survival and Olafr's heroic death and added at the end of her letter:

The centre where kings play cannot hold it seems, Sigrid, and all is change there, but the edge can, and Thorgils, Ulf, and I thrive on our island at the edge of the world.

You didn't want or plan to Sigrid, but despite yourself you too have lived bravely, travelled widely and accumulated wealth as a good Norse heroine should. You are a secret Viking. The only part you are missing is fame – no one can speak your true name and your heroism and adventures are unsung.

Thorgils tried to forget how his shoulder companions were in earth's grip, grave-grasped. He told the skalds he did not want to hear tales of Svold for one full year, and yet after that year had passed he was still heavy with friend-loss and it was a long time before his hall was filled again with cheerful uproar and throng-noise, forgetful of the quiet dead.

# 35

# Poitiers

## 1003

Guy came to visit Adalmode and his son, Ademar, on his return from the Holy Land, and his visit made her life more bearable for a while. After the required public welcoming and feasting in the hall, she finally had her brother to herself in her chamber and could really speak with him. Looking around her, as Guy embraced Ademar for as long as the boy would allow, Adalmode thought again how the lavishness of her chamber – hung with yellow silk, red and green tapestries, loaded with furs and cushions – felt like somebody else's room. None of it was her choice. It was all Guillaume. Still Guy could not see any of its details and made no remark on his surroundings. He bounced on the bed next to her, and took her hand, smiling.

'Things do not stay still,' she said, 'with a new Emperor in the east, Henry II, and a new Pope, John XVII.'

He nodded. 'Yes, everything changes.'

'How did you find things in Limoges? Is there change there? How are Aina and Bernard?'

'No, little change in Limoges, everything is well. They are both very well and Aina sends her apologies not to be here but she is much occupied with our three other sons. Bernard is growing into a fine boy, Adalmode.'

She smiled warmly, sitting close where he could see something of her face. 'And how *is* your marriage, Guy? You thought Aina was not inclined to the match during your long betrothal.'

'Yes, that's true. I'd entirely forgotten that,' Guy said, a look of surprise on his face, 'because, Adalmode, I am entirely happy. *We* are happy I believe. Aina is understanding and helpful about my eyesight too. I couldn't be happier.'

'I am very glad for you, Guy.'

'You deserve to be happy too, sister,' Guy said frowning and lowering his voice. 'Are things no better between you and the Duke?'

'No,' she said brightly putting a mock cheerful expression on her face. 'They can't be and they won't be Guy. I loved Audebert with a love far deeper than the pit he was imprisoned in at Montignac and no man could follow on from that. Least of all Guillaume. Simply, I do not like him nor ever will.' She took Guy's hand. She could see his distress at her words, knowing he had been party to forcing her to the marriage. 'But I am not without consolations. I have you. I have Bernard. I dearly love your son Ademar. And I am a good Duchess I believe. I am not entirely unhappy Guy.'

Guy told her he met Fulk of Anjou in Jerusalem. 'He travelled there to atone for burning his first wife Elisabeth.'

'Little good that did her,' Adalmode said, her expression grim.

'And King Robert has had to put aside his wife, Berthe.'

Adalmode raised her eyebrows in query.

The King has been under great pressure from the Church,' Guy told her, 'because of the close kinship between them. So Berthe is repudiated now and Robert has married Blanche of Anjou's fifteen-year-old daughter Constance of Provence.'

Adalmode raised her eyebrows again. 'Constance, Blanche's daughter! I was at her birth in Brioude.'

Guy nodded. 'This is a peace offering to Fulk from the King, since Constance is Fulk's niece.'

'The Angevins continue closely aligned with the Frank throne one way or another. It's not right that clerics should involve themselves in these ways in our business, forcing the King to repudiate his wife.'

Guy said nothing in response and Adalmode saw he did not wish to discuss this topic of consanguinity further, since it touched so closely on his own marriage. 'The Norman Duke

Richard has arranged the marriage of his sister Emma to the English King Athelred whose kingdom is much plagued by Vikings,' said Guy.

'Oh here too!' exclaimed Adalmode. 'I knew there was something else I meant to tell you!'

'Vikings here?' asked Guy. 'When was this?'

'Earlier this year they came to Saint Michel en l'Herm again, where Aina was taken.'

'What happened?'

'When news came of their landing, my husband mounted a defence of his lands,' said Adalmode, her tone heavy with sarcasm. Her brother took a gulp of wine, knowing that he was in for a good story.

'The Vikings dug concealed pits in front of the Abbey where they were feasting and Guillaume rode his horses straight into the trap.' Adalmode allowed herself a brief smile at her husband's ineptitude and Guy snorted.

'What happened?'

'He narrowly escaped with his life whilst many of his entourage were captured. He had to pay exorbitant ransoms to get them back.'

Adalmode enjoyed giving Guy her frank assessment of her husband's court. 'It is full of pomp. He preens about his meetings with the Pope, the Emperor, King Canute, that come of his annual pilgrimages and mentions their names in connection with his at every opportunity. He is well regarded by Bishops to whom he is generous, but he is not so well regarded by his own local lords such as Hugh of Lusignan, Radulf of Thouars and William of Parthenay, not mention his neighbour, Fulk of Anjou. All pay him lip-service as the great Duke, recognising him as suzerain, easily manipulating his vanity, and paying him little attention in their deeds.'

Guillaume heaved a sigh of relief that he disguised as a sigh of distressed emotion, as his mother's last breath left her mouth and the priest commended her soul to God. Guillaume tried not to think about how God might react to that. 'Protect the Abbey of

Maillezais Guillaume, in eternal memory of me,' she had whispered to him. There had been so little Christian kindness in his mother, and she had committed so many crimes against others, but he could not waste time to think about the suffering she would undoubtedly be going through in her transition into the afterlife, perhaps in Hell. He would pay for prayers to be said for her, of course, that was his filial duty, but he doubted that a million prayers would help her and he had too many other things to think of and do now that she was gone.

The news that Boson of La Marche had died arrived last week. The messenger reported the claim that he had been poisoned by his wife. The woman was waiting in the hall below now, for Guillaume's judgement. He needed to take action over the inheritance of La Marche and Périgord. He already knew what he would do. He had planned it from the start. Perhaps if Adalmode had been kinder to him, if she had tried harder to give him an heir, he would have changed his mind and kept his promise but no she needed to be taught a lesson and he needed to protect his own interests. Never again would he be threatened by a Count of La Marche, as he had been threatened by Audebert and shamefully made to run for his life from his own city, a laughing stock.

Adalmode was waiting in the hall for him, smiling ecstatically into the face of her son, who she was seeing for the first time since her marriage. Bernard was twelve and already favouring Audebert dramatically – it was like looking at the man himself as a boy on the verge of manhood. Guillaume tried to ignore the knot of fear in his stomach that he experienced at the sight of the boy. Also in the hall were Boson's wife and two sons. He would show them all justice. He would show them all that he was Duke. The three most favoured friends in his entourage were also there, as instructed, Cadelon of Aulnay, Boso of Châtellerault, and Raoul of Thouars, and their presence bolstered him up for what he must do.

Boson's sons rose at his entrance and he gestured for them to take their seats. Boson's wife stood but did not look up, keeping her head down. Her sons sat apart from her whereas Adalmode was hanging onto Bernard's hand, as if he were a small child. The boy stared boldly at Guillaume who found himself having to avoid his blue eyes that reminded him so of Audebert.

'I come with the sad news that my mother has just in this last hour died and gone to meet her Maker,' Guillaume said and all in the hall crossed themselves and murmured commiserations, although none, Guillaume knew, had ever liked her.

'Shall we postpone this hearing, then, my lord?' Adalmode asked. 'Prepare for your mother's vigil and burial?'

'No,' Guillaume said quickly. 'That is all going on, but we shall see to this business nevertheless. Countess Cecilia, it has come to our notice that you have been accused of maliciously and criminally murdering your husband, Count Boson of La Marche and Périgord, with poison. Do you deny this charge?'

The dejected woman shook her head and her two sons shifted further away from her on the trestle.

'Speak,' Guillaume said, 'you need to speak.'

'No,' she said, swallowing and looking up now, looking to Adalmode and speaking in her direction. 'I did kill him and I repent that it was a sin, but the man was cruel and unkind to me all my life. He took mistresses and flaunted them in my face. He beat me.'

Guillaume watched the sons drop their heads and stare blankly at the floor. Yes the woman was clearly speaking truth and he knew from Adalmode that Boson had troubled her too.

'Whatever his crimes to you, you had no right to take his life,' he said.

'I know my lord and I am greatly sorry for my sin.'

Guillaume paused at length. It was necessary to introduce some theatricality into these situations, to give his words their proper weight. 'You will be confined in the nunnery at Maillezais and the nuns will work with you to bring you to absolution if they can.'

'Thank you lord.'

'She should burn for the murder of my father,' the eldest son burst out.

Guillaume quelled this disruption to his dignity with a cold stare and the boy hung his head again. A tear trickled down the face of his mother and Guillaume saw that Adalmode was looking with pity on the woman. She had such a vast lake of kindness available for anyone but him. Had he not done penance enough to earn her love by now. Why could she not pity and love *him*.

'Lady Cecilia's fate will be as I have decreed and there will be no further debate on the matter.'

The boy did not look up and Guillaume settled further into his throne with satisfaction, placing his arms along its broad wooden struts, wrapping his hands around the balled claws. His feet touched the ground when he sat back thus in this chair, but only just, he thought with irritation, sitting a little forward again in case anyone should notice that he was having to reach down with the toe of his boot.

'There is the matter of the disposition of the counties of La Marche and Périgord,' he said.

'My son, Bernard, is the heir to the Counties,' Adalmode stated in a loud, clear voice and Guillaume squirmed irritated on the chair.

'You will be silent,' he said, turning to her fiercely. 'I am the Duke and I will say what the disposition of these vassal counties are.'

'The Count of La Marche and Périgord gave you no fealty, nor any other man,' Adalmode said.

'If you are not silent, Lady Adalmode,' Guillaume said coolly, 'I will have you removed to your chambers.' He glanced towards Cadelon, Boso and Raoul, implying that they would physically do the removing if he commanded it. He saw Adalmode's mouth set in a straight line and she gripped her son's hand with both of her own. She did not want to be removed from *him*.

'It is my decision that Bernard will inherit his father's county of La Marche,' Adalmode opened her mouth but Guillaume quelled her with an angry look, 'and the county of Périgord I give into the hands of young Helie, the son of Boson who was my faithful vassal, before he was so direly murdered by his wife.'

Boson's sons and Lady Cecilia looked up in surprise. Guillaume waited with satisfaction. Adalmode would object and he would enjoy her dismay. He looked at Bernard while he waited for her response, and was alarmed to see the expression on the boy's face. There was no fear or subservience there. His expression had hardened into cool dislike. Before Adalmode could gather herself to address him, the boy himself spoke: 'Both counties belong to me. They are my rightful inheritance from my father. My uncle

349

Boson was merely Regent during my minority. I ask them both of you now, Duke Guillaume.' His voice clenched on the word ask, implying a demand rather than a request.

'I have made my decision,' Guillaume said. 'Further since you are still a minor, Count Bernard, I am sending you to Bellac with two guardians who will take care of you and your inheritance: Lord Humbert and Father Pierre will accompany you.'

'He needs no such guardians,' Adalmode found her voice and Guillaume felt a shiver at his neck at the ice in it. 'I will stand as Regent for him and go with him to Bellac.'

Guillaume shifted in his chair to face her directly. 'No you will not. Your place is here with me.'

'You renege on the agreement brokered by my brother and Fulk of Anjou at the time of our wedding,' she stated. He watched a pulse throbbing in her neck and thought how he would like to place his fingertips there, or better his mouth, and feel her passionate blood beneath his lips.

'A lord should not stand in the way of a man obtaining the honour which had been in his kin's possession,' Bernard said boldly to Guillaume and he saw how Adalmode looked proudly at him. 'My father *possessed* La Marche *and Périgord* and much more besides,' he asserted, hinting at the fact that Audebert had briefly possessed Poitiers, Tours, Gençay and most of Aquitaine too. 'These two counties are both rightfully mine and I state a claim for all of my father's lands.'

'My decisions here are final and absolute,' Guillaume said rising. If he allowed this discussion to go on he would start to lose ground. He should have had the boy murdered along with his father, he thought regretfully and then his own son, if he ever had one, could have inherited both counties. He looked coldly at Adalmode. Her beauty still moved him and he would never let her leave him, but he knew now that she would never love him.

'Thank you Duke, for your justice,' young Helie was saying as Guillaume moved past him.

'Justice!' he heard Adalmode spit incredulously behind him and he quickened his pace to get through the door and away.

That evening Guillaume sat in his chamber with a tremendous blaze in the hearth. It was a little too hot, and he was a little drunk he admitted to himself. He heard a noise at the door and looking up was surprised to see Adalmode standing there, swathed from her shoulders to her naked ankles in a heavy shawl and wearing thin silver slippers on her feet. Her hair was loose and he saw the threads of white in it now at her temples. There were tiny crease lines at the corners of her eyes and her mouth, yet she was still the most beautiful and desirable woman he had ever seen. She never came to him of her own free will. He always had to go to her and she never received him with anything except duty and revulsion.

'My Lady?'

She stepped into the room.

'Some wine?' he asked. He found this usually helped in their marital encounters and could almost create the impression some-times that she was a willing recipient beneath him. She shook her head and he swallowed at the cold expression on her face.

The room was very hot and she let the shawl slip a little from her shoulders and throat. Beneath the shawl she wore only a low nightgown of thin white cotton and Guillaume looked hungrily at the swell of her breasts, her skin a golden-olive warmed in the firelight.

'Are you here to render your marriage debt to me, wife?'

'No I am here to treat with you.' She shook her head at his gesture to the stool close to him. 'Repudiate me,' she said bluntly. 'If you will not let me go to Bellac as Regent, then repudiate me and I will go into a nunnery.'

'Er,' Guillaume was thrown by this unexpected request. 'Er, do sit down wife, please.' Reluctantly she sat and he poured wine for them both. He threw back his own wine in one gulp. She did not touch hers.

'I cannot do that Adalmode,' he said, leaning forward and clasping her hand tightly, though she tried to extract it. 'I love you. You are my dear wife.'

She wrenched her hand free and red scratches where visible on her fingers where she had scrapped her flesh against his rings. She sat back looking coldly at him, saying nothing.

'I'm sorry if I have pained you with my decisions today . . .'

'You are not.'

'They are for the best, dear. Your son is young yet.'

'You deliberately divided his father's inheritance. You rob him and you have robbed me every day for the last six years with your lies. You renege on the promises you made at our marriage. If necessary, I will ask Count Fulk and my brother to enforce your promises that they were witnesses to.'

'I think we should renew our marriage debt, now,' he said, furious at her threat. He saw her mouth set and her hand grip the arm of the chair. What was the point in trying to woo her, hoping she might willingly return his feelings. There was no hope of that left. Yet he needed to treat her carefully. He wouldn't put it past her to leave him, as his mother had left his father, and return to her brother, and he did not want to drive her to that.

'If you were to give me an heir, Adalmode,' he said making his voice and face gentle, 'then we could discuss the possibility of your taking the veil if that were still your wish, but you know that I must have an heir and you must give him to me.'

She stared at the fire but he could see the resignation and the misery in her face. He could keep her a while longer.

'This is Ademar of Chabannes,' Guillaume said to Adalmode, introducing a young monk standing eagerly before them, his brown habit spilling overlong onto the pale white slabs paving the Great Hall. The monk looked small and inconsequential, dwarfed by the great expanse of the hall stretching empty behind him. 'The Count of Angoulême has commissioned him to write a history of Aquitaine. A splendid idea don't you think? He will do some of his research in our Library.'

Adalmode did not answer. She stared down the hall, past the monk, unseeing, only half-listening to the conversation between the young man and her husband about the research he planned to undertake. She held her hand on the mound of her stomach. She had thought to go to a nunnery even though Guillaume had refused it, but now that she was carrying a child again, what could she do? Perhaps this child would drop from her also and then she could go. Her maid had told her of a woman in the poor quarter of Poitiers who sold pennyroyal to women who could not afford another mouth to feed, but Adalmode could not muster adequate courage for that crime, that sin, and if the child lived, she knew that she would be unable to abandon it, and it would keep her here, with him.

Guillaume dismissed the monk from their presence and reached out a hand to place it on top of hers with satisfaction. 'God willing you will carry this one,' he said. 'You must be confined throughout the pregnancy this time. I will send my mother's old midwife to organise everything.'

Adalmode wanted to object but she had no energy. Perhaps when she was over these first few months of sickness she could muster herself to take action and resist Guillaume's arrangements.

'Richard, the new Duke of Normandy has sent a chest of books to us as a gift, dear,' Guillaume said. 'Your maid can look through them and find something for you and bring it up to your chamber. It will be a long confinement I know but I will visit you every day and you will have anything and every thing you want.'

Adalmode stared at him stonily. She wanted to be done with him, to be in Bellac with her son and her memories of her first husband.

The thought of being confined to her chambers for the next six months, cared for by unfriendly servants, was not appealing, but she grit her teeth, determined not to show her feelings. If she lost this child too it would be soon and then she could steal away to the nunnery. Her body would reject this one just as it had rejected all the other spores of Audebert's murderer.

# 36

# Limoges
## 1009

Aina's mother, Lady Melisende, as far as anyone knows *my* mother, died and my grief at her funeral was real enough for I loved her dearly from the first moment I smelt her lemon scent in Tallinn when she bought me and took pity on me, sheared raw away from my brothers as I was. I ached to be with Aina when she received the news of Melisende's death. I had been terrified to hear of the Saint Brice's Day Massacre of Scandinavians in Engaland, sanctioned callously by their king Athelred. I waited anxiously to hear from Aina but when her letter came she reassured me the wave of anti-Norse feeling had not reached far into Bretland. 'Now that my mother is dead,' she wrote, 'there is no one left alive there who knows who you truly are.' No one except me, I thought, me and my lies.

Guy's sister, Adalmode, bore an heir at last for the Duke of Aquitaine. Guy says that he is a fine boy, six years old now, and past the threats of infancy. Count Fulk of Anjou too finally has an heir named Geoffrey. When Guy told me of Fulk's pilgrimage to Jerusalem to atone for his cruelty to his first wife, Elisabeth of Vendôme I burst out, 'That will not give her life again, or take away the agonies she suffered. What kind of a religion would offer forgiveness for such actions just because a man gets on a horse or a boat and travels a long way.'

'Aina!' said Guy, 'I do hope you continue to only voice such bizarre opinions to me.'

'I have some sense, husband,' I said crossly. 'Plenty.'

A bright new star was seen in the sky in 1006 and some took this as yet another indication of the Second Coming and Judgement Day. Abbo of Fleury's recalculation of the End of Time to 1004 proved to be the end of time only for him, when he was murdered by resentful monks who he was intent on reforming. 'The Church grows mad over this notion of the End of Time,' I said to Guy but he told me I should not speak impieties.

Hilduin continues to advise Guy to separate from me. In my bleak moods I fear that I will lose my husband for a consanguinity that does not exist, for fear of a hell that I do not believe in. My lies tangle me more and more, even though Guy assures me he does not heed Hilduin's counsel on this nor ever will.

I have been waiting anxiously for Guy's return from Roccamolten where he has been assisting his sister's son, our foster-son Bernard, to oust the 'tutors,' Pierre of Dorat and Humbert Drus, that Duke Guillaume thrust upon him, and I am relieved to hear the sound of many horses arriving below. Delighted I run to the window to see him come, but draw my head back quickly when I see not only his dear face looking up to my chamber window, but also beside him, the golden head of his sister, Adalmode, also looking upwards. I sit down with a thump onto a low birthing stool, my heart beating. I have to avoid her. Guy sent me no warning that she would accompany him. If I claim to be ill she will come to nurse me, unless my illness should endanger her. I know she is carrying her second child by the Duke of Aquitaine. 'Hilde!' I call to my maid. 'Quickly girl. You must take a message to my husband immediately in the hall below.'

'Won't you greet him my lady?' She looks taken aback. She knows how I have looked out for him every day and longed for his safe return.

'Tell him, Hilde,' I look at her intently and firmly. 'Tell him that Lady Adalmode must on no account enter my chamber for I am only lately recovered of the spotting sickness that kills babies in the womb. I know that she is with child.'

Hilde gapes at me. 'But Lady Aina?'

'As you love me, Hilde, you must do this, now.'

She closes her mouth, swallows and nods, her eyes wide on my face, that of course shows no signs of the spotting sickness at all, although there has been an outbreak recently in the town and Guy knows of this. I nursed several cases and Fulayh told me of its fatal effect on unborn babies.

In the Great Hall of the Limoges Motte castle Guy sat with Adalmode, who was expressing her dismay that yet again she would have to miss seeing Aina.

'This is great bad luck. When this child is born you and Aina must come to visit me in Poitiers.'

Guy smiled his agreement to her suggestion.

'How are your Annals Guy? It seems that it is always likely to be the End of Time.'

He smiled. 'I have little time for writing them now, but yes there is plenty to record this year.'

'My husband you know is harbouring Charles of Lorraine's penniless son Louis in Poitiers, saying that he is the rightful king.'

Guy raised his eyebrows. 'He means to pursue this?'

Adalmode shook her head. 'He is only doing it to annoy King Robert, whilst this young man Louis, will no doubt suffer for these assertions one day. My husband is a pompous fool, Guy,' Adalmode whispered, leaning close to his ear, 'who loves to play at kingmaker but will not follow through with any risk to himself.'

Guy laughed and hushed her. 'I think the King has plenty of other things to annoy him.'

Adalmode nodded. King Robert's friend, Hugh of Beauvais had lately urged him to repudiate Queen Constance, and she in retaliation had organised Hugh's murder, some said with the aid of her uncle, Fulk of Anjou. Despite the heirs that Queen Constance had given him, the King hoped the Pope might annul his marriage to Constance and allow him to remarry his first wife, Berthe, but the Pope had recently refused. Constance was now restored as Queen and reported to be thick in intrigues with her uncle Fulk.

'Yet even the ructions at the royal court,' Guy said, 'are nothing compared to the news from Jerusalem that the Egyptian Caliph, Al-Hakim, has destroyed the Christian Church of the Holy Sepulchre.'

Adalmode pressed his hand in agreement. For Christians everywhere this was seismic news. 'Yes. My husband's next planned pilgrimage to Jerusalem cannot take place now,' she said. 'I will have to send him to Compostela instead.'

Guy laughed and stood. He had business to see to in the courtyard with his steward.

Adalmode watched her small son, Guillaume, playing with Guy's sons. She looked around at the hall remembering her own history here: her father and mother finally regaining their honours, Audebert being freed from the dungeon by Geoffrey of Anjou, standing before them all starved, his ankle ringed with sores, asking for her in marriage and declaring that he would take no other. She remembered Guy being made Viscount and the help she had given to him during the years of Aina's captivity with the Vikings, and then finally, she remembered Audebert striding up the hall towards her and Guy to claim her as his bride. Her recollections were suddenly dispelled by a deliberate cough close to her. She looked up and recognised the young monk, Ademar, who had been undertaking research in the library in Poitiers, writing a history of Aquitaine. She smiled a greeting to him, 'Brother Ademar isn't it? You are living here in the Abbey of Saint Martial?'

'Yes, lady. I wondered if I might have a private word with you.'

Adalmode looked quizzically at him, 'Concerning?'

His face showed embarrassment. A monk asking to engage in conversation alone with a woman might be misconstrued, but she indicated that he should take a seat at the trestle.

'You may not be aware my lady that my father was related to the viscounts of Limoges, to your family.'

Adalmode smiled briefly, politely. It must have been a very distant claim to kinship since she had never heard of it. The monk had a round, pock-marked face with large brown eyes and a small mouth. Despite his youth, there were dark circles and baggy skin beneath his eyes.

'My father's grandmother was the daughter of the Viscount of Aubusson and . . . related to bishops and abbots,' he ended lamely, apparently not receiving the impressed response from her that he was hoping for.

'You come of good stock, Brother,' she said curtly to conciliate him, but wished that he would get to the point.

'My grandfather was Ainard of Dorat,' he said.

'Ah yes!' Adalmode's expression and tone warmed now. 'My husband, my first husband, Audebert, spoke warmly of your grandfather. He was his good adviser and ally.'

The monk was nodding happily now, pleased it seemed that she had recognised a bond between them.

'Yes! I could have been trained as a warrior, instead of given as an oblate to the church,' he said wistfully.

Adalmode felt some pity for the young man sitting before her. No doubt he had no choice when his family decided to give him to the church at seven, and it seemed it would not have been his choice. She looked at the soft flesh of his face and hands. 'Your family aspired for you to make your way in the church,' she said. Perhaps this was what he wanted from her, patronage on his road to becoming an abbot. 'What are you working on here at Saint Martial's?'

'I continue working on my history of Aquitaine, Lady Adalmode, and I also write music and act as *custodes* for the crypt of the saint.'

She nodded, forcing a look of interest onto her face. So he was managing the hordes of pilgrims that flocked here, lecturing them on Saint Martial, unlocking the church doors to them for the nocturnal vigils when the pushing crowd streamed in wanting to see and touch the saint's candelit tomb.

'You wished to speak to me on a particular matter?' Adalmode asked, growing impatient again.

'Ah yes! I confess I am experiencing great reluctance in broaching the matter. It is something I found in the Poitiers library during my research, my lady. It concerns a person of your acquaintance and I find myself in need of your advice as to how to proceed with this discovery.'

Adalmode was intrigued. Perhaps it concerned Audebert. He would undoubtedly play a part in the monk's history but if

Guillaume had editorial control, which he would have, she doubted that Audebert's story would be told truly. If she could do anything about that . . . She signalled to her maid to keep an eye on the boys who were playing with a stuffed toy horse and called for a jug of wine.

'You intrigue me Brother Ademar. How can I help you?'

'I found a letter inside one of the books I was examining,' he said, pulling a small jewelled book from the sleeve of his habit. He opened the book and slid out a folded parchment. He placed the book on the trestle before them, placed the parchment flat on his knee and both of his hands on top of it.

'You took this book from Poitiers without permission?' Adalmode asked.

The monk's face clouded with embarrassment. 'I . . . borrowed it merely for my research. The letter I found inside is written in Norse I believe, with a truly execrable Langue d'Oil translation accompanying it.'

'Norse?'

'It is from King Olafr Tryggvason to the Duke of Normandy.'

Adalmode frowned. She had heard the name before and could not recall where.

'It was inside a book that was in a chest which I believe the Norman Duke sent to your husband as a gift sometime ago, but I imagine with the heavy duties of state he has not had time to peruse every book there yet. It was near the bottom. I saw it glinting there with its beautiful jewelled cover – and when I reached it from the chest, the letter fell out.'

They both looked at the small jewelled book on the table. 'I see,' Adalmode said, still wondering where this might be tending. It seemed unlikely that it was anything to do with Audebert. He had few dealing with Normandy as far as she could remember.

'It concerns Lady Aina of Ségur, the Viscountess, your sister by marriage,' Ademar said.

Realisation dawned on Adalmode. 'Ah, yes! This Olafr was the man who kidnapped her long ago, before she married Guy.'

Ademar was hesitant now and Adalmode knit her brow in concern at the tone of his voice. 'Yes, precisely so, my lady.'

'Well?'

'May I read the letter to you? It may shock you I fear.'

'Yes, get on with it.'

The monk pouted at her irritation, but he pulled himself up straight, unfolded the parchment and read:

> From King Olafr Tryggvason to Richard, Duke of Normandy, greetings.
>
> I write in grief to tell you of a great betrayal that has fallen upon me from a source I did not look for – from my best warrior and foster-brother, Jarl Thorgils, who lives now on Kelda Ey. Since my father was murdered, my mother set me upon the knee of this Thorgils' father and we grew together as foster-brothers, suffered misfortunes in company with each other, sailed and fought valiantly together. Yet he has betrayed me over a woman and over this matter of the ransom of Lady Aina of Ségur. Now that I am Christian, as are you, I cannot have this lie upon my conscience and so I write to tell you of it. Thorgils lay with the lady and would not give her up when I ordered it and he sent, unknown to me, his sister, Sigrid in her stead to wed the Viscount for his silver. So you have taken a cuckoo to this Viscount Guy and we are deceived by my erstwhile most trusted companion. I leave you to decide what action to take. Good health to you and your wife.
>
> Olafr, son of Tryggve, great-grandson of Harald Finehair, King of all Norway, Iceland and Greenland.

Ademar refolded the letter, placed it back beneath his crossed hands on his knee and looked up into Adalmode's shocked face. Yes, she thought, everyone suspected that Aina must have lain with her Viking captors before being returned to Guy, even though Guy assured Adalmode that his wife had come to him as a virgin. It would be easy to deceive him in that, but she had not imagined a deceit of this extent. She looked down at her own knees for some time, trying to order her ideas, remembering the Norse maid, Sigrid.

'Thank you for bringing this to me, Brother. Give me the book and the letter.' She held out her hand.

'Lady, will you act upon it or should I take it to your husband, the Duke?'

Adalmode stared angrily at him and she watched Ademar quail at her expression.

'Give them to me, monk.'

His courage failed him and he passed them to her. She did not doubt that he had made a copy of the letter in any case.

'I will act on it as I see fit and you will keep your counsel on it if you would receive a reward,' she said, her voice becoming more gentle and conciliatory.

'Of course, lady.'

'Come to me tomorrow morning here after breaking fast when I have had time to consider this fully.'

'Yes lady.' Ademar rose and left her.

Adalmode opened the letter and looked down at the words there. The Norse made no sense to her and as the monk had said, the Langue d'Oil was almost indecipherable. Perhaps it did not say what the monk had told her: that Aina, Guy's wife, was not Aina, but Sigrid, her Norse maid. Why would they have run the great risk of swapping the women? Had Aina perhaps died in childbirth and that was the way for the Viking to still get his silver. Guy would have known . . . but then, Adalmode considered, perhaps not. She had to find out more and she had to keep that odious monk's discretion under her control. It was clear that he wanted a reward but in her experience that could mean he would keep on wanting a reward, over and over. She must avoid the public exposure of this story for Guy's sake. If it were revealed it would be completely humiliating for him. And what would be the standing then of Guy's four sons? This woman, masquerading as his wife, she would have to pay for such a crime of deception. Adalmode lifted the hem of her skirts and set her foot on the bottom step of the staircase that led to the chambers of the Viscountess.

For several days I have been safe from Adalmode's eyes, hiding here in my chamber, occupying myself with sewing and issuing orders for the feasting and household matters through Hilde. Yesterday Guy had come to commiserate with me on my sickness and marvelled that there was no trace of it on my skin now. What was one more lie to him to add to my great hoard of lies?

'Yes I am fully recovered and am quite safe,' I assured him, 'but Fulayh says I must have no contact with any pregnant women for at least two weeks.'

Luckily for me Fulayh is away from Limoges undertaking some business of his own with a friend in Charroux.

Guy was greatly disappointed for his sister's sake. 'She was so looking forward to seeing you Aina. She says it has been twelve years since you last met, before the kidnapping, but I fear she cannot stay here beyond a week.'

I gaze with remorse at a great bunch of gay flowers standing in a pottery jug near the window that Guy brought to me, to cheer up my 'sick-chamber.' The door creaks. 'The list for the kitchen is on the chest near the door, Hilde,' I say, without looking up from a difficult part of the embroidery that is occupying me. It is an overcast day and the light is not good.

'Hello Aina.' Adalmode's voice.

I drop the veil on top of my head to cover my face and rise, my heart thumping. If Adalmode should recognise me now my whole life will collapse around me. I will lose everything: Guy, my children, likely my life, and would Aina and Thorgils be safe?

'Lady Adalmode please!' I say holding out my hand to stay her progress into the room. Her green gown is stretched over the protruding round of her belly. 'I fear for your child with my recent illness.'

'I have a charm against that Sigrid.'

'But if the charm should not prove efficacious . . .' I stop, realising that she has called me by my name.

'No more lies, Sigrid.'

I look down for a moment at the stone flags of the chamber at my feet, then I raise my head to look at my sister-in-law, lift the veil from my face and drape it back over my head. I see her grimace of recognition. She knows and she does not bother with pretence and now neither will I. 'I am so tired of lies,' I say. For a long moment we stare at each other. Emotions pass swiftly over her face, so swiftly that I have difficulty reading them: anger, disgust, confusion? 'Will you take some wine with me?' I ask and she nods, sitting and arranging her skirts carefully around her, placing her hands beneath her belly to support its weight and ease it from her back. I call to Hilde and she comes with the wine jug and goblets. Hilde looks silent, bewildered questions to me, knowing as she does how hard I have sought to avoid a meeting with Adalmode, but I ignore Hilde's curious expressions and focus on the jug and goblets until she goes out quietly closing the door behind her. I can feel Adalmode's regard on my bowed head and averted face like heat. I take a small sip of wine for form's sake, and so does she.

'I didn't think all this time how strange it was that I never encountered my sister-in-law Aina, after all we were both much occupied with our children and our households. How is it Sigrid that you have deceived my brother and married him in Aina's place?' Her voice is low but the anger in it seethes.

I look her earnestly in the face. 'The deceit was not intended to harm your brother, Lady Adalmode. I have been a good and loving wife to him.'

Adalmode nods but her face is stony.

'When Aina and I were kidnapped from Saint Michel en l'Herm, the Norse raiders took us to the Scottish Isles to await the payment of the ransom,' I say, lying again, and intending never to reveal where Aina and Thorgils truly are to anyone. 'As you know it was a long wait. Three years.'

'My brother could not find such a huge sum in a hurry,' Adalmode says defensively.

'I can understand that. I was amazed to discover that our kidnappers were my brother, Thorgils, and my foster-brother, Olafr, who I had been separated from in Tallinn, when I met Lady Melisende and Lord Ademar.' I falter over my last words. I do not want to remind Adalmode that Melisende bought me in a slave market.

Adalmode is looking at me with interest. 'Your brothers?'

'So of course Lady Aina was treated well, and I was full of joy to be reunited with my kin. During those three years Aina grew greatly fond of my brother, Thorgils and he of her and she became his wife.' I pause and see that Adalmode is listening intently, her eyes cast down on her hands on the round of her belly.

'Go on,' she says, looking up at me.

'Olafr sent word that the ransom was waiting for collection finally with the Duke of Normandy and that Thorgils should return Aina to Rouen. Olafr did not know of their relationship.'

'I see.'

'By this time, Aina was with child.' I pause again but cannot read what Adalmode's response to the tale is. Her face is averted and she gives no indication of her reaction. I can only carry on. 'My brother lost a wife and child before this. He was distraught and so was Aina. She could not leave Thorgils and she could not return to your brother, great with another man's child.'

Adalmode sits back and regards me. 'No.'

'I suggested that I come in her place and try to pass myself off as Aina long enough to make them safe from Olafr and from anyone here.'

'You left your brother and your friend.'

'Yes. I could not see any other way.'

'You deceived *my* brother.'

'Yes and I am sorry for it. I am not proud of my cunning perjury. I am no Odysseus, heroic in his lies. I did not laugh behind Guy's back that I had gulled him. I love Guy. With every fibre of my being I love Guy now, and I believe that I make him happy. I am so worn down by lies and fears.' Tears roll down my cheeks now, as I begin to experience a mixture of my fear that I will lose him and relief that I am finally able to speak the truth.

'Guy has told me many times you *do* make him very happy. You and your children: the four sons you have borne to him as Aina of Ségur.'

I should perhaps hang my head in shame but no, instead I touch the serpent at my belt and decide to fight for what I love. 'Lady Adalmode, I throw myself and my children on your mercy. I am no serf. I was nobly born in Norway. My father served a queen and he was foster-father to Olafr who was King of all Norway. I am worthy of your brother and the name of Viscountess that I have taken, even though I have not taken either in a worthy fashion.'

She looks at me a long time. 'You acted honourably and bravely for your friend and your brother and you have, as you say, made my brother happy. You truly love him, Sigrid?'

'Yes, I truly do.'

Adalmode looks down again and after some minutes of silence, I see that she is weeping and I reach out my hand to her, confused, 'Adalmode?'

'Just so you took my hand when I told you of him long ago, and how our marriage was thwarted, and I loved you for your words of kindness then.'

I realise that she is speaking of her first husband, Audebert.

'He told me,' she says looking up and forcing a smile to her face, wiping one hand across her wet cheek, and leaving her other hand in mine. 'He told me about Brioude.'

I am confused for a moment. Brioude – eighteen years before – when I had seen her outside in the secret embrace of Lord Audebert. I nod my head slowly. The memory of my feelings then rush back on me, of him speaking to me in the darkness, both the threat and the humanness of him.

'You kept our secret then, Sigrid.'

I look at her with understanding and hope. 'Yes,' I say.

'I will keep yours.'

I feel as if a suffocating shroud has been lifted from me. 'I am grateful . . .' I break down, spluttering and losing control of my emotions, my hands covering my wet face.

'But, Sigrid,' Adalmode has to raise her voice above my noise, 'I insist that you tell Guy. If he loves you, he will forgive you, but you are not safe unless you tell him, and as you say, the weight of the lies is pressing on you.'

I regain control of myself and look at her. She is right but the thought of telling him is tremendously fearful. 'I will, but he will repudiate me.'

'I believe your son Ademar is soon to be made Associate Viscount and married to Senegundis of Aulnay, daughter to that Aldearde who was beloved by the old Duke of Aquitaine?'

I nod and she smiles, embracing me. 'Tell Guy, Sigrid, and see how he responds. Only one other person knows of this: a monk of Saint Martial's named Ademar who is researching in the library at Poitiers and found a letter from King Olafr in a book that belonged to the Duke of Normandy. It seems that nobody had read it before now. The Duke died and my husband never looked at the books that Duchess Gunnora sent as a gift after his death.'

I look at her concerned. 'I heard of that letter from Thorgils and Aina and we always wondered why it had never been delivered.'

'I will deal with the monk Ademar. By controlling the written records these monks establish what the past was and will be,' she says. She rises, lifting me with her, holding both my hands and kissing my cheek. 'I will deal with Ademar of Chabannes sister, and his Chronicle.'

The monk came to Adalmode in the hall the following morning at the appointed time. She looked around her, ensuring that Guy was nowhere to be seen and that the servants and any other people were well out of earshot. 'Sit,' she said to him curtly, and watched him frown, but his frown disappeared, replaced by an avid look when she held out to him a heavy purse of silver and the beautiful jewelled book that the letter had been concealed within. He took them, placed the purse in the scrip at his belt, and kept the book on his lap, fingering its jewels. 'Look inside,' she commanded, 'you will keep your counsel on this matter and speak to no one of it.'

'I am most grateful, my lady, but . . .' He fell silent abruptly and his face clouded as he read the inscription she had written in a fine script, with her signature and seal beneath it:

> To Brother Ademar for his kind service to Lady Adalmode of Limoges, over the matter of Olafr Tryggvason's letter in this book, and for his unfailing discretion.

Adalmode watched him stare at the inscription, digesting its meaning. If he took the book and there was a later dispute, Adalmode would be able to show the inscription and claim he had lied and concealed the evidence. If he did not take the book, she could still show the inscription if it ever became necessary. She had him caught. The book was costly and beautiful, and she could see he coveted it. 'How firmly does your grip on your quill equate with reality?' she asked.

He lifted his head and gave her a defeated smile. 'I am truly grateful, Lady Adalmode, for your generosity, and you may rely on my unfailing discretion.'

'Do not forget that the writing of recent history can pose serious dangers, Brother Ademar.'

He nodded, suppressed petulance on his mouth again.

'I have stories to tell you for your Chronicle too, Ademar.'

His face lit and she was glad to see that this monk was at least as interested in scholarship as he was in money and baubles.

'There is the story of how my father kept my first husband in a deep dungeon and that is how we met and I grew to love him. And the story of how his brother blinded the Priest Benedict and how he was captured by my father and brother and thrown into the dungeon for many years.' The monk nodded, his expression growing more and more avid as she went on: 'And the story of Count Audebert's alliance with Fulk of Anjou in their war against the Duke and the King. And how the King demanded of Count Audebert: Who made you Count? and Audebert retorted: Who made *you* King?'

The monk could not control a snigger as he averted his eyes at this scandalous treason that he would no doubt greatly enjoy transcribing. She saw that she would control him best by being a real patron for his work on the Chronicle.

'I will return tomorrow with parchment and pen to write these stories down in all their detail.'

She smiled graciously and dismissed him. Spinning true tales of Audebert and Guy for this monk's history would be a welcome distraction for her. Her son Bernard needed her advice as he grew into command of La Marche and her little son, Guillaume, needed her guidance and affection too, along with whoever this was now that shifted and kicked like a feather in her belly. A daughter perhaps? Adalmode looked down at the heavy rings on her fingers. Now she could have a relationship with Guy's wife, now that she had a new sister to talk with and grow close to, perhaps she could survive Guillaume a little longer.

To tell my husband is the hardest thing I have had to do in my life, harder even than leaving Aina and Thorgils. I watch his face crumple and want to comfort him, but he holds me away from him and does not speak for several minutes.

'I knew,' he says eventually, turning his beautiful, vague eyes to me. 'I do not know what to call you . . . I think I must continue with Aina.'

I am confused. What did he know? 'I don't understand.'

'When you first came to me with Richard of Normandy, returned from your imprisonment as a hostage, I think I knew then, but I wasn't entirely sure. I had seen so little of Aina as a woman and your . . . her mother, Lady Melisende, accepted you as her daughter and I thought I must be mistaken, and yet I did know.'

'How could you know?'

'Your voice – there was still, then, the faintest strange trace in your accent. As soon as I heard you speak I began to wonder. I told myself, that perhaps Aina would have picked up a trace of a Norse accent, living amongst them for three years, but there was a doubt in my mind, all along.'

'Why did you allow our sham marriage to go ahead then!' I burst out angry with the pain I had caused us both over the years.

'It was, is, no sham marriage, wife,' he asserts. 'I'll not have you say that.'

I hang my head and slip my fingers into his and he does not resist my touch. 'Not for me. Never for me.'

He cups my chin and forces me to look at him. 'Nor ever for me. I needed so badly to marry Aina of Ségur, else the Duke of Aquitaine was threatening to remove my family's rights to Limoges again, and there you were after three years that had seemed so hopeless, there you were, and I wanted you to be Aina. You had to be her. I smothered the doubt before it became a conscious thought. Then I forgot my doubts in loving you,' he says simply, and pauses to look at me with affection. 'And why did *you* do this? Come here as Aina, come to me and make me your husband? Did she die, Melisende and Ademar's daughter? Was it to gain the ransom for your kin?'

'No! No! You think I would act from venery?' He shakes his head and gentles me with his hands, stroking my cheek, my hair, my shoulders. 'You think I would leave my brother and my countrymen that I had longed for all my life just for silver!'

'What then? I know you would have had a good, an honourable reason.'

I tell him then, in a great relieved rush, the whole story of Thorgils and Aina and their child and Olafr's fury and how I had persuaded Melisende to help me, because there was no help for it. 'I'm so sorry,' I begin, but he puts his fingers to my lips.

'No. No sorries, Aina, my love,' he says with the greatest gentleness. 'I know that you did this for love of your brother and your friend. I know that you did not intend any harm to me or deceive me for malice.'

I shake my head desperately.

'I cannot but love you Aina-Sigrid,' he says smiling and I know that everything will be alright as the weight of my deception drops from me like the heaviest anchor plummeting into the deepest sea and wallows down there in the deeps where I can no longer see it and I weep loudly against his chest, shaking and soothed. 'I have been a Viking serpent in your breast,' I moan and hear a strangled noise from Guy. I look up to see he is trying, unsuccessfully, to smother a great fit of laughter, and then I am laughing with him and swallowing my salty tears.

# 37

# Kelda Ey

## 1009

On Kelda Ey a ship from Dublin has come into harbour bringing news that Angharad is to wed Llewlyn of Powys and they mean to challenge usurpers in Dyfed for her father's kingdom. The ship also carries a package from Normandy for Aina that comes from Sigrid in Limoges. Aina unwraps the layers of packaging, thinking that Sigrid has gone to great pains to keep its contents safe on the voyage and how like her to be so over-careful. Inside is a letter in Occitan and a parchment scroll in Latin in an unknown hand. Aina reads aloud the title of the scroll: 'Ademari Cabannensis, Chronicon, Liber Tertius, Capitula XLIV.' She looks up at Thorgils. 'It says Ademar of Chabannes, Chronicle, Book Three.'

She frowns at him perplexed as to why Sigrid has sent this to her, and shrugging her shoulders, she begins to slowly read the Latin text. After a while she begins to laugh. 'Listen to this, Thorgils! It is written here:

> Aina of Ségur was kidnapped by Vikings from the monastery of Saint Michel en l'Herm and held hostage for three years abroad until Viscount Guy of Limoges paid a huge ransom and then, the Viscountess was returned and conveyed to her marriage in Limoges by Richard, son of the Duke of Normandy and an escort of the best Norman warriors.

She glances at him and continues: 'And in her letter Sigrid writes: "See Aina we are not unsung, just wrong sung! And we can't blame anyone but ourselves for that."'

Thorgils smiles with Aina, watches her read and re-read both the parchment and the letter and watches her expression change.

'I will never see Sigrid again will I?'

Thorgils knows that Aina weather this morning will be bleak and grey. 'I don't think we will see her, no, much as we long to.'

'I would have liked her to meet Ulf.'

'She has met him in her heart and in her mind's eye.'

This kind of Aina weather is best left to pass over in its own time and so he leaves her alone in the hall, while he goes down to the beach to carry on the work on the ships he has in hand. Carrying out these tasks that he knows so well always gives him good thinking time.

'Come on, Aina,' Thorgils says, rousing her from the bed. 'Get dressed. I want you to see something.'

Thorgils leads Aina up the beacon hill. They reach the top and Aina holds her hand flat between her breasts, catching her breath after the long climb. She looks around at the stupendous view that is now so familiar and she remembers running up here with Sigrid on their first day on the island, whirling round and round. 'I came here with Sigrid often,' she says.

'I know. Look over there.' Thorgils points to the headland.

Aina looks where he is pointing. There is a new standing stone, the height of a woman. She glances at Thorgils in wonder and runs over to the stone. She traces its snaking runes with her fingertips slowly translating them in her head, making sure she has them right and then she laughs aloud, throws both arms around Thorgils and hugs him with all her strength so that he groans, 'Oof!,' as she punches the air from him.

Over his shoulder she sees that the snake shape of the runes mimics Sigrid's serpent brooch. 'Thank you,' she says fiercely, looking into his freckled face and holding the gaze of his sea-green eyes. 'Oh Thorgils! You can feel the vehemence of life up here, a vehemence that you, me, Sigrid and Olafr have known!'

He laughs at her delight and kisses her. Aina pushes him away and walks to the very edge of the cliff so that he has to put his fingers into her belt in fear for her, and she shouts out the runes that Thorgils has carved on the standing stone, out to the sea, into the wind:

'Thorgils Thorolfsson and Aina Ademarsdottir raised this stone for the courage of their sister Sigrid Thorolfsdottir, who went on the Swan Road and lived with the Franks as a secret Viking and a free woman!'

# Historical Note

In 1028 the monk Adémar of Chabannes, who lived in the monasteries of Saint Martial in Limoges and Saint Cybard in Angoulême, completed his *Chronicle of Aquitaine and France*. The *Chronicle* described the kidnap of Emma of Ségur (or Aina in this novel), wife or betrothed wife of Guy of Limoges. Adémar reported that Emma was kidnapped by Vikings from Saint Michel en l'Herm monastery and held hostage overseas for three years before Viscount Guy could raise and pay her ransom. The *Chronicle* also described the marriage of Guy's sister, Adalmode of Limoges, to Audebert of La Marche who had been imprisoned for a long period of time in her father's dungeon. Adémar of Chabannes' elliptical accounts of these two historical events were the starting points for this novel.

Most of the noble characters in this story of late 10th and early 11th century Europe, focussing on Aquitaine (modern south west France) and Dyfed (Pembrokeshire in modern Wales), principal events such as marriages, wars and deaths, and the contacts between Scandinavians, Franks and Welsh are based on the lives of real historical people. Which Vikings kidnapped Emma of Ségur, where she was held, and what happened to her during that time is not recorded. Before he became King of Norway, some sources have Olafr Tryggvason sold into slavery with Thorgils Thorolfsson. Sigrid Thorolfsdottir, however, is a fictional character, as are all the characters who are not noble-born. The story draws on historical research, but this is nevertheless a historical novel rather than a history and much of the detail and all of the psychology and emotions are imagined.

There is some disagreement amongst historians over the identity of Duke Guillaume V of Aquitaine's first wife Adalmode. Adémar of Chabannes, the primary source, informs us that she was Adalmode of Limoges, sister of Viscount Guy of Limoges, and widow of Audebert of La Marche. Pierre de Maillezais, however, writing in 1060 claimed that she was the daughter of Adelais-Blanche of Anjou and a number of later historians have followed this identification (Bachrach, 1993) and assumed that Audebert's first wife, the sister of Guy of Limoges, died and Adalmode was his second wife and Fulk's cousin. Cawley (Medlands) and Settipani (2004) argue that Stasser (1997) disproved this. I have worked on the assumption that she was Guy's sister and Audebert's only wife. The history of this period is a moveable feast and many 'facts' about it are debateable, with an abundance of documents being forgeries – not least some by Adémar of Chabannes – the main chronicler for 10th and 11th century Aquitaine, who was notorious for forging the life of a saint and supposed apostle.

The Swan Road was a Norse kenning meaning the sea. One sea route, frequently used by Norwegian raiders and traders, came from Norway skirting Scotland and the islands, threading down past the Isle of Man, between Ireland and Wales, past the Scilly Isles, towards the island of Noirmoutier, and down to the coast of Aquitaine.

Place-names, archaelogical finds and scanty written accounts evidence Viking raids, bases and settlements along the Pembrokeshire coast. The Vikings knew Wales as Bretland and named the Welsh inhabitants, the Bretar. Kelda Ey is a fictional mix of the real islands of Caldey and Skomer which were occupied by Vikings in the 10th century. Caldey was known as Kelda Ey – Island of the Spring – to its Viking inhabitants, or Kaldr Ey – Cold Island. Llanteulyddog is an old name for Carmarthen. Dinbych-y-psygod is the Welsh name for Tenby. The Viking raiders, mercenaries and settlers undoubtedly played some part in the unstable dynastic rule in Dyfed, and in depicting them I have tried to unpick the demonisation or romanticisation that often imbues accounts of Vikings, to portray them in feasible relationships with people from other cultures.

This was a period of Christian evangelism. The Dukes of Normandy were descended from marauding Vikings who had so successfully harassed the King of France that he ceded Normandy to them. In the 10th century they were consolidating their power, shifting from their pagan beliefs to Christianity, and integrating with their reluctant Frankish hosts. Olafr Tryggvason was purported to have accelerated the slow process of converting Norway and its colonies in Iceland and Greenland to Christianity, although this is disputed as heroic legend by some historians. There is a particularly enjoyable dismantling of the legends surrounding Olafr written by Gwyn Jones (1968) where he argues that we cannot believe in the story of Tryggvason's slavery.

As Wendy Davies points out 'sovereignty is not a concept which has much applicability in the early middle ages' (Davies, 1990, p. 16) and this is true of both Aquitaine and Dyfed with various lords violently, or through negotiation and marriage, vying for control and expansion. In the 10th and 11th centuries the southern counties of France were effectively independent of the northern French king and ruled by various Dukes and Counts. The novel covers the period of time in which the Carolingian line of Kings, descended from Charlemagne, came to an end. In Wales Kings and Princes vyed with their own kin for control of territories, and contested with Viking invaders and encroaching Anglo-Saxon forces.

The early Middle Ages was a surprisingly international experience for some people: sailors, soldiers, traders, pilgrims, missionary priests, slaves, and some brides. All Scandinavian peoples (who we now distinguish as Norwegians, Danes, Swedes, Finns) spoke mutually intelligible forms of Old Norse. Matthew Townend argues that Old English and Old Norse were also mutually intelligible (2002). Old Welsh would have been understood by Cornish and Breton speakers. Children born to Welsh slave mothers and Norse fathers might well have been bi-lingual.

This was a highly stratified and unequal society. Slavery was a flourishing trade until at least the 12th century and there was still a high demand for slaves at the turn of the 11th century and little attempt by Church or State to intervene. From the 9th century some elements in the Church tried to suppress the sale of Christians into pagan territories but this was motivated by a concern for souls rather than any notion of inhumanity during the lifetimes of those unfortunate enough to find themselves enslaved due to birth, capture in war, raiding, destitution, or as a sentence for a crime.

The meaning of the term hostage in the Middle Ages was different from our contemporary understanding (Kosto, 2012). Now we would consider someone kidnapped and taken for ransom as a hostage, but in medieval Europe that person was a prisoner and a kidnap victim but not a hostage. Similarly Audebert, imprisoned for a crime, was a prisoner and not a hostage. A medieval hostage was given as surety for a promise. A prisoner was taken, a hostage was given. There could be some blurring when for instance a person was kidnapped and held for ransom and then released in exchange for another person, a hostage, as the guarantee of future payment by the original prisoner.

I have drawn on a wide range of literary and historical sources published in contemporary English and French, from translations of Adémar of Chabannes writing in the 11th century and Snorri Sturlsson writing in the 13th century, to recent historical scholarship including Bernard Bachrach, Eric Christiansen, Wendy Davies, James Graham-Campbell, Judith Jesch, Gwyn Jones, Kari Maund, Mark Redknap, Peter Sawyer, Christian Settipani, and many others. Some key sources are listed in the Selected Bibliography.

Amongst the historical people my characters are based on: Adalmode of Limoges, Duchess of Aquitaine, died in childbirth shortly after the period covered by this novel; Guillaume, Duke of Aquitaine, had two subsequent wives and a long reign; Adalmode and Audebert's son Bernard, held the county of La Marche through turbulent times; Fulk went on many penitential pilgrimages and was a strong ruler in Anjou; Angharad's husband and son were amongst the most successful of the Welsh princes; Guy ruled Limoges until his death in 1025; and his wife, the Viscountess, died the following year. Count Audebert of La Marche and Périgord and Adalmode of Limoges were the grandparents of Almodis of La Marche who is the heroine of my first novel, *Almodis: The Peaceweaver* (Impress Books, 2011).

# Genealogies

Genealogies for characters in the novel (shown in **bold**) who are based on real historical people. Dates of accession to titles are shown. These are selected rather than comprehensive genealogies (not all of Harald Finehair's wives are shown for instance.)

# CAROLINGIAN KINGS

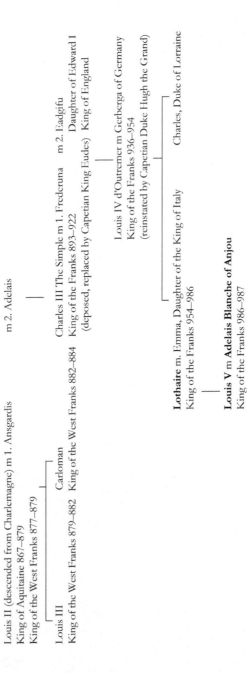

Louis II (descended from Charlemagne) m 1. Ansgardis     m 2. Adelais
King of Aquitaine 867–879
King of the West Franks 877–879

Louis III     Carloman
King of the West Franks 879–882     King of the West Franks 882–884

Charles III The Simple m 1. Fredecruna     m 2. Eadgifu
King of the Franks 893–922     Daughter of Edward I
(deposed, replaced by Capetian King Eudes)     King of England

Louis IV d'Outremer m Gerberga of Germany
King of the Franks 936–954
(reinstated by Capetian Duke Hugh the Grand)

**Lothaire** m. Emma, Daughter of the King of Italy     Charles, Duke of Lorraine
King of the Franks 954–986

**Louis V** m **Adelais Blanche of Anjou**
King of the Franks 986–987

# CAPETS

Eudes m Theoderada
King of France 888–898

Robert I m Beatrix of Vermandois
King of France 922–923

Emma m Raoul Count of Bourgogne
King of France 923–936

Hugh 'The Grand' m 1. Judith of Maine   m 2. Eadhil   m 3. Hedwig of Germany
Duke of Burgundy 936–956                 Daughter of Edward I
                                         King of England

Hugh Capet m Adelais of Poitou     Emma of France m Richard I Count of Normandy
King of France 987–996                              d. 968

Robert II, The Pious     m 1. Rozala   m 2. Berthe of Burgundy   m 3. Constance of Arles
King of France 996–1031                                          Daughter of Adelais Blanche of Anjou

# KINGS OF NORWAY

Harald I Finehair    m 3. Swanhild   m 6. Ragnhild
King of Norway 872–930

Erik Bloodaxe                        m Gunhild
King of Norway 930–936               Daughter of Gorm, King of Denmark
King of Orkney 936–937
King of York 948–949; 952–954

Harald II Greyskin
King of Norway 960–965

Olaf
King of Viken 934

'Tryggve m Astrid
King of Viken 946–968

**Olafr Tryggvason**
King of Norway 995–1000

m 1. Gyda            m 2. Gyda           m 3. Gudrun    m 4. Thyric
Daughter of the      Sister of the King of                Daughter of King Harald
King of the Wends    Dublin                                Bluetooth of Denmark

'Thora, Mistress

Haakon
King of Norway 936–960

# KINGS of DEHEUBARTH (South West Wales)

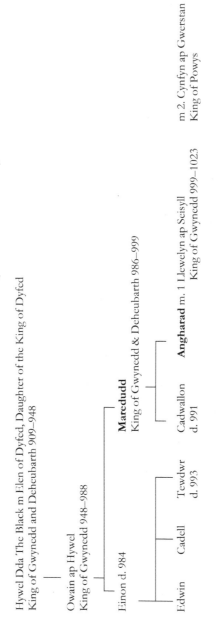

Hywel Dda The Black m Elen of Dyfed, Daughter of the King of Dyfed
King of Gwynedd and Deheubarth 909–948

Owain ap Hywel
King of Gwynedd 948–988

Einon d. 984

**Maredudd**
King of Gwynedd & Deheubarth 986–999

Edwin    Cadell    Tewdwr
                    d. 993

Cadwallon
d. 991

**Angharad** m. 1 Llewelyn ap Seisyll
King of Gwynedd 999–1023

m 2. Cynfyn ap Gwerstan
King of Powys

# LIMOGES HOUSEHOLD/ SÉGUR HOUSEHOLD

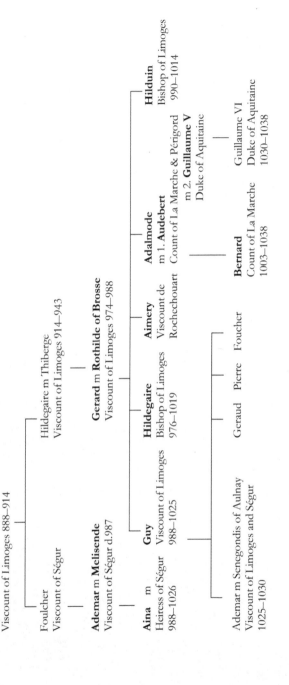

Audebert m Adaltrude of Aurillac
Viscount of Limoges 888–914

Foulcher
Viscount of Ségur

Hildegaire m Thiberge
Viscount of Limoges 914–943

**Ademar** m **Melisende**
Viscount of Ségur d.987

**Gerard** m **Rothilde of Brosse**
Viscount of Limoges 974–988

**Aina** m
Heiress of Ségur
988–1026

**Guy**
Viscount of Limoges
988–1025

**Hildegaire**
Bishop of Limoges
976–1019

**Aimery**
Viscount de
Rochechouart

**Adalmode**
m 1. **Audebert**
Count of La Marche & Périgord
m 2. **Guillaume V**
Duke of Aquitaine

**Hilduin**
Bishop of Limoges
990–1014

Ademar m Senegondis of Aulnay
Viscount of Limoges and Ségur
1025–1030

Geraud    Pierre    Foucher

**Bernard**
Count of La Marche
1003–1038

Guillaume VI
Duke of Aquitaine
1030–1038

## LA MARCHE HOUSEHOLD

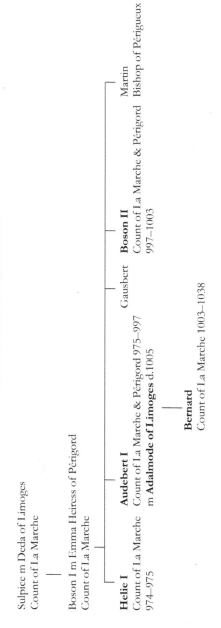

Sulpice m Deda of Limoges
Count of La Marche

Boson I m Emma Heiress of Périgord
Count of La Marche

**Helie I**
Count of La Marche
974–975

**Audebert I**
Count of La Marche & Périgord 975–997
m **Adalmode of Limoges** d.1005

Gausbert

**Boson II**
Count of La Marche & Périgord
997–1003

Martin
Bishop of Périgueux

**Bernard**
Count of La Marche 1003–1038

# AQUITAINE HOUSEHOLD

Guillaume III m Adela of Normandy
Duke of Aquitaine, Count of Poitou 934–962
Monk 962–963

**Guillaume IV 'Strongarm'** m **Emma of Blois**
Duke of Aquitaine, Count of Poitou 963–993
Monk 993–996

**Guillaume V 'The Great'** m **Adalmode of Limoges**
Duke of Aquitaine, Count of Poitou 993–1030

Guillaume VI 'The Fat'
Duke of Aquitaine 1030–1038

Adelais of Poitou m **Hugh Capet**
King of France 987–996

# ANJOU HOUSEHOLD

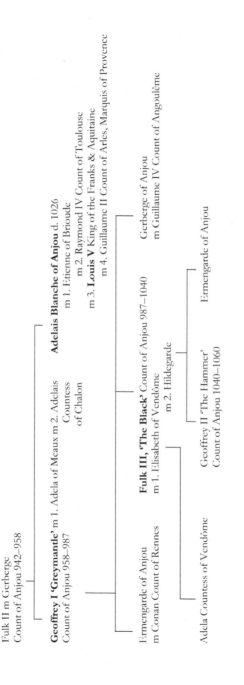

Fulk II m Gerberge
Count of Anjou 942–958

**Geoffrey I 'Greymantle'** m 1. Adela of Meaux m 2. Adelais
Count of Anjou 958–987                          Countess
                                                of Chalon

**Adelais Blanche of Anjou** d. 1026
m 1. Etienne of Brioude
m 2. Raymond IV Count of Toulouse
m 3. **Louis V** King of the Franks & Aquitaine
m 4. Guillaume II Count of Arles, Marquis of Provence

Gerberge of Anjou
m Guillaume IV Count of Angoulême

Ermengarde of Anjou

**Fulk III, 'The Black'** Count of Anjou 987–1040
m 1. Elisabeth of Vendôme
m 2. Hildegarde

Ermengarde of Anjou
m Conan Count of Rennes

Geoffrey II 'The Hammer'
Count of Anjou 1040–1060

Adela Countess of Vendôme

# NORMANDY HOUSEHOLD

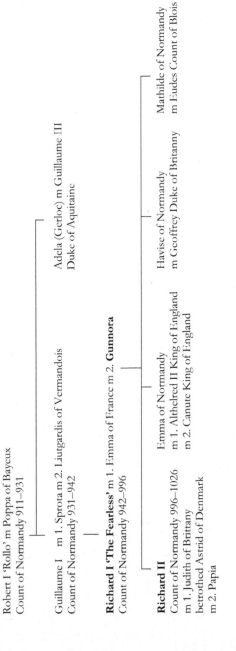

Robert I 'Rollo' m Poppa of Bayeux
Count of Normandy 911–931

Guillaume I   m 1. Sprota m 2. Liutgardis of Vermandois
Count of Normandy 931–942

Adela (Gerloc) m Guillaume III
Duke of Aquitaine

**Richard I 'The Fearless'** m 1. Emma of France m 2. **Gunnora**
Count of Normandy 942–996

**Richard II**
Count of Normandy 996–1026
m 1. Judith of Brittany
betrothed Astrid of Denmark
m 2. Papia

Emma of Normandy
m 1. Athelred II King of England
m 2. Canute King of England

Havise of Normandy
m Geoffrey Duke of Brittanny

Mathilde of Normandy
m Eudes Count of Blois

# Selected Bibliography

The epigraphs at the beginning of the three parts are from the following sources:

Part One: Adalbero of Laon, quoted in Fichtenau, Heinrich (1991) *Living in the Tenth Century*, transl. Patrick J. Geary, London: University of Chicago, p. 403.

Part Two: Edmund Spenser, 'Amoretti LXXV: One Day I Wrote Her Name upon the Strand,' Smith, J.C. & de Selincourt, E., eds. (1977) *Spenser: Poetical Works*, Oxford: Oxford University Press, p. 575.

Part Three: Anonymous, from the *Poetic Edda*, translated in Jesch, Judith (2013) *Viking Poetry of Love and War*, London: British Museum, p. 70.

In Chapter 26 Guy's description of spring in Aquitaine is a quotation from Freda White's wonderful book: White, Freda (1984) *Three Rivers of France: Dordogne, Lot, Tarn*, London: Faber & Faber.

Some of the primary sources I looked at were:

(1912) *The Anglo-Saxon Chronicle*, trans. Rev. James Ingram and Dr J. A. Giles, London: Everyman, online at http://omacl.org/Anglo/

*Annales Cambriae (The Annals of Wales) 447–954*, online at http://www.fordham.edu/halsall/source/annalescambriae.asp

De Chabannes, Adémar (2003) *Chronique*, 3 vols., trans. Yves Chauvin et Georges Pon, Turnhout: Brepols.

Dudo of St Quentin, *Gesta Normannorum*, 1015, online at http://theorb.net/orb_done/dudo/dudintro.html

Fanning, Steven and Bachrach, Bernard S. (2004) *The Annals of Flodoard of Reims 919–966*, Orchard Park: Broadview Press.

Giles, J. A. (2000) *Gildas*, Ontario: In parenthesis.

Some of the other significant sources I looked at were:

Abel, Mickey (2012) 'Emma of Blois as Arbiter of Peace and the Politics of Patronage' in Martin, Therese, ed. (2012) *Reassessing the Roles of Women as 'Makers' of Medieval Art and Architecture*, Leiden/Boston: Brill, pp. 823–861.

Ackroyd, Peter (2012) *The History of England Volume I: Foundations*, London: Pan.

Adams, Jonathan and Holman, Katherine (2004) *Scandinavia and Europe 800–1350: Contact, Conflict, and Coexistence*, Turnhout: Brepols.

Bachrach, Bernard S. (1993) *Fulk Nerra: The Neo-Roman Consul 987–1040 – A Political Autobiography of the Angevin Count*, Berkeley: University of California Press.

Cawley, Charles, Medieval Lands: A Prosopography of Medieval European Noble and Royal Families, online at http://fmg.ac/Projects/Medlands

Christensen, Eric (2006) *The Norsemen in the Viking Age*, Oxford: Blackwell Publishing.

Davies, Wendy (1990) *Patterns of Power in Early Wales*, Oxford: Clarendon.

Duby, Georges and Goldhammer, Arthur (1993) *A History of Private Life: Revelations of the Medieval World*, Boston: Harvard University Press.

Fletcher, Richard (1998) *The Conversion of Europe from Paganism to Christianity 371–1386 AD*, London: Fontana.

Graham-Campbell, James (2001) *The Viking World*, London: Frances Lincoln.

Hadley, Dawn M. (2006) *The Vikings in England: Settlement, Society and Culture*, Manchester: Manchester University Press.

Herlihy, David (1985) *Medieval Households*, London: Harvard University Press.

Jesch, Judith (2001) *Ships and Men in the Late Viking Age*, Woodbridge: Boydell Press.

Jesch, Judith (1991) *Women in the Viking Age*, Woodbridge: Boydell Press.

Jones, Gwyn (1968) *W.P. Ker Lecture: The Legendary History of Olaf Tryggvason*, Glasgow: University of Glasgow.

Jones, Gwyn (2001) *A History of the Vikings*, Oxford: Oxford University Press.

Kosto, Adam (2012) *Hostages in the Middle Ages*, Oxford: Oxford University Press.

Landes, Richard (1995) *Relics, Apocalypse and the Deceits of History: Adémar of Chabannes 989–1034*, Cambridge, Massachusetts: Harvard University Press.

Lavergne, Maurice de Bony de (1965) *Une Descendence des Seconds Rois d'Austrasie les Vicomtes de Limoges*, Dordogne: Clairvivre.

Maeterlinck, Maurice (1912) *The Life of the Bee*, trans. Alfred Sutro, New York: Dodd, Mead and Company.

Matthews, Jane, ed. (2011) *Skomer: Portrait of a Welsh Island*, Cardiff: Graffeg.

Maund, Kari (2000) *The Welsh Kings: Warriors, Warlords and Princes*, Stroud: The History Press.

Power, Eileen (1997) *Medieval Women*, Cambridge: Cambridge University Press.

Redknap, Mark (2000) *The Vikings in Wales*, Cardiff: National Museum & Galleries of Wales.

Rosenwein, Barbara H. (1998) *Anger's Past: The Social Uses of an Emotion in the Middle Ages*, Ithaca/London: Cornell University Press.

Sawyer, Peter (1982) *Kings and Vikings*, London: Routledge.

Sawyer, Peter, ed. (2001) *The Oxford Illustrated History of the Vikings*, Oxford: Oxford University Press.

Searle, Eleanor (1988) *Predatory Kinship and the Creation of Norman Power 840–1066*, Berkeley: University of California Press.

Settipani, Christian (2004) *La Noblesse du Midi Carolingien: Études sur Quelques Grandes Familles d'Aquitaine et du Languedoc du IXe au XIe Siècles*, Oxford: Prosographica et Genealogica.

Simpson, Jacqueline (1967) *Everyday Life in the Viking Age*, London: B.T. Batsford.

Stasser, Thierry (1997) 'Adélaïde d'Anjou: Sa Famille, Ses Mariages, Sa Descendance', *Le Moyen Age*, 103, 1, pp. 9–52.

Sturluson, Snorri (2009) *The Saga of Olaf Tryggvason*, Valde Books.

Townend, Matthew (2002) *Language and History in Viking Age England: Linguistic Relations between Speakers of Old Norse and Old English*, Turnhout: Brepols.

Verlinden, Charles (1977) *L'Esclavage dans l'Europe Médiévale*, Brugge: De Tempel, 2 vols.

A full bibliography of my research is on my website: http://tracey-warrwriting.com

# Acknowledgements

I am grateful to Richard Willis, Tamsin Ballard and everyone working at Impress Books for their support and the excellent effort they put into producing their books. Many of the readers of my first book, *Almodis*, encouraged me in the writing of this book by urging me to get a second to them. Maggi de Rozario helped with French sayings and road trips. Bodil Humphries got me started on Vikings, and Andrew Humphries told me about tidal gates and streams. Lola Rose, Jack Turley, Julie Turley, Misha Myers, Gloria Myers and Rob La Frenais were my insightful first readers. Bob Smillie was my muse as ever in Wales and France. I am grateful without measure to my family and friends for their support.